Trinket and her pals are, once again, caught in the middle of a murder scene...

"Professor Sturgis is dead."

"Hah!" replied my cousin/best friend/partner in mayhem. "I'm not that lucky."

"It's true," I said as I pointed to her son's dorm room closet. "Look for yourself. But I warn you—it's not a pretty sight."

My warning did not deter Bitty Hollandale from peering into the closet where the dead professor was propped against a shoe rack. She immediately recoiled. "Good lord! I thought you were joking . . . it . . . how horrible!"

I didn't say "I told you so" although I could have. I was still too rattled myself to take a verbal swing at Bitty. What I'd thought was an untidy pile of clothing tumbling out of the closet turned out to be a professor with whom Bitty had just quarreled that very morning. This was not a good thing.

Bitty peered at him again, and asked after a moment's silence, "But what is he doing *here*—in Clayton's closet?"

"You're asking me? How would I know?"

"Well, you're the one who found him."

I gave myself a mental slap to the forehead. "That doesn't mean I know how he got here."

"Fine. So now what do we do?"

Since my previous experience at finding dead men in closets was limited to one, I wasn't really up on all the protocol involved. So I decided to try what *hadn't* happened the last time I'd been presented with a similar scenario: "Leave him right here and call the police."

Bitty was horrified. "We can't do *that!* He has to be found somewhere else."

I rolled my eyes. Apparently, this time was not going to be much different than the last time. I wasn't that surprised.

Virginia Brown's Novels from Bell Bridge Books

The Dixie Divas Mysteries
Dixie Divas
Drop Dead Divas
Dixie Diva Blues
Divas and Dead Rebels

The Blue Suede Memphis Mysteries
Hound Dog Blues
Harley Rushes In
Suspicious Mimes
Return to Fender (2013)

General Mystery/Fiction
Dark River Road

Historical Romance
Comanche Moon
Capture the Wind

Divas and Dead Rebels

Book 4 of the *Dixie Diva* Mysteries

by

Virginia Brown

Bell Bridge Books

This is a work of fiction. Names, characters, places and incidents are either the products of the author's imagination or are used fictitiously. Any resemblance to actual persons (living or dead), events or locations is entirely coincidental.

Bell Bridge Books
PO BOX 300921
Memphis, TN 38130
Print ISBN: 978-1-61194-205-7

Bell Bridge Books is an Imprint of BelleBooks, Inc.

We at BelleBooks enjoy hearing from readers.
Visit our websites – www.BelleBooks.com and www.BellBridgeBooks.com.

10 9 8 7 6 5 4 3 2 1

Cover design: Debra Dixon
Interior design: Hank Smith
Photo credits:
Shoe - © Jaguarwoman Designs

:Ldrd:01:

Chapter 1

"Professor Sturgis is dead."

"Hah!" replied my cousin/best friend/partner in mayhem. "I'm not that lucky."

"It's true," I said as I pointed to her son's dorm room closet. "Look for yourself. But I warn you—it's not a pretty sight."

My warning did not deter Bitty Hollandale from peering into the closet where the dead professor was propped against a shoe rack. She immediately recoiled. "Good lord! I thought you were joking . . . it . . . how horrible!"

I didn't say "I told you so" although I could have. I was still too rattled myself to take a verbal swing at Bitty. What I'd thought was an untidy pile of clothing tumbling out of the closet turned out to be a professor with whom Bitty had just quarreled that very morning. This was not a good thing.

Bitty peered at him again, and asked after a moment's silence, "But what is he doing *here*—in Clayton's closet?"

"You're asking me? How would I know?"

"Well, you're the one who found him."

I gave myself a mental slap to the forehead. "That doesn't mean I know how he got here."

"Fine. So now what do we do?"

Since my previous experience at finding dead men in closets was limited to one, I wasn't really up on all the protocol involved. So I decided to try what *hadn't* happened the last time I'd been presented with a similar scenario: "Leave him right here and call the police."

Bitty was horrified. "We can't do *that*! He has to be found somewhere else."

I rolled my eyes. Apparently, this time was not going to be much different than the last time. I wasn't that surprised.

My name is Trinket Truevine, and my cousin Bitty Hollandale and I have lately made it a habit to become entangled in murder cases. Bitty, who is five-two without her stilettos, likes to claim that if not for her and me and our group of friends known as the Dixie Divas, no murder committed in our hometown of Holly Springs, Mississippi would ever get solved. You can imagine how well that goes over with the Holly Springs Police Department.

I had no reason to believe it would be any different with the campus police at Ole Miss in Oxford.

It's mind-boggling how Bitty and I seem to end up in the company of so many dead people lately. Who would have thought that our visit down to the University of Mississippi would create another scene from *Sixth Sense*? A phrase from that movie, "I see dead people," was taking on a whole new meaning.

And now Bitty intended a replay of a past transgression that hadn't gone well at all. I shook my head rather vigorously.

"No. I'm not doing anything you suggest. I remember how it turned out the last time I found a dead-man-in-a-closet and listened to you. I don't want to go through the same thing again."

"For heaven's sake, Trinket! I was never married to *this* man. It's not at all the same thing."

"Bitty, it's much too close for comfort."

She looked bewildered. "Why? This isn't even in my house. It's a dorm room."

"It's a dorm room that belongs to your sons. People saw or heard you and the professor arguing this morning. Several hours later he's dead. You know they'll make that short leap to the next logical conclusion."

Bitty blinked her baby blue eyes at me. I could tell she hadn't a clue what I was talking about. Sometimes she does that just to annoy me, but maybe finding her son's professor—who had just flunked him—dead in Clayton's closet robbed her of enough common sense to follow the dots.

I sighed. "We really have to call the police, Bitty."

"Oh no, we don't," she said emphatically. "The police might think Clayton had something to do with killing him. You don't suppose Sturgis died a natural death, do you?"

I made myself look at the body again. It was an ugly sight, and I winced. Professor Sturgis had a wire coat hanger tied so tightly around his neck that it could barely be seen beneath folds of skin. The loop jutted incongruously along his collarbone. His face had turned deep purple, his eyes bulged and his tongue stuck out one side of his mouth. Since his hands were tied with duct tape, I rather doubted it was a natural death.

"No," I said bluntly. "Not unless he had a heart attack while someone was killing him."

"Oh." Bitty looked back at the closet and put her hands on her hips. "Well, can you believe the nerve of that man? Coming here to my son's room to be murdered!"

"I'll call the police while you mourn the professor's loss, dear," I said dryly. "I hope you can manage to contain your grief long enough to explain to law enforcement that you really didn't mean any of those things you said to Professor Sturgis outside his office today. Where everyone at Ole Miss could—and probably did—hear you."

She looked thoughtful. I hoped she intended to give in and do the rational thing. I should have known better. After a short silence, during which I was sure I smelled smoke and heard the faint crackle and pop of brain waves, she crossed the room and seized a canvas-sided bin like those motels use for dirty laundry. This one had Motel 6 printed on white canvas in bold black letters. It had probably been confiscated from the motel by a student. There could be any number of reasons it had ended up in her sons' dorm room.

"Here, Trinket," she said, and rolled it right up to the closet. "Help me get him into this laundry cart. He's not that tall. He should fit, don't you think?"

"I'm not doing this," I said. "This is obstruction and tampering with evidence and disturbing a crime scene and probably a half dozen more charges."

"Don't be silly. No one will ever know he was even in here if we move him somewhere else."

"And where do you suggest? In front of the Lyceum? Out in The Grove?" I said, naming two very public areas of the large campus. "This isn't *Weekend at Bernie's*, you know. We can't haul around a dead man as if he were still alive."

"This is no time to be talking about movies. Here. You take his legs, and I'll get his . . . oh, his . . . well, maybe we should just wrap him in a blanket or something before we stuff him in the cart."

"I . . . am . . . not . . . moving . . . him."

Bitty ignored my carefully enunciated refusal. She tugged at Professor Sturgis until she managed to get him a few inches out of the closet. I recited one of the police codes I've memorized about tampering with evidence. Bitty dropped the professor's feet to the floor. I quoted police code about disturbing a crime scene. Bitty took the blanket off one of the twin beds and draped it over Sturgis. I mentioned obstruction charges. Bitty rolled Sturgis up in the blanket and tucked in one end like a burrito.

By that time she was panting. Her blonde hair stuck to perspiration at her temples and neck. She straightened up and looked at me where I stood with my arms crossed over my chest and my mouth set in a determined line.

Her eyes narrowed, and I swear they turned as red as her scarlet lipstick. I thought for a second I saw steam come out of her ears. Then she said, "If you don't help me get him out of here so my son doesn't get charged with murder, I'll tell everyone in Holly Springs that in our senior year you got so nervous when Danny Ray Bell tried to give you a hickey on the neck that you threw up on him."

I shrugged. "So? Do you think anyone will care what happened thirty-five years ago?"

Bitty looked disgusted. "You have no shame. I'd just die if something like that was said about me."

"No, you wouldn't. You'd lie your way out of it."

"True." She thought a moment, then a smile of pure evil curved her collagen-filled lips. "Help me, or I'll buy your parents two round trip tickets to Cairo."

"Illinois or Egypt?"

"What do you think?"

I gasped. "You wouldn't!"

"Try me. They'd love riding a camel along the Nile."

I narrowed my eyes at her, but she didn't back down a bit. She knows how to get to me, and using my parents—who are reliving their youth and forgetting their bodies are still pretty much in their seventies—was a very effective threat. I went for cajolery: "Bitty—think about it. We aren't in Marshall County. We're in Lafayette County. This is Oxford, not Holly Springs. We don't know the local police here. If you move this body and get caught, you're liable to end up in jail."

"I'm less likely to get caught if I have someone helping me," she said tartly. "And besides, do you really want your nephew to be blamed for something he didn't do?"

"Of course not. But neither do I want his aunt—me—to go to jail for something she got caught doing."

Technically, her twin sons are my second cousins. In the South we find it much easier to refer to such close blood relatives as aunt, uncle, niece or nephew rather than go through tortuous explanations. Not that Bitty always observes the finer points.

"Don't be selfish, Trinket. Here. Grab his feet."

I looked down at Professor Sturgis. For a smallish man, he had really big feet. Or big shoes, anyway. They stuck out from under the blue plaid blanket, cordovan wingtips with the scuffed soles showing a lot of wear. There was no way I wanted to touch him.

When I stood there staring, Bitty said, "Oh for heaven's sake, Trinket. When did you get so squeamish? Here. I'll cover him up so nothing shows. We've got to hurry and get him out of here before someone else shows up. Otherwise, it'll be a big mess."

"It's going to end up in a big mess anyway, Bitty. Trust me. I know these things."

"As long as it's a big mess somewhere besides my sons' dorm room, I don't care. Now, are you going to help me or not?"

I wanted to say "or not," but I didn't. That's a big character flaw of mine; I don't always act in my own best interests.

After Bitty had Professor Sturgis completely covered from view, I found myself hefting him off the floor as far as I could get him. Don't ever wonder if the phrase "dead weight" isn't realistic. I can relate from my own experience that an inert object such as a corpse is heavy, bulky and troublesome to move around.

Bitty and I huffed, puffed, muttered really ugly words, and finally got the former professor up and over the side of the laundry cart. Then Bitty dropped her end. He didn't sink down into the cart as we had hoped. Instead, Professor Sturgis contrarily stuck over the side like a tree limb. Apparently, after death the body goes through profound alterations. Like rigor mortis. The professor's covered head and shoulders caught on one side of the cart while his feet and ankles jutted out on the other side. He'd become a straight, nearly inflexible plank.

Bitty looked exasperated. "Isn't it too soon for him to be so . . . rigid?"

I counted back the hours since we'd last seen him. Somehow, in the time between our noisy encounter with the professor and our unpleasant discovery of him, he'd been murdered. "Six hours, more or less," I replied. "Time enough, it seems."

"Well," said Bitty. "What do we do now?"

"Call the police," I suggested again, even though I knew she'd ignore me.

She did. I could almost see the cartoon light bulb go on over her head.

"I know . . . we can pile up laundry all around him so that it looks like we just have a lot of dirty stuff to wash. Help me strip these beds. Oh, and we can use the boys' clothes as filler if necessary."

"Why not packing peanuts? Then we can just wrap this entire contraption up in brown paper and mail it to an address in New Guinea."

I swear, I think Bitty actually considered it for a moment before shaking her blonde head so hard I heard her teeny, tiny little brain rattling around inside all that space.

"Won't work. Unless we stick him in a freezer, he's liable to start drawing flies fairly soon."

"Bitty, really—aren't you being terribly inconsiderate with Professor Sturgis? I mean, he's dead, Bitty. *Murdered.* Someone killed him right here in your sons' dorm room, and you're acting more like he's an inconvenience than a victim."

Busily stripping sheets and blankets off twin beds, Bitty didn't answer for a minute. She piled the linens atop Sturgis and stuffed what she could down into the cart so that it looked overflowing. Then she leaned so far into the cart that her voice sounded like it came from a deep well: "Yes, Trinket. I *have* thought about the professor's untimely death. But if I dwell on it, I won't be able to do what's necessary to keep my son from being accused of his murder. I have to prevent that first."

I had to say it. Someone would eventually, and it'd be best coming from me.

"But what if Brandon or Clayton did kill him?"

Bitty never paused in tucking linens around the body. "They didn't. I'm sure of it. For one thing, I doubt Sturgis was killed in here at all."

"And how did you come to that conclusion?"

"Because," said Bitty as she straightened up and looked at me, "Sturgis has a wire coat hanger tight around his neck, and my boys don't use those. They have only wooden hangers in their closets. See?"

When she pointed, I looked and saw that she was right. Not a single wire hanger could be seen.

I nodded. "Very good, Holmes. You're getting better at this deduction stuff."

"Thank you, Doctor Watson. Now here—help me push this cart out into the hall."

That's how I found myself pushing a dead professor in a stolen laundry cart down a hallway to an elevator. As luck would have it, a student caught the elevator doors right before they could close and slipped inside to stand next to us. I focused on shiny walls and what was probably a hidden camera in the ceiling, while Bitty flashed the young man a smile. She can't help herself. She was born a belle. Belles flirt with any unrelated male of all ages, whether they even mean to or not. Of course, it wasn't a flirtation of the come-on, sexual type; Bitty may be many things, but she's not a pervert or deviant. We are in our early, *early* fifties, after all, and the student was around the age of her sons, in his late teens or early twenties.

"Hey there, sugar," she said to the young man. "Are you doing all right today?"

He smiled back at her. People of the male persuasion tend to do that.

"Yes, ma'am. Doing great, thanks."

"I'm glad to hear that," said Bitty. "It's too nice a day not to be doing great, don't you think?"

"Yes, ma'am, I sure do."

Such a polite, meaningless exchange to have in an elevator while hauling around the body of a dead professor. Who knew it would come back to haunt us?

When the elevator doors opened at the lobby level, Bitty and I shoved the heavy cart forward while the nice young man courteously held the doors open. Sunshine spread light through the lobby windows and backlit ancient trees on the campus as we pushed on through the front door and out onto walkways that dissected the lawns. It was the Friday before Game Day, and expensive motor homes already lined the streets. Nearby, The Grove—a large greensward dotted with huge, ancient oaks—was being sectioned off for the tailgating parties. Spray paint delineated its walkways and roadways for emergency vehicles, and all other areas were open for the array of tents to come. Very shortly, The Grove would look more like a refugee camp for the well-heeled than a peaceful campus lawn. Foot and vehicle traffic had already begun to increase.

"Which way?" I asked my fearless leader. I had no intention of being responsible for any decisions she made one way or the other. I was just an accomplice, not the master mind behind this idiocy. Not that the distinction would prevent me from drawing just as long a prison sentence as it would the master mind, of course. Maybe even longer. After all, I *know* better than to move anything at a crime scene. So does Bitty, but she pretends not to understand the law or recognize that there are penalties for civil disobedience.

My fearless leader looked temporarily indecisive. She gazed across the grounds with a confused expression. By that, I mean her Botox-riddled brow had the merest suggestion of a wrinkle. Then she turned to look at me, and all indecision ceased.

"You're too noticeable, Trinket. Try to be inconspicuous."

I lifted my brows. Unlike Bitty, I can't afford nor do I want Botox, so I have no problem moving my facial muscles.

"Am I on fire or something? Why do you think I'm too noticeable?"

She made an impatient motion with one hand. "Because you're an Amazon. Can't you crouch down a little?"

Now, I think I'm fairly normal in the height range. I'm five-nine and still working my way down from being twenty pounds overweight to something more manageable. I'm not exactly King Kong material.

"I'm not that tall," I said in my defense. "You're just so short it seems like I'm tall to you."

"Amazon," Bitty insisted, and it irritated me.

"Midget," I shot back.

Bitty's eyes narrowed slightly. "That's not politically correct."

"Excuse me. Vertically challenged, brain cell deficient—uh oh. Is that Brandon and Clayton I see coming this way?"

In the distance two young men in matching hoodies with the school colors of dark blue and red walked with a blonde girl toward Dormitory

Row. The tall students each had blond hair as well, and the easy stride of confidence. We'd recognize them anywhere and from any distance.

"Omigod—they can't see us, Trinket! Push, push!"

The approach of her sons triggered an end to our disagreement. Bitty grabbed one end of the cart and started pushing, and caught up in her panic, I helped.

"Does everything at Ole Miss have to be at the top of a hill?" I muttered as the cart surged forward with a life of its own.

"Always complaining," Bitty shot back, but I noticed that she was having as much trouble as I was hanging on to the cart. We manhandled the blamed thing down the steep sidewalk at a speed much faster than the rickety little wheels on their four corners could manage, around a bend and out of sight. Just as we got to a curb, one wheel locked up, the cart tilted, and we—and our passenger—hit the pavement. I just knew we were done for.

As usual, however, Fate smiled on Bitty. I have no idea why. Not only were no cars passing, but there were no pedestrians nearby to ask why two mature women—one of whom wore six-inch stilettos—were bobsledding a laundry cart down a sidewalk.

Fortunately, the professor did not come fully untucked from his burrito-blanket swaddling. Save for one shoe, he remained firmly encased in blue plaid. We wasted no time in getting up and rewrapping him and sticking him back in the cart. Our desperation released an enormous rush of adrenalin, because we didn't have nearly as much trouble as we'd had in the privacy of the boys' dorm room. I can completely understand how people are able to lift cars off loved ones when it would normally be impossible.

By the time we rounded another corner and the dormitory was well behind us, we were both too winded to talk. I sagged against the cart gasping for air, and Bitty brought it to a halt. Since she was trying to breathe too, she just pointed. I turned and looked.

There, parked against a curb in the parking lot of a concrete and red brick building with former Mississippi senator Trent Lott's name on it, stood an empty moving truck. The sliding overhead door was open about three feet, and a pile of moving blankets were stacked neatly at one corner. It seemed to be the perfect answer to our problem. All we had to do was figure out how to get our load the rest of the way down the hill, into the lot, then up and over the high back and onto the truck's floor. Those trucks sit pretty far off the ground.

Wordlessly, we headed for the moving truck. If only we could get there before it left, and if we could be nonchalant in loading up the professor as if he were a pricey rug, we might be able to pull this off.

By the time we got to the big yellow truck, I was wheezing for air and certain that someone would call the campus police to report two suspicious characters. Three, if they counted the corpse in the cart.

"What now, O Great Leader?" I asked when I could speak, and Bitty launched the next phase of her plan guaranteed to get us ten to twenty-five in Parchman Prison.

"Do you think you can lift the door a little bit more so we can shove him in there where no one will see him?"

"I can lift the door okay. It's the professor that I can't lift."

"Don't be silly. We got him in here, we can get him in there. Now hurry up before someone comes out and sees us."

I looked around. What were the odds no one was watching us? I figured about ninety-ten. Not in our favor. Classes may be in session, but not all students had the same classes at the same times. Foot traffic was erratic. Traffic was steady. Maybe we could blend in. After all, it was home game weekend, and lots of people were loading and unloading stuff. I looked at Bitty.

"If we're lucky," I said, "only a half-dozen people are watching us right now. Act like this is normal."

"Act like what's normal? Shoving a dead man into the back of a truck? I'm not so sure there's anything at all normal about that."

I couldn't argue with her logic. I sighed and grabbed the blanket-wrapped body by the shoulders. As I heaved, Bitty grabbed the bottom end, and we both just lifted and heaved-ho at the same time.

It wasn't as difficult as I'd first thought. Since the professor was as rigid as a two by four, we were able to use gravity and physics to leverage his body up until he slipped right on into the opening. Bitty tucked the blanket ends around his feet. I grabbed the strap and closed the door. Then we stood there gazing at each other in mild surprise for a moment when no one came out and asked what we were doing, or tried to arrest us.

"What now, Mrs. Dillinger?" I asked as it sunk in that no one was watching.

Bitty gave me another blank look. "Who?"

"Dillinger. You know, John Dillinger, the infamous criminal back in the thirties. Johnny Depp just played him in a movie a year or so ago."

"Well good heavens, Trinket. I'm not as old as you are. How would I know who John Dillinger was?"

Bitty likes to pretend that there are a few years difference in our ages, but there are really only a couple months between us. So I rolled my eyes.

"It's not like *I'm* old enough to have been his girlfriend, but I paid attention in high school, so I learned something other than which spoon to use for dessert," I retorted.

"You and I obviously did not take the same classes," said Bitty, unperturbed by my retort, "and one uses the dessert spoon provided, of course. It depends upon what kind of dessert is served."

"*Excuuuse* me, Miss Manners."

Bitty smiled. "Why, of course you're excused, dear. Now come along. Grab hold of the cart and help me pilot this thing on over to my car. I should never have listened to you and left my car at the hotel. Now we have to do all this walking around, and my feet will be killing me by suppertime."

"That's what you get for wearing nine-inch heels. Remember, I suggested you wear something more practical."

"One must be well-dressed when meeting with professors, even such ill-tempered boors as Professor Sturgis."

"Whatever happened to that old adage about not speaking ill of the dead?" I asked aloud.

Bitty waved a dismissive hand. "That was only meant for people who deserved it, I'm sure. Sturgis did not strike me as a very . . . considerate individual."

I ignored that and said, "Let's just take this stuff back to the boys' dorm room. No point in trundling it all around town now."

"Oh no, we have to make sure there's no trace evidence left on any of their blankets or clothes. Don't you watch *CSI? Criminal Minds? Cops?*" Bitty came to a sudden stop, and the laundry cart wobbled on its little wheels. "Trinket, I have a better idea than both of us pushing this cart all the way to the hotel."

"No," I said without waiting to hear her idea. I just knew it would not be an idea that would benefit me. "I'm not doing it."

Bitty smiled kindly. "That's fine. Of course, it would probably save us a lot of walking, but why do that? We'll just carry on like this."

"Good," I said. We went another yard or two, and I sighed. "Okay, what's your idea?"

"You stay here with the cart, I'll get a taxi and go get my car, then I'll meet you in an alley where we can transfer the boys' things to my trunk."

"No." I shook my head. "Once you leave here you're liable to forget I exist. We stay together. That way I know we'll either escape together or hang together."

"A grim thought. Are you sure? Think of your poor feet."

"My poor feet aren't in ten-inch heels."

"Well then, think of *my* poor feet."

"You're used to heels. You even wear them to bed. No, Cinderella, no coach and six white horses for you while I stay with the mice."

"Honestly, I think you're getting dementia in your old age. I'll be visiting you down at Whitfield before long, I just know it."

"Visiting me? You mean sharing a padded room with me."

Bitty shot me a dark look but just said, "No, let's go this way. We can cut through The Grove and get there much faster."

I stopped and looked at her. "Didn't you notice all those people working to put out the boundaries when we passed earlier? You know, the guys with cans of spray paint? Are you sure you want to push this cart past so many potential witnesses?"

"Why not? It's a laundry cart, not a stolen car."

As usual, Bitty missed the finer points of my concerns, so we ended up doing it exactly as she wanted. By the time we passed, the go-ahead had been given for people to stake out their spot in The Grove. So we rolled the laundry cart past a huge crowd, up and down sidewalks, all the way over to the parking lot of the Campus Inn and right up to Bitty's car, unloaded the blankets and clothes into her trunk, then returned the cart to the dormitory laundry room. By that time we were worn out and dragging badly. It was quite a hike.

"I'm not cut out for this," Bitty said in between huge gulps for air. "It's too much work. Whoever said crime doesn't pay well was right."

"I think that saying has an entirely different meaning. However," I said as my breathing slowed and my heart rate approached something close to a normal speed, "it can certainly apply to this situation. You do realize we've committed a crime, right?"

Bitty flapped one hand in dismissal of my observation. "Nonsense. We didn't do anything other than divert attention to the actual victim instead of creating problems for innocent people."

"Tell that to the driver of the truck. He's liable to be arrested."

"That's ridiculous. All the driver has to do is tell them he didn't have anything to do with it."

Right. That would stand up in court for less than a nanosecond.

"Well, we can only hope the judge sees it your way," I said after a couple more minutes went by, and we had reached the second floor dormitory room of her boys. "If he doesn't, maybe our prison cells will be next to each other."

"Honestly, Trinket, you worry too much about things that never happen. Try not to be so obsessive, okay?"

Before I could form a proper response, the dorm room door opened, and Brandon said, "You're not going to believe this, but someone came in and stole all our clothes and bed linens!"

"Really," said Bitty calmly. "Well, don't worry about it. We can go shopping to get you some more."

Clayton appeared next to his brother as we entered the room. It was a mess. I felt a twinge of concern. Then my concern changed into horror when Clayton said, "I already called the campus police. They'll be here any minute to investigate."

I looked at Bitty, and she looked back at me. Uh oh.

Chapter 2

There have been a few times in my adult life when I nearly wet myself. Only twice can I recall passing the "nearly" mark and sliding into "soggy." This was almost one of those times. I barely made it to the dorm bathroom in time. Students are not the neatest people. It was like stepping into a primeval swamp. If some prehistoric creature had risen out of the showers, I would not have been the least surprised. Nevertheless, it did not deter me from my mission.

When I returned, two campus policemen were standing in the middle of the dorm room taking down information. Bitty was listing missing items on her fingers. Light from the windows made her huge diamond rings sparkle as she named off L.L. Bean bedding and Ralph Lauren towels. I held my breath waiting for lightning to strike her. It should. She had more gall than anyone I knew to stand there lying to law enforcement like she did it every day.

"But I have no intention of filing a claim or anything," Bitty said while the young officer wrote on his small notepad. "I'll replace all those items myself."

"Yes, ma'am," he said politely. "I'll note that as well."

The other officer was older and not quite as deferential. He studied Bitty, then the dorm room, and looked over a few items left behind by the bedding thieves. Laptops. CD and DVD players. Thirty-inch flat screen TV with an X-Box or Wii or whatever that was hooked up to it. He had the look of a man who recognized when something didn't fit.

"All that was taken was bedding and some clothes?" he asked abruptly, cutting off the young policeman who had started to speak.

"Why yes, as I was telling this *polite* young man," Bitty said, "it looks like all that's been stolen are garments and luxury bedding."

Her unuttered reproof against his rudeness was not wasted on the officer. He put one hand on his hip, far too close to the buttoned-down holster of his gun, in my opinion. I took two steps back, just in case.

"Ma'am," he began, "there's something fishy about—"

"My name is Mrs. Hollandale," Bitty interrupted with one of those feline smiles that can portray bitchiness even better than words. I don't know why she does that at the worst possible moments. All I can figure is that she has a death wish. Or at the least, an incarceration wish.

The police officer gave her a look but said in a civil tone, "Mrs. Hollandale, is it normal for your sons to leave their dorm room unlocked when they go to class?"

Bitty batted her baby blues at him. "Gracious, I'm sure it isn't, but they can answer that much better than I can. Boys, please answer the officer's questions."

Brandon and Clayton, who are used to their mama's quirks by now, just nodded. It was Brandon who said, "We always lock up. And I thought the same thing, sir. Why take just stuff like blankets and sheets and towels instead of our laptops or the TV? We've got all these expensive games lying around . . . it just seems weird."

The officer agreed. "Is there anyone who may be pulling a practical joke on you?"

Clayton grinned. "That's always possible. I never thought of that—do you think Heather might know something, bro?"

The last he addressed to his brother, since Brandon was seeing a rather nice young lady named Heather Lightner. I had once suspected her of murder, but I was completely wrong about that. Among other things. I don't usually mind admitting I'm wrong. Unlike a certain person who shall remain nameless—Bitty Hollandale. Okay, so I have issues with her stubborn inability to admit when she's wrong most of the time.

"I'll ask her," said Brandon, and he reached for his cell phone to call Heather. As he walked toward the open door into the hallway, one of his friends showed up.

"Hey, everything okay?" the young man asked. His eyes got a little wider when he saw the campus police standing in the middle of the room. "Uh oh, nobody's dead, I hope."

I thought Bitty was going to have a rigor right there. Her eyes bugged out, and her mouth dropped open, and I had to say something quick or there's no telling what she may have blurted out. So instead of giving an answer that made some sense, I came out with: "The only thing dead in here is the Latin language."

As jokes went, it flew right over the heads of everyone there except the young police officer. He's the only one who got it.

"Latin has been a dead language for a lot longer than *my* college days," he said, and I smiled gratefully. Everyone else just stared at me as if I had been speaking in . . . well, Latin. Truthfully, pig-Latin is the only foreign language I can remember.

The boys' friend only looked confused, shook his head, and disappeared down the hallway. I wondered what on earth they were teaching students these days.

I didn't finish college, though I had attended Ole Miss for a semester before I met my future husband and decided that sit-ins for causes like Greenpeace and Save the Whales was a lot more important than a degree. How foolish the young can be at times. I don't have the husband anymore, but I do have our wonderful daughter, who's married and living in Atlanta with her engineer husband. She's smart enough to have gone back to school for another degree, even though it's only at night right now.

Bitty had finished her college education at Ole Miss with a degree in Liberal Arts. I'm not sure what that was supposed to prepare her for, but it wouldn't have mattered anyway because she married a popular football jock with a penchant for making money. Unfortunately, Frank Caldwell wasn't picky about minor things like the law and got himself into trouble with a pyramid scheme that cheated quite a few people. He's still doing fifteen to twenty-five in a Federal prison, while Bitty divorced him, gained full custody of their twin sons, and went on to marry again. Three more times. She's either an eternal optimist or a horrible judge of proper husband material. I lean toward the first assessment.

Her current male companion, however, makes up for all the former mistakes. He's an excellent attorney with offices in several towns and absolutely adores Bitty. I'm quite sure that feeling is returned, although Bitty is being extremely cautious this time around. Her last divorce was a doozy. People still talk about it, especially since her senator ex-husband ended up murdered, and she was briefly a prime suspect in his death. That can traumatize some people.

Fortunately for her, Bitty is not "some people." Instead of being traumatized, she ignored reality while I and the rest of the Dixie Divas were left to try to sort out things. Which we did rather clumsily. Now we have a local reputation for getting involved in murders. Well, I think what's *really* being said is that we've intruded in so many police investigations we're lucky we're not in prison. Bitty has always led a charmed life. With all that in mind, Bitty is somewhat justified in thinking that we can get away with disturbing a murder scene. I, however, have a more pessimistic view of the situation.

So there we were, standing in the dorm room where we'd found—and moved—the body of her son's ancient history professor, talking to police about the theft of missing blankets. Try as I might, I can never quite match Bitty's insouciance in the face of deception.

Apparently having recovered from her moment of fright, Bitty said cheerfully, "I declare, all this fuss about some missing bed linens is enough to make my head hurt. It's really nothing, officers, and I'll replace their things before I leave Oxford. I'm not about to let a little thing like this ruin my visit, and especially the big game. We're favored to beat

Mississippi State by six points."

The older officer flipped his book closed and nodded. "I hear ya on that score."

If there's one thing men understand, it's football. The game inspires a dedication bordering on obsession with far too many of them. Bitty knows this. All Southern women know this, whether young or old, married or single. Football ranks right up there with beer, guns, fast cars and Jesus. Not necessarily in that order. The Top Five of Southern males rarely varies. It doesn't really matter which brand of beer, caliber of gun, race car driver or religious preference, pigskin loyalty is unwavering.

Those of us who attended, or have family who attended, Ole Miss are just as fervently loyal as anyone else in the country is to their alma mater. Ole Miss and Mississippi State are long-time rivals. While they aren't that far apart geographically, fans are about as far apart as you can get when it comes to their home team. This football game was about old rivalries as well as a ranking in the SEC.

It wasn't until Bitty had walked the officers across the small room to the door and held it for them while they exited with a farewell recommendation to keep the doors locked that I drew in a deep breath. I think I'd been holding it too long. I felt definitely lightheaded.

Bitty shut the dorm room door, flipped the lock, then turned and leaned back against it. "Good God, I thought we were sunk for sure," she said, and I didn't know what to say in response.

Did she mean to tell Brandon and Clayton what we'd done? I wasn't sure that was a good idea. But then, neither had been the idea of shoving a dead man into the back of a moving van, and I'd helped do that, so maybe my judgment was impaired.

"Boys," Bitty said as she pushed away from the door and crossed to her sons, "did you leave a . . . mess . . . in your room before you left for class? Either of you?"

"Well," said Clayton, "I admit it was pretty messy when we left, but we meant to get back in time to clean it before you got here."

"Clay has cleaning duty this week," Brandon said promptly. "I did our laundry."

"Is that why the laundry cart was in your room?" I asked.

Brandon looked puzzled. "Laundry cart? Oh, you mean that Motel Six thing that some of the guys brought back? No, ma'am, it was out in the hallway when we left this morning. Why would someone bring it in here?"

"It's not the laundry cart that worries me," Bitty said tartly, and both boys looked at her in surprise. "What do you know about the man in Clayton's closet?"

They both looked stunned, but it was Brandon who said, "What? Someone was snooping in here? Why didn't you tell the police? That was probably who stole our—"

Bitty held up a hand. "*I* took your blankets and clothes, and I'll tell you why in a few minutes. Right now I want your sworn word that neither one of you knew anything about the man in your closet."

"No, ma'am!" they both said in unison.

Clayton added, "Why would we let some guy mess around in our closet, anyway? It sounds stupid."

The expressions on their faces were genuine, I thought, and I'd spent a lot of the summer in their company and felt pretty sure I could tell if they were lying. Not that I'm an expert on liars, because quite a few people have managed to fool me, I can tell you that. It's embarrassing how many, in fact.

"Bitty," I said, "I'd like to speak to you privately, please."

"In a minute, Trinket."

"No, we need to talk *now*. Before you say anything else."

She looked around the rather small dorm room. "I don't know where you think we can go to talk privately, unless you mean the closet or the dorm bathroom."

"Neither one is clean enough. I'd rather stand neck-deep in a Louisiana swamp. No offense, boys."

"None taken, Aunt Trinket," said Brandon.

"It's not *that* bad," Clayton defended himself. "I cleaned up a day or so ago."

We all just looked at him, and he shrugged and gave a sheepish grin. "Okay, I forgot. But I meant to clean. I've been studying for exams, though, so that should count for something."

"Not much," said his brother, and Clayton smacked at him with a spiral notebook. That started one of their frequent tussles and provided a perfect distraction.

"Just step outside in the hall," I said to Bitty. "This won't take but a moment."

Once in the hallway, I looked at her and said, "Don't involve your boys. The less they know, the safer they are, and the better it is for all concerned."

Bitty thought about it for a moment, then nodded. "You're right. I'll just pretend nothing happened."

I stopped her before she went back into their room. "Uh, Bitty— you've already told them we found a man in their closet. We better think of some way to fix that."

"True. Hm. Oh, I know—we can say that it must have been a practical joke. That should explain it."

"Somehow, I think your boys will find flaws in that explanation."

"Oh for heaven's sake, Trinket, just let me handle it. I'll think of something."

Bitty tends to forget her boys aren't ten years old any longer, so I had no great expectations for her concocting a viable explanation.

She must just love to astound me.

"Listen," she said when she got their immediate attention by snapping her fingers at them as they wrestled on one of the stripped beds, "Trinket just reminded me that I had your clothes and bedding picked up to be cleaned, and that's probably what the man was doing in your closet. I'd forgotten all about those arrangements, so your things will be returned as soon as the dry cleaners finish with them."

"Why didn't the laundry guy say something then?" asked Brandon skeptically. His face was a bit flushed and his blond hair tousled from wrestling. "It seems to me that if some guy had a woman asking him why he was in our closets, he'd have said so."

"You'd think that, wouldn't you?" Bitty replied. "But he must have been startled, because he didn't say a thing about it. He just left without the rest of your things. I'll be sure to talk to the laundry about it. Now, Trinket and I are going back to the hotel and rest before we go eat supper. We'll meet you later at Proud Larry's if you two want to drop by for a drink and music tonight."

The last was said more as a question than a statement, and Clayton replied, "I've got other plans earlier, but I'll be by there later."

Brandon said, "Heather and I will come by after we finish helping her sorority mom get stuff together for the Sigma Kappa tailgate party tomorrow."

"Good. It's going to be fun, just like always. Now, don't you boys get into any trouble while I'm here, or I'll be angry at you, you hear?"

"I hear, Mama," they chorused, then looked at each other and shrugged. It was Clayton who said, "Did you talk to Professor Sturgis about my grade in his class?"

"I did, and he's a dreadful, dreadful man to try and reason with, I swear. But don't be too upset, sugar, because things will work out. They always do."

I guess Bitty's boys are so used to her whimsical impracticality that they accepted it without more questions. That can be a good thing sometimes.

Once Bitty and I were downstairs and outside the dormitory again, I said, "You're going to have to take all their things to a laundry to be cleaned, you know."

"I know. There are plenty in Oxford."

"There's Washboard Coin Laundry on University," I said, "but I don't know if that's the smartest place to go. Someone might remember if you drag in a lot of clothes and linens. You don't want anything to connect us to the blanket around the professor."

"Well, there's Starbrite or Oxford Fluff and Fold. Starbrite has a couple different locations. We'll take their stuff to the one farthest away."

"It's a shame that we've become criminals," I observed. "We're even beginning to think like criminals. We're covering our tracks. Now we just have to figure out some alibis."

"Why? We weren't there when the professor was murdered, so we shouldn't be suspects at all."

"That's just it, Bitty. We have no idea when or even where he was murdered. All we can say for certain is that he was alive for his scheduled parent meeting this morning. Not to mention, for his rather loud . . . debate . . . with you over Clayton's failing grade in his ancient history class."

Bitty sniffed disdainfully. "Wretched man. He wouldn't even consider makeup tests or extra work, even though Clayton had a doctor's excuse for his absences those days. He was a very unreasonable man. No wonder someone killed him. Bless his heart."

Those last three words are usually used to lessen mean things said about someone else. It's considered sort of an amulet to ward off the same fate, I suppose. A modern version of garlic and St. John's Wort in a much tidier—and less fragrant—package.

A brisk wind picked up some red and orange fallen leaves and sent them flying in a spiral across the campus lawn. November isn't known as a very cold month in this part of the South. There have been times of freezing temperatures, but more often lately we just have cold nights and mild days. Really cold weather doesn't arrive until January or later.

"We're taking the bus back to The Inn," I said when Bitty took out her cell phone to call a taxi. "It's cheaper and probably much quicker than waiting for a taxi during home game traffic."

Bitty lifted one eyebrow at me and dropped her cell phone back into her purse. "If you insist, dear. Let's wait at the bus stop near the student center. It's probably the quickest."

Unsuspecting creature that I am, I agreed. "Okay."

"Where are you going?" I asked when Bitty veered toward the path we had taken earlier with Professor Sturgis in the laundry cart. It occurred to me then what she was doing. As she trotted down the hill in her Prada stilettos, I guess I panicked. "No, Bitty no, don't even go close! Criminals always return to the scene of the crime, and we don't want to—Bitty!"

I stopped where I was on the curb, but Bitty steamrolled onward.

"I just want to see if he's still there," she called back to me, and I looked around to see if there was anyone close by. Traffic had picked up considerably. Cars decorated in school colors rolled past us, pedestrians strolled sidewalks and waited at red lights, and anyone looking out a window could have seen everything. That thought alone made me shiver. What if we were reported as having been seen stuffing a roll of blankets into the moving van?

I just don't know how or why I get myself into predicaments like these, I said to myself, but really—that's a lie. I do know how and why. I'm a lemming. A rat to Bitty's Pied Piper call. I seem to follow along with whatever mad scheme she concocts. To be fair, she does the same for me. Not all my schemes have worked out well. But at least I plan mine more carefully. I'm not sure that's a recommendation in my favor.

I ambled along the sidewalk toward a glass and metal bus stop. White, or blue and white buses with GPS systems powered by solar energy make it convenient to get around the campus and housing areas, and I intended to catch the next one and get myself back to The Inn as quickly as I could. I was tired, my feet hurt, and I had visions of spending years in the same eight-foot-by-eight-foot jail cell as Bitty. I'd probably end up strangling her.

Bitty joined me at the bus stop to report that the moving van was gone. "Now they'll find him far from Clayton's closet," she said with obvious satisfaction.

"And far from the actual murder scene, too," I pointed out. "How will the police know where to investigate?"

"We could always send them a little note," Bitty suggested.

I stared at her in disbelief. "That says what? 'Excuse us, but we moved the body of Professor Sturgis from the dormitory where he was really murdered'?"

"Honestly, Trinket, you're always so pessimistic. Things will work out. As long as my sons aren't implicated, it doesn't really matter to me who the killer is. The police are very good at finding out that kind of thing. We probably need to hurry to get to the dry cleaners before they close, so I hope this bus arrives soon. Sure you don't want me to call a taxi?"

"Yes," I said as I saw the bus lumbering toward us. "So I'm just to forget that we ever saw a dead man, that we ever moved his body, and that you're crazy as a Betsy bug. I'll erase all those memories from my mind and be a clean slate. Right?"

"You're so dramatic sometimes. Just try to have a good time tonight and forget all about Professor Sturgis. He'll be found, and the police will track down his murderer. It's what they do best. Good lord—how am I supposed to get on this thing?" she ended as the bus wheezed to a stop, and the door swooshed open.

I eyed her snug skirt and high heels with rather petty satisfaction. "Just hike up your skirt and hop on. I'm sure the bus driver's been flashed before."

I waited until we were sitting in her car and driving toward the dry cleaners before I said, "I think we're becoming too blasé about dead bodies. We've seen so many in the past year that we don't properly appreciate the horror or magnitude of murder."

"Nonsense. If anything, I appreciate the awfulness of it much more than I would if I was sitting at the breakfast table reading about it in the paper. I just don't let that cloud my judgment at the moment."

"Well, isn't that handy. I haven't perfected that talent just yet."

"That's okay, honey. You'll get it sooner or later."

I shut my mouth so tightly my jaws ached. We turned on to Jackson Avenue right in front of an oncoming car, but my jaws didn't unclench in time to scream. The car missed us by maybe a foot. I just closed my eyes. There was absolutely no point in trying to get Bitty to see the error of her ways. There never had been, but I still kept on working at it as if somehow I'd get through to her. But then, that would probably change her entire personality, and I didn't really want to do that. I just wanted her to be a little more wary of getting in trouble with the police. The best way to do that, I've found, is to follow the law.

Too bad other people don't believe in that. Until recently, I'd never thought about murder much. Since returning home to Holly Springs, I'd come into close contact with more murder victims than I had ever dreamed possible. Not that Marshall County has experienced a dramatic rise in number of murders. No, not all the victims were killed in Marshall County.

Divas have branched out to other Mississippi counties with our involvement as well. We are not always appreciated. Law enforcement at the state level has been notified of our efforts, I'm told, so Divas had better have an excellent reason for getting involved in any future murder cases.

Apparently none of that mattered much to Bitty. We were now involved in a murder that hadn't been discovered yet, and I was pretty sure that when it was—we'd be in it up to our necks.

Chapter 3

Football at Ole Miss is more of a religious experience than a sports game. If football is a religious experience, then the tailgating parties at The Grove are as close to heaven as a person can get without dying. A favorite saying of Ole Miss students is, "We may not win every game, but we ain't never lost a party."

Despite the double negative, it's nice to know some things never change.

Although it had been years since I'd attended the University of Mississippi, there are some rituals and friendships that are never forgotten. Attending tailgate parties is an activity that's easy to catch up on despite an absence of thirty-odd years.

Bitty has annual reservations at The Inn at Ole Miss on the campus. This makes the trip to and from the Vaught-Hemingway Stadium for the big game feasible, and even easier to get to The Grove for the tailgating parties. Drinking and driving is always a big no-no, and especially so in Oxford. Police there have very strict guidelines and swift consequences for those who flaunt the rules. In the bars, closing hours are much earlier than normal; Monday through Wednesday, they close at midnight. Thursday through Saturday, they close at one AM. On the university campus itself, no beer is allowed except east of Gertrude Ford Boulevard. However, liquor is welcome over the entire campus.

Don't ask *me*. I didn't make the rules.

Liquor cannot be seen in bottle form; it must be in a container. Beer is generally overlooked by campus police as long as it isn't seen. In other words, coolers must remain closed, and beer and liquor must be in a cup. Fairly simple rules for the initiate.

Early that Friday evening we dined at the City Grocery on the Square. While Bitty wanted to eat in the fine dining area, I and my bourgeois taste buds opted for upstairs and maybe a seat on the balcony if we were lucky. The downstairs is incredibly crowded, with tables an arm's length apart. Normally that convivial atmosphere might be lovely, but I was suffering an immense amount of guilt at my part in our afternoon activities. I ordered a Rebel ale with my cheese grits and shrimp, and Bitty ordered Jack and Coke with her fried pimento cheese salad. An abundance of alcohol should take care of any tendencies toward getting "bound up" as my mama would say about so much cheese.

At any rate, we were fortunate enough to sit out on the small balcony that looks over the Square. Oxford Square is lovely, with old southern architecture and an elegance most often seen in New Orleans. In some ways, it's reminiscent of that old city to the south. People have been known to call Oxford "The Little Easy" for its ambient lifestyle and laid-back attitude that mimics New Orleans. Of course, the "Big Easy" reputation of New Orleans also includes some pretty high crime statistics.

Although they didn't know it yet, The Little Easy had just gotten a rise in crime statistics, too.

Leaning forward, I said to Bitty across our table, "How can you sit there as if nothing has happened?"

"What do you want me to do—leap off the balcony? Beat my breast and do a soliloquy of contrition? *I* didn't kill him."

"For heaven's sake, don't beat your breast. You'd cause a seismic episode," I said rather crossly. Bitty's breasts are—in the words of her third husband—"most magnificent mammaries" or some ridiculous thing like that. He just meant she's well-endowed.

I never did care much for him.

Bitty knocked back her Jack and Coke and set it on the table so the waiter would see it and bring her another. "Really, Trinket, you have a terrible tendency to dwell on things far too much. No one has said anything, and he's long gone from the campus, so no one probably will while we're here. You need to get over this."

I stared at her. "Get over . . . Bitty, he's dead. D. E. A. D. Dead. What do you think is going to happen when he doesn't show up at home for dinner tonight?"

"How on earth should I know? I imagine they'll call for the police—yes, thank you, another one, please—" That last was said to the waiter who showed up to take away her empty glass. She leaned forward to finish more quietly, "—and the police will realize he's nowhere to be found, and then they'll start looking for him."

"By then someone will probably have found him in the back of a U-Haul."

"I think it was a Penske," Bitty corrected me, and I rolled my eyes.

"Whatever. There he'll be, wrapped up like a burrito in L.L. Bean blankets. What if they trace the blankets to you?"

"What if they don't? Honestly, Trinket, you're getting on my nerves. We have a lot of fun to get to tonight, and you'd better not ruin it. I've been looking forward to this for ages. Isn't it just like some nerdy professor to go and get himself killed on the very day I get here to have fun? It's not like we know who did it, or even need to know. All we have to do is pretend we don't know anything."

I gave her a sour look. "That's usually much easier for you to do than me."

"Are you saying I don't know anything?"

"If only it were that simple."

Truthfully, I didn't know what to do. Telling the police was obviously out for us now since we'd already committed a crime by moving the body. But I kept looking at the well-lit courthouse across the street and expecting a cop to come out to arrest us at any minute.

When I said, "We'll probably be arrested before we finish eating," Bitty flapped a hand at me.

"If it hasn't already happened, I doubt it will. Now finish your food, and we'll wander on over to Proud Larry's to listen to a little music."

I wasn't sure I wanted to hear any music, but I knew by then that crossing Bitty when she has her mind made up is usually an exercise in futility. Frankly, I thought we should get the hell out of Dodge. If for no other reason than that I had a guilty conscience and was in danger of throwing myself at the feet of the next Oxford cop I saw to beg for mercy. I get like that sometimes.

The band at Proud Larry's club was a rhythm and blues group, and for a while I was able to just enjoy the music and put everything else to the back of my mind. It wasn't as easy for me as it is for Bitty, but I'm always grateful for small blessings. Of course, Bitty immediately met up with some alumni and former sorority sisters, and proceeded to have more fun than is legally possible in most places. Oxford is a wonderful place to do this, as long as you can handle your liquor and don't get out of hand. I freely admit, I had fun just watching Bitty in her element.

My element is more comfortable in jeans and tee shirts rather than stilettos and diamonds, but that doesn't mean I can't have a good time observing how the other half lives. And I had some lovely conversations with a few people I vaguely remembered from my brief college days.

One of them used to live in the same dormitory as Bitty and I had in our freshman year. Freshmen are required to live on campus and of course, follow the rules, and we had delighted in constant attempts at breaking those rules—within reason. My daddy would have been livid if I'd gotten kicked out for acting up, so I kept it reasonable. Not that we didn't have loads of fun anyway. Unfortunately for me, I had to really study to keep up my grades, while Bitty seemed to breeze through all her classes, so she had a lot more time for fun than I did.

Bitty has always led a charmed life.

Right before midnight, a small group of ladies came in and made their way to our tables. Introductions were made all around, but one name stuck out in my mind as if put there with a hot iron: Emily Sturgis. Surely, it was a coincidence, I thought. I mean, it's not as if Sturgis is a terribly common name, but neither is it unusual. There could be two Sturgises living in Oxford, Mississippi, I assured myself, right?

But then Candy Lynn Stovall said to me, "Emily is married to Spencer Sturgis who teaches ancient history, and she hasn't been here long, so you may not know her."

Candy Lynn was a little intoxicated, so I asked Emily, just to be certain, "Your husband is a professor here at Ole Miss?"

Emily nodded. She looked much more sober than her companions. "Why yes, he is. Do you know him?"

"Oh, I know of him," I said with a vague wave of my hand. "I think one of my nephews was or is in his class."

Emily smiled. "I'd be interested in knowing what your nephew thinks of him. I have heard some diverse opinions on his classroom . . . shall we say . . . skills."

"Really? Why, I've never asked him how he feels about the professor, but I've never heard him complain, either."

That was the truth, as closely adhered to without stepping over the line as possible. I'm not as good as Bitty at doing the "belle," so didn't even attempt it. She can bat her eyelashes and switch to belle mode in a heartbeat, saying the most outrageous things in the sweetest voice, smiling all the time so that the person she's talking to or about has no clue they've just been terribly insulted until they stop and think about it later.

Emily Sturgis looked to be in her forties, about five-six, I'd say, slender with a nice figure, and much prettier than I would have thought the professor could manage. Of course, I only saw him twice, and the first time he was furious, so his face was beet red, and the second time he was dead, so his face was plum purple. On neither occasion did he strike me as a particularly handsome man.

Mrs. Sturgis laughed. "That's very tactful of you, Miz—I'm sorry, I didn't catch your name?"

"Truevine, and you may call me Trinket."

"Trinket. I just love Southern whimsy. Such colorful names." Emily smiled at me, but I caught a hint of condescension in her tone.

"Thank you, we love it too, obviously, or we wouldn't do it." I smiled back at her and again considered batting my eyelashes before I thought better of it. I'd probably look like I was having some kind of fit. "Where are you and your husband from, originally?"

"Spencer is from the shore in New Jersey, but *I'm* from New York."

"Really? I lived in the Catskills for a while. It was lovely. Are you from around there?"

It was true; I had lived in the Catskills one summer when my husband found a job as a waiter at one of the upscale lodges, and I worked there in reservations and at the front desk. But since we were playing a game of socialite tag, I left that part out.

Emily said, "No, I'm from the Hamptons. Wainscott."

"Wainscott? That's in Suffolk County, isn't it? It's been so long since I visited Long Island I just don't remember the area very well."

Emily nodded politely. I figured she wasn't that impressed with my knowledge of New York's high-dollar real estate. I'd pretty much said all I knew about the ritzy shores where the wealthy played and the rest of us got paid to work for them.

"Mississippi is certainly different from the Hamptons," I remarked for lack of any intelligent comment to ease the sudden awkwardness between us.

Emily Sturgis arched a brow. "Yes. It certainly *is* different."

Her tone left me in no doubt that the comparison wasn't very flattering to my home state. I couldn't help saying, "We have a more relaxed way of life down here, more time for the little courtesies so often lacking in certain areas of the country. Don't you think?"

Even though I smiled and didn't attempt a fluttering of eyelashes à la Belle-mode, Emily still got my meaning. She murmured an innocuous reply, then pretended to answer a question from one of her companions, and we drifted apart. It was a big relief. Only opening my mouth to change feet can get tiresome. And embarrassing.

I sucked in a deep breath and looked across the table to find Bitty watching me with a faint smile. She lifted her whiskey tumbler in a silent salute that let me know she'd heard at least part of our exchange and approved. She would. Bitty is the mistress of catty comments. I saluted her back, realized my glass was empty, and went to find a waiter.

The place was packed. Somehow I got detoured and found myself at the restrooms instead of the bar. No, it had nothing to do with how much I'd had to drink, but everything to do with the press of people crammed into one small area. Since I was that close to the restrooms I decided to take advantage of the situation to make a pit stop.

When I came out, I had to push my way between people to locate the bar. As I sucked in my stomach to make more room between myself and the other patrons, I heard a man say in a low, angry tone, "He's dead, I tell you. I don't care if he hasn't been found yet. Now you just keep your end of the bargain and—"

That was all I heard before the press of people squeezed me forward, and I popped out at the end of what seemed to be a long tunnel of laughing, talking, partiers. I tried to turn around to see who had been speaking, and who they'd been talking to, but I found myself carried along on a wave of people surging toward the bar. Or maybe the band. I wasn't really sure. I just know that by the time I got near our table I was breathless, and I was pretty sure that someone had felt me up along the way. I didn't know whether to be indignant or flattered. It's not like I'm a young, firm coed anymore, so I decided to feel a little sorry for the person who had expected ambrosia and got pudding instead. It must have been a dreadful shock.

When I reached our table, Bitty was up dancing with one of her sons. He turned slightly, and I was pretty sure it was Brandon. As he and Clayton are identical twins, I still have trouble telling them apart sometimes. It's not like my twin and me, who are fraternal instead of identical. Emerald is petite and blonde like our mother, and I inherited the Truevine height and coloring. In other words, I am Bigfoot to Emerald's Princess Leia. It's the luck of the genetic draw. I'm pretty content with the way things turned out; I've noticed a tendency in some men to be overprotective of small, delicate females, and I would go crazy at being smothered with constant attention. I like my space.

Since there was very little space where we were, I tapped Bitty on the shoulder and asked her to come outside with me for a minute. She was in the middle of a dance-step that involved being swung about by her son, and I had caught her as she was whirling past.

"What?" she yelled at me as she spun toward the wall, then came back toward me like a Tilt-a-Whirl at the annual fair. My first instinct was to duck, but Brandon caught her in time and spun her toward another wall. I decided to wait out her dance and talk to her when she was too exhausted to move. It'd be safer for her, me, and the other patrons.

That moment came fairly quickly. Not even Jack Daniels can keep Bitty going indefinitely. Of course, she's not one to admit defeat even when her blonde hair straggled into her face, and her complexion had turned red as an autumn apple. Instead, she hung over the table gasping for breath as she reached for her empty tumbler.

"Oh . . . dear," she managed to say with a little difficulty, "I'm . . . empty."

"I'll get you another one, Mama," Brandon said, polite young man that he is. And so good to his mother. He took bartending classes just so he could keep up with her social affairs since she likes to show off her sons to other ladies in the garden club and on the many committees she attends. Not to mention, it comes in very handy with the Divas.

While Brandon went toward the crowded bar I said quickly in Bitty's ear, "I have to talk to you!"

Still dragging in air to fill her depleted lungs, she nodded. "O-kay. Talk."

"Not in here. Somewhere private."

Bitty leaned forward to rest with her palms on the table, but blinked at me. "What is it . . . with you—and the privacy thing?"

"Oh, for heaven's sake," I said, and took her by the arm to drag her toward the door. It took me a couple minutes to find the door since it seemed to have been covered up by people, but I finally succeeded and got her outside with me.

We stood for a moment in the street outside Proud Larry's while Bitty caught her breath. Then she said, "What on earth are you doing? I was having a good time in there."

"And you can go right back in as soon as I tell you what I just overheard."

She put her hands on her hips. "What did you hear that's so important you have to drag me away from all the fun?"

"I think I just bumped into the professor's murderer," I said in a tone just loud enough for her to hear but not loud enough for anyone else. When Bitty's eyes got bigger, I said, "I heard him telling someone that he's dead but just hasn't been found yet."

"Oh my gawd—are you sure that's what he said? He said Professor Sturgis is dead and hasn't been found?"

"Well . . . he didn't say the professor's name, but I'm sure that's who he meant. It has to be. Who else could he have meant?"

Bitty glared at me. "He could have meant his dog, or cat, or even boyfriend for all we know! It could be anything. It's not like you to be so nervous, Trinket."

"Excuse me? What do you mean it's not like me? It's *just* like me to be nervous when we've done something stupid! I'm always nervous! I hate waiting for the other shoe to fall, and when it does—"

Since I had started waving my arms around and had gotten pretty loud, I noticed a few people glancing our way. I put my arms down at my sides and finished primly, "—when it does fall, it never falls on you. I'm always the one who gets hit in the head with it."

After a brief moment of silence between us, Bitty said calmly, "Do you feel better now that you've gotten all that out?"

I thought about it a second, then nodded. "Yes, I think I do."

"Good. Okay, let's start over. I agree that I think it's possible whoever you heard may be referring to—" She glanced around before saying in a low tone, "Professor Sturgis."

When I started to speak she lifted one hand palm out and shook her head. "Let me finish, Trinket."

I shut my mouth, folded my arms across my chest, and nodded at her to continue.

"However, it's just as possible," Bitty said, "that it's about something else entirely, and you're all worried for nothing. There's no way we'll know for sure until . . . until it's out in the open, know what I mean?"

I nodded silently as a couple passed us on their way up the street. We stepped back into the shadows of the building a little, and Bitty shook her head. "We just can't go around all crazy as usual. No one else but us and the murderer seem to know the truth, and unless we want to get all involved again, we need to pretend nothing has happened."

Really, she was making sense. I was very proud of her. And extremely cautious.

"You're right," I said at last. "I guess I just panicked. I'm too old for this kind of thing. Actually, I don't think this kind of thing is good at any age. I'm having to buy more hair dye than usual lately, and I know all this stress is making me prematurely gray."

Bitty looked up at my hair. "Well, it's definitely a most interesting shade of—what is that color? Never mind. I wish you'd use my hairdresser."

"Thank you for reassuring me," I said sarcastically, and she sighed.

"Cheap hair color from Walmart isn't nearly as good as a trained professional, you must admit, Trinket."

"Professional—do you suppose that's who I overheard? A professional hitman?"

"I thought we weren't going to worry about that any longer?"

"In your dreams. You know me. Do you really think I'll be able to put this out of my mind for longer than ten or fifteen seconds?"

Bitty looped her arm through mine and turned me toward Proud Larry's front door. "I know just the thing to get you to relax and have fun without all the worry, honey. Come on with me. I'll fix you right up."

I should have known anything Bitty concocts—or has a bartender concoct—is quite likely to be lethal. Fortunately, this just put me into a kind of coma while I was still standing up and talking to people. I understand I was pretty entertaining.

I remember very little of it. Thank heavens.

By nine o'clock Saturday morning The Grove, which the day before had been empty save for spray-painted lines, was full of tents and people. Red, blue, and white tents sprouted from the ground like dozens of silk mushrooms. Girls in designer dresses and young men in designer duds roamed from tent to tent like army ants, devouring delicacies and leaving laughter and high spirits in their wake.

While cars are no longer allowed to park in The Grove for tailgating as they did in my day, it's still a huge crowd that gathers to celebrate the coming game. Saturdays when there's a home game are akin to the Sabbath in Oxford. Everything is slanted toward the approaching rituals. Since food cannot be cooked in The Grove as no fires are permitted, some people have their tailgate party catered, and others just bring old favorites. Tables are set up under the tents, tablecloths are spread, flowers bedeck tables and loop in lovely garlands, and platters of epicurean delights that would please even the Greek gods are presented for consumption. Pimento cheese sandwiches stacked three high may fill a solid silver tray, while next to it fresh fruit spills out of a crystal bowl. Crunchy okra sits next to watermelon slices; bowls of chips have several kinds of dip; pasta salads in all different colors dot tables, and of course, hoagies, barbecue, and other sandwiches may fill up plastic trays with the Ole Miss motif printed on the surface. Baked goods are decorated in the blue and red colors of the university, and some are baked in the shape of a giant M.

Bitty, of course, carried a sterling silver cup engraved with her name and filled with bourbon, simple syrup and mint—a Mint Julep. While I didn't have a sterling silver cup engraved with my name, I did have a sterling silver cup engraved with Bitty's ex-husband's name: Philip Hollandale. I didn't care. I doubted seriously that Philip would need it where he was, although he might think about it wistfully. And I needed it badly. I had awakened with a horrible hangover that Bitty insisted upon treating with "hair of the dog that bit ya," and I felt as if I had been pretty badly mauled, not just bitten.

Amazingly, a little vodka and tomato juice made me feel much better. Almost every tent where we paused had plenty of refills for our cups, too. It was a good thing. I wore stilettos at Bitty's insistence, and I honestly don't think I could have managed it if not for vodka. It gave me just enough false courage to pull it off. Normally, I'd rather wear live alligators on my feet than five-inch heels. But Bitty harassed me until I bought some very nice shoes at one of the resale shops before we came down to Oxford.

"It must be meant for you to wear those, Trinket," she'd said, "because I never would have thought anyone else has feet as big as yours. Maybe they came from a drag queen with good taste."

"You mean like that dress you're wearing?" I'd responded, and we'd both smiled. It pleases us to insult each other.

At any rate, I wore navy stilettos and a navy blue sophisticated dress, and Bitty wore a red Gucci dress and Christian Louboutin sandals that were dark blue and white gingham on the uppers, with red and white striped knot bows and dark blue and white striped stiletto heels. I felt instant lust for the shoes but not the nearly nine hundred dollar price tag. I'm funny that way. Still, I was glad Bitty had insisted I wear stilettos since almost every female I saw teetered on at least four inches of heel. If one of us tripped, it wouldn't have surprised me at all to find us all toppling like dominoes.

Bitty and I flitted from tent to tent in our fancy footwear like giddy butterflies, occasionally stopping to greet someone we knew—or more likely, that Bitty knew—and sample their food and, of course, their libations.

It was a lovely autumn day with warm sunshine gilding the skies and the leaves turning colors, and seemed to be one of those perfect times in life. If I hadn't had the worry in the back of my mind that somehow our foolish act of moving a corpse would come back to haunt us, I would have had a wonderful day. Just like Bitty.

Two and a half hours before game time, Ole Miss football players appeared under an arch that named it the Walk of Champions; they strolled down the brick pathway between all the tailgaters. The coach walked with them, and the entire crowd went crazy. Over all the hollering and Rebel yells could be heard the Ole Miss Hotty Toddy cheer:

Are you ready?
Hell yes! Damn right!
Hotty Toddy, gosh almighty,
Who the hell are we? Hey!
Flim flam, bim bam,
OLE MISS, BY DAMN!

Even though I was a little surprised I still remembered it, I fell right in with all the others and yelled so loud my throat got dry. That called for another sip from my sterling silver cup, of course. Throughout the rest of the afternoon before the big game, I heard the Hotty Toddy countless times. All it took was one person yelling *"Are you ready?"* for the rest of us to chime in.

Really, Bitty can be right about some things. It was a lot more fun to lose myself in the enjoyment of the camaraderie and familiar rituals than it was to think about a dead professor.

I should have known the Law of Retribution would catch up with me sooner rather than later.

Chapter 4

By the time Bitty and I returned to Holly Springs the next day, I was exhausted. Ole Miss had won their game, the boys had their new bedding, their laundry had been cleaned and returned, and no one had said anything about a dead professor.

Maybe Bitty was right. Maybe I was OCD and just worried for nothing most of the time.

It was still before noon Sunday morning when we pulled into the driveway of Six Chimneys, her sprawling antebellum home with front and side-porches. An iron railing fence encloses a small front yard, and her triple-wide driveway ends at a four car garage behind and to one side of the house. My car, a five-year-old beige Ford Taurus, sat on the concrete and brick drive where I'd left it.

Huge iron or concrete planters held pansies, purple kale and maiden grass, with tendrils of ivy trailing over the edges. Bitty has a gardening service that makes sure her home is always up to date with the current season. Her house is pink with cobalt blue shutters and white trim on the gingerbread scrolling. Crystal chandeliers hang from the porch ceiling, but they're the outdoor kind that weather well.

Bitty also has an alarm service, but she rarely remembers to set it. This time I'd reminded her, so she opened the front door and started punching in numbers. It beeped at her a couple times until I told her the code. She entered it and then looked at me.

"How do you know my code?"

"Simple. I know you. It was easy to figure out."

Her eyes narrowed slightly. "No, it's not."

"Really, Bitty, anyone who knows you could figure it out pretty easily. You should use something unusual, not your dog's name."

"I only used part of her name."

I rolled my eyes, Bitty muttered something rude, and I set down my overnight case and asked if she had anything cool to drink.

"Mimosas sound okay?" she said as she started toward the newly remodeled kitchen.

"Only one of those for me, since I have to drive home. I see no point in giving our local police an excuse to stop me."

"Hah. As if they need an excuse. Do you know that Rodney Farrell stopped me the other day for something he called a 'rolling stop' at the stop sign? I told him there was no such thing, and I had no intention whatsoever of letting him write me a ticket."

While Bitty got out the orange juice and a bottle of champagne, I took glasses down from one of the cabinets.

"Did he write you a ticket?" I asked as I held out the glasses for her to pour in the juice and sweeten it with champagne.

"No, but he was fixing to until I told him that I'd tell his grandmother how rude he'd been to me."

"There *is* such a thing as a rolling stop, you know," I said when my glass was full. "It's a traffic violation."

"Oh, don't be silly." Bitty recorked the champagne bottle and put it back in the cooler. "I never heard of it. If they go around making up new laws, they should put out some kind of announcement about it."

I nodded. "It's on the driver's license test. A driver must come to a complete stop at a stop sign, regardless if it's a three-way, four-way, or even one-way stop."

Bitty gave me a sour look. "Well, aren't you little Miss Traffic Cop today. How do you know this, may I ask?"

"Because when I came back home I had to change my driver's license from one state to another, and they required me to take the test since it was time for me to renew anyway. I had to study the Mississippi driver's manual. Would you really have told his grandmother?"

"Probably not. But he didn't know that."

I pictured Officer Rodney Farrell's horror at Bitty's threat. He reminds me of a character or two from the old *Andy Griffith Show* reruns, since he acts like Barney Fife and looks like Opie Taylor. Bitty and I have vast experience with old TV shows and old movies. We frequently finish one another's sentences when quoting lines from oft-seen television reruns.

I said, "Well, he probably just wanted to 'nip it, nip it'—"

"'Nip it in the bud!'" we both finished together and laughed at our own silliness in quoting a line used by the fictional Barney Fife.

Once we were seated in Bitty's small parlor and had our feet up on ottomans, she asked, "What new plans do Aunt Anna and Uncle Eddie have in mind lately?"

Aunt Anna and Uncle Eddie are my parents. My father's brother was Bitty's father, now deceased. My parents have come down with a bug in their later years—the travel bug. While I sometimes suspect them of luring me home just so I can take care of their neurotic dog and feral cats while they go climb Pike's Peak and gamble at Cripple Creek, it's more like I'm a temporary custodian. They're usually only gone a week at a time, and I'm usually so glad to see them return I forget the horror I've endured while they were absent. It's something similar to childbirth; once the baby gets here, labor pains fade from memory. That just about describes my feelings about caring for their creatures.

"It's so near the holidays," I replied to Bitty's question, "that they haven't made any new plans that I know of. I should be safe until after the first of the year. Then I can start worrying about them taking off for the pyramids or Machu Picchu."

"Bless you."

I looked at her. "What?"

"Didn't you just sneeze?"

I thought a moment. Then I shook my head. "No. I was just telling you that my parents have sent off for brochures again, this time adding Machu Picchu to the list."

Bitty stared at me. "They sent off for brochures to *where?*"

"Machu Picchu. It's an ancient abandoned village atop a mountain in Peru."

"Oh. Good gawd. I'd hate to think of them traipsing around mountains and all. They're in their seventies. Why don't they go somewhere flat?"

"I'm hoping they don't find out they'll need passports until it's too late. That may slow them down a little bit."

"Speaking of ancient history," Bitty began, "I think that professor just had it out for Clayton for some reason. Why wouldn't he allow him to take his exam, or do some extra work or something to make up those missed days? Why just flunk him for no good reason?"

I'm getting pretty good at following Bitty's swift conversational sidebars.

"Were his grades good up until then?" I asked.

"Not too bad. Some Cs but more Bs, and he usually turned in all his assignments on time. By flunking him, Sturgis could really have hurt Clayton's future chances."

"At what?"

"Who knows? My boys have changed their major so many times, I can hardly keep up with it, but good grades are almost always required in most cases."

"Is Brandon still determined to be an attorney?"

Bitty shuddered. "Yes, so he says. Jackson Lee is delighted."

"He would be. He's an excellent attorney. So why aren't you pleased about it?"

"Law is all right for some people, but I'd like to see my son go into a field that's more respectable."

"What's disrespectable about the law?"

"All those lawyer jokes, for one thing."

I rolled my eyes. "Honestly, Bitty, and you accuse me of being OCD. You're much more illogical than I am."

"Am not."

"Are too."

We stuck our tongues out at each other, laughed, and took another drink of our mimosas. Regression to childhood is always more fun with a companion.

Since it was early afternoon on a Sunday, we decided to go to brunch at Budgie's. The current name is really the French Market Café, but Budgie used to own it and is still the manager, so locals still refer to it as Budgie's. Old habits are hard to break.

There were several tables still available, so the lunch crowd hadn't yet shown up when we arrived. Since Budgie had recently been forced to implement a No Pets rule, we were without Bitty's usual furry accessory, and I anticipated a quiet, leisurely meal with no puggy interruptions. Not that Chen Ling isn't cute in her own, inimitable way. It's just that meals are so much more palatable without her porcine snorts as she gobbles down whatever she can reach on Bitty's plate.

After the stress of our discovery at Ole Miss, I decided that something fattening was in order. Truthfully, I don't need an excuse. I eat stuff that's bad for me all the time. It just doesn't seem fair that artery-clogging fats should come in so many delicious flavors.

I ordered fried okra, fried green tomatoes, chicken fried steak, black-eyed peas with fatback, cornbread sticks with butter, and sweet tea to drink. For dessert, I planned to order butter roll and coffee. That should encompass all the main food groups in recipes from the South: butter, salt, sugar and grease. Vegetables, meat, fruit and grains are just accidental in my favorite meals.

For those unfamiliar with butter roll, it's similar to a cobbler without fruit. Or to a cinnamon roll swimming in custard sauce. Legend says it originated in slave cabins years ago, and they were kind enough to share the recipe and ingredients with other poor families who passed it along. It's delicious and an excellent way to end a meal.

Bitty didn't seem stressed at all, so she stuck to a light meal of fried catfish and hushpuppies, with a side order of coleslaw. Sweet tea is *de rigueur* at Budgie's. As Dolly Parton said in the movie *Steel Magnolias*, "It's the house wine of the South." Amen.

"No dessert?" I asked when it seemed as if she might pass up some calories. I like to share my excess with others.

"I'm thinking about having buttermilk pie."

I smiled. "Let's order extra plates."

"Don't we always?" Bitty chirped.

We do. When it comes to dessert, just one isn't usually enough. We each order a different delicacy, then half it on an extra plate so we can indulge ourselves with both and yet not require either an insulin shot or a pacemaker to get out of the café. Gluttony can be bad for your health, I've heard.

Besides, I'd lost five pounds and didn't really want to add it back on at one meal. With only fifteen more pounds to go, I had hope of fitting back into clothes I'd saved from the eighties. Why not? Padded shoulders and caftan sleeves will be popular again one day, I'm sure. These styles seem to recycle every few decades. Of course, if the mini-skirt and no bra fashions come back, I'll have to opt out. Unless I wear the mini-skirt over my chest, innocent spectators could have their eyesight irreparably damaged.

Budgie had just delivered our desserts when Rayna Blue came rushing into the café. She paused, then she saw us and made a beeline for our table. I don't know how I knew it, but all of a sudden I was certain catastrophe came with her.

Sometimes I really am psychic.

"You're not going to believe this," she started out, and I put up my hand palm out to stop her.

"No. Please. I just started my dessert and coffee, and I don't want to hear anything I won't believe right now. Can't it wait until I've finished?"

Rayna looked nonplussed for a second, then nodded. "I suppose. But hurry up. I have to get back to the office pretty quick."

Recently, Rayna had been drafted to help her husband, Robert Rainey, with his business. Rob is an insurance investigator and bail bondsman. It was his job at the last that got him in a predicament a couple months back, but everything worked out and he's back on the job tracking down people who skipped out on their bond, and investigating insurance claims to keep people honest. Or catch them being dishonest. I admit to being amazed by how many people try to defraud insurance companies, and at their sheer stupidity in concocting wild schemes. It's the last that intrigues me, since Divas are prone to creating our own wild schemes. Not that we need any new ideas.

Bitty, however, couldn't wait to hear what Rayna had to say. She continued with her work of cutting our desserts in half to share as she asked, "What on earth is it, Rayna? You look right frazzled."

Rayna is medium height, slender, and has dark hair she either wears brushing her shoulders or in a ponytail. Today she had it loose around her pretty face. Her denim jeans and long-sleeved cotton blouse had paint smears on them as usual, since Rayna is an artist of some note in our area. She's also right around our age and one of the founding members of the Dixie Divas group.

"Well, I am frazzled," said Rayna, and she pulled out a chair from the table to sit down with us. Bitty automatically cut some of the desserts to include her in our feast.

"So tell us what's happened, for heaven's sake," Bitty said, and pushed some pie, butter roll, and a clean fork toward Rayna. "Don't keep us in suspense."

When Rayna glanced at me I shrugged. "I don't care, just as long as it doesn't interfere with my buttermilk pie and butter roll."

"*Well,*" began Rayna as she scooted the dessert plate closer, "you know how Rob has had me helping him these last few weeks, tracking down people who skipped out on their bond for whatever reason, while he does his insurance investigations."

She took a bite of butter roll, briefly closed her eyes in what I could only assume was ecstasy, and then opened them again with a smile to continue. "So when I turned on the police scanner, I heard there's a guy down in Oxford that's gone missing. His wife claims he should have been home on Friday night, but he hasn't shown up. Well, the Oxford police were reluctant to call it a Missing Persons case since he's only been gone thirty-six hours, but they put out a BOLO for him anyway."

"What on earth is a BOLO, and why should I care about some husband who's probably still drunk under a table somewhere?" Bitty wanted to know.

"Be On the Look-Out for," answered Rayna. She scooped up a bite of pie, and said, "He's not just *some* husband, Bitty. He's very well known in Oxford, and no one has seen him. I wouldn't think it was so strange, except that he disappeared in the middle of the day. I did a little digging of my own, and he didn't make any of his afternoon classes Friday, and despite being expected at a function Friday night, he was a no-show. His wife is convinced something has happened to him."

While Rayna paused to take another bite of dessert, I had a sinking feeling I knew where this was going. Not even a huge bite of buttermilk pie got rid of the rock sitting in the pit of my stomach.

"So what actions are the police taking now?" I asked.

Rayna looked up from her dessert plate. "Here's where it gets even more strange. The wife was staying at a friend's house for the night to help with festivities for the next day, but when she couldn't reach her husband she called the police. When they got to their house in the wee hours of Saturday morning, everything in the place was torn upside down and sideways, with no sign of the professor."

Bitty stopped shoveling butter roll in her mouth for a second to echo, "Professor?"

Rayna waved an impatient hand. "Yes, one of the professors at the university, but here's the best part—there are rumors he's been kidnapped. Can you believe it? A professor at Ole Miss has probably been abducted, and you two were right there when it happened! I'm surprised y'all didn't hear anything about it, but they did keep it quiet in case he turned up or kidnappers called with a ransom demand. Of course, his wife is afraid he's been killed, but the police are still going with a Missing Person at this point. Well, I tell you, the newswires got a hold of it, and now it's all over the state about this guy."

Bitty looked slightly relieved and started eating butter roll again. "It's probably one of those money things, you know. I never knew professors made a lot of money, but I guess you never really know about those kinds of things, do you?"

"By any chance," I asked without really wanting to know the answer, "is this professor's name Sturgis?"

My question caught Rayna with a mouthful of buttermilk pie, and she just nodded.

Bitty's fork clattered to her dessert plate as she dropped it and put a hand over her mouth to stifle a gasp of surprise. I just looked at her. I tried to signal with my eyebrows that she should keep any unwise responses to herself so as not to compromise Rayna, but apparently she thought I meant for her to blurt out everything she knew.

"Professor Sturgis wasn't kidnapped," she said in a voice much louder than a whisper. "He's dead!"

I sighed, and Rayna looked momentarily startled before she said, "But there was no evidence to support that theory, Bitty. No blood or anything at the scene, I mean."

"That's because he was strangled with a wire coat hanger," my clueless cousin replied with a nod of her head. At least this time she lowered her voice.

Rayna glanced at me as if for explanation or confirmation. I briefly considered my inclination to disavow any knowledge of the professor's fate, then realized that it would only be postponing the inevitable. So I nodded.

"It's true. We saw him."

"You . . . *saw* him?" Rayna looked horrified.

"Somebody hid him in Clayton's dorm room closet," rattled Bitty, "so of course, we moved him elsewhere. They'll find him eventually, I'm sure."

Nonplussed, Rayna put down her dessert fork and looked from me to Bitty and back. "This is really true, Trinket?"

"I'm afraid so."

"Oh my."

I managed a smile and pointed to her dessert plate with my fork. "Don't waste the pie or butter roll. You'll be sorry later."

Rayna picked up her fork, but I could tell she'd lost interest in food. "Didn't you think about telling the police?" she asked in Bitty's direction, but her eyes were on me. I nodded.

"I did, I did, but I was out-maneuvered by . . . my traveling companion."

Naturally, Rayna looked right at Bitty, who was scooping up her last bite of pie. After she finished her last bite of butter roll, she looked up, saw us staring at her and said, "What? Have I got food on my face?"

She put up one hand to brush away imaginary crumbs, and while I shook my head, Rayna said, "Bitty, you . . . you *moved* him?"

"Didn't you hear me say he was in Clayton's closet? Of course we moved him. I wasn't taking any chances someone would think he'd been killed there by my son."

"But . . . but . . ." Rayna seemed at a loss for words and looked back at me. Since I couldn't think of a thing to say that would help her understand, I just shrugged.

She leaned back in her chair again. Finally she said, "Do you remember the last time we disturbed a crime scene?"

"There have been so many times—refresh me on which one you mean," said Bitty.

"Okay. Let's talk about the time we moved another body. Do you recall how that worked out?"

Bitty thought for a moment, then a light came on in her upstairs windows—by that I mean her eyes got brighter—and she nodded. "Oh yes. Philip. He ended up moved around a lot more than I intended, I do recall that very well. He should have been that quiet and agreeable when he was still alive."

"Right. Okay. So then, you do remember that the police were very upset with us for tampering with evidence, disturbing a crime scene and moving a corpse? If not for Jackson Lee, we would all probably still be in jail."

Nodding, Bitty said, "Jackson Lee is wonderful, isn't he?"

"Bitty," I said, "I think the point Rayna is trying to make is that we've once more become involved in activities that could put us in jail."

"Well for heaven's sake, Trinket, you've only said that about a dozen times."

I looked at Rayna. "Do you see what I was dealing with? She had a convenient bout with memory loss every time I tried to stop her from moving the professor. I will say this, I think Bitty was right when she said the professor was murdered elsewhere. It sounds as if he was killed at his home, from what you just told us."

"See there?" Bitty beamed at me. "I was right!"

"Don't strain anything patting yourself on the back," I said, "because that's the only time the entire weekend that you were right."

"Not true. I was right about the Rebels beating the Bulldogs, wasn't I? Even though the score was really close, Ole Miss won the game. The Colonel was done proud."

"He's not the mascot anymore," said Rayna. "Remember? The Rebels are now represented by a black bear and not the Colonel."

Bitty waved one hand at her. "I know, I know, but Colonel Reb was at The Grove anyway, so it's not like he's gone forever. But it's best that all the students be okay with things, I suppose, and not feel uncomfortable about their mascot. Ole Miss will always be the Rebels, even if our mascot is in a black bear costume next time."

"Can we get back to what happened to the professor?" I asked when she paused to take a breath, and Bitty looked a little surprised.

"What else is there to say, Trinket? He's dead, and now the police will find it out, and then they'll find the killer, and everything will be okay, just like I told you."

"Uh, Bitty—aren't you forgetting a small detail?" I asked, and she blinked at me a couple of times before slowly shaking her head.

"No, I don't think so, Trinket. That pretty much sums it up."

I leaned over my dessert plate to whisper loud enough for her and Rayna to hear but not so loud people at the next table heard us: "We found the professor dead in your sons' dorm room, so the killer probably put him there. Why?"

"Oh, well . . . *oh lord!* Someone's trying to frame my boys for murder!"

"Keep your voice down, Bitty," Rayna said. "People are starting to stare."

Bitty snatched up her black Chanel tote and began digging inside it. "I'm calling Jackson Lee, that's what I'm going to do. He'll take care of this."

"Stop," I said, "and wait just a minute. Do we really want to involve him in this situation? As an attorney, he'll be honor bound to report it to the authorities, or insist that you do. I'm not sure that's the best thing at this point."

Rayna agreed with me. "Let's go ask Rob what to do, Bitty. He might have a reasonable solution to suggest."

Still digging in her tote, Bitty slowed down the frantic search for her cell phone long enough to realize it was safely tucked into the neat little pocket just for cell phones. Chanel does convenient things like that for their customers. Those who can afford to drop a couple thousand on a purse, anyway.

"I don't know if we should," she said. "Rob may feel the same way Jackson Lee would feel. Oh my . . . what if the killer thinks my boys know who he is and goes after *them?*" She looked suddenly frantic, and her fingers dug into the soft leather purse like cat claws.

I put my hand over hers where it still clutched the top of her purse. "Calm down, sugar. That's very doubtful. The killer probably just chose their room at random."

"Do you really think so?"

She sounded so hopeful I had to say yes. "Of course, honey. It was just chance that the professor was left in their room. Once the police find the killer, it will be just fine, you know it will."

When we both turned toward Rayna, she had her head tilted to one side and a skeptical expression on her face. "Maybe we need to get some objective opinions."

I knew what she meant.

"Okay," I said, "I'll call Cady Lee and Deelight, you go ahead and call Gaynelle and Cindy. Bitty, you call Sandra and Marcy. I'll stop by the lingerie shop and tell Carolann and Rose. Where should we meet?"

"My house, of course," said Bitty. "Rob will be too nosy if we have an emergency meeting at Rayna's, and I'm afraid Aunt Anna and Uncle Eddie will hear us if we have it at your house, Trinket. Say, in three hours? That should give everyone enough time to be free."

"Got it," said Rayna. "Five o'clock your house, Bitty. Don't bother about food or drinks. I'll tell everyone to bring something."

Bitty nodded. "That gives me enough time to get over to Luann Carey's house for Chen Ling, then get back home. We need to figure out a strategy."

"What we need," I said bluntly, "is to figure out how to put the body back where it was originally and turn back the hands of time."

I swear, when Bitty looked at me, I think she was actually trying to figure out how to do that.

Chapter 5

Divas come in all sizes and all stages of life. Our youngest Diva is Marcy Porter, who at thirty just had her third child this summer. Cindy Nelson is only a couple years older than Marcy and lives with her husband and several kids in Snow Lake, about fifteen miles east of Holly Springs. Sandra Dobson is in her early thirties, a registered nurse, and lives between Snow Lake and Holly Springs. Gaynelle Bishop is currently our oldest Diva; she's a retired school teacher in her sixties and lives in a cute bungalow a block away from Bitty. Cady Lee Forsythe, whom I've known since grade school, is now married to Brett Kincade, whose family owns a chain of department stores. I still call her Cady Lee Forsythe most of the time. It's hard to break old habits. Bitty Hollandale is my age—that is to say, we are ageless ladies in our very, *very* early fifties. Okay, fifty-two. Don't ask Bitty her age, though. She still claims she's "nearly fifty" and justifies that white lie by pointing out that two years over the fifty mark is just as close to fifty as two years under the mark. Arguing with her logic is a futile thing, so don't bother.

I stopped by Silk Promises, the real name of Carolann Barnett's lingerie shop, though the locals all just refer to it as Carolann's. She and Rose Allgood, her business partner in the shop, are our newest Divas. Carolann is a year younger than I am, a little chunky in size, and addicted to the New Age lifestyle. Or maybe just clothes style. While her shop has the most up-to-date designer garments in lingerie and silk blouses, Carolann wears tie-dyed peasant dresses and beads with peace signs around her neck. She has red, curly hair and an infectious laugh.

Rose is tall, slender, and a cool blonde. She manages the Blue Velvet Room in the shop and sells exotic panties without a crotch and rainbow colored, sometimes iridescent, dildos. There's other merchandise in her retail cases, but those are the two things that stick out most in my mind. They stick out on her shelves, too, lined up like happy little—or big— soldiers.

Anyway, both Carolann and Rose said they would be at Bitty's at five, since on Sunday afternoons the shop closes at four. It's a small town, and she makes the hours that suit her and her clients best.

"Oh my," said Carolann, "an emergency Diva meeting again so soon?"

It hadn't been an awful long time since we'd had another emergency meeting to help cheer up one of our Divas.

"Bitty needs some advice," was all I said, and Carolann nodded.

"Just as long as it's not about murder, I can offer all the advice she needs."

I smiled.

Rose picked up on my smile, somehow, or maybe it was the fact that I didn't say it wasn't about murder, because she lifted her eyebrows at me.

"Oh no," she said, her voice a cool contrast to Carolann's louder tones. "Again?"

"Well . . . not really. At least—I mean, it's nothing like the last time. We just need a few extra opinions on what should be done, that's all."

Rather dryly, Rose observed, "Maybe I should bring my lawyer."

I shrugged. "It couldn't hurt."

Carolann said, "Good lord!" in a tone so loud it rattled the glass prisms of one of her pretty overhead chandeliers. "Is this about another murder?"

"Be prepared to discuss many topics tonight," I said, "and I'm sure one of them is going to be about murder. Oh, and bring something chocolate."

Chocolate and murder, I thought when I went back to my car parked across the street on the court square; as incongruous as the latter may be in conjunction with a nice evening with friends, they're becoming a regular ritual at our Diva meetings. It could be worse. If we ran out of chocolate, for instance.

First I stopped at the Pig—our local name for the Piggly-Wiggly grocery store—to buy something delectably chocolate for the evening, then I leisurely made my way down 311 Highway toward my ancestral home named Cherryhill. I share the house with my septuagenarian parents, who are very active. It's where I grew up, and I have many fond memories of my childhood with my twin sister and two older brothers. We may not have had a lot of money, but we did have a lot of fun.

My sister Emerald lives across the continent in the Pacific Northwest, my brothers both died in Vietnam when I was still very young, and Mama and Daddy are usually off to some part of the country they always wanted to see but never had the money or time. I am the pinch hitter; that means when they take off for a trip, I hold down the fort at home. It might be easier if all I had to do was ward off invading hordes of Vikings or whatever while they're gone, but my time is spent feeding and caring for feral cats, and to render my services to their spoiled, neurotic dog. Brownie makes Chen Ling look like a piker. Both of them shamelessly manipulate the women who adore them. It's simply not true that dogs cannot reason. I have seen canines at work far too many times.

That said, I was looking forward to the holiday season this year. Last year I'd still been moving when Thanksgiving arrived, and by the time the Christmas season rolled around I was still numb from the trauma. Moving isn't a picnic, but I thought at the time that getting a divorce and moving simultaneously must have a ranking *somewhere* in the nine levels of hell described by Dante.

Looking back, I can truthfully say that I had no idea what was in store for me. The shock of finding my parents much more mobile—and prone to escapades of an intimate nature in unexpected places—than I had been led to believe was barely absorbed before I was introduced to my first corpse. From that point onward, it has been a roller coaster ride of often unbelievable thrills and chills. It is not a ride I recommend to the faint of heart.

Mama was already in a tizzy when I walked into our kitchen, and as I paused to survey the array of baking ingredients spread upon the countertops, Brownie greeted me by throwing up on my shoe. I'm his favorite receptacle for all things unpleasant.

Of course, Mama was immediately concerned and rushed to the rescue.

"Oh, my poor baby," she crooned. "Mama's here. It will be okay."

I knew better than to think she was talking to me. I reached over to take a roll of paper towels from the counter to wipe off my shoe. It was an icky mess.

"Do you think he's eaten something bad for him again?" Mama asked as she tried to pry open Brownie's jaws to check.

My reply was a bit grumpy. "If he's awake, then I'm certain he's eaten something bad for him again. Probably a tin can or a roll of toilet paper. You should have named him Billy Goat Gruff. It's much more suitable."

Brownie, a part-beagle, part-dachshund, closed his brown eyes and quivered with his best show of distress. The little faker.

I watched while he wrapped my mother right around his left front paw. Ignoring me, she patted him and spoke softly to him until he allowed her to get his maw open wide enough for her to be sure he didn't have anything he shouldn't have in his mouth—like a table leg. Jewelry. Watches. Dental bridge. Those are just a few of the things he has ingested since showing up on my parents' back deck one cold, icy night a few years back. Since then he has turned his big-eyed waif act into a thriving career. The single fact that my father—after years of not allowing animals in the house—actually lets this dog not only in the house, but in his bed every night, speaks volumes for Little Brown Dog's repertoire of beggar tricks.

He doesn't fool me. And he knows he doesn't fool me. We get along quite well when my parents are gone, because I generally don't cater to him, and he generally lets me bump along in my selfish way until my mother returns. We have an unspoken truce. It works pretty well for both of us.

"Excuse me," I said to my mother, "I need to reach the garbage can with this mess I took off my shoe."

"For heaven's sake, Trinket, go around that way. Just don't let it drip. Did you see anything in it that could have caused him to throw up?"

I stopped dead in my tracks and looked at my mother, who still knelt on the floor with Brownie cuddled up against her. "I have no intention of looking through it to see. If you'd like, I can hand this to you."

Mama looked up at me, and then she laughed. "I guess that is asking a bit much of you, isn't it."

"Yes. Oh yes. I'll put it in the garbage can and take the can outside. What are you baking?"

"Pies that will freeze well. I have two chess pies in the oven already. We've asked Emerald and Jon if they want to come for Thanksgiving this year."

I had already pulled the garbage sack out of the can. My mother's statement made me drop it, and trash spilled across the floor. "What?" I said.

Mama turned to look at me. "Emerald and Jon. I asked if they'd like to come over for Thanksgiving dinner this year. Are you all right?"

"Yes, I'm fine . . . you say that as if they live just around the corner. They live all the way across the country, for heaven's sake. If they come for Thanksgiving, will they bring all their kids, too?"

"My goodness, Trinket, what are you thinking? Of course they will. That's one reason your father and I said we'd pay their way, because it's so expensive to travel with a large family. Are you sure you're all right? You look funny."

"I'm fine. It's just . . . the spilled garbage. I'll get it. Yes. That's what I'll do. If they bring all those kids—how many is it again? Six? Seven?— where will they sleep?"

"Oh, we'll find places to tuck them here and there. Yours and Emerald's old room still has a good bed in it, of course, and the boys' room . . . I've kept it with twin beds in it that will sleep at least two of her boys. That would be nice, don't you think, to have boys in Jack and Luke's old room again?"

"Well," I said, "I guess her boys can't be any more destructive than Jack and Luke were. Their room's still in one piece, so I doubt Emerald's kids could destroy it in only a few days. It is only a few days, right?"

"What's the matter with you?" Mama asked me as she got up from kneeling on the floor by Brownie, who seemed to have fully recovered from his brief bout of nausea. "You don't sound very excited."

"I don't? Hm. Are you aware that one of her kids set the house on fire a while back?"

Mama looked at me. "So did Bitty not so long ago."

Good point. I tried again.

"It wasn't too long ago that she told me her youngest twins are going through the terrible twos. They screamed the entire time she was on the phone with me."

"I didn't get more than an hour's sleep at a time from the day I brought you home from the hospital until you and Emerald started kindergarten," Mama countered. "And her youngest twins aren't two anymore."

Drat. She trumped me again.

"They'll probably torment Brownie," I said in what was a desperate attempt to delay the inevitable. "You know he doesn't like kids."

"He bites. They'll learn."

I gave up. "You're good," I said, and she nodded sweetly.

"I know. It'll be just fine, Trinket. You can always hide at Bitty's house when the kids get to be too much for you."

"That will be about four minutes after they arrive," I said glumly. "I never could handle a lot of children at once. That's why I had just one. And there were times I got crazy with only one child."

I finished picking up the trash I'd spilled, holding my breath so I wouldn't gag, and took the bag outside to dump it in one of the big plastic bins. My twin sister would be here for Thanksgiving. Really, that's not a bad thing. I love her and miss her. It's just that she has so many little rug rats that my head begins to pound and my eyes begin to twitch, and they make fun of me. One of them insists upon calling me "Auntie Tinkle." She giggles when she says it, so I know that she thinks it's naughty. She's my favorite.

I sucked in a deep breath of fresh air before I went back inside the house and tried to keep my left eye from twitching too badly. Then I pasted a big ole smile on my face and went in to put another plastic bag into the garbage can.

My mother insists upon coordinating her winter clothing with my father's, and also with Brownie. Since Brownie was wearing a blue plaid sweater, and Mama wore a blue plaid cardigan, I assumed my father must also be wearing a blue plaid sweater. I felt out of place in my black jeans and green blouse. While Mama is dainty, with porcelain skin that has probably never seen a blemish of any kind, and her once-blonde-now-silvery hair is usually well-coifed, I am more like my father's side of the family. Daddy is pretty tall, even though his over-six foot height seems to have slightly shrunk in the past few years, and his once-dark hair is now snow white. We're both big-boned. Really.

Mama patted me on the arm as she passed me on the way back to the kitchen sink where she washed her hands, then dried them on an old towel. She picked up a flour sifter and began sifting flour into a stoneware bowl. I saw the red food coloring sitting near the bowl and knew that she was making one of her specialties.

"Red Velvet Cake?" I asked, and Mama nodded.

"Is this for Emerald? I mean, Thanksgiving is still three weeks away, isn't it?"

"This is for our church social," said Mama over her shoulder. "I'm baking a Lane cake for Emerald."

"A Lane cake!" I drew in a breath of ecstasy. Maybe my sister coming home for a few days would have unexpected perks. It *had* been a long time since I'd seen her, even if she was going to show up with kids in tow. Most of my family knows I avoid children in any groups larger than one. Emerald's children were, the last time I spent longer than five minutes with them, beautiful to look at but hard on anyone who still had their hearing. And their sanity.

Emerald seems not to notice when her offspring bounce on couches, walk across coffee tables, or pee in her potted plants. I suspected my sister of being a bit "potted" herself a time or two. She just smiles serenely and goes on with whatever she's doing at the moment, whether it be peeling a child off the ceiling or escorting a terrified guest to the front door. That last would be me.

"You do realize Emerald's children are much older than the last time you saw them," Mama pointed out while I was still reminiscing about the little darlings.

"Oh. Yes, I guess they are. So . . . the oldest ones are somewhere around the ages of Bitty's boys, I suppose? And that would make the youngest . . . ten? There are a couple more in there somewhere. Good lord. She's too old to have kids that young. What was she thinking?"

"Change of life babies," Mama said as she sifted in baking powder and salt. "It's a miracle they got here in perfect shape. But I suppose medicine has come so far now that the risks aren't as great for mother and baby."

"Twins at forty-two," I thought out loud, and shook my head as I realized just how lucky I've been in my life. "I'd have left them at the hospital."

"Oh, Trinket, the things you say. You know you'd have done no such thing," Mama said, and I wondered just how it was my mother could be so blind to who I really am, especially lately.

I decided to let her drift pleasantly along in her fantasy world and went upstairs to my bedroom to change clothes and unpack my overnight bag. Daddy must have taken it from the hallway and brought it upstairs for me, since I couldn't recall having done so myself. I was pretty sure I hadn't, but then, strange things have been happening to and around me so much lately, I wouldn't place a bet on even a sure thing. My mind plays terrible tricks on me.

I sat down on the edge of my bed after unpacking my overnight bag and thought about not only my twin sister, but Bitty and her new habit of carting around corpses. That was not a situation that would mesh well with my sister's visit. Emerald had never been that adventurous, and as a child had been a terrible tattletale. My brothers and I could never resist tormenting her, so of course, we always stayed in trouble.

Not that Emerald was an innocent victim all the time. Oh no. She was just sneaky. She put itching powder in my brothers' underwear and socks. She substituted liquid food coloring for one of my spray perfumes, so that I looked like a Smurf right before my date came to the door to get me. She used my best fingernail polish on the barn dog's toenails.

All that aside, if Emerald got even a whiff of what Bitty and I had encountered in Clayton's dorm room, it would be all over town. She's worse than Cady Lee Forsythe, who has the biggest mouth of all the Divas. Not the loudest, just the biggest. I'd better let Bitty know she was coming home for a visit.

"You're not calling to cancel, are you?" asked Bitty when she answered my call. I had finally given in and gotten a cell phone, and now she always knows it's me. Caller ID is not the best of modern advances, in my opinion.

"No, I just thought I'd let you know that Emerald is coming home for a visit."

Silence on the other end.

"Bitty?"

"I'm here. I'm just torn between being glad to see her again, and fear that she'll get involved in our current . . . project."

Trust Bitty to whitewash murder with an innocuous name like "project."

"She'll be here in three weeks. With her husband and kids."

"Gawd. How many kids does she have now?"

"Six. But the oldest ones are Brandon and Clayton's age, and the youngest ones are ten. So we don't have to worry about diapers or tantrums."

"Not that I would anyway. So now we just have to worry about smoking and cussing."

I thought about it a moment. "Probably. You're referring to the ten-year-olds, right?"

"Of course. Kids today are much more precocious. I think it has something to do with all the stuff the government puts in our food to make it grow. It makes our kids grow up too fast."

"Bitty, have you been on the Internet again?"

"Not this weekend. We've been a bit busy, if you'll recall."

"Right. Okay. I have chocolate, and I'll be there at five."

"Bring hard liquor."

She hung up before I could remind her that drinking and driving was a lot worse than doing a rolling stop at a stop sign. Officer Rodney Farrell should be glad I'm such a conscientious person about some things.

Of course, no liquor store is open on Sundays in Holly Springs, nor are grocery stores allowed to sell anything stronger than beer. Wine is sold in grocery stores only if it's 6% alcohol or less, and even then, the Blue Law that prohibits the sale of spirits is being stretched. Just a few years back—okay, over forty—the entire state of Mississippi prohibited the sale of any kind of liquor at all. A few of the counties are now half-dry, half-wet. There are still dry counties in our state that forbid alcohol to be sold in any form. Naturally, the citizens there go to the neighboring counties to leave their money. A blind eye is turned toward responsible drinkers in those counties, but woe be unto you if you mess up and get caught drinking and driving. Or creating a disturbance fueled by any kind of alcohol. Only politicians or judges can get by with that.

So I wisely refrained from adding to any cache of bourbon that Bitty already had tucked away in her basement—she has a wine cellar complete with temperature controls and an index—and kept to my chocolate rule for the evening. It would probably be more than I could handle with or without the added alcohol anyway.

Divas usually meet by the dozen. There are few rules to being a Diva, but one very important rule is that no men are allowed unless they serve a purpose such as to wait tables or as entertainment. Normally, there are twelve Divas. Due to a few changes in the past year, the number now stands at eleven. Carolann and Rose are the newest, and before them, I was the last to be inducted into the Diva membership. It's not that we're a fancy, exclusive club or anything, because really, the essential requirement of being a Diva is an excellent sense of humor. And a high tolerance for chocolate and spirits.

Lately, I have also suggested keeping bail money at hand. While we have collectively developed a knack for getting involved in crimes, getting arrested is more of an individual talent.

I blame that on the ringleaders: Bitty Hollandale, Rayna Blue, Gaynelle Bishop, and Trinket Truevine.

Yes, I have included myself among the guilty for the simple reason that I have been guilty of leading forays into danger and disaster. It's a latent talent that has bloomed under the tutelage of my companions. We bring out the best—some have suggested the worst—in one another.

So it wasn't at all surprising that once we had all the greetings out of the way and had settled into comfy chairs with our choice of beverage and form of chocolate, that my dear cousin Bitty brought the group to order. She set Chen Ling on the settee next to her and stood up to get everyone's attention. Still holding her champagne glass in one hand, she made a gesture with the other as if striking a gavel, and everyone laughed.

"Divas, we have a problem," she said with her most charming smile. "As some of you may know, Trinket and I went down to Oxford this weekend to the football game—Ole Miss won, of course—and while we were there, something awful happened." Bitty looked at me and held out her free hand. "Trinket will tell you all about it."

I had just begun to suck down some sweet tea when she made that announcement and nearly choked before I could get it all the way down. I gave Bitty an evil look, but she had already sat back on her uncomfortable settee next to her dog. Chen Ling, a cross-eyed, bow-legged, pigeon-toed pug, returned my evil look since Bitty declined to even glance in my direction. Chen Ling—occasionally I refer to her as Chitling—has cleverly developed a keen sense for trouble of any kind. She has been known to bite the offender. This is not usually a problem since she has only three of her front fangs, but it does sting.

With everyone now looking at me, I wiped tea off my chin and managed a smile. "I'll try to make this brief," I said, "so forgive me if I leave out a few details. First, as you all know, what's said with the Divas, stays with the Divas, right?"

Of course everyone agreed, some just with nods, others with "Of course!"

I continued, "This past Friday, Bitty and I went to her sons' dorm room to see if they were back yet from their morning classes. Earlier that morning Bitty had a parent meeting with Clayton's ancient history professor. It did not go well."

I paused, uncertain quite how much to divulge at this point. I didn't want to say anything that would put either Bitty, Clayton, or any of the Divas at an uncomfortable disadvantage should they be interviewed by the police. There always seems to be that point to consider lately.

So I said, "Imagine our surprise when we arrived at their dorm room to find it unlocked and neither boy there. Instead, there was the professor whom Bitty had argued with only a few hours before about Clayton's grades." I paused before adding, "He was in the closet and very, very dead."

Someone gasped, someone else groaned, and I was pretty sure it was Cady Lee Forsythe who muttered, "Here we go again . . ."

"Seeing as how he was in her sons' dorm room," I said as soon as the gasps and groans had died down, "there seemed to be only one thing to do so no suspicion could be directed at one of the boys."

"Oh . . . my . . . *gawd*," said Sandra Dobson. "You didn't! Not again!"

Sandra had been briefly involved in the last case of the traveling corpse and still shuddered when it was mentioned.

"Oh, yes," Bitty piped up, "it was the only thing to do."

"Needless to say," I said loud enough to drown out anything incriminating Bitty might say next, "matters have progressed rather rapidly. Rayna has come across some new information . . . do you want to share it, Rayna, or would you rather I did?"

"I can, if you'd like." When I nodded, she stood up with a glass of wine in one hand and a fudgy brownie in the other. "It's like this. Oxford police think the professor was abducted since his living room is torn up pretty badly. There's no sign of blood, so they assume it's an abduction for ransom. We know otherwise."

"Are you sure it's the same guy?" asked Cindy Nelson. "It could be one of those terrible coincidences."

"Very sure," said Rayna around a mouthful of brownie. She chased it with a sip of wine before continuing. "For one thing, Bitty and Trinket recognized him when he was found dead. For another, his wife is supposed to be near hysteria and saying the worst, that someone has probably killed him. It's the same man."

"Why does she think he's dead if the police think he's kidnapped?" Marcy asked. "If that was my husband, I'd hope for the best. Wouldn't you?"

She looked around at the others, who all nodded except for Bitty, Gaynelle and me. While Bitty and I have been married and divorced, Gaynelle has never married. None of us would qualify to answer that question, I thought. I was then proven wrong.

"You may hope for the best," said Gaynelle after a moment, "but you might also fear the worst. Some people are better than others at holding in their emotions."

I thought about Emily Sturgis; she was someone whom I would have picked as able to hold in her emotions. Tragedy affects everyone differently, I suppose. And since police usually suspect the spouse when a partner is murdered, maybe she feared the worst for that reason, too.

"So what you're wanting from us," began Deelight Tillman, "is an idea on what to do next?"

"Right," said Rayna with a nod. "Should Bitty and Trinket go down and inform the Oxford police how and where they found the professor—which, of course, entails giving them the reason they moved him—or should they just wait to see what happens?"

The consensus was almost unanimous: Wait to see what happened next.

"After all," said Deelight, "it's not as if anyone knows he's already dead. It's best just to let it play out. I'm sure someone will find him soon, and then the police can change their investigation to homicide instead of a kidnapping."

"Keep in mind," Gaynelle said, "that while the police are investigating the wrong kind of crime, a dangerous murderer is getting away."

We all looked at each other in silence. Gaynelle had a point. By delaying, maybe we would give a killer enough time to make a complete getaway.

It was Bitty who said, "Nonsense. The murderer won't get any farther than if the professor had been found an hour after the murder. It's not time that matters so much in something like this, as it is who had the motive, means and opportunity. Maybe the killer is feeling safer by the hour, but that doesn't mean he'll get away. Police have a way of finding out things, and besides—I'm pretty sure I know who killed him."

For a moment no one said anything. I'm sure we were all equally stunned by her calm announcement. Finally I dredged up the courage to ask, "So who killed Sturgis?"

Bitty said calmly, "His wife, of course. It's always the wife."

Gaynelle said flatly, "That kind of blanket statement is unproven by facts. I doubt it can be applied to every murder case, Bitty."

"Nine times out of ten, then."

"Bitty," I said gently, "don't you remember when you were a suspect in your husband's death?"

"Of course, I do, Trinket. I'm the one out of ten who happened to be innocent. And he was my ex-husband anyway."

I refrained from rolling my eyes. Gaynelle cleared her throat, and Rayna drained her glass of wine. Several Divas followed Rayna's lead.

"Do you really think so, Bitty?" asked Cady Lee Forsythe. "I met Emily Sturgis once at an alumni fund raiser. She seemed like a mousy little thing."

I thought of the professor's wife a bit differently. She hadn't seemed at all mousy to me. But what did I know? After all, I'd only seen her in a crowded bar.

"I don't know about mousy, but she's definitely got the motive and opportunity," Bitty replied as she inspected her manicured nails with a frown. "I'm not sure about this color. What do you think, Divas?"

"What's her motive?" asked Rayna, frowning at Bitty, who stopped inspecting her nails to reply.

"For one thing, he's a horrid little man with a big ego and small brain. For another thing, he must be doing something wrong, or he wouldn't have been murdered. Nice people just don't usually get murdered for no apparent reason. Do they?"

I figured most of us must consider Bitty's last question to be rhetoric since no one answered. The only sounds in the room were the ticking of a fussy ormolu clock on the fireplace's carved mantel and the rather wheezy snorts from a fat pug.

Deelight Tillman finally broke the silence. "And the opportunity?" she asked. "Do you think his wife killed him right after his meeting with you?"

Bitty blinked at her. "Why would I think that?"

"Well . . . because you and Trinket found him dead only a few hours after your meeting with him that morning. So somewhere in there is when he had to be . . . you know. Murdered."

"How odd. Well, I suppose Emily could have done it during that time," said Bitty with a thoughtful nod of her head. "I mean, it's quite possible, don't you think?"

"Anything is possible," said Gaynelle firmly, "but not everything is probable."

"I hate it when you talk in riddles," Bitty said crossly.

"She *means*," I said, "that Emily Sturgis may have had the time, but it's not likely that she's the murderer."

Bitty looked faintly astonished. "Why on earth would you say that, Gaynelle? I had no idea you knew Emily that well."

"I don't know her that well, but I do know that she's a small woman and not at all capable of overpowering a man in order to strangle him with a coat hanger."

"Sturgis isn't—wasn't—that big a man. Heavens, *I* could have taken him if I'd tried."

"Bitty!" three Divas chorused simultaneously.

I rolled my eyes and muttered into my empty tea glass, "I swear, she's bound and determined to end up in prison one day."

While Bitty frowned at me, Gaynelle said practically, "I'm quite sure the police forensics team will investigate all possibilities. Really, it's out of your hands now, so the best thing to be done is nothing. Do we all agree on that?"

Of course we all agreed, even Bitty, who suddenly seemed to find conversation with her pug more fascinating than the discussion of murder.

That should have been my first clue.

Chapter 6

It's always amazed me how often I can be so wrong, yet still manage to escape serious harm. I'm not necessarily referring to physical harm, although that's always a big consideration. Psychological trauma can be infinitely more frightening. I think it's the whole "waiting for the other shoe to drop" aspect that most scares me—the fear of what's to come, the unknown factor of . . . well, Bitty and what she might say or do.

Bitty hasn't always been wrong in what she says or does, but her timing is quite frequently amiss. I say this only because it's true.

A prime example of this? Bitty's insistence upon returning to the scene of the crime. Or more accurately, to the scene of *our* crime.

Two days after our emergency Diva meeting, Professor Sturgis was found in the back of the moving truck. By then he was in really poor condition, according to the county coroner's office. I figured they knew what they were talking about. He hadn't looked so good when I'd last seen him, either.

"We have to go down there immediately, Trinket," Bitty called to say early that morning. I held my cell phone out from my ear and rolled my eyes. Cell phones can be a nuisance. I'm not always in a position to speak freely.

"Hold on, Bitty," I said, and looked over at my mother who was busily creating a pan of lasagna larger than our oven could hold. "Mama, do you still need me? I'll be back in a minute."

Mama looked at me with her brows lifted, and I knew what was coming: "You tell Bitty that whatever it is she's got in her mind to do—*don't*. It's too near the holidays to have to spend time in jail."

"I'll tell her," I promised, and as I left the kitchen, I dutifully repeated Mama's warning. "Don't do it, Bitty. Mama says it's too near the holidays to go to jail."

"Oh for heaven's sake, Trinket. You didn't tell her what I said, did you?"

"Since I don't know sign language, and you didn't hear me divulge your risky plans, you have to know I didn't. Are you crazy? Never mind. That was a rhetorical question. I know you're crazy. Haven't you ever heard of playing it safe?"

"That's what I'm trying to do. We need to get down to Oxford this morning so the boys don't end up as suspects."

I put my hand over my eyes. I don't know why. Blocking out Bitty is impossible even when she's five miles away.

"How can they end up as suspects?" I asked her. "There's absolutely nothing to tie them to the professor other than Clayton being one of his many, many students."

"One of his students who was flunking."

"Nobody murders someone because of bad grades, Bitty. I mean, it just isn't done."

"Just because it's not usually done doesn't mean it isn't *ever* done, Trinket."

She had me there. I uncovered my eyes and looked down at the floor. Brownie sat there staring at me suspiciously. Sometimes I think he understands everything that's said, and at other times I'm convinced he hasn't a clue.

"She's crazy, you know," I said to him, and his tail thumped once against the floorboards. That encouraged me and I continued, "She convinces herself that danger lurks just behind the next door and gets me all involved, and it usually turns out that we only make it worse."

Brownie cocked his head to one side and perked up his ears. I'm sure he knew exactly what I meant.

"Who are you talking to now, Trinket?" Bitty demanded. "I can hear what you're saying about me, you know."

"Yes," I said. "I know. I was talking to Brownie. He keeps secrets pretty well most of the time. Although it's not exactly a secret that you're crazy."

Bitty huffed into the phone, and I smiled. If she was going to drag me off into some foolish enterprise, the very least she could do was let me annoy her.

"I'll be there in an hour to pick you up," she said after a moment, and I sighed.

"Okay. I don't know why I let you talk me into these things, but I guess I'd better go with you to keep you from doing something stupid."

"You mean, from doing something like moving a corpse?"

Sometimes Bitty doesn't play fair at all.

"Yes," I said a bit irritably. "Something like that."

"I've got goosebumps of anticipation. Be ready. Oh, and wear something nice."

She hung up before I could ask her why I had to wear nice clothes. It's not that I don't have anything nice. I do. Unfortunately, my nice clothes are not only out of fashion by now, but two sizes too small. I've lost weight, but not enough to take me back twenty years. Or twenty pounds. So I ended up wearing a nice pair of slacks and a sweater set suitable for my part-time job working at Silk Promises. It would have to do.

Of course, Bitty disagreed.

She eyed me when I came out of the house and got into her black Mercedes. She calls it the Franklin Benz, since her third husband's divorce settlement purchased it, and his name was Franklin.

"Is that what you consider nice, Trinket?" she asked after scanning me from head to toe.

"Yes. It is. I don't want to hear what you consider nice. This will have to do. My jewels are being cleaned, and my furs are in cold storage. In Russia. Besides, you're wearing a gussied-up pug. Anything I wear is only anti-climactic."

"I don't *wear* Chen Ling. She is my companion, not an accessory."

"Really." I returned the inspection, my gaze lingering deliberately long on Chen Ling's diamond dog collar. "So you say. And yet . . . her outfit matches yours."

That was true. Along with the diamonds, Chen Ling wore a deep purple velvet dog dress, with a small tulle bow anchored with what looked like a huge crystal bead on the front. She sat in smug comfort in a cashmere-lined basket seat-belted to the middle of the leather front seat. I was left enough room on the passenger side if I didn't want to use my arms. Bitty wore a deep purple velvet outfit, matching stilettos, I was sure, and her diamond bracelet caught the sunlight in tiny refractions so that it looked like she was plugged in to electricity. I felt definitely dowdy next to these two sparkling creatures.

"You're blinding me," I said, and slammed shut the passenger side door. "Did you bring enough batteries for those floodlights you're wearing?"

"Did you bring a change of clothes?"

"Don't be a snob. These are nice navy slacks, and the sweater set is Sag Harbor. I look very nice."

Bitty started the Benz. "Well, thank heavens you're pretty, or you'd never get away with that outfit where we're going."

My head began to buzz. I wasn't sure if my reaction was because she'd actually given me a back-handed compliment, or because the phrase "where we're going" held a sudden connotation of danger.

"Where are we going?"

"Why, didn't I tell you? To Oxford.'

"I know *that*, Bitty. Where in Oxford? I thought we were going to see the boys?"

"Well, that too, of course, but first we're going to the professor's house. Alumni, staff, and friends are invited to a sort of wake for Sturgis."

The buzzing in my head got so loud I looked around for a bee hive. Nope. All in my head. That was scary enough. Just the thought of me, Bitty and Chitling at a wake for Professor Sturgis was enough to catapult me over the edge right into panic.

I grabbed hold of the car's expensive dashboard and braced my feet against the floorboards as if I were being dragged. It was my metaphorical protest since Bitty had the Benz rolling fairly fast down our driveway.

"No," I said. "I'm not going. Let me out here. I'll walk back up to the house."

"Don't be silly, Trinket. We need to show proper respect for the dead. You don't want people to talk about us, do you?"

"Bitty, I'm quite certain people talk about us no matter what we do now, so that's not exactly a great concern of mine. Showing proper respect for the dead should include not rolling him around in a laundry cart, as well as popping up at his house later as if we knew nothing about his death."

"Well, we don't know anything about how he died. Except, of course, that he was strangled with a wire clothes hanger and hidden in Clayton's dormitory closet."

"That's probably more than the Oxford police know right now," I pointed out. "Stop the car. Let me out. I don't want to go."

"If I thought you meant that," Bitty began as she aimed the car toward the road, swerved into a turn and picked up speed down the hill, "I'd be very upset. However, I know you don't want to disappoint me."

"I do. Oh, I do. If it means having to stand in the professor's living room and offer his wife my condolences when all the time I'm waiting for someone to ask me why we were pushing a gigantic laundry cart across the campus, I want to disappoint you. I can't stand the suspense. You know that. You know I hate waiting on bad news."

"You're such a pessimist. Good heavens—where did all those houses come from? I haven't seen them before, have I?"

"I assume you're referring to the subdivision we're passing. You've been passing them for about five years now. Daddy sold the cow pasture to some land developers. Stop trying to distract me, and do stop the car. I can still get back to the house before dark if I walk really fast."

"Nonsense, Trinket. It's not even noon yet. You'd be back at the house before lunch if I let you out."

"Are you? Going to let me out?"

"Of course not. We need to stick together. I talked it over with Gaynelle, and she thinks going down there and seeing if anything out of the normal is said or done is a fine idea."

"Gaynelle's in her sixties now. She's probably getting senile dementia."

"If you really think that, you can tell her yourself. We'll be at her house in about five minutes to pick her up."

"She's going with us?"

"I thought it best. Since she's an academic, she can mingle with the professor's associates."

"Why do *I* have to go if Gaynelle is going?"

Bitty glanced over at me. "Are you whining again? I declare, I don't know what's gotten into you lately. You're beginning to act like a spoiled child."

She sounded like my mother giving me a good scold. To add insult to injury, her dog growled at me. I gave Chen Ling what I considered to be a withering glare, but it just rolled right off her. She lifted one paw and licked it daintily. Her toenails were a nice shade of purple. *My gawd*, I thought, *she's turning into a furry Bitty* . . .

"Did you paint Chitling's toenails?" I asked instead of responding to Bitty's unkind and far-too-close-to-the-truth remarks.

"No, Regina did. At the doggy spa. Why? Isn't the color right?"

"The color is perfect, Princess Glitter. Y'all match beautifully. Does your dress have a tulle bow, too?"

"Yes. And don't give me any guff about it, either. Your own parents are just as bad if not worse than I am about putting clothes on a dog."

Alas, Bitty spoke the truth. It's a source of great concern at times, although I realize that just because I never dressed up my cat or dog that doesn't mean I'm deficient in the area of pet ownership. Or so I've convinced myself.

"Why is it important to dress up if we're just going to the professor's house?" I asked. "It's not like they live in a mansion. Do they?"

"Where they live isn't important, Trinket. It's who they are. You want to be well-dressed, but not over-dressed. Of course, you obviously don't have to worry about that last point."

"Velvet and tulle is not over-dressed for a wake? Good lord. What madness have I become involved in?"

"Since it's still daytime, you'll probably pass inspection by the skin of your teeth. Or your cheap slacks."

"Bitty, you are such a snob sometimes."

She became immediately indignant. "I am not! I just like to dress appropriately."

"Then stop making snide remarks about my clothes. I'm always clean, and I strive to wear suitable styles at the suitable times. Slacks and a sweater set are just fine for going to someone's house in the afternoon. I'll bet you'll be the only one there in velvet and tulle."

"And you obviously don't know the ladies of Oxford."

"True. Now I'm not sure I want to."

"It's just that there's a certain code for the alumni and professor's wives, and it includes dressing up for affairs. I'm no more dressed up now than as if I was going to a garden club meeting."

"I'm not sure what that says about Holly Springs garden club members."

"Trinket, this may *look* dressy, but it's a pantsuit, not an evening gown. I'm not even wearing stilettos."

I peered down at her feet. By golly, she was right. Instead of ten inch high heels, she wore nice, low-heeled pumps that matched her pantsuit.

"Badgley Mischka?" I guessed, and she shook her head.

"Manolo Blahnik. Fall collection."

"Cute. I like the suede flower on the toe. And the heels aren't so high you look like you're walking on stilts."

"I'd say thank you, but I'm not sure that's a compliment," said Bitty as she nosed the big black Mercedes against the curb in front of Gaynelle's neat little house.

She must have been watching for us, because the front door opened immediately, and Gaynelle stepped out onto the porch and turned back to lock up. She wore a sensible tweed jacket with a matching skirt, low-heeled shoes, and a silk blouse with a froth of ruffles at the throat. Gaynelle's hair was a lovely chestnut color this week. It framed her face nicely and made her look years younger than her sixties.

"See," I said, "Gaynelle isn't dressed in satin or velvet either."

"Gaynelle isn't related to me. You are."

"Ah, so you're only a snob with blood relatives."

"Yes. I suppose that's true. It's a reflection on the Truevine name, you know."

"Lucky me, to be related to you."

"Indeed you are, my dear, and one day I'll get it through to you that clothes may not make the man, but they definitely make the woman."

I rolled my eyes and stuck out my tongue at Chitling. She barked fiercely at me, and I smiled. Really, Bitty's right: I revert to childhood much too often these days.

"Hey, Gaynelle," I said as she opened the back door and slid onto the leather seat.

"Hey, Trinket, Bitty." She slammed shut the door and strapped her seatbelt. "I'm ready, so let's go brave the Oxford matrons."

"Are they really that bad?" I asked as Bitty put the car into gear, and we shot forward on the narrow street. It's not that I doubted Bitty's assertion, but an objective point of view is always welcome.

"Oh, no. Most of them are very nice, very down to earth people, but a few of them consider themselves a cut or two above everyone else. Did you put a rinse on your hair, Trinket?"

I reached up to touch my hair self-consciously. If I don't put a rinse on it every six weeks or so, Brownie looks at me as if I'm hiding his enemy the squirrel on top of my head. I think it has to do with the gray color it gets and wearing it pulled back into a ponytail. I've tried to do better about letting myself go, especially since I started keeping company with Kit Coltrane. The handsome vet is enough to make any woman reconsider her options. Just the thought of his smile when he sees me gives me shivers and makes my stomach flip. In fact, just thinking about him at all has the same effect.

"Don't you like it?" I asked, half-turning to look at Gaynelle. "Is the color off?"

"No, not at all. And I do like it. I just noticed that it was different than it was a few days ago, that's all. Is that a medium auburn you're using?"

"Yes. It's the closest I can find to my natural hair color."

"Your natural hair color is gray," Bitty said. She's unwilling to be left out of any conversation for very long. I still thought it tacky of her to say that.

"My natural color has always been auburn," I corrected her firmly. "It's just lately that I've been getting gray. Since I came home and starting hanging around with you, as a matter of fact."

"Don't be so rude, Trinket. You were gray when you drove across the Memphis-Arkansas Bridge. Don't try and blame it on me."

"Bitty, is that outfit by Gucci?" Gaynelle interrupted. I recognized her attempt to stop what could degenerate into a long exchange of insults.

Bitty glanced at her in the rear view mirror. "Why yes, it is, Gaynelle. Do you like it?"

"I do. I never thought blondes could wear that color, but it suits you."

"It's called Eggplant. I like it anyway. And my shoes match, too . . ."

Complimenting Bitty on her style choices usually soothes the savage beast in her, and it worked this time, too. We got into an involved conversation about shoe styles, the insane prices charged, and if they were really better than less well-known designers. Before I knew it, we were on the outskirts of Oxford. Engaging Bitty in a discussion about shoes and/or clothes is always a guaranteed time-consumer.

"Here we are," said Bitty, and slowed the Mercedes down in front of a nice house with a front yard full of old trees and a driveway full of expensive cars. "Looks like we're not the first ones here."

"You *think?*" I murmured as I noted the Jaguars, Mercedes, Acuras and Lexus all parked neatly in the wide, wide driveway. Ivy climbed old stone walls, liriope circled the oak trees, and bright yellow and rust-colored mums dotted the carefully cultivated grounds. I began to think Bitty had been right. I didn't know a thing about Oxford matrons.

Bitty quickly checked her makeup—after all, we'd been in the car for a good forty-five minutes—added some lipstick, then unfastened Chen Ling from her basket.

"You're really going to take that dog inside?" I asked even though I was pretty sure a court order wouldn't have stopped her. "Is she on the guest list?"

"Of course she is," Bitty replied, undeterred by my mockery. "Her name is right above yours."

"Hunh," I said because I couldn't think of anything better at the moment. I just undid my seatbelt and got out of the car. It was a little past noon, and weak sunlight slid between thick oak branches. Clouds had started to gather overhead, and I figured it would probably rain all the way back to Holly Springs.

As Bitty had predicted, everyone in the Sturgis home was dressed expensively. I should have felt out of place, but I've been around Bitty too much lately to let it bother me. Since no one gasped and pointed at me, I figured no one but Bitty noticed or cared that my entire outfit cost less than any one of their keychains.

Only a couple of men were there, and one of them greeted Bitty about three seconds after we entered the front door.

"Elisabeth Truevine, is that you?" he asked, his voice lower than usual because of the solemnity of the occasion.

"It's Hollandale now," said Bitty, matching his tone with just the right amount of decorum. "I'm a widow."

I barely kept from rolling my eyes. Bitty and Philip Hollandale had been divorced for over a year when he got himself murdered, so that hardly classifies his ex-wife as a widow. Bitty, however, has taken to referring to herself that way no matter how many times I've pointed out the truth.

Turning to me, Bitty said, "This is the man I would have married had Frank not stolen my heart first. I know you've heard me speak of him—Breck Hartford."

Of course, I played my part to perfection. Since I had never heard the name before in my life, I said, "Not *the* Breck Hartford?"

Bitty smiled. "The very one. Star halfback on the football team, Captain of the Varsity Club, and now assistant coach right back here at

Ole Miss. How you been doing these past few years, Breck?"

She turned back to him to ask the last question, and I saw out of one corner of my eye a vaguely familiar face that seemed riveted in our direction. It took me only an instant to recall her: Mrs. Sebastian Sturgis. Wait. *What was his first name?* I wondered as she detached herself from the small group of ladies and came toward us. It wasn't until she reached us that the name came to me.

Gaynelle greeted her first. "Perhaps you remember me, Mrs. Sturgis? I worked briefly with your husband on a refresher course of ancient history a few years ago. You invited me here for lunch."

"Oh yes, of course. Gaynelle Bishop, is that right?"

Gaynelle nodded. "Yes. I'm sorry we must meet again under these circumstances. Please accept my condolences."

Emily Sturgis nodded, and her gaze flicked across Bitty and Hartford for a moment before settling on me. "I believe we've met before?" she began, and I nodded.

"I'm so sorry to hear about your husband," I said, taking the hand she offered to me. "Everyone says Spencer was a wonderful man."

Emily Sturgis inclined her head slightly to acknowledge my condolences. "Thank you. His loss is . . . well, dreadful. Please forgive me, but I've forgotten your name?"

"Trinket Truevine," I supplied as we released our brief clasp of each other's hand. "I'm Bitty Hollandale's cousin."

"Yes, yes, of course. I'm so sorry. It's just that everything has been so . . . so hazy since we found out about . . . Spencer."

Tears welled into her eyes. She managed a faint smile as she looked at Bitty, then at Hartford. I felt very bad for her. Maybe I hadn't liked her that much when I first met her, but no woman should ever have to suffer the loss of her husband to a violent death. It made me feel even worse that I knew something about how he died, and that I'd known it even when she didn't. I had to fight the sudden urge to tell her everything.

Maybe Bitty sensed what I was feeling, or maybe she felt it herself, because she locked on to my arm with a Vulcan death grip and said, "Emily, if ever there's anything I or Trinket can do for you, please feel free to call."

I would have added my assurances, but since Bitty had her claws sunk into the flesh of my forearm so deeply that any sound I made would be a shriek, I clamped my jaws tightly together and just nodded. Chen Ling, safely tucked under Bitty's other arm and far enough away from me that there was no danger of her biting, added her own doggy utterance as I peeled Bitty's hand off my arm. I swear I saw part of my sweater and maybe a little bit of my skin stick to her fingernails.

Breck Hartford apparently had his chivalric impulses stirred, for he went at once to Emily's side and slid an arm around her shoulders. "My dear, you know Victoria and I will be here for you as well. She's so sorry she couldn't come with me today."

Emily Sturgis leaned into him a little and brought up a delicate lace handkerchief to dab at her tears. It was artfully done. "You and Vic have been my rock since this awful thing happened," she murmured, and turned her face against his chest.

Hartford, tall and lean, wore a gray tweed jacket, button-down shirt with a sweater vest, and dark slacks. He was good-looking in that way men are when they have flecks of silver at their temples. On women, those same flecks would be considered a sign of age. On men, they're considered distinguished. Go figure.

Anyway, he patted her rather awkwardly on the back, seeming embarrassed and at the same time, a bit flattered. I wanted to roll my eyes, but I refrained. Conversation in the room was subdued, and just to keep my eyes busy and unrolled, I glanced around to see if I knew anyone there. Candy Lynn Stovall stood across the room, and I managed to detach myself from our small group and head her way.

"Trinket," she said warmly, and we leaned toward each other to do one of those half-hugs and air-kisses. "I'm so glad to see you again. Of course, the circumstances aren't very nice."

"No, it's a shame about the professor. Have any suspects been arrested?"

One of the women standing next to Candy said, "As far as I know, the police don't have any idea where to look. I mean, they thought he was abducted at first, and then when that moving company found his body—well, it's just anybody's guess who might have killed him."

"So he was found by a moving company?" I asked as innocently as possible. "How odd."

"Apparently he was killed here . . . right in this very room," said Candy in almost a whisper. Of course, we all looked at each other and shivered. I tried not to look around for signs of blood or violence. That would be so tacky.

Candy, however, glanced toward the stone fireplace and took a step away from it. "Then the murderer stuck him in a moving van for God only knows what reason. It's crazy. Police are interviewing everyone on campus, especially students in the boys' dormitories. Do you suppose they think a student killed him?"

"Whose moving van was it?" said the other woman who'd spoken earlier. I tried to think of her name since I had met her at Proud Larry's, but it eluded me. Really, I should never have let Bitty buy me a drink unless I watched what went in it. The woman lowered her voice. "I heard it was rented by one of the students Spencer flunked out of his history class. And I heard he's probably the one who killed him, too. You know. Revenge."

"For a failing grade?" I couldn't help saying.

"Oh, but grades are everything, Trinket," said Candy Lynn. "Things have changed a lot since you were here. Now grades determine a lot more than just what college will take you after high school. They can affect the job you get after graduating from college."

"Okay, grades are important. But important enough to kill for? That doesn't make a bit of sense to me."

"Or to me either. But *we're* not killers. Someone on this campus *is* a killer."

Candy Lynn's response was louder than she realized. It had the effect of halting all conversations around us. The sudden silence felt heavy and awkward.

Trust Bitty to find a way to make it worse.

"Oh for heaven's sake," she said, sounding faintly annoyed, "of course there's a killer on the campus. How else would Professor Sturgis have been murdered in his own home? He wouldn't let just any random stranger inside."

Deep silence got deeper. People exchanged embarrassed glances, and no one dared look at Emily Sturgis. Except, of course, Bitty.

"Well?" she said. "*Would* he let in a total stranger?"

This last was directed at Emily, and she sucked in a sharp breath and shook her head. "No. No, Spencer wouldn't do that. Especially when he was working. He always wanted complete quiet and total privacy when he worked on his thesis or graded papers."

"But it's so safe on campus," protested Candy Lynn.

"Technically," said Gaynelle Bishop, "this home isn't on the campus. It borders it. Would there have been any security available, Emily?"

"Well, we have our own security system, and all the doors and windows are hooked up to it, but it has to be activated to send a signal to the monitoring company. If Spencer . . . if he was able to get to the keypad, he could have set off the alarm."

"So you don't usually keep it on?" Gaynelle asked.

"Not until we go to bed at night. Oxford is such a safe, quiet place to live. There's been no need for it. This isn't New York."

Gaynelle nodded understanding. "Yes, you're right about feeling safer in a small town. The reality, however, may be otherwise."

"Apparently so," Candy Lynn said wryly. "Oh, I'm sorry, Emily. That may have sounded insensitive. Have the police given you any indication of who is responsible?"

Emily shook her head. "No. They just say that it's under investigation."

"Police are usually as close-mouthed as clams," said Bitty, and she nodded her head wisely. "We've had to deal with them a great deal lately."

Emily looked at Bitty. "You have? Why?"

It was a simple question, but I was sure Bitty would give a complicated answer, so I said quickly, "Her former husband was murdered several months ago."

"Oh yes. I think we heard about that. He was a senator, wasn't he?" Emily asked.

Affecting a sorrowful expression, Bitty nodded and sighed. "Yes. It was terrible. One never expects their husband to be murdered, you know."

It was Candy Lynn who said, "Oh my no. I mean, it's expected that you'll just be together forever. Or at least until your lawyer gets you a nice alimony settlement."

Candy Lynn and Bitty exchanged a smile of understanding. I made a mental note to ask Bitty later about Candy Lynn's matrimonial status.

Gaynelle immediately diverted my attention by saying to Emily, "Do you know anyone who might have been angry with Spencer? Angry enough to do him harm?"

Emily hesitated, then said gently, "Spencer did not always worry about how he said things to people. He could be quite abrasive at times. In the past he's been the brunt of several students' anger at receiving failing grades."

"Not to mention his on-going association with a faculty member's wife," said a brunette woman whose name I couldn't recall. Everyone turned to look at her, and she lifted a martini glass in acknowledgement. "Well? You all are dancing around it, but you know someone's bound to talk about them sooner or later. Love turned to hate? Could that be a reason for his murder?"

Still standing close to Emily Sturgis, Breck Hartford cleared his throat. "Victoria may not be present to defend herself, so I'll say for her that's a preposterous suggestion. It has no merit at all, and you must know that, Catherine."

"So why isn't she here tonight? Wait. I know the answer. She's off on another one of her triathlon jaunts. Or so she said. That leaves you and your son alone, right?"

"If you're insinuating that—"

"Please. Spare me, of all people, the melodramatic denials. Maybe your family's extracurricular activities need closer inspection."

"You make it sound as if you suspect Victoria of murdering Spencer."

Catherine merely smiled. "Did I? Maybe I didn't mean your *wife*, Breck dearest. But don't underestimate the police. They'll get around to you soon enough."

Breck glared at her. "Are you suggesting that I had anything to do with Spencer's death?"

"Now, why would I do that?"

Breck sucked in a harsh breath, took a step forward, then seemed to recall that he was surrounded by other people. "I cannot imagine why you do any of the things you do, Catherine," he responded evenly. "This is hardly the time or place for your venom. Do try to contain it for once."

"Breck darling," she purred, "I find it most amusing that you dare to talk to *me* about restraint."

A deep silence fell. I stared at Catherine in fascination. She behaved so coolly and indifferently to Breck's anger. No one else moved or spoke in defense of either Catherine or Hartford. *My, my,* I said to myself, *there are definite undercurrents here.*

It was Chen Ling who broke the tension that gripped everyone. She barked into the silence, startling several people who either hadn't noticed or had ignored the velvet-clad gnome clutched tightly in Bitty's arms.

Somehow the pug managed to wiggle free of Bitty's tight grasp and leap to the floor, providing a definite distraction when she went straight for a plate of *hors d'oeuvres* set upon a low table near the fireplace. The sight and smell of cocktail weenies speared with toothpicks had apparently overtaken her. Bitty barely managed to catch her before she could gobble down half the plate, toothpicks and all. The brief skirmish that followed did the job of easing the tension and turning the tide of conversation to laughter mixed with horror.

While people tidied up the overturned platter and its aftermath, I decided to follow Gaynelle. She'd moved toward the hallway and disappeared from sight. Nosy creature that I am, I wanted to see what she was doing. I caught up with her a few doors down a wide corridor that had several rooms opening off it, with a staircase tucked above an ell.

"What are you doing?" I asked her as softly as I could, and she turned to look at me.

"Snooping. What else?"

I put a hand over my mouth to stifle my laughter. Sometimes when I get tickled I snort. It's always a dead giveaway.

Gaynelle put up a hand to point. "Look."

I turned to look at what had caught her attention. For a moment nothing struck me as particularly noticeable. "What?" I asked.

Rather impatiently, Gaynelle took a few steps toward a partially open closet door. "Don't you see?" She rustled the plastic laundry bags protecting what looked like shirts hanging from a small hook on the door. "Freshly washed, starched and ironed."

"So?"

"Look at the hangers, Trinket."

Still not quite comprehending where she was going with her observations, I looked at the wire coat hangers that held the clean shirts. Then it came to me.

"Oh! Do you think the professor was stra—" I stopped and looked behind me. No point in letting any eavesdroppers hear that I knew details that would only be known to the killer and to police.

"Yes," said Gaynelle softly. "Not only that, but probably with one from one of his own shirts."

Possibilities skipped quickly through my brain. I leaned close to say, "Maybe the professor was killed by someone posing as a laundry man."

"Spencer would have allowed him into the house," Gaynelle agreed. "Most of the time he probably didn't even look at who delivered his cleaned clothes. It would be an excellent method of gaining entry."

"But maybe these were just delivered," I said, and Gaynelle rustled through the thin plastic coverings until she found a ticket.

"Ah. Just as I thought. This tag is dated the same day he was killed."

For a moment I stood there in the gloomy shadows of the hallway with its dark wood wainscoting and trim and considered several options. There were a few things that came to mind, but it seemed to me that the most important evidence pointed to some kind of planned murder instead of just an overwrought student losing control enough to kill the professor. I looked back at Gaynelle.

"So who wants to ask his widow if they had laundry delivered, and if so, did it arrive before or after the professor went missing?"

"I will," Gaynelle said firmly. "Just leave it to me."

Rather relieved that the responsibility was going to be hers instead of mine, I just nodded. "Fine with me. How well do you know her?"

"Only in passing, really. As I said earlier, I had attended a seminar with Spencer and was invited to a luncheon here at the house afterward."

"Did you ever notice anything unusual between the professor and Hartford's wife? I mean, Catherine certainly did hint that they hated each other."

"I find it odd that she'd say that. Spencer and Victoria always seemed to get on well with one another. But of course, that was a year ago. Anything could have happened to turn them into enemies since then, I suppose."

I said, "I remember Victoria from our freshman year. She was in our dorm. Kind of a hateful girl back then. She never made it to her sophomore year. And now she's married to the star football player from the old days," I added.

"So why would she have a relationship with Professor Sturgis, and then later say that she hates him?" Gaynelle wondered.

I shrugged. "Beats me. Sturgis definitely has—had—a combative personality. He was quite rude to Bitty, and his staff seemed afraid of him."

"Afraid?"

"Oh, not in the usual sense, like he would attack them or anything, but as if they didn't want to anger him or they'd be fired. That kind of afraid."

"Yes, I can see that," Gaynelle said. "He did have that kind of personality."

I looked at her curiously. "Did you know him very well?"

"Oh no. Spencer Sturgis was not the kind of man one wished to know very well," she said rather firmly. "Still, I admit to being surprised that he was murdered."

"Why?"

"Because he just didn't seem important enough to murder, if that makes any sense at all."

It did. In my very brief acquaintance with the man, I'd developed a keen dislike for him, but nothing even close to the kind of passion it must take to murder someone. Not even Bitty had felt that way, although of course she had a bad habit of making inappropriate remarks. Sturgis just seemed like an annoying, rude man who got under the skin of those he taught or met. It would take a lot more than irritation or anger at a failing grade to kill a man, I was just positive.

Life, I have since realized, is an educational process that never stops.

We'd been standing in the dimly lit hallway whispering, so when Gaynelle saw someone approaching, she said loudly, "I just know the powder room is somewhere close by."

Breck Hartford paused in the hall archway. "To your left, ladies. Second door on the right."

"Thank you," said Gaynelle with a smile, and we turned to our left and went down the hall.

I could feel him watching us, and when I chose to wait outside while Gaynelle went into the powder room, I looked toward him. Hartford had an expression of utter rage on his face. That's the only way I can describe it. When he saw me staring, he give a start, his expression cleared, and he smiled, but the impression lingered even after he turned and walked up the stairs at the end of the hall.

Apparently, he was still upset by Catherine Moore's tacky comments about him and his wife.

Catherine, I decided, was definitely someone I needed to talk to; she seemed to have all the good gossip. And gossip often turned out to have a kernel of truth that could lead to killers . . .

Chapter 7

Catherine Moore stood in the kitchen fixing herself a very dry martini with two olives when I found her. She glanced at me. "Martini?" she offered, and I shook my head in reply.

"No, thanks. I don't do so well on straight vodka before dark."

She laughed, a throaty sound. "How inconvenient for you. I don't do well without it before dark. Too many annoyances, you know. So what really brings you down to Oxford today? I know it's not to comfort a grieving widow."

A little nonplussed by her astute comment, I decided to go with truth. "Bitty made me come with her."

Catherine took a sip of her martini, folded her arms across her chest and leaned back against the kitchen counter. She was really an attractive woman. Her dark hair was beautifully styled, her clothes obviously expensive, and her makeup artfully applied. She reminded me of Anne Bancroft, the lovely actress who played Mrs. Robinson in the film, *The Graduate*. Catherine had the same blend of self-possession and wry humor.

"Bitty is a force of nature," said Catherine with a smile. "She hasn't changed at all since college."

"That's a rather daunting thought."

"Isn't it? Yet she makes it work. I know she isn't that friendly with Emily, so there has to be another reason you all came down from Holly Springs today. Should I try to guess?"

"If you want," I said with a laugh. "Or I could just tell you that Bitty likes to keep up appearances."

"I'm sure she does. As long as it's convenient." Catherine took another sip of her drink then said, "I heard that Bitty and Spencer had a major row the day he was killed. I don't suppose her showing up today has anything to do with that?"

"Why would it? It's a little late to make amends with the professor."

"Um," she replied with an arch of her brow. "I came today just to make sure that Spencer is really dead. He's no loss to the academic community, I can assure you of that. I hope there's an open casket service so I can see for myself that it's him and not some other jerk being planted six feet under."

"I take it you weren't one of his biggest fans."

She smiled. "Hardly. He was an obnoxious, selfish, horrid beast of a human being with forged credentials that got him this position. But then, maybe I'm a bit prejudiced."

"*Forged* credentials?"

"Yes. He was under closer inspection when he was lucky enough to be murdered instead of tossed out on his ear."

"Who found out his credentials were forged?"

Catherine smiled again. "I did. I always knew there was something off about that little toad, so I checked up on him. It's true that he attended Harvard as he claimed, but he never graduated with a master's degree, a PhD, or any other degree for that matter. I can't imagine why no one found it out before I did."

"I thought the process was more careful."

Catherine drained the last of her martini and turned back to the counter to make another one. "It usually is. That made me wonder just who Sturgis bribed to get on as a professor."

Her caustic comments opened up an entirely new train of thought, and I began to see a host of reasons why the professor might have been murdered.

"Did you decide on the bribee?" I asked after a moment, and she laughed her soft, husky laugh again.

"Yes, I certainly did. But don't worry. I fully intend to take that up with them in my own time."

For some reason the only reply I could think to make to that comment was, "Be careful."

Catherine winked at me. "Sugar, I always am. It takes a lot to scare me."

Bitty chose that moment to find me in the kitchen. Chen Ling was in her usual place on Bitty's chest, peering at me with a disgruntled expression. Yes, pugs have facial expressions.

"Who's scared?" asked Bitty as she joined us.

"Me," I promptly replied. "The growth on your chest is glaring at me."

"Pooh. Chen Ling doesn't glare. She's always sweet to those who are sweet to her."

"Ah, so that's the trick to it. Thanks for sharing."

"Hi Cat," Bitty said to Catherine. "Those olives take up too much room in that glass, don't they?"

Catherine laughed. "I soaked them in vodka first."

Bitty nodded approval. "Perfect. Trinket," she added, looking at me, "we need to go visit the boys if I'm going to catch them between classes.

Are you ready to leave?"

Since I was more than ready to leave but not quite ready to relinquish my talk with a source of valuable information, I nodded and said, "Catherine, I'd love to have a drink or lunch with you one day soon. We can finish our conversation."

"Call me Cat," she said. "All my friends do. Bitty has my numbers, so just give me a call, and we'll meet somewhere for lunch."

I nodded and said I would, then followed Bitty and Gaynelle out to the car after making my goodbyes to the recent widow. Sunshine flirted with clouds, and patches of light wavered here and there as we drove away from the Sturgis home. Tree-lined streets were quiet and orderly, with no hint of the murder that had recently disturbed the peace.

"Well," said Bitty, "you and Cat seemed thick as thieves. What on earth were you two talking about?"

"Murder," I said. "What else?"

Gaynelle laughed. "It's certainly the main topic these days. Did you find out some good information?"

"Maybe. Cat seems to think Sturgis bribed someone to get his position as history professor."

"Good lord," muttered Bitty, "why on earth would anyone pay money to teach ancient history to disinterested students?"

"I don't know, but she does. And she knows who the bribee was, too."

Bitty looked at me. "Who?"

"That's what I hope to find out if and when I have lunch with her. Maybe Sturgis made a threat to reveal the person who got him his fake credentials or accepted him as a university professor, and they murdered him."

"If he did that," said Gaynelle, "he would have been revealing that he'd given a bribe to get his position."

"Good point." I thought for a moment. "What did you find out about the laundry delivery?"

"An interesting fact. Emily said they don't have their laundry delivered. She just assumed Spencer picked it up on his way home."

"What laundry?" asked Bitty.

"Spencer's," replied Gaynelle. "But I'm sure the police have already made that discovery."

"Probably," Bitty said as she made a rolling stop at a four-way inter-section. "The police usually figure out everything long before we do. I say let them have at it, and we stay out of it."

"Bitty, that's the most intelligent thing I've heard you say in some time," said Gaynelle.

I turned to look at her in the back seat. "Don't hold your breath that she does it. She changes her mind more often than Congress."

"I just want to make sure my boys are safe, that's all." Bitty slowed down for a yellow light and looked over at me. "That's all I want."

I patted her arm. "An admirable goal."

We found Brandon and Clayton in the Student Center. They were in the outer lobby area with a group of kids their own age and were laughing and teasing one another like college-age kids usually do. Across the lobby, a bookstore sold tee shirts, books and everything Ole Miss, from bumper stickers to coolers.

"Look at them," Bitty grumbled, "like they haven't got a care in the world. Here I am worrying myself to death that they're all upset at being suspects."

"Maybe they don't know they're suspects," I suggested. "It's not like anyone has told them what was in their closet."

"True. Do you think we should—"

"No!" I said before she could finish her sentence. "The less they know, the safer they are, remember?"

"All right. But I hate keeping secrets from them."

"Nonsense," Gaynelle said calmly. "You do it all the time."

Instead of arguing, Bitty just nodded acceptance. About that time one of the boys looked up and saw us standing near the entrance, and nudged his brother. Both of them got up from their seats, said some goodbyes, and then started toward us.

"Such handsome young men," Gaynelle commented, and Bitty beamed with pride.

"Aren't they? And smart, too. Even if Brandon decides to go into law, I'm very proud of both of them."

I still hadn't heard what Clayton had decided to do after college and hoped that he took after Bitty and not his father. Or maybe took after his grandfather or uncle. Bitty's brother had a business of his own down in Jackson and manufactured something like grommets for engines. I think. Truthfully, it's a rather dull thing to do, but he makes good money, so I guess I'd prefer Clay take after him rather than, say, Frank Caldwell.

"Mama, I hope everything's all right at home," said Brandon when they reached us, and Bitty nodded.

"Everything's fine at home, but how are you two doing here?"

"You mean because Professor Sturgis was murdered?" asked Clayton. "Police came around and asked us all questions about where we were Friday morning and all that, but as far as I know they still haven't found out who killed him."

"Are you okay with all this?" I asked, and Clayton shrugged.

"It doesn't bother me, but it is kind of creepy that he was murdered and nobody knew about it for a couple days. I heard that Randy Klein might be involved, since the professor was found in the truck he'd rented."

"Who's Randy Klein?" Bitty asked, and looked from Clayton to Brandon. "Do you know him?"

"No," Brandon said at the same time Clayton said, "Not real well." They looked at each other, and then Brandon continued, "Clay has a few classes with him. I don't."

"Is there somewhere we can go and talk without having to stand up?" Gaynelle asked. "Not that I'm tired, but I feel rather conspicuous lurking here just inside the door like an old dragon."

Brandon grinned. "Miz Bishop, you fit right in with the rest of us. Come on with me, and I'll show y'all where Heather and I like to sit sometimes."

We ended up sitting on a curved concrete bench situated in a quiet spot near the Lyceum. The Corinthian-columned building rises majestically on a small hill at the apex of a circle roadway. It's the symbol of Ole Miss. Built between 1846 and 1848, the Greek Revival style structure first housed classrooms and a lecture hall, and during the Civil War served as a hospital. Now it houses the offices of the Chancellor, Vice Chancellors, and the university's Provost.

Warm sunshine lit the grounds; it was one of those lovely autumn days that never seem to last long enough. The air held a hint of crispness, and somewhere someone had a fire going. The fragrance of burning logs drifted on soft currents of air. I tilted my head back to look up at patches of rich blue sky. Dark clouds gathered in the distance, but for the moment no storms marred the day.

Brandon sat on the grass, his long legs crossed at the ankles, and leaned back with his weight on hands pressed into the still-green lawn. With blue eyes slitted against the bright light, he drawled, "Sturgis managed to get himself killed at a time nobody would notice for a while, y'know?"

"What do you mean by that statement?" asked Gaynelle.

Shrugging, Brandon said, "Well, everybody who wasn't in class was busy getting ready for the home game and tailgate parties. Nobody would notice him missing unless they went looking for him."

"The professor didn't usually participate in the festivities?" Gaynelle pressed.

Brandon shook his head. "Sturgis has a reputation for being a big jerk."

"How did you hear that?" Gaynelle asked him next. "Did he have any well-known enemies? And are you personally acquainted with him?"

Clayton spoke up. "I am. I've got him for ancient history class. Bran's right. He's a jerk. And that's one of the nicest things he's been called. Especially by me."

Bitty gazed at her sons for a moment, and I saw that she was troubled. So was I, although I wasn't sure it was for the same reason.

"You aren't in the habit of telling everyone how you felt about Sturgis, are you?" I asked Clayton. "In light of what's happened, that could be, uh, detrimental."

I swear, when Clayton looked at me with his blue eyes opened wide, it was almost like looking at Bitty in one of her clueless moments. Apparently, not only do apples not fall far from the tree, they occasionally bonk some people on their heads when they do.

"What do you mean?" asked Bitty's clone. I mean son.

"I mean that if you tell people you didn't like him, the police may show up asking you where you were when he was killed."

"Oh. I never thought of that. So what do I do if I already told people I'm glad he's dead?"

I smiled gently at him, and in the kindest voice I could manage asked, "Did you share that opinion of the professor with anyone in a uniform, honey?"

"Uniform?"

"You know, firemen wear them, soldiers wear them—and policemen wear them."

Sitting next to him, Brandon rolled his eyes and jabbed Clayton in the side with a sharp elbow. "She's asking if you already incriminated yourself with the cops, dude. You might as well fess up. Or I'll do it for you."

A tingle of alarm went through me, and a swift glance at Gaynelle saw that she was also thinking along the same lines. Bitty sat quite still. If not for the rise and fall of the pug she wore on her chest, I wouldn't have known she was breathing a little fast.

Clayton scowled and ran his hand through his hair, fingers spreading the thick blond and brown mass so that it looked rumpled. For a moment he seemed almost twelve again, a boy instead of a young man of twenty-one.

"They just kept asking me all these questions, y'know?" he began. "I mean this one cop, he acted like he thought I had a feud going on with the professor. But the other cop was kinda cool, y'know? I didn't mind talking to him as much."

Brandon groaned. "You fell for the oldest trick around, dude. Good cop-bad cop."

Clayton smacked his brother on the arm with a balled-up fist. "Did not. It wasn't like that."

"Yeah, you know it was," Brandon said, and ducked another fist by rolling away on the grass. He grinned widely. "Admit it, dude. You got played."

Of course, Clayton admitted nothing. Male pride is fiercest when bruised. He started to lunge toward his brother but was brought up short by Gaynelle saying in her sharp schoolteacher tone, "Stop that this minute! We have more important matters to deal with than that sort of nonsense."

Brandon and Clayton immediately sat up straight and looked at her. They know when to stop playing around and hush up, I'll say that for them.

"What exactly did you say to the policemen?" Gaynelle asked Brandon. "I'm interested in what questions they asked of you, as well."

Running a hand through his thick blond hair in a gesture very close to that of his twin, Brandon shrugged slightly and said, "They asked the usual stuff, you know, where I was between ten and two, who I was with that could verify my actions, and if I had any personal opinions about the professor."

"What'd you say?" I couldn't help breaking in to ask.

"Just that I didn't know him, but had heard he was a jerk."

"And you?" I looked at Clayton and asked. "Exactly what did you say?"

Clayton hesitated, then looked a little sheepish. "I guess it wasn't too smart, but I said what I thought. I told them Professor Sturgis might be smart enough, but he couldn't teach worth a damn, and that he had personal favorites in the class that got away with a lot while other students didn't. And I said I didn't like him and felt like we were all better off with him gone."

Brandon rolled his eyes and made a disgusted sound. "Why didn't you just tell 'em that you killed him, you dumba—uh, idiot."

"No," Gaynelle said when Clayton started to punch Brandon on the arm again, "I think you did exactly the right thing, Clayton. It's always best to tell the truth. It usually comes out anyway."

Bitty, who had been unusually still and quiet for the past few minutes, stood up. "I need to call Jackson Lee."

"There's no need in being precipitate," said Gaynelle quickly. "Clayton isn't a suspect, and any attention drawn to him unnecessarily would be unwise."

Bitty sat back down. Chen Ling gazed out of her baby sling and yawned. Clayton looked around at us with a somewhat mystified expression.

"Hey, what's going on here? Would anybody really think I had anything to do with the professor's murder? Maybe I said a few stupid things to the cops, but I was in classes most of the morning he was killed."

"Except for between eleven and two," said Brandon. "Remember? Sturgis cut the class and so did a bunch of you guys. Y'all went off-campus for a while."

"Yeah, but I was with Beau and Rand. They can vouch for me. Why would I need an alibi anyway?" He looked over at his mother. "Mama, what's going on?"

Bitty adjusted Chen Ling in her soft chenille and velvet cradle before she looked up and said, "Murder is a rather ugly crime that touches everyone who knows the victim. If I need to, I'll get you a lawyer, but both you boys must be careful what you say and who you say it to, you hear? Clayton?"

"Yes ma'am, but I haven't done anything," protested Clayton. "Why do you think I might need a lawyer?"

Bitty drew in a deep breath. "I'm your mother. I panic easily. I imagine every student on this campus who had any connection to the professor is asked the same kind of questions by the police. You have to be cautious who you confide in, or even who you let confide in you, all right?"

Shaking his head slightly, Clayton said, "All right, Mama, but I think you're making too much of me being in the professor's class. There's probably a couple hundred other students in his classes, too."

"And maybe they don't have anyone telling them to watch what they say, either," said Bitty. "You boys do. Now. We came down here to pay our respects and to make sure you two don't let all this unpleasant business distract you from your studies. Do you need anything before we leave?"

"No, ma'am," they both said at the same time. Gaynelle and I discreetly walked a couple yards away so Bitty could talk to her sons privately.

"She did well," I said to Gaynelle, who nodded agreement. "I'm shocked. Bitty can definitely say what must be said without melodrama when she chooses."

"Bitty loves those boys to death. I certainly hope neither of them ever gives her any heartache."

I looked curiously at Gaynelle. "Why do you say that?"

"Well, I met their father several times, you know. A charming, devilishly good-looking young man, and he could talk the bark off a tree if he chose. Bitty adored him. He hurt her deeply when he decided that conducting business honestly was far too much trouble and too slow a method to making a fortune. Of course, she never knew about it until he was arrested. Not only was she humiliated, but she had to protect her sons. I know she'd be heartbroken if one of them was ever involved in crime like their father."

I thought of the past summer and the twins' visit to their father at the Federal prison where he's doing his time. Supposedly he's a model prisoner. But Gaynelle's assessment of him was right on the mark, too.

"Well," I said, "genetics don't count for everything. Bitty's instilled honesty in them as well as making them earn their way when they were kids. Both of them had part-time jobs as teenagers and always had chores to do at home. When they're home in the summers, they still do chores. Maybe they're a little spoiled in some ways, but I think they're both good boys."

Gaynelle nodded. "So do I. But there are people who will choose to remember that their father isn't honest, you know."

"Yes, I'm afraid you're right." I paused before adding, "Bitty's right, too. We need to do all we can to protect her boys."

I changed the course of our conversation when I saw Bitty start toward us across the lawn. She looked okay, not terribly worried as she had earlier, and I felt a little better.

"Are they coming with us?" I asked, indicating Brandon and Clayton with a nod of my head in their direction.

"No, they have classes to attend." Bitty adjusted the gnome she wore like an extra appendage, and something about the dog caught my attention.

For a moment I puzzled as to what was wrong, then I realized, "Chitling has lost her bow."

Bitty looked down. "Oh my—she had it on just a few minutes ago. What'd you do with your bow, precious?"

Precious looked decidedly grumpy about being questioned. Bitty investigated the baby sling, feeling gently around the fat little dog, but to no avail. The big crystal was still there, but her tulle bow had been lost somewhere.

"It's all right," I said, "y'all still look a lot alike."

Instead of being insulted as most women would be at being compared to a squash–faced pug with wrinkles no amount of Botox could help, Bitty just nodded agreement. "I hope so. It definitely costs me enough money to have our clothes match."

Gaynelle put up a hand. "Don't even mention a figure. If I didn't know you to be one of the most generous people in Mississippi, I'd feel it necessary to scold you for wasting so much money when there are starving children in the Appalachians."

"There are?" Bitty looked startled. "Oh my. I should put them on my list, then. I'll bring it up at our next Ladies Social Welfare Meeting."

Bitty belongs to any number of charitable foundations, as well as the Holly Springs Garden Club and Daughters of the Confederacy. If she could wrangle it, I'm sure she'd belong to the Daughters of the American Revolution as well, but she hasn't yet decided if she wants to acknowledge the fact that some of our ancestors were Yankees. It isn't necessarily a sticking point, but Bitty is somewhat reluctant. Go figure.

While I've met my share of northerners who consider the South to be a backward, ignorant area rife with barefoot residents whose brains are slower than their drawls, I've also been fortunate enough to meet the nicest people in my travels, whether it was in the northeast or the northwest. It seems those who band together in clubs of some sort often nurture prejudices *en masse* against their fellow citizens. Rather like Congress.

I'm just glad the Dixie Divas are eclectic in our likes and dislikes. As a social club, we harbor resentment against no one because of their origins or chosen preferences. If we did, every meeting would end in a brawl, I'm sure. We like to keep our brawls low in number, but memorable in content.

On the way back to Holly Springs the rain started. By the time we reached Bitty's house, it had turned into a monsoon. When we'd stopped to let Gaynelle out at her curb, the wind had caught the door somehow and blown rain in on us, and Bitty, Chen Ling and I were uncomfortably damp. To add to our misery, the temperature had dropped to a chilly 54 degrees.

"You know that once we get out of this warm car we're going to end up soaked to the bone," Bitty observed as we sat in her Mercedes and stared at the curtain of rain obscuring her garage. Unfortunately, it's not an attached garage. That meant a mad dash toward the door, whether we parked at the front of the house or at the back. "It's twenty-eight steps from the front curb up to the porch, and only twenty-two from the driveway to the sunroom. What do you want to do?"

"You counted the steps?" I asked as I squinted out the window at the driving rain.

"Yes. I vote we take the lesser of two evils."

"Did you bring an umbrella?"

Bitty looked at me. "No. Let's just make a run for it."

"Is your sunroom door unlocked?"

"Good lord, Trinket, you can sit out here all day and ask questions if you want to, but I'm going inside. Are you coming?"

"I'll wait until you get the door unlocked."

"Fine. You can carry Chen Ling, then, so she doesn't get too wet."

I looked at the little dog, who stared back at me with suspicion in her dark brown bug-eyes. Even without the tulle bow she looked imperious, a queen to be cosseted and kept dry. Easy decision. I held out my hand.

"I'll unlock the door. Give me your keys."

"Are you sure?"

I looked at the dog again. "Very sure. Chitling is ready to either bite me or pee on me, and I'd rather get rain-wet than endure either of those doggy activities."

Bitty handed me the keys. "It's the one with the square head. Marker, I think. It'll open the security door, and I don't ever lock the wooden one."

"No wonder Jackson Lee insisted on updating your security system. He just didn't take into account the fact that you refuse to lock doors."

"Well, it's hard to get used to it when we never locked doors growing up. Times have changed, I guess, but I don't like it."

I put my hand on the door handle. "Neither do I, but there's no point in inviting trouble. We get into enough uninvited trouble as it is."

Bitty's sunroom used to be the kitchen way back when it was dangerous to have kitchens attached to the main house. Fire was always a huge concern. Now it's a large sunroom that was attached to the house during renovations about a hundred years ago. It probably should have remained unattached since Bitty made the mistake of trying to cook breakfast not so long ago and nearly burned down the entire house, but it serves its purpose as a sunroom very well in cold weather. In warm weather, Bitty opens the glass windows so it's a screened porch.

Six Chimneys is renovated Victorian in style, with cupolas and curlicues and old shingles that make it very appealing. What it lacks, however, are decent rain gutters. Once I got out of the car and dashed across the driveway and up the bricked path to the wrought-iron security door, I had to stand beneath a steady drip of rain off the first floor roof. I said a few awful things under my breath, finally got the key into the lock and turned, and then had to use all my strength to open the heavy door. Damn that Jackson Lee. He must have had the door reinforced with ninety pounds of iron! I think I strained something pulling it open.

If I hadn't paused to see if I'd pulled a muscle, I wouldn't have been run over by a short blonde female with a fat brown pug running to get out of the rain. As it was, she propelled herself through the door like a torpedo, spinning me around so that I ended up outside again. More gutter-free rain dumped on my head.

"You could have waited," I grumbled once I regained my balance and staggered through the door into the shelter of the sunroom. "I barely got the door open."

"I declare, Trinket, you've been really whiny lately. You're upsetting Chen Ling."

"Nothing upsets Chitling. Unless you're out of food." I stuck my fingers in my hair and tried to shake it free of rainwater. It felt sticky.

Bitty looked up at me, and her eyes widened a little. "What?" I said. "Why are you looking at me like that?"

"Did you do something *different* to your hair?"

"Just color. Why? What's the matter with it?"

"Oh . . . nothing. It just looks a bit—fried."

"Fried?" I remembered I'd used a new hair gel earlier. "Oh, it's a new product I tried. I guess it's not compatible with water."

"Oh no, it'd be fine if you plan to never wash your hair again. Honestly, I wish you'd let me treat you to a day at the spa."

As I followed her up the shallow stairs to the kitchen door I said, "There is no spa in Holly Springs. We'd have to go up to Memphis or Collierville."

"Or Olive Branch or Southaven. They have spas." Bitty turned the doorknob and pushed open the kitchen door, and we entered a world of heavenly fragrances. "Sharita must be here," said Bitty. "I'd forgotten she switched days this week. I guess I didn't see her car at the curb."

"Neither did I. Does Sharita have a key?" I wondered aloud.

"Of course. So does Jackson Lee, the pest control company and Maria. Of course she comes so early to clean everything I'm always here anyway."

"Who doesn't have a key to your house?" I asked. "And probably knows your alarm code, too? Not that you ever set it."

"Don't be tacky, Trinket. It's an unpleasant habit."

"My, my," I drawled, "it's so vairy vairy wahm in heah . . ."

My retort was an old one; we use it whenever we don't want to continue the topic under discussion—or to get out of conversational quicksand. It worked. We both smiled.

Chen Ling began to struggle, and Bitty set her down on the floor. The prissy pug immediately headed for the origin of the delicious smells. She knows a good thing when she smells it. We peeled off our outer layer of wet clothes in Bitty's laundry room and changed into thick terry cloth robes fresh from the dryer before following the pug.

Sharita Stone is in her late twenties, I'd say, and already has her own business. She owns a small bakery that provides muffins and homemade jams to customers, as well as a clientele who pay her to come to their homes and prepare a week's worth of food at a time. She also caters parties and banquets, and on occasion, Diva meetings. Bitty would starve to death if not for Sharita.

I'd weigh three hundred pounds if I could afford her. It was bad enough that my mother had been on a cooking marathon the past few days. I could almost feel my thighs growing more cellulite every time I stepped into our kitchen.

Chitling beat us to Sharita, but we weren't too far behind. Bitty caught up the dog and pulled off her wet doggy dress, then took it to the laundry room. I got to the kitchen first. Sharita stood at the granite counter in a professional looking white apron, her curly black hair pulled on top of her head and secured with a rainbow of elastic bands.

"Whatever you're cooking smells delicious," I said in a shameless attempt to get a taste. When she looked at me, I waggled my eyebrows.

Sharita's dark eyes lit up with amusement. "You'll have to wait until it's ready. I thought Miss Bitty might like some cold weather food now that the weather's turned."

"Italian," I guessed, and she laughed.

"Some of it. And some of it's just good plain food like Miss Sarah used to cook."

Miss Sarah was Bitty's mother. She'd left a legacy of recipes that might as well have been written in Egyptian hieroglyphics for all the good they'd do Bitty, but Sharita made good use of them.

"I smell pot roast," said Bitty on her return from the laundry room, sniffing the air just like her dog would do. "Veal Parmigiana? Beef Stroganoff?"

"Very good, Miss Bitty, and if you want me to finish up here before I have to go to my next appointment, you'll scoot out of the way and leave me be."

We're accustomed to Sharita's scolds. She's forced to do that a lot. Otherwise, we'd both be under her feet in the kitchen while she prepares meals.

"I'd forgotten you changed days," said Bitty, stalling as she eyed the rich tomato sauce Sharita was stirring. "I didn't see your car out front."

"My car's in the shop over at Brewster's. My brother gave me a ride here, and he'll pick me up. Don't even try that, Miss Bitty. I see your spoon. You know I don't allow no double-dippin'."

"Just *one* teeny-weeny taste?" Bitty begged, and Sharita rolled her dark eyes. I stayed close just in case. After some more wheedling, Sharita gave in, and we managed to wrangle a taste of Parmigiana sauce before she shooed us out of the kitchen.

"She's good," I commented, still licking my lips as we headed for Bitty's small parlor off the front hall. "I thought for a minute there she was going to smack your hand with that big wooden spoon."

"So did I. It wouldn't have been the first time."

I didn't doubt it. Sharita has a no-nonsense way about her, although she's usually smiling and cheerful.

"Everyone says she's an excellent businesswoman and is doing quite well," Bitty added as we reached the parlor. "Her catering and shop haven't suffered much at all in this economic decline."

"That's because she sells delicious foods at fair prices. Just like Budgie. Turn on a lamp," I said when I stepped into the parlor. Gray light seeped through wooden window shutters, barely illuminating the room. "It's dark as a tomb in here."

"That's a ghoulish thought," muttered Bitty. "Especially after everything that's happened lately." She reached across an overstuffed chair under the window and turned on the antique brass lamp on the table at one side. Then she flopped onto the snowy white chair cushions.

"You haven't changed your slipcovers from summer yet?" I asked as I mimicked her actions by flopping onto the matching chair across the room. "It's November."

"I know, I know. My other slipcovers were too frayed, so I'm having new ones made, and it's taking longer than expected. When did you become the designer police?"

"What a testy little thing you are," I said mildly. "It's just that I know how you are about having things done at the proper times."

"Sorry." Bitty folded her right arm over her face in a dramatic gesture that made me roll my eyes while she couldn't see me. "It's all this worry about my precious sons, and if they'll end up arrested for a murder they didn't commit—I tell you, Trinket, my life will just *end* if something happens to them, I swear it will!"

"Oh Bitty, nothing is going to happen to them, it just can't. You know they're not mixed up in the professor's murder, so I doubt that anything at all comes out of Clayton being one of his many students who didn't like him."

Her arm dropped from over her face, and her expression was so genuinely anxious that I couldn't tease her when she said, "You think so, Trinket, you truly do?"

"Of course, I do, honey."

Bitty looked relieved, and I felt a twinge of concern that I wasn't quite as sure as I pretended. Oh, I didn't think either boy was guilty of anything like murder, but there was always the chance that they'd cover up for a friend.

So to change the subject I asked, "Where's the ornament you usually have around your neck? You know, the furry queen of flatulence?"

"Don't be tacky, Trinket," Bitty reproved. "Chen Ling has digestive issues. It's quite a worry to Dr. Coltrane."

Just the mention of Kit's name gave me one of those stomach flutters that often accompany heat flashes when in his presence. There should be a law against men who can cause such reactions by long distance.

"I'm sure her digestive problems have nothing at all to do with her scarfing down half a platter of cocktail weenies whenever possible," I said. "Toothpicks and all."

Bitty looked indignant. "She did not. I got to her before she could. Although that tacky Catherine Moore said dogs belong outside, not in nice company, she behaved very well after that, too."

Catherine Moore . . . "How well do you know her?" I asked Bitty. "And how does she fit into the Ole Miss academic circle?"

"I imagine she fits in horizontally with all the male professors," Bitty replied with a twitch of her brows. Botox doesn't allow much more than twitching these days. "She's in Admin and thinks she runs the entire school single-handed."

"What does Admin do?"

"Administration. You know, in charge of all the pesky details that go with such a large campus. She says she coordinates everything from landscaping to library."

"Hm. Would she really be the one to order books for the library?"

"Oh for heaven's sake, Trinket, *I* don't know! All I know is that she thinks she's the queen of Ole Miss when she really isn't anything more than a toady. Let's talk about something besides that wretched woman, okay?"

"Truthfully," I said, "I'm a mite chilled."

"I can light a fire, if you want."

"That's all right. This bathrobe is warm. I'm just damp from our run in the rain."

"Well," said Bitty, "you do look rather like a half-drowned rat."

I don't know why it is, but when she makes a comment like that, my hand goes automatically to my hair. It was wet and stringy. Earlier it had been brushed into a soft curve against my face; now it felt matted and sticky. I flexed my toes and then grabbed a plush chenille throw draped over the back of the matching overstuffed chair where I sat. "Thank you," I said in reply to her comparing me to a half-drowned rat. "A pity we can't all be impervious to the rain like you. I assume you spray all that lacquer on your hair to keep your brain dry? Can't have it getting through all those holes in your head."

Bitty patted her hair. I thought I heard some of it break, but she merely said, "It works, and that's all I expect of my hair spray. If you had a style, I'd suggest you use it as well."

"I do have a style. It's called casual." I fluffed up the chenille throw and covered my still-damp feet. "How do you sleep in that hair helmet, anyway? I'd be afraid it'd just pop right off one day."

Really, I know how Bitty sleeps. She wears little pink satin caps and blinders over her eyes. She looks like a bottle of Pepto-Bismol.

"I sleep very well, thank you. At least when I get up the next morning I don't look like rats have chewed on my hair while I slept."

"Rats? What is this thing you have with rats? You know I don't like rats."

"Yes." Bitty smiled. "I know."

I made a face at her. "Keep that up, and I'll change the subject to slithery snakes." Bitty's shudder was genuine. "Ouch. So how did you like the Oxford academic society?" she asked in an obvious effort to change the topic of conversation.

"I had no idea I'd know so many of them. I hadn't seen Candy Lynn Stovall in a coon's age until the night before the game. She hasn't changed much since your college days."

"Well, they were your college days, too, for a little while anyway. Do you ever regret not finishing school?"

I thought about it a moment. "Sometimes. I can't say I regret meeting Perry, because then I wouldn't have my wonderful daughter, but I've often wondered what I would have done or where I'd be if I'd had sense enough to get a college education."

"You haven't done so badly, though. I mean, you had a career in the hospitality industry for a long time."

"Right," I said wryly, "and look how far I've come. Now I sell underwear, and on occasion, rubber penises for a living."

We both laughed, then Bitty said more seriously, "Well, I finished school but still did something foolish. As you said, though, I could never regret marrying Frank because I wouldn't have my boys. And they are good boys, they really are. Don't you think?"

I realized what she was really asking, so I said firmly, "They are both good boys, and neither one of them would ever do anything to make you less than proud of them. All this worry about the professor's murder will soon be over when they find the killer, and then you can go back to worrying about whether or not Clayton will graduate and if Brandon will be a lawyer."

Bitty looked relieved. She sat up and swung her legs over the side of the chair. "You're right. I'm being silly worrying about something that will never happen. I'll go see if Sharita can make us some coffee. Maybe Irish coffee?"

I opened my mouth to answer, but two things happened simultaneously: Chen Ling barreled into the parlor, and the doorbell rang. Ordinarily, the pug's entrance would not have created much of a problem. But this time she happened to be pulling something along behind her.

Sharita was in hot pursuit and looked flustered when she came to a halt just inside the parlor door. "There's something the matter with her," she said while pointing at the dog. I thought, but didn't say, that the only thing the matter with the dog was Bitty.

Bitty seemed perplexed at first. Before she could get off the chair, Chen Ling launched her fat little body up onto the white slipcovers next to her. I saw a flash of what looked like a faded red ribbon behind her. While Chitling snuffled and huffed, and turned in a couple of circles atop the cushions, her doting parent let out a scream.

Now, I have been privy to some awful sights in my lifetime, but I cannot think of a more startling sight than a faded tulle ribbon knotted with . . . well, poop, and hanging out of a dog's rear end. Whenever Chitling turned, the ribboned poo swung behind her and left skid marks across Bitty's expensive white slipcovers.

The more Bitty shrieked, the faster the pug spun around, until the bothersome extra tail whipped across the chair with a life of its own. Sharita stood just inside the doorway, transfixed by the entire thing, while I burst into rib-bruising laughter.

Since I have the rather embarrassing habit of snorting when I laugh, a sound that Bitty once described as resembling a choking goose, I imagine the noise emanating from the small parlor did sound rather like a confrontation of some sort. That would explain why Marcus Stone, who happens to be Sharita's brother and an officer on the Holly Springs Police force, swung open the front door and thundered down the hallway with his pistol drawn.

"Halt! Police!" he barked as he confronted a hysterical Bitty and twirling pug. His sister grabbed his arm, but had started laughing so hard she couldn't explain there was no need for gunfire. It's a good thing Lieutenant Stone is quick on the mark, because once he realized there was no danger, he slid his pistol back into the heavy holster and put his hands on his hips. "What the hell?" he demanded of no one in particular.

At that moment, Chitling must have decided that her mommy was of no help at all in the situation, because she leaped down from the chair and darted toward the parlor door. As she went by, Marcus Stone glanced down, saw the trailing ribbon, and put his black boot right on it. With a muffled pop, the ribbon disengaged from the pug, and Chen Ling went on her merry way. I heard her little toenails click indignantly against the old wood floors in the hallway.

"Well," I said when I was able to stop laughing, "the mystery of the disappearing bow has been solved at last."

Bitty did not appreciate my humor. She said something quite pithy. I chose not to take offense. After all, she had quite a mess to clean up, and I had no intention whatsoever of helping. My monthly quota of dog messes that require cleaning up had been reached.

"Do you need help, Miss Bitty?" Sharita asked with a straight face.

"No, I won't ask you to do that. I'll get it." Bitty glanced at the lieutenant. "I think Sharita's almost through cooking. You can have some coffee if you don't mind waiting a moment."

Lieutenant Stone shook his head. "I didn't come to give Sharita a ride home, Miz Hollandale. I came to talk to you."

Uh oh.

Chapter 8

Bitty is the mistress of stall tactics. She should have been elected to Congress instead of her late husband. She can talk more and say less than anyone I've ever met. Lieutenant Stone, it turned out, was immune to this kind of thing. Maybe because he has three sisters, or maybe because he's had to deal with Bitty before, but he cut short her circuitous conversation pretty quickly.

After the ribbon incident and clean-up, we had all gathered in Bitty's kitchen to drink coffee. Mine was flavored with French Vanilla, Bitty's was flavored with Bailey's. As far as I know, Sharita and her brother drank their coffee with just sugar.

Just as Bitty started relating a story about Miranda Watson's pet pig eating all the flower heads off bouquets for sale at the local farmer's market, Lieutenant Stone cleared his throat.

"Miz Hollandale," he began, and Bitty looked at him sharply over the rim of her cup. Stone's voice had an authoritative tone to it that she obviously recognized. She set down her cup.

"Yes, Lieutenant?"

Any other time she might have called him by his first name since she'd known him for a long time. But when a police officer addresses you formally, you just know that something's up.

Marcus Stone rubbed his chin with one hand. "I'll get right to the point. There's a police investigation down in Oxford. I'm here to get an official statement from you about what you were doing with a laundry cart."

My stomach dropped. I think I gulped. I hoped no one noticed.

I think Bitty's gotten better at keeping her cool than she used to be, because she just lifted a Botoxed brow and said, "Why, I have no idea what you're talking about."

Now, I've always considered it rather dangerous to lie to law enforcement for any reason. For one thing, they almost always know when you're lying, and for another thing, it really does work against you when you need them to believe you. But I had to admire Bitty's chutzpa in the face of certain disaster. After all, if a policeman is asking questions, he probably already knows the answers.

Lieutenant Stone shook his head. "Now Miz Hollandale, I don't think that's quite true. Think about it a minute. Or we can always do this over at the precinct. Or in Oxford. If you won't talk to me now, I'm sure the Oxford police will arrange to get you down there for a statement. You'll get a free ride in one of their cruisers."

Bitty and Lieutenant Stone stared at each other for a moment. He took a casual sip of coffee, his eyes never leaving hers. Sharita and I stood there like statues. The only sound in the kitchen was Chitling snuffling along the floor in search of lost crumbs. She had apparently completely recovered from her earlier trauma.

"A *laundry cart*? Really, I—oh wait. Do you mean a big white tub like motels use sometimes?"

Bitty sounded very convincing. I wondered for a brief moment if she really had managed to forget all about trundling Professor Sturgis around in a laundry cart. See what I mean? She really is good at subterfuge.

If Lieutenant Stone guessed she was stalling, he didn't let it show. He just nodded agreement. "Yes, that's the kind of laundry cart I mean. What can you tell me about the one in your sons' dormitory basement?"

"What a peculiar question to ask." Bitty took another swig of her coffee fortified with enough Bailey's to register her alcohol content at an illegal level. "What do you want to hear about it?"

I recognized that this little play could go south pretty quickly. Before I could stop myself from getting even more involved than I already was, I said, "Oh Bitty, don't you remember that cart we found in the dorms? It had *Motel Six* printed on the side, I think."

Bitty nearly choked on her coffee, but managed to say sweetly, "Oh yes, I think I do recall that. It was blocking their doorway, I believe." She looked over at Stone with eyes wide and guileless. "Is that the one you mean?"

Stone sighed. "Yes ma'am, that's the one I mean. Exactly where in the dorm did you find it, and what did you do with it?"

"Oh for heaven's sake, I can't remember *exactly* where it was when we found it. Trinket seems to recall that better than I do."

This time I nearly choked on my coffee. Bitty, as always, looked completely guileless. I, as usual, probably looked guilty of everything from murder to bank robbery. I cleared my throat and tried to think of an answer near enough to the truth to be plausible, and far enough away from it not to be incriminating.

"It seems to me that it was near Brandon and Clayton's doorway," I said when the lieutenant looked at me. "We had to move it, of course."

All that was true. I just didn't specify which side of the door it had been on. And we'd had to move it; I just left out the part where we moved it to facilitate the loading of a corpse into its canvas depths.

Marcus Stone set his coffee cup down on the gleaming granite countertop. "Let's get past this real quick, ladies. You were both seen in an elevator with the laundry cart. I want to hear why you had the cart, where you took it, and what was in it."

Really, it's a good thing he was looking at Bitty when he said that, because I was pretty sure I had guilt written all over my face. Bitty, however, said, "Well, we did what one does with a laundry cart. We moved laundry."

"So this laundry cart that you didn't remember existed just a few seconds ago, you now remember moving laundry with it? Whose laundry? Where? Why?"

Stone sounded irritated now. Prevarication can only be carried so far before police tend to get cranky. Even Bitty recognized that.

After she set her coffee cup on the counter, she said quite seriously, "I know that you're a good policeman, Marcus, and a good person. I've never held it against you that I was the chief suspect for a while in Philip's murder. Circumstances were what they were. I ask now that you believe me when I tell you that I have no idea who murdered Spencer Sturgis or why. I may know who *didn't* do it, but I have no evidence as to who did."

Lieutenant Stone sighed. "Miz Bitty, I've known you most of my life, and for the most part, I always thought you were pretty harmless. But lately, you've been involved in some pretty weird stuff, you have to admit. So when I get a call from Oxford police saying there was a murder on campus, the victim was moved, you were seen pushing a laundry cart around the campus, and someone has said you and the victim had a loud argument, I've got to come ask you questions. You know that. And believe me, the Oxford police are gonna get an official statement. There's a witness who says he had a conversation with you in the dorm elevator where your two sons reside, and that later he saw you and Miz Truevine here pushing the cart past The Grove."

He held up a hand when Bitty opened her mouth. "No, just let me lay this out for you before you come up with some lame excuse."

Bitty looked slightly indignant, but kept her mouth shut, thank heavens.

"Professor Sturgis was found in the back of a moving truck that had been parked in plain sight in back of a building. How did he get there without someone seeing the murder, we had to ask, and a logical answer would be that he was killed elsewhere and transported to the dump site. But no witnesses. Then came the information that two older ladies were seen pushing a curiously heavy laundry cart around. Fingerprints were found on the cart. AFIS came up with your name." He looked over at me. "While your fingerprints aren't on it that we can find, you were seen with

Miz Bitty pushing the cart."

"So you're saying that I'm a murder suspect again?" Bitty burst out.

Stone shook his head. "No ma'am, I'm not. You might be a little crazy, but you aren't strong enough to have killed the professor." He shifted position to lean against the counter with his back to it and his elbow propping him up. "Here's what I think. I think you found the professor's body, went and got the laundry cart, and moved the body to keep it from incriminating one of your boys."

Bitty went white as a bleached cotton sheet. A cold chill gripped my throat and all the way down to my knees. I shivered.

"My boys would never—" Bitty began, but the lieutenant cut her off with a lifted hand as he agreed.

"I know your boys, known 'em all my life, and I agree that neither one of them is the kind to commit murder. But I'm not the one you have to convince. This didn't happen in my jurisdiction.

"What you have to help me do is figure out what happened, and you can do that by telling me the truth. The *whole* truth, Miz Bitty. Not even a little white lie."

There it was, laid out plainly so that even Bitty had to see the sense in it. I made up my mind that if she didn't tell the truth, I'd have to, but she beat me to it.

"Trinket, would you mind getting some more coffee and bringing it out to us in the living room?" she asked. "Oh, and maybe a little of that pound cake with raspberry preserves Sharita's mama made."

Turning back to the lieutenant, Bitty said, "I'd have you in the parlor, but as you know, it's a mess right now, so we can talk in the living room well enough, I think."

It turned out that all four of us sat in the living room eating pound cake drizzled with raspberry preserves and drinking coffee while Bitty sorted out what she wanted to say. The uncomfortable horsehair stuffed antique settee was occupied by Bitty and Chen Ling. Sharita, the lieutenant and I sat in antique chairs drawn up to the Turkish ottoman that did double duty on occasion as a coffee table.

The silver tray was set with Bitty's serviceable china and accessories, and I thought the lieutenant looked way too big and bulky to be sitting in the Louis XVI chair he occupied. He balanced a rose-patterned china plate on his knee that held pound cake, but had held on to his mug instead of drinking from one of the Royal Albert tea cups. Men can be intimidated by fragile china, I've observed.

Once Bitty started explaining the events of our day the morning the professor was murdered, Stone put down his plate and took out a small notebook and pen. He scribbled a few things in it, then began writing furiously when Bitty got to the part where we found Sturgis dead in Clayton's dorm room closet.

"Why in God's name did you move him?" the lieutenant asked in a brief pause. He sounded cranky. "You should have called in the police immediately."

"I didn't want anyone to think Clayton had anything to do with him being dead," she explained. "You know how it would look to people."

"Now it looks even worse," Stone said dryly. "It looks like a conspiracy. Or at best, a cover-up."

"Well, that's just ridiculous. Of course it isn't. Clayton has no idea that Sturgis was stuffed in his closet like a Christmas turkey. I mean, all tied up, you know."

"Yeah. I got that." He glanced over at me. "One of you should have thought this through more before you did something so stupid."

"One of us did," I replied, but didn't have to clarify. Stone is pretty quick on the uptake.

"Hunh," he grunted, shaking his head as he jotted down more notes in his little book. Finally he looked up at Bitty. "Okay, this is the way I understand it. Stop me if I'm wrong about anything. First, you and Trinket got down to Oxford at approximately eight-fifteen Friday morning on the fifth. You went immediately to Professor Sturgis's office for your eight-thirty appointment. At approximately nine ten, the professor allowed you into his office for a pre-arranged meeting to discuss your son Clayton Caldwell's failing grade in his ancient history class."

"Can you believe he was so rude as to keep us waiting that long?" Bitty cut in with an indignant sniff. "Definitely low-class."

Stone ignored her interruption and comment, and went on. "During this meeting, the professor suddenly became highly irate at your insistence he should allow Clayton to make up a test he had missed for medical reasons. He began yelling and ordered you to leave his office immediately. Whereupon you did so, but returned to his door to tell him that you intended to report him to the board of directors and to the alumni association so they could remove him before tenure. At that, the professor ran after you down the hall and proceeded to scream what you deemed to be threats. You then said—and this is a direct quote: 'You'll be long dead before that happens.' Is this correct so far, Miz Bitty?"

She nodded thoughtfully. "Yes, except I really wanted to slap some sense in him, too. If not for the fact that he'd already made such a scene, and Trinket was trying to pull my arm out of socket, I think I would have done just that."

I rolled my eyes, Sharita seemed suddenly interested in the contents of her coffee cup, and Marcus Stone just stared at Bitty for a moment before shaking his head.

"That information isn't necessary, so I advise you to keep it to yourself. I have here that, after meeting with Sturgis, you and Miz Truevine took a taxi to the Square and did some shopping, then had lunch at Old Venice Pizza and later returned to your sons' dorm room to see if they were out of class. You said you have credit card receipts for your purchases and lunch and are willing to give them to me. At approximately three-fifteen, you found the door to the dorm room unlocked and your sons still absent."

Now he turned to me. "Miz Truevine, in your statement you say you noticed what appeared to be an unusual pile of clothing on the floor in front of Clayton Caldwell's open closet, so stepped closer to look at it, is that right?"

I affirmed it, and he went on. "Upon closer inspection, you realized it was the body of Professor Spencer Sturgis. He lay halfway inside the closet with a wire clothes hanger wrapped tightly around his neck, and his hands and ankles bound with duct tape. You did not touch him at that point, realizing he was deceased. Is this correct so far?"

"Yes," I said. "It appeared that the coat hanger had been attached to the closet rod at one point but had come loose so the professor just sort of . . . *leaned* into the closet."

Stone wrote in his notebook, then looked back over at Bitty. "That is when you decided to remove the professor from the crime scene to another location to prevent your sons from being involved. You then proceeded to place the professor into the laundry cart you found in the hallway, and—"

"No," I interrupted. "The laundry cart was already inside the room. Over behind the door."

"Was it. Ah." Stone wrote some more in his book and looked up, his eyes going from me to Bitty. "That's when you placed the body into the cart and disguised it with clothing and linens, right? Then you took it downstairs in the elevator, during which you had a brief discussion with Randy Klein, a student and resident of the dorm. After leaving the dormitory, you headed east until you saw a moving truck. That is where you left the professor's body. He was wrapped up in two L.L. Bean blankets, one blue plaid and the other a red plaid."

"No," said Bitty. "Two blue plaid blankets."

Stone checked his notes again. Then he frowned. "Are you sure?"

"Of course, I'm sure. I bought them, after all, and I always buy the boys matching blankets, pillows and sheets for their beds. Just like here at home."

After ruffling the pages of the notebook for a moment, Lieutenant

Stone said, "I must have it written down wrong. No problem."

After a couple more questions, the lieutenant flipped his notebook closed and put his ballpoint pen into his shirt pocket. He wore an open vest and what looked like body armor under his uniform shirt. Even in small towns, police have to be wary of people off their medication or on the run, I suppose.

"Miz Bitty," he said, "I'll make sure the Oxford police get a copy of my report, but you can expect that they'll want you to come down and make a complete, official statement. If you weren't who you are, they'd probably have you in the back of one of their units right now."

"Well, I'm grateful for your intervention," said Bitty. "I do wonder, though—how did they decide that just because my fingerprints were on the laundry cart that it was used to move the professor?"

"Did I say that?"

"You said that my fingerprints were found on the cart."

"I did say that, yes."

Bitty looked up at him with slightly narrowed eyes. "You tricked me into telling you what happened, didn't you."

"Think of it more as asking the right questions. I'll mention that you cooperated fully in my report."

We walked him toward the front door while Sharita grabbed up the bag she used to carry supplies for her customers. Rain still dripped outside, mostly from the eaves now instead of the downpour of earlier. Marcus Stone paused and turned to look down at Bitty when we reached the door.

"By the way," he said, "one of my patrolmen reported that he gave you a warning about a rolling stop down at the corner. Just so you know, next time you run that stop sign, it will get you a ticket."

Bitty put her hands on her hips. I wondered if she knew she looked just like an indignant chicken all fluffed out in her white terry cloth robe and her hair glued atop her head.

"Honestly. I never knew police could be so picky about small things that don't matter worth a hill of beans!"

Stone looked at her with an expression of weary patience. "It'd matter a lot more than a hill of beans if another car had the right of way and slammed into you. What may seem a minor infraction to you could end up being a pretty serious accident. So come to a complete stop at all stop signs. That's why they're called *stop* signs."

I thought for a moment that Bitty might continue to argue, but it surprised me when she took a deep breath and nodded. "Yes. You're right, of course. I promise to do better from now on. Please tell Officer Farrell that I won't say anything about him to his grandmother."

That last sentence earned a lifted brow from the lieutenant, but if he meant to say anything, he didn't as Sharita appeared in the entrance hall wearing a raincoat.

"I called Alfie," she said, "and told him you're picking me up so he doesn't have to." She fluffed out the collar of her raincoat and looked at Bitty. "Chen Ling's special food is in its usual place, but I think you should take her to the vet anyway. If she ate a bow, no telling what else she might have gotten into."

"Oh, I will," Bitty assured her. "I'm pretty sure it was just the bow she wore to Oxford with us today, but I don't want to take any chances."

After they left, Sharita climbing into the front seat of her brother's patrol car, I looked at Bitty. "Are you really going to take her to the vet?"

"Don't you think I should?"

I thought about it a moment. "Well, it was just a bow, and it seems to have passed naturally. Of course, if you're worried we can call Kit."

Kit is short for Christopher. Dr. Coltrane has only been a vet at Willow Bend Animal Hospital for about a year and the main man in my life for less time than that.

Bitty hesitated. "Well, it's not like she hasn't done this kind of thing before. Just not all over my white chairs."

I tried not to laugh. "She's probably fine. From what I could tell, all the ribbon came out."

For a moment Bitty just stood there, then she shook her head and started to laugh. That made me laugh, too, of course. By the time we finally subsided, we both had tears in our eyes. At some point we'd fallen into each other's arms to hold ourselves upright. Chen Ling looked up at us with a disgusted expression. Not that she doesn't look at me like that most of the time anyway.

"Right now," said Bitty ruefully as she wiped at her eyes, "I'm just as worried about my white slipcovers. How will I ever get that . . . that *stuff* to come out? It's all purplish and probably soaked into the material so it won't ever come clean."

"Bleach," I said. "Lots of bleach."

"On linen?"

"Oh. Call your dry cleaners. They'll know what to do."

I hooked my arm through Bitty's and led her toward the kitchen. "As for Chitling, have I ever told you about the time Brownie ate my earrings?"

"Only about a dozen times. He ate your emerald earrings, and you had to follow him around the back yard wearing plastic gloves in case he pooped them out, yadda yadda, yadda."

"Ah, I see you haven't learned the moral of the tale," I replied instead of giving her a good shake.

"There's a moral?"

When we reached the kitchen I released her arm and headed toward the laundry room. "Yes," I said over my shoulder, "the moral is not to expect small furry creatures to act like rational human beings. In your case, that would be like me, not you."

I think I heard her say something quite rude as I went into the laundry room, but decided not to ask her to repeat it. There are some things it's best not to know.

Despite tumbling around in Bitty's dryer, my clothes were still a bit damp when I reached home. Mama and Daddy had a small fire lit in the living room fireplace, and were cuddled up together watching a 1950s movie with Carmen Miranda wearing a pile of fruit on her head. Brownie, of course, was nestled between them, warm in his sweater matching my parents' cardigans. Really. It boggles my mind how my parents treat their dog like a small, furry child. I'm sure Brownie is in their will, his name right above mine and Emerald's. He'll probably get the house, I'll get the cats, and Emerald will get any money left, if my parents don't spend it all buying clothes for the dog. Not to mention money spent feeding a battalion of stray cats they also get fixed so there isn't an army of new kittens every spring.

It's not that I'm not an animal person. I've had pets of my own in the past, and if not already surrounded by furry creatures I'd probably have one of my own now. But there can be too much of a good thing, I keep telling my parents. They just smile and nod, and pay me no mind whatsoever. That's okay. I don't really pay them any mind when they warn me about Bitty and her latest scheme. It evens out.

Mama looked at me over the back of the couch when I paused in the living room doorway to look in on them.

"Hey, sugar," she greeted me. "Busy day?"

"Always, when I'm with Bitty," I replied. I heard Daddy chuckle, but Mama just nodded at me. "We went down to Oxford for a visitation with the widow," I continued. "It rained on us all the way back."

"A visitation?" Mama seemed surprised. "I didn't think he'd be back from down in Jackson so soon."

She referred, of course, to Professor Sturgis's body being released by the state coroner's office in Mississippi's state capital.

"It wasn't that kind of visitation," I said. "We just went to comfort his widow. I think he'll end up being buried in New Jersey anyway, since that's where he's from."

"His family must be pretty upset by this. A terrible thing to happen. I don't know what the world's coming to lately, all these murders and crazy goings-on," Mama said with a sorrowful shake of her head.

I murmured agreement and escaped as quickly as I could before Mama got around to asking me more detailed questions. The less my parents know about things like this, the better it is for all of us. Not that the Holly Springs grapevine isn't efficient, but if I could manage to keep them ignorant of my involvement in the professor's corpse getting moved, the better it would be all the way around. Right now, only the Divas and Sharita knew about it. Oh, and Lieutenant Marcus Stone. Surely, none of *them* would spread the gossip.

Oh, how foolish I can be at times . . .

Chapter 9

I left early the next morning to go to my part-time job at Silk Promises, the shop belonging to Carolann Barnett and Rose Allgood. I usually work in just Carolann's part of the shop; she sells beautiful lingerie by name brand designers, soaps, candles, pretty blouses, consignment jewelry and other nice things for a woman's personal use. Since Jennie's Florist and Gift Shop across the town square sells exquisite items like baby bedding, fine china, silver and crystal, and gifts suitable for wedding showers, Silk Promises focuses mainly on nightwear and underwear.

Not to mention Rose's side of the shop, the Blue Velvet Room. I usually just call it the Blue Room. As mentioned before, Rose sells *very* personal items. She usually rings them up herself, but on occasion I've taken care of her customer's purchase and bagged the item. You'd be absolutely amazed at what kind of "marital aids" there are on today's market. I know I certainly was.

At any rate, I hadn't been at work an hour before my cell phone rang, and my mother wanted to know why I hadn't mentioned that I'd carted the professor's body out to The Grove for the tailgate party. For a moment I was stunned into silence. Even if she'd gotten the information correct, how did she get it so quick?

"Well?" Mama prompted me. "Didn't you think I'd want to hear something like that from you instead of—from where I did hear it?"

"Estelle Weaver," I said. "You had to hear it from her. She's the only one I know who'd dare call you with gossip like that." Estelle and my mother have been friends since the fifties. They tell each other everything.

"It doesn't matter where I heard it. Why didn't you tell me yourself?"

"In the first place, we did not cart the professor's body out to The Grove for the tailgate festivities. That's ridiculous. It would have been in the paper and on *CNN Headline News* if we'd done that kind of thing. Secondly, I didn't want you to worry."

"Oh, *lord!* So just where did you take the body? And why?"

There was a plaintive note in her last question, and I sighed. "The professor was already dead in Clayton's dorm room closet, so we just moved him. Bitty didn't want any suspicion to fall on Clayton, of course."

"Oh, Trinket."

The way Mama said that made me feel like I was fifteen years old again and in trouble for skipping class.

"Listen," I said as several customers came in at the same time and hovered near a rack of lacy thongs by Vera Wang, "I have to go right now. We're getting busy. We can talk about this later when I get back home."

"We certainly can," Mama said rather tartly, and I sighed again as I clicked off my cell phone and dropped it back into my pocket.

"May I help you?" I approached the ladies and asked in my most helpful tone. "I see you're looking at *Simply Vera*, our lovely line by Vera Wang. She's designed some very beautiful lingerie, hasn't she?"

One of the women I judged to be in her late thirties or early forties nodded as she chose a black and red lacy thong. She held it up. "Tell me, does this little string just go up between your butt cheeks? I mean, is that comfortable?"

I hesitated. Dare I confess that I'd never in my life worn a pair of thongs, nor did I intend to? It might be the truth, but it definitely wasn't a sales point. So I smiled.

"My customers tell me they're very comfortable. We sell quite a lot of them."

One of the other women dug an elbow into the customer's ribs. "Ask her."

I kept the smile on my face, anticipating a query about the quality, sizes, or if they had matching bras. Instead, the woman holding up the thongs looked at me and asked, "Are you the woman who keeps moving dead bodies around?"

For a moment her question took me off-guard. I mean, as questions go, it wasn't one I'd been asked before. I wasn't sure how to respond. So I just said, "Do you want me to ring those up for you, or do you want to look around some more?"

The woman who'd used her elbow apparently grew bolder. "Well, are you? We heard that you and your cousin stuck the body of a teacher into a wheelbarrow and rolled it around the Ole Miss football field."

"Did you?" I managed to respond. "How odd. We did nothing of the sort. I can't imagine why anyone would say we did."

The three women looked definitely disappointed. I grabbed a bra off a rack and put it with the thongs. "These are a good match. Why don't you look around some more, and if you have any questions about the merchandise, I'll be glad to answer them."

I walked off, not looking back, hoping I got away before I exploded. Whoever was spreading rumors needed to be stopped at once. This was definitely getting out of hand.

When I called Bitty to warn her about what was being said, I got her answering machine. I called her cell phone, and it went straight to voicemail. I wouldn't be a bit surprised if she wasn't getting the same kind of questions I had just gotten.

Carolann came out front from the back of the shop, smiling until she saw my face. "Are you all right?" she asked, her voice lowered. "You look . . . strange."

"This is my mad expression. As in angry, not insane. Not yet, anyway. Do you mind if I take my lunch break early? I need to talk to Bitty. I'll tell you all about it in a little while."

"Of course, honey, you go take care of things. It's a slow day anyway. Are those ladies buyers or shoppers?" she asked, indicating the three women looking at thongs.

"Interrogators," I replied. "Don't be shocked by anything they ask you, and don't answer any of their questions that don't pertain to underwear."

Although she looked puzzled, Carolann nodded, and I headed for the back door. I was steaming. Someone was deliberately causing trouble by running their mouth. This would only end up making Bitty and I look foolish, and once again tarnish the Dixie Divas' reputation. Of course, the thought ran through my mind that Miranda Watson had somehow learned about our statement to the Holly Springs police. But as far as I knew, she had no close connection to the police department, only *The South Reporter*, our local paper. As a weekly gossip columnist, Miranda could be counted on to report innuendos as well as relate Who went Where with Whom in Marshall County.

It took less than five minutes to reach Bitty's house. Her red Miata was parked in the driveway instead of the garage, so I knew she'd already been up and about. And it wasn't even noon yet. I parked in front of the house at the curb and left my windows down. After all the rain the day before, it had turned out sunny and mild. A red maple had turned scarlet in the next door yard, and there was a crispness in the air that promised autumn had arrived.

Bitty's front door was open, so I just walked in. I could hear her chattering away to someone for a few seconds before the pug alarm went off. Maybe Bitty was right. Why bother with a security system when she was armed with a very loud pug?

Chen Ling barreled toward me from the direction of the kitchen, her shrill barks making my ears ring. I ignored her as I headed for the kitchen where no doubt Bitty still talked on the phone. That was my guess. I couldn't hear a blessed thing for the dog at my feet. By this time, Chitling had worked herself into a frenzy of barks and yowls. It was as if she were telling me I'd ignored the courtesy of ringing the bell or knocking. Or maybe it was just her way of greeting me. At least she didn't throw up on my shoes.

When I reached the kitchen, Chen Ling apparently gave up announcing my arrival. She gave a final snort in my direction, then trotted toward her food bowl. Peace fell again upon Six Chimneys. Relative peace, anyway.

Bitty had the refrigerator door open, and leaned into it. I could see her backside sticking out and the refrigerator light illuminated her feet. No stilettos. Just a pair of nice suede loafers that probably cost more than a small car.

". . . that's right," she was saying to whoever was on the other end of the phone, "she thought it best to move the body instead of leave it there to incriminate Clayton. One just never knows what the police will think, you see."

I figured someone had asked her the same questions I'd gotten this morning, and shook my head. This tidbit of gossip had certainly gotten around quickly. Since I was pretty sure the Holly Springs Police Department hadn't put out a statement informing the world of all the details of our confessions, I leaned toward the notion that one of the Divas must be the source. Sharita would never be so unwise as to spread gossip, especially what she heard in the company of her brother in his capacity as an officer of the law.

But which Diva? Usually, Cady Lee Forsythe is to blame. Of all the Divas, she's the one who can least resist telling a good piece of gossip. As soon as Bitty hung up with her call, I'd ask if she'd talked to Cady Lee.

About the time Bitty chose an item from the chilled depths of her state-of-the-art refrigerator and stood up straight, I grasped the door to keep her from closing it. I wanted to see if she had any sweet tea left. She evidently thought I was a murderous intruder.

She screamed. So I screamed. Chitling barked at both of us.

"Dear gawd," Bitty said when she saw it was me, "why did you sneak up on me?"

"*Sneak?* Are you kidding? With your pug alarm going off?"

Bitty dismissed that with, "Oh, she's always barking at something. I don't hardly pay her any attention anymore. No, everything's okay, dear. Trinket just scared the liver out of me, that's all."

I assumed that last was to her caller.

When she hung up I said, "Bad news travels fast."

Bitty put a plastic container on the counter and popped the lid. "Oh, I think it's all over town now. It took long enough. Want some Chicken Parmigiana?"

"Yes. What do you mean, it took long enough?"

While Bitty fussed with the plastic container and the microwave, she said over her shoulder, "Well, I've been working at it since you left yesterday."

I began to feel a bit lightheaded. "Excuse me?" I said after a moment of shocked silence. "You've been what?"

"Working at it. You know. Making sure everyone hears exactly what happened. I don't know what setting to use on this blamed thing. It's confusing. This is a pretty big dish. Do you think the Entrée setting is right?"

My brain began to spin. I actually felt dizzy. I looked down at my cousin—without her stilettos she's very, very short—and wondered if she had finally gone over to the dark side.

"Are you all right, Bitty?" I asked as gently as possible. I've heard it's never wise to frighten a mentally unstable person. "No headaches, or . . . fits?"

Bitty's renovation expert had installed an over-the-range microwave when redoing the kitchen a few months before and hadn't taken into account his client's short stature. She had to stand on tiptoes to reach the microwave keypad.

"Of course not, Trinket, why ever would you ask me a thing like that?" she replied without looking at me. "I think the Entrée button is that one on the top . . . there. That should do it."

She turned around. Her light sweater was festooned with glittery swirls; maybe a less well-endowed woman wouldn't have the same problem, but I swear, the reflection was a bit glaring.

I put up a hand to shield my eyes and said a trifle irritably, "Your boobs are winking at me. Make them stop."

"What? Oh, my sweater? You don't like it?"

"The sweater's fine. It's just that all those rhinestones seem to be centered right at the front of your . . . rack. Really. It looks odd."

"Honestly, Trinket, you say the strangest things." Bitty put both hands on her hips. "Why are you here? I thought you were working today."

"I am. And I'm here because I've already been interrogated by my mother and three complete strangers about why I trundled a corpse to a football game. No mention was made of you, I noted. Can you tell me why that is?"

"For heaven's sake, how would I know?" Bitty bent down to scoop Chen Ling into her arms. She seemed a little nervous. Bitty, not the dog. Chen Ling doesn't have a nervous bone in her body, I'm sure.

I leaned against the kitchen counter and smiled. "Oh, I think you have an idea why that is," I said calmly. "You know, I came over here to warn you that someone—and I had no idea who—has been spreading gossip about what happened in Oxford. I wanted you to be prepared just in case someone said something to you. It never occurred to me that you're the big mouth spreading ridiculous rumors."

"I did not." Bitty was indignant. "I simply wanted our side of the story to get out before people started saying all kind of crazy things. That's all."

"And yet, oddly enough, people are saying all kind of crazy things. About *me*."

"Are they? Why . . . how odd." Bitty buried her face in Chen Ling's furry neck. I narrowed my eyes.

"What have you been saying, Bitty? C'mon, you can tell me. And you might want to be the one to tell me before I hear it from someone else. Or read it in the paper."

"Well . . . I might have left out a few parts here and there to a couple people."

"Ah. A few parts here and there. I assume you mean the parts where *you* were involved in the incident of the traveling corpse. Right?"

"No, not really. Well. Not much. Oh Trinket, you know how it is, people just say mean things. I knew all this would come out now that we've had to make a statement about our part in it, and I didn't want anyone to think Clayton had anything to do with the professor's murder. If they thought I was behind moving the professor's body, then they might think Clayton is guilty. That's all. I didn't think people would assume you did it all by yourself. I really didn't."

I wanted to be mad. Instead I just fixed myself a tall glass of sweet tea. It took a couple minutes to do that, and by the time I had taken a few sips, the entrée was ready. I really do love most aspects of modern technology.

"Are you mad at me?" Bitty asked when I took the plate she offered me.

"Not anymore. I'm over it. I just wish you'd told me what you were doing. Then I could have been more prepared. Does the police department know you've been telling people details of the case?"

Bitty gave me a blank look. "I have no idea," she said after a moment. "I never thought to ask. Do you think it matters?"

"It might. If it does, I imagine we'll hear from Lieutenant Stone again." I took a bite of the Chicken Parmigiana and closed my eyes in ecstasy. Sharita really is good. I carried my plate from the counter to the small table and chairs under a corner window. The only window covering is wooden shutters that were open to allow in sunlight.

Bitty followed me. "Well, we've given our official statement, so we should be left out of this from now on. I mean, it's not like we know for sure who killed him."

"Thank god," I mumbled around another bite of chicken and tomato sauce. "But I don't think we're completely out of the equation yet. Oxford police may want to talk to us, too, remember."

Bitty made a dismissive motion with one hand. "Oh, they can just go by the statement we already made."

"Right. Let's hope they come to the same conclusion," I said. She gave me an inquiring look, so I added, "That no one we know is a suspect. Or at least, no one in our family."

Bitty nodded. "Amen to that, sister."

We finished our early lunch, and before I left to go back to the shop, I told Bitty not to make any more phone calls. "Let people call you. Everything gets twisted around anyway. By the time it gets back to the source, they'll have us both riding the corpse into the football game. That's not fair to his widow or to us. We need to let this die down as quickly as possible."

"I thought I was doing the right thing to protect Clayton," said Bitty with a sigh. "I guess I just made things worse."

"Well, not for him. And I can handle what's said to me. By the way, you might want to give your boys a call and explain things before the gossip gets to Oxford."

Bitty looked stricken. "Oh, I hadn't even thought about that. I'll call them right now."

When I left, I was just sure she'd be more careful about what she said to whom. I can be so stupidly optimistic.

By the time I got home that afternoon it was already dark. Approaching winter closed in early these days, and with my car window down I inhaled chilly air rich with the scents of wood fires and burning leaves. I parked in front of what used to be a stable of sorts that had been reinvented as a garage. Mama's big Lincoln and Daddy's Ford truck were in the garage; there was room for two more cars, but I parked outside so I didn't have to maneuver past stacks of old fertilizer, wheelbarrows and various yard equipment that should be stored in the barn but wasn't.

Instead of going around to the back, I went in the front door. Brownie met me in the hallway, barking ferociously.

"You can't scare me," I said to him. "I've already been hassled by a fat pug."

For some reason that admonishment made him happy. He put his ears back on his dachshund head and his front paws up on my skirt. Since he has the longer legs of his beagle ancestry, this put him at my kneecaps. Rather surprised at this greeting, I bent to pat the top of his head. He promptly grabbed the cuff of my blouse and began to tug. No amount of discouragement convinced him to let go, and I was debating on whether to call for help or lift him high enough in the air to cause vertigo when my father appeared at the end of the hall.

"Brownie," he said calmly, and of course, the little sniper immediately let go of my cuff.

"I was ambushed," I said, frowning at the now frayed edges of my sleeve. "He used a bait and switch tactic on me."

Brownie looked up at my father adoringly. His tail thumped the floor a few times, and I could tell from Daddy's face that I'd already lost this battle.

"Never mind," I said with a sigh.

"How was your day?" Daddy asked when we reached the kitchen. He sounded a bit strained and kept clearing his throat.

I looked at him a little more closely. "I've had better," I answered cautiously. "Is everything all right?"

Daddy looked around, then leaned toward me and said in a low voice, "Your mother has been on the phone most of the day."

"Oh lord."

He nodded. "I'm sure you have a good explanation. You know. For things."

Things translated to trouble. I sighed again. "I do have an explanation. I'm not sure she'll think it's a good one. I'm not sure I even think it's a good one. It's just the truth."

Daddy nodded. "Then it'll do."

"I hope so."

Actually, my mother was much more understanding by the time she came into the kitchen with a fistful of cut flowers. A few mums, some fading hydrangea blooms, and an assortment of wildflowers were put into an old blue canning jar and set in the middle of the big oak table before we sat down to talk. I told her exactly what had happened, and she nodded when I finished.

"After the fifth phone call with a different wild story about what you and Bitty did down in Oxford, I began to figure out that something was screwy about all this." Mama reached over to pat my hand. "I do think you need to stop going to places where there are dead people, however. It's beginning to look very odd."

"Well, there goes my volunteer work at the county morgue," I joked, and my mother winced. So much for trying a little levity.

"Trinket, these recent activities of yours and Bitty's are going to end up getting you hurt very badly one day, I fear."

I started to answer, but felt a sneeze coming on and paused. My nose itched, and my eyes began to water. I wrinkled my nose a couple times and took a deep breath. Then I sneezed loudly. Mama handed me a tissue.

"Bless you," she said, and I nodded.

"Are any of those wildflowers goldenrod?" I asked a bit wetly.

Mama looked at the bouquet in the blue canning jar. "Oh. Yes. I didn't even think about your allergies. I'll throw them out."

"No, that's okay. I'll just move them to the counter. Look," I said around the tissue I held to my nose, "I'm sure everything will be fine. Bitty and I have talked to the police, and they know everything we know."

"Really?" Mama turned to look at me where I stood by the counter. "You've both talked to the police?"

I nodded. "We have. Lieutenant Stone. He was pretty nice about it all. I'm sure this will all blow over soon. It usually does."

"Yes, but sometimes between 'will' and 'soon' a lot of other things happen. I just don't want you or Bitty to run into any more killers. It's a terrible habit to have."

"I completely agree. Fortunately, this killer is down in Oxford, and Bitty and I are in Holly Springs. There's absolutely no reason that should change."

Mama nodded in relief. "I hope so, sugar. By the way, Dr. Coltrane was out here today, and he said to tell you he's still planning on picking you up tomorrow evening, so call him if plans have changed."

Kit? Pick me up? Apparently we had a date I'd completely forgotten about. I'd call him.

When I went upstairs a few minutes later, I kicked off my shoes and sank down on my bed. I flopped backward onto my pillows and dialed Kit's cell phone number. I felt somewhat like a teenager again, lying across my bed and talking to a boyfriend. It didn't seem that long ago since I'd done this kind of thing, or felt this kind of excitement while I waited for him to pick up. It must seem silly, me being in my fifties and as giddy as a girl about a boy, but I guess some things don't change that much just because of gray hair and a few extra pounds.

Kit answered, and his deep voice ignited heat that raced through my veins. "Hi, sexy," I said in my most sultry tone, and he laughed.

"Hi yourself, beautiful."

See why I get giddy? Any man who can call me beautiful and mean it ranks right up there with Elvis and Steve Perry, in my book.

"So what's on our agenda for tomorrow night?" I asked when I could breathe normally again.

"Movie and drinks, or dinner and dancing," he said. "Your choice."

"Hm. Are there any other options? I mean since we're doing multiple choice here, there should be at least an option C."

"Ah, I know a cozy spot on a rug in front of a fire, free drinks included. Does that make a good option C?"

"You bet. Let me see . . ." I pretended to weigh my options for a moment, and so said, "The only movie I really want to see is one of those cartoon graphics by Disney or Pixar, I can't recall which, and my dancing shoes are in cold storage, so that leaves—why, I guess that leaves option C."

"Seven o'clock, my house?"

"I'll be there," I promised.

We talked aimlessly for a few minutes while my toes finally began to uncurl, and my heartbeat returned to a more normal pace, and when we hung up, I couldn't stop smiling. I probably looked like an idiot, but since there was no one in my room to see, I didn't care.

I stood up and stretched lazily. A hot shower would be relaxing, and afterward I could go through my wardrobe and try to find something that didn't shriek *outdated* or *ugly*. Maybe Bitty was right. I really did need new clothes.

Just as I put my cell phone on my nightstand, a Hank Williams song announced another call. Kit, probably. I answered in my most sultry tone: "*Hellooo* there."

I got a staticky silence. Then a voice said, "Yes, hello? Trinket?"

It was a female voice, so I said, "Yes, this is Trinket. Who's this?"

"Cat. Catherine Moore. Listen—we need to talk. There's something important I need to tell you."

She sounded stressed, her voice strained and a bit lower than usual. I said, "Sure, Cat. What's up?"

"No, I don't mean now. It's . . . I don't trust phones. Tomorrow. Will you be free for lunch?"

"I'm off tomorrow, so I can meet you somewhere. In Oxford, or—"

"No! Not Oxford. God no, not here. It has to be somewhere else. I know. There's a place in Tupelo. The Grill on East Main Street. Meet me there about eleven thirty. Okay?"

"All right—are you okay? You sound stressed."

Catherine laughed a little. "That's putting it mildly. Look, come alone, okay? And don't tell anyone you're meeting me. It's not safe."

"I won't. Heavens, you make it sound like espionage."

"It's worse than that. See you tomorrow."

Before I could ask her anything else she hung up. I looked at my cell phone, and out of curiosity, thumbed back the Caller ID to see her number. It came up unlisted. How strange.

I didn't get much sleep that night, wondering what on earth was so urgent that Catherine Moore had to meet with me in such secrecy. Surely she hadn't found out who killed the professor? If she had that kind of information, she should go to the police, and I'd tell her just that very thing if it turned out she'd learned the killer's identity. It wasn't safe to keep that kind of knowledge to yourself, I knew that much.

Chapter 10

Finding the restaurant was easy. Waiting for Catherine was annoying. Truth be told, I've never been very good at waiting. I'm an impatient person. Oh, I try not to let it show, but I get fidgety when forced to wait for someone to arrive, or for the other shoe to fall. When I get too fidgety, I tend to do unwise things.

"Another drink, ma'am?" my server asked in a solicitous tone, and I nodded.

"Please."

Normally I stop at two drinks, especially when driving. I figured that food would soak up the alcohol, however, once Catherine arrived and we ordered. I checked my watch a couple times, then verified it was still working by asking a lady at the next table if she had the correct time. I drummed my fingers against the table, sipped my spritzer slowly—surely the amount of alcohol in a wine spritzer was negligible—and huffed big sighs a few more times before I decided to call her.

The number I had been given for her was apparently wrong. It rang several times with no answer, not even a canned voice offering to take a message. How odd. Maybe it was her home number, not her cell phone. But the cell phone she'd called me on the night before was unlisted. How was I supposed to reach her?

I did the unthinkable. I called Bitty.

"Do you have a cell phone number for Catherine Moore?" I asked when she answered.

"For Cat? I'm sure I have it somewhere—why?"

"Because I want to write it on a wall in the men's bathroom, of course," I said rather testily. "Why do you think I want it?"

"Well, aren't you the little ray of sunshine today," said Bitty calmly. "You've interrupted me in a garden club meeting, you know. But I'll be the bigger person. I have her number in my address book if you'll wait just a minute."

"Sorry," I said. "I'm just . . ." My voice trailed off as I remembered that our meeting was supposed to be private. Secrecy is not my best talent. I try, but far too often find myself blurting out things best left unsaid.

Bitty gave me the number, then said, "You're just what?"

I sighed. "I'm just supposed to call her. That's all I can say for now. Okay?"

"Are you snooping around without me?"

"Would I do that?"

"Aha! You are," Bitty accused.

"Not really. Frankly, I'm not at all sure what this is about. It may be something completely different than—" I paused, looked around me to be sure no one could hear me and finished in a low tone, "—murder."

"But you don't really think so."

"I'm not sure what I think."

"Hunh. I could tell you what to think."

"I'm sure you could. Oh, never mind. I think I see her coming now. Talk to you in a little while."

I hung up before Bitty could ask more questions or give more unwanted advice. To my profound relief, Catherine Moore wound her way through tables and joined me, dragging out a chair and sinking down into it with feline grace.

"Sorry I'm late," she said. "Gawd, I need a drink."

She lifted her chin, and a waiter appeared at her elbow. "Vodka martini, dry, two olives," she said as she pulled off a pair of expensive leather gloves. She tossed them carelessly into her open purse, removed expensive sunglasses to toss them inside as well, then set the designer bag on the empty chair next to her. I recognized it as a Jimmy Choo tote bag only because Bitty had one very similar. They start at a thousand dollars.

I watched in total fascination. Catherine Moore was one of those women who had the presence of a Hollywood star, and would even if she wore clothes from Walmart instead of designer duds. Her movements were casual yet graceful, her air one of utter boredom with her surroundings. If not for the faint frown lines that tucked her waxed—and probably Botoxed—eyebrows together, one would have thought her without a care in the world. Her husky voice reminded me once again of Anne Bancroft when she leaned forward and said, "You didn't tell anyone about meeting me here, did you?"

"No," I said, because it was true. I'd only asked Bitty for her cell phone number and not given any other information.

"Good. People have a nasty way of putting two and two together and coming up with five. Do you mind if I smoke?"

Without waiting for me to reply, she pulled a small case out of her bag and extracted a slim brown cigarette. While I anticipated choking to death on the second-hand smoke, she lit it with a practiced snap of her lighter and blew out a long stream of smoke that smelled like cloves. A rather pleasant surprise.

The waiter brought her drink and an ashtray, so I figured we must be in the smoking section. She took the glass in her free hand and swapped back and forth between drinking and smoking as she began telling me why she had asked to meet.

"You know I have no love for Emily Sturgis, nor did I like her boorish husband. It doesn't bother me that he's dead, but I don't want all of Ole Miss to suffer because of his idiocy." She blew out another stream of clove-scented smoke. "Too much negative attention can be bad for a university. We already had that controversy over Colonel Reb, and just barely got that settled when Spencer had to go and get himself murdered."

Despite her outward calm, I noticed that her left eye had started to twitch a little, and the hand holding her drink trembled ever so slightly when she lifted it to her lips. I waited for her to continue. She drained half her martini before doing so.

"After meeting you at that farcical commiseration with the grieving widow, I got the feeling you and I are kindred spirits of a kind."

Rather astonished, I gaped at her, and her lips curved with wry humor.

"*Of a kind*, I said. Of course, I'm much more cynical than you, but I could tell that you weren't all that impressed by the show Emily put on."

While I wasn't at all sure I knew what she was talking about, I nodded as if I did and agreed.

Catherine took a deep drag of her skinny cigarette. "Even a legally blind person could tell exactly what Breck Hartford was up to, and neither he nor Emily fooled any of us for a second."

Now I was really confused. Did she mean Breck and Emily were . . . intimate? Or partners in crime? I didn't especially want to display my ignorance to someone who had assumed I was smarter than I was, but neither did I want to miss out on any possible clue that might point in the direction of the killer.

"They were having an affair?" I asked.

"More like a competition, I'd say. A 'who can get away with what for how long' kind of thing."

That sounded promising. So I said, "Breck's wife—does she know?"

Catherine lifted her brows. "I doubt Victoria knows that gravity is a law, but she can't be so stupid as not to know her husband plays around on her. She pretends not to notice. Not that I blame her. If I had to live with a man as dedicated to drama as he is to wearing women's panties, I'd play stupid, too."

My confusion only deepened. What were we talking about here? A cross-dressing Romeo or a devious killer?

Maybe my expression registered my confusion, because Cat leaned forward and said, "You do realize, don't you, that Breck and Emily have been having an affair almost since the time she and Spencer showed up in Oxford? It's one of those things that everyone knows but no one wants to admit, just in case the police start poking into their own affairs a little too closely. Now *that* would be theater at its best."

She sat back and took another drag off her cigarette, again spicing the air with the scent of cloves. After a moment, she said, "Breck Hartford hated Spencer. They had a history, though, even before Sturgis got to Ole Miss."

"So you think Breck is responsible for killing the professor?" I asked.

"I do. He's not the only one with a motive, but he's the only one I know who's capable of committing murder. I just can't prove it."

I was already fascinated, but now I felt she was finally edging around the reason for our "lunch" date in Tupelo. I tried to sound as nonchalant as she did. "So how do you think I can help?"

Catherine blew out another stream of smoke and smiled. "Breck is smarter than to leave an obvious trail of evidence. I think he's covered up as much as he can, but there's always something that's overlooked. There really isn't such a thing as a perfect murder. I need someone who isn't too close to the situation, and whom Breck would never suspect, to get to the truth and find the evidence. It's there. We just have to dig it up."

When she said "we" I knew exactly who she had in mind. I wasn't so sure I wanted to be involved, however.

"I can't imagine what kind of reason would be enough to commit murder," I said. "*Why* would he kill Professor Sturgis?"

A faint smile touched the corners of her mouth. "It's been my observation that the main reasons people become killers involve love, fear and/or personal gain. The last can be either money or advancement of some kind. Love is the silliest reason for murder, in my opinion, but people do get overwrought about it. Now, fear . . . fear is a huge motivator for murder. Fear of being found guilty of something, fear of losing your job, your home, your freedom, or even fear of failure. Fear of—dying."

She paused to take another drag from her cigarette, then leaned forward slightly to crush it into a glass ashtray. "I think you know where I'm going with this, don't you?"

I wanted to say yes. I really did. But to be honest, I hadn't a clue. I was torn between being honest and looking foolish, and pretending I knew what she was talking about and probably ending up looking foolish anyway.

Fortunately, she saved me.

Catherine's hand shook slightly, and her eyes widened as she made eye contact. "Breck Hartford knows how to manipulate people. He may seem charming, but he is a barracuda, believe me. Once, we were lovers. Now I'm his enemy. And he seems to have recently cultivated a habit of eliminating people he considers his enemies."

Catherine had kept her tone low, and I noticed the twitch was back at the corner of her eye. Still, what she suggested sounded preposterous.

"But you're talking about multiple murders. Is he a serial killer?" I asked.

She leaned back in her chair and shrugged. "He certainly has the right personality for it. Breck has no conscience whatsoever. He could kill someone and then go to dinner without turning a hair. He could manipulate a student, who would never commit a crime, into covering up a murder. Do you see what I mean?"

After a brief pause, I shook my head. "No. Not really. It's unimaginable to me that anyone would do something totally against their nature just because it was suggested by another person."

It occurred to me as soon as I said it that I did things totally against my nature all the time. If not for Bitty, I would never have moved corpses. Or maybe even met corpses.

"But it's happened before," said Catherine. "An *accident* that was really a murder, and there was a cover-up."

"I had no idea," I said. "When did this happen?"

"A couple years ago. Another student's murder was ruled an accidental death. I know Breck Hartford was responsible for it, however."

"Then . . . shouldn't Breck have been arrested?"

"In a perfect world, yes. There was no proof. Police concluded the investigation and ruled it an accident. But I know better. The witness intended to go to the police with what he knew, but he didn't have a chance. Then it was too late."

"So it could be possible that Breck Hartford was innocent, right?"

Catherine sounded slightly impatient. "Possible. Not probable."

I remembered Gaynelle saying the same kind of thing. It had made sense when she'd said it, but with Catherine Moore, I just didn't know whether or not to believe her.

"This witness to a murder was the student you mentioned, right? Is he still attending Ole Miss?" I asked.

Catherine shook her head. "No. He's dead."

"Dead! What happened to him?"

"Suicide. Or that's what it was ruled. I don't believe that for a second, either."

"But you obviously knew the witness. Wouldn't the police listen to you if you told them what he said?" I asked.

"Apparently not. They thought I was . . . overwrought." Her lips twisted in a bitter grimace. "Sometimes living in a small-town atmosphere can be a disadvantage. Too many people know your private business and are willing to share the information."

"I see," I said even though I really didn't. There was obviously something she wasn't saying.

Catherine shook her head. "No, you don't. I don't blame you. It's too bizarre even to me, and I've lived with it for far too long."

"This all sounds like the plot of a really bad TV movie," I said after a moment, and Catherine smiled.

"Exactly like it. But this is true. I can't prove it, but I know it happened. Just like I know Breck is behind the murder of Sturgis. Not that I blame him much. Spencer was an obnoxious little man."

"No one deserves to be murdered," I said rather primly, and Catherine's smile reminded me of one of Mama's feral cats. Her nickname suited her.

"Please. I can name five world leaders right off the top of my head that deserve to be killed. However, that's not why I'm telling you this."

"Yes, why *are* you telling me this when you should be telling the police?"

"Because the police have already closed the case of Monty's death and ruled it a suicide. They aren't going to listen to me again, and they aren't likely to reopen it without strong evidence. You seem to have a way of ferreting out the truth about mysterious deaths. My other reason is purely vindictive. I'd love to see Breck Hartford living in a small prison cell with a mountainous inmate named Bubba."

"Forgive me, but this seems too much like a spurned lover, a quarrel that's turned to hate. It happens all the time. That may be why the police aren't investigating it. Are you sure some of your accusations aren't motivated by bitterness?" I asked, and this time her smile was positively feline.

"Honey, you're absolutely right. I *am* bitter. But despite what some may say, I'm not crazy. I didn't invent this. I know Breck a bit too well for that."

"Then you should be able to get the information needed to prove that he's the killer. If you know him that well, it might be easier for you."

"He'd know immediately what I was doing. It has to be someone he doesn't know well. Maybe this is my way of making sure he doesn't kill me next."

A beat went by while I tried to absorb the implications. "Why would he kill you?"

"I know too much."

"About a murder?"

She hesitated and reached inside her purse for another cigarette. I waited until she lit it before I said, "I know I keep saying this, but if you have any information that the police should know, I think you should either tell them yourself or get an attorney to do it for you."

"And I told you I've already tried that. It hasn't helped. I need you to find proof that Breck is involved in not just the murder of Spencer Sturgis, but two others."

I was aghast. "*Three* murders? Are you serious? And the police won't do anything about him? Surely if what you're saying is true, they're at least investigating."

Catherine sighed, a heavy, frustrated sound. "The first two deaths have been ruled on by a coroner. The first was an accident, the second a suicide. Unless I can come up with solid evidence, he'll get away with not only their murders, but that of Sturgis as well. I don't put it past him to have covered his tracks very well. He's used to weaseling out of situations. And if I don't pursue this, no one else will. He needs to be in jail. He's dangerous."

A shiver went down my spine at her tone. She sounded serious. Dead serious.

"Why aren't you afraid?" I asked.

Catherine hesitated. "I can't afford to be," she said after a moment. "Breck's the kind of man who feeds on the fear of others. The worst thing I could do is let him know that he terrifies me." She leaned forward and said softly, "But he does terrify me. I know what he can do."

"My God," I said, matching her low tone. "You *must* go to the police! They can protect you and—"

She cut me off with a harsh laugh. "Right. They think—or say—that I'm seeing guilt where none exists."

"I don't understand. Why won't they take you seriously?"

She waved a hand, and then said, "Because I had a breakdown a year ago. I went Looney Tunes, okay? I spent some time in a hospital sorting things out. I'm fine now. Or at least, I can hide my 'paranoia' better."

She sounded very bitter. I didn't know what to say that wouldn't sound trite or too placating.

So I said simply, "I didn't know."

"Not many people do. I told everyone I was going on a cruise. Some people are like sharks. If one sees a little blood in the water, they all try to take a bite. I'd just as soon not have to deal with that."

"I don't blame you."

Catherine's smile was brittle. "So here I am, asking for help from an almost total stranger. I don't know where else to turn. There are days when I think I should just give up and let it go, but then, who would be left to see justice done for Monty?"

"You're talking about the student who committed suicide."

She lifted one finger. "The death was ruled suicide. It was murder."

"Have you tried hiring a private investigator? They have all kinds of techniques to get information. Access to private records, even recording devices that can get valuable evidence to give to police gives them an edge I wouldn't have."

"That could be fatal. Some stranger going around asking inconvenient questions would just give Breck Hartford the warning he'd need to get rid of evidence. Not to mention getting rid of more witnesses. Like me."

"You saw—?"

"I didn't have to *see* it done to know what happened. I saw the aftermath. It was brutal. Look. You're smart, and you're familiar enough to people not to arouse suspicion."

Since I wasn't at all certain I was the kind of smart she needed, I said, "I don't know that I'm who you need to do this, Catherine."

"I do. I'll pay you. I have money. Just name your price."

There was such desperation in her tone that it took me back. All I could think to say was, "What did the student's parents have to say about his death?"

Before she could reply, I knew what she would say. It hit me suddenly, that the pain and desperation in her eyes could only mean one thing: "Monty was my son. My only child."

The raw emotion in her voice left me speechless and understanding a lot more than I had up until this point. So I nodded.

"You'll help me?" she asked hoarsely, and again I nodded.

Relief flooded her face, and she actually smiled. It was a genuine smile, not the bitter or cynical smiles of earlier.

"Thank you, Trinket. It means a lot to me that you're going to help. I have a lot of notes I've made since Monty died, and I'll bring them to you. I would have brought them with me today, but . . . but I wasn't sure you'd help, and I didn't want to risk someone else getting their hands on them. I keep them hidden. I even use codes."

It was faintly startling that she'd resorted to codes and hidden information for fear of discovery. Hartford had seemed arrogant when I met him, but not especially evil. Had I misjudged him, or was Catherine creating guilt where there was none?

"Do you really think Breck Hartford would do harm to you? Is he that dangerous?"

"He's that manipulative. He likes to be in control of everything—the people around him, his job, his athletics department . . . and his lovers. He may come across as charming, but he's always on a power trip. Breck would have no compunction about getting rid of those he considers his enemies."

"But—*murder?* Are you sure?" I asked.

"I suppose it's the ultimate challenge for him."

"He certainly does hide it well. I would never have guessed."

"Very few would. You'd have to know him well to realize what he is."

Catherine stood up and leaned over to gather her Jimmy Choo tote and sunglasses. My head was whirling with everything she'd said.

"How are you so sure Breck was responsible for your son's death?" I asked as she slid Gucci tortoiseshell sunglasses over her eyes.

For a moment she didn't reply, just stared at me through the dark lenses. "Because Monty wouldn't have hung himself for *any* reason," she said at last.

"Had he been depressed, or seen a doctor recently? A recent breakup with a girl, maybe? He could have been sick, or—"

"No. None of those things made him hang himself from his closet rod while I was out of town. *I know that.*"

The last three words were said so harshly that I recoiled a little. "I'm only asking questions that the police either will or have already asked you," I said. "These are things that may have contributed to his death being ruled a suicide instead of—"

Catherine interrupted softly, "Monty had no signs of depression, no tragic loss, no mental imbalance, just an overwhelming need for approval from a father figure."

"Breck Hartford," I said, and she nodded.

"Yes. And Breck used him, then discarded him when he was done. He deserves to pay for that." She slung her tote bag to her shoulder, paused, and said fiercely, "I want to be a witness at his execution!"

For several minutes after Catherine left, I sat staring into space, mulling over all she'd told me. If she was right about her son being murdered, then it was possible that Hartford was also involved in the death of Professor Sturgis. But what motive would be enough to kill a respected, if not loved, professor? A love triangle made the most sense. But that didn't take into account the deaths of two other people. What was really the fatal link between all of them? Someone else should know about it, someone who wasn't as close to Sturgis and Hartford as Catherine obviously was. Maybe that was who I needed to talk to next. I needed a fresh, unbiased perspective.

Instead, I left Tupelo and went straight to Bitty's house.

Chapter 11

"I thought you went to lunch," Bitty said, watching me as I scrounged through her refrigerator for something to tide me over until my date with Kit.

"I did. I had several wine spritzers and some bread. How old is this?" I held up a plastic dish for her to see.

"If it's not green and fuzzy, it's edible. That's Chen Ling's food, by the way," she added when I started to pop the top. "Oatmeal, long-grain rice, veggies and chicken. It's not bad."

I stuck the plastic dish back in the meat drawer. "Thanks anyway. If I eat after your dog I might start barking and sniffing butts."

"A vast improvement of your social skills. Oh for heaven's sake— move out of the way, and I'll get you something to eat."

"Never mind. I'll just eat some of this." I paused before I peeled back the foil on a container of fruit and yogurt. "This isn't Chitling's food too, is it?"

"Don't be silly. She only eats plain yogurt."

I rolled my eyes and didn't care if she saw me. "I hope I come back in my next life as your dog, Bitty, I swear I do."

Bitty smiled. "So do I, dear."

After a mental eye roll, I found a spoon and dug into the raspberry-yogurt cup. As I leaned back against the granite counter, I thought about whether or not I should share what I'd learned with Bitty. Most of the time she's a help, but the times that she isn't can have catastrophic consequences.

Bitty put both hands on her hips. "Okay, don't even think about not telling me what you've been up to. I know you had lunch with Catherine Moore, and now I want to know why and what you said. Or she said."

"When did you take up mind-reading?" I asked around my raspberry-yogurt.

"When you came in the door with that secretive look on your face. So spill it. Is Cat trying to get you to help her prove that Monty's death wasn't a suicide?"

I must have looked astonished because she said, "Your lower lip is hanging. Don't dribble yogurt on my clean floor, please. Well? Is she?"

"How did you know?" I managed to ask while wiping raspberry colored yogurt off the front of my blouse.

"Everyone knows Cat was devastated by his death. She can't or won't believe that it was suicide."

"What do you think it was? Suicide or murder?"

Bitty paused a moment before saying, "Well, Monty certainly had everything to live for, but isn't that true of most suicides? He was very bright and always made the Dean's list until not long before he died. Cat pushed him, but she was a single mother who had big plans for him, and I can't fault her for that."

"What about Monty? Was he ambitious as well?"

"He must have been. You'd have to ask the boys. They'd know more than I would about it. You know how college kids are, letting everyone but their parents know what they plan on doing."

That was true. When I'd quit college to go roaming around the country with Perry, my parents were the last to know. Fortunately, my daughter kept me in the loop about her plans, so I wasn't surprised when she cut her education short to get married and go to work. Now she's back in school and going for a degree in Business Ed. She's a lot smarter than I was about that kind of thing.

"So there's no reason Monty would kill himself?" I asked Bitty when my mind wandered back to the subject at hand.

"Like I said, none that I can think of. Why so many questions? What is Cat up to now?"

"You were right. I promised I'd help her find out who killed Sturgis and why," I said after a moment. "She thinks his murder is linked to her son's death."

"No!" Now Bitty looked astonished. "But how? I mean, Monty died a year and a half ago, and Sturgis only a week and a half ago. How could they be connected?"

"That's what I'm supposed to find out. Catherine has her theories, of course, and some evidence she's gathered that she's going to share with me."

Bitty perked up. "Evidence? What kind of evidence? You mean like bloody shoes or fingerprints or something like that?"

"I rather doubt it. If she had something like that, she'd have given it to the police. I hope." I put my empty yogurt cup in Bitty's trash compactor and moved to the sink to dump the spoon and wash my hands. Bitty followed me.

"So when do we start?"

"*We?* Have you got a mouse in your pocket, Cochise?"

"Funny girl. You know I always go along with you."

"Unless it's before noon or conflicts with your hair and nail appointment."

Bitty said, "I have my standards, of course. So. When do we start?"

I dried my hands with a paper towel and surrendered to the inevitable. "Tomorrow morning. I'll be here at nine."

"Ten."

"Nine thirty, and you have the coffee on."

"Done." Bitty smiled. "What fun!"

"Right. Can you be trusted not to tell anyone what we're doing?"

Bitty made the motion of zipping her lips shut, and I rolled my eyes. "Like that's ever worked before."

"I won't breathe a word, Trinket. I promise."

"Pinky promise?" I asked, and she grinned as she held up her right hand with the pinky finger stuck out. I immediately reverted to third grade and curled my little finger around hers. "Honestly, I can't believe us sometimes. Last time we did this, I didn't have to worry about your forty-carat diamond slicing into my hand. Now—"

"Shut up and say it," Bitty interrupted.

We locked eyes and said simultaneously, "I swear that if I break this promise I'll cut off my pinky and bury it by an old stump under a full moon."

We solemnly lifted our entwined hands in the air twice, then let go at the same time. Then we both burst into laughter.

"Oh," I said after a moment, "we forgot to spit."

"Don't you dare, Trinket Truevine. Maria just cleaned this morning."

"Ah, the mysterious, mythical Maria. I'm still not sure if she exists, or you just invented her to cover up a deep-seated obsession with cleaning."

"Spit on my clean floor, and you'll find out," Bitty warned. "I think she installed hidden cameras, because she always seems to know how something got so dirty."

"Tomorrow morning," I reminded as I headed for the front door. "Coffee ready."

"I'll want a full report of your night with Kit," said Bitty as she followed.

Just before the door shut behind me I said over my shoulder, "Ain't gonna happen!"

By the time I went home, showered, changed into comfortable clothes that I was pretty sure Kit hadn't seen too many times, and put on make-up again, I was running late. Since I'm a properly reared Southern girl, I know better than to show up at someone's house without a gift for the host. Fortunately, I had a lovely bottle of wine that both Kit and I liked, and even if it didn't go with whatever he planned to serve for dinner that night, it wouldn't go to waste.

Daylight Savings Time had ended already, so it was dark when I left the house. Daddy's advice to lock my car doors and not stop for any hitchhikers still rang in my ears as I pulled out of our half circle driveway and onto blacktop road. Truevine Road winds back through countryside and eventually into Holly Springs if one wants a scenic route, but 301 Highway gets me there a lot faster. After leaving our road, there aren't any streetlights again until closer to town. That never bothers me, because I've traveled this road all my life and know it like the back of my hand. It didn't take long for me to get familiar with it again once I came back home.

While our house, Cherryhill, is about three miles outside the Holly Springs city limits, our post office address is still listed as Holly Springs. It's been that way for as long as Truevines have been in Marshall County.

Kit lives in the middle of Holly Springs. He's still looking for a house and a few acres out of town a little ways. I think the house he's in now suits him just fine. It's got that masculine feel to it despite the graceful lines of architecture that hail from an era long past.

I parked in his narrow driveway, and before the engine even died he was at my door, opening it for me, ready to envelope me in a warm embrace. See how lucky I am? How could I possibly resist a man who treats me like a special lady?

Kit Coltrane is six-four, and being taller than me is a definite plus. Not only that, his arms go all the way around me, and as I'm still battling at least fifteen extra pounds that have somehow homesteaded my five-nine frame, that's another big plus.

Nuzzling my neck, he murmured, "I have a fire going and wine breathing. Let's go inside."

He didn't have to ask me twice.

It's not that I'm suggestible. I just know a good thing when I hear it.

Later that evening—yes, much later—we sat on a really cushy rug in front of the dwindling fire and talked. Kit told me about a parcel of land he'd found that might be just right for him, and I told him about moving a corpse in a laundry cart.

He stared at me. "Not again," he said after a moment, and I had to nod.

"Yes. Sorry. You know how Bitty is. Nothing else would do."

Kit slapped a hand to his forehead. "I don't understand why both of you aren't serving life at Parchman. If anyone else had done half the things the two of you have done just in the short time I've known you—"

"No, really, I'm fine. Thank you for asking," I interrupted.

Groaning, he shook his head. "You do know that you don't have to do every nutty thing she wants, right?"

"You've met Bitty, haven't you?" I countered.

Check. My queen to his bishop. We sat in silence for a few moments. Then he looked up at me with a faint smile. Firelight reflected in his dark brown eyes.

"I suppose I should be grateful she didn't insist on taking him to the football game," he said wryly, and I nodded.

"It was suggested." When he shot me a startled look I said, "Kidding. But that's some of the gossip going around. I'm surprised you haven't heard it yet."

"So am I. I'll have to talk to some of the vet techs and tell them they're falling down on their job. Gossip is the glue that holds this town together."

"Isn't that true in every small town?"

Kit grinned. "Probably, but I'd have to say the gossip quality in Holly Springs is hard to beat these days. Murders, midnight skulkers, mobile corpses—just those three things alone elevate Holly Springs to the top of any list."

I pointed out that the last mobile corpse had actually occurred in Oxford, but Kit failed to make the distinction. He shook his head.

"Nope. Still qualifies since two of Holly Springs' finest citizens were responsible."

"Ah, I see there are rules to this gossip game. I'll have to brush up."

He leaned forward to press his forehead to mine. My heart leaped, and my mouth got too dry to swallow as he murmured, "Just stay safe, sugar. I worry about you."

There's just something so nice about being made to feel special by someone who isn't a blood relative. It'd been a long time since I'd felt this way, and I freely admit that I relished every moment. Why not? Even fifty-something women past their prime, but not their youthfulness, need to feel special.

Still, I felt I should say, "Oh, don't worry about me. Everything always turns out fine."

"Right," he said wryly and planted a kiss on my forehead before he leaned back to shake his head again. "It's all turned out fine so far, but one of these days, you ladies may run into something or someone you can't escape. I can't help but worry about that."

I smiled. "The police finally gave Bitty back her pistol, so we'll be armed if we run into any trouble."

Kit groaned. "Is that supposed to be comforting? And how the devil did she get it back? Never mind. I know. Jackson Lee. He must really be in love to give in to her like that."

"Does that mean you wouldn't give me back my pistol if I had one?" I couldn't help asking.

"You're not Bitty. If you were—well, I doubt I'd be in this relationship."

Somehow, I found that very reassuring. It's not that I view Bitty as competition, necessarily, but she's always been the "star" of the show. I rather liked feeling that I was the star in this particular show.

Just as I was thinking about how to reward Kit for saying all the right things, my cell phone rang. Now, I'd resisted modern technology for as long as I could. If my well-meaning parents—and AT&T—hadn't made it too easy to surrender, I'd have still been cell phone free that night, and Kit would have been an extremely happy man the next morning.

But then, maybe a murderer would have gone free, and that would have been too awful to think about.

Chapter 12

"Trinket," said a husky voice I barely recognized as Catherine Moore's once I dug my cell phone out of my purse and answered, "he knows! *Omigod*, he's found out that I have proof of what he did . . ."

"Catherine," I said quickly, "where are you? Are you alone?"

She gave a half-sob, half-laugh. "Aren't I always? I'm locked in my bathroom. I think . . . I think he's downstairs in my office."

"Call nine-one-one immediately," I said. "If someone is in your house—if it's Breck Hartford or not—call the police!"

"They'd never get here in time. I have a gun. I know what he's looking for . . . all the evidence against him. But he's too late. All I have left is the evidence to give to you, and he won't understand it but you will . . . *no!*"

I heard a sudden loud banging, as if a fist against a door. Catherine screamed, and a loud bang like a gunshot nearly deafened me. There was a crash, then silence.

"Catherine," I said several times before I realized that our connection was gone. I looked up at Kit, who'd sat up and was pulling on his shoes. "I'll call her back. Maybe it's okay. Maybe it's all a big mistake."

I dialed her number twice and got the recording both times. Kit had already laced up his tennis shoes and was holding out his hand for me to take. He pulled me up and steadied me with his hand under my elbow.

"Call the Holly Springs police while I get my car keys. Do you know where she lives?"

I nodded. "Oxford."

"Oh," he said, and paused. "Call the Holly Springs police anyway. They can get through to the Oxford police much faster than we can."

I got Sergeant Maxwell on the phone, and after I identified myself I told him, "I was on the phone with a friend in Oxford when someone broke into her house. Shots were fired. Can you help?"

He took down her name and cell phone number, then warned, "Do not attempt to get more involved, Miz Truevine. Do you understand me? I don't want a single one of you Divas messing around in any more investigations."

"Yes, Sergeant," I replied, "I understand you. But you are going to let me know if my friend is okay, right?"

Silence. Then, finally, a grudging, "Yeah. We'll let you know."

He hung up, and I looked at Kit. "Well, now what do I do? I can't just sit here and wonder what's happening, if she killed someone, or if someone killed her—oh lord. I'm getting just as bad as Bitty, aren't I?"

Kit put out a hand to stop me since I was pacing the floor, and he folded me into his arms. "I'll make some coffee. We may be up a while waiting on the police to let us know about Catherine."

"Do you think I should call Bitty and let her know?" I asked as I went with him to his kitchen. "After all, she's known Catherine a lot longer than I have."

"Are they good friends?"

I had to think a minute. Then I said, "Not what I'd call good friends, but they've known each other a while."

"Maybe you should wait until you know something definite to tell her," Kit said as he measured out coffee beans into a grinder. "Right now all you could say is that she's in some kind of trouble, and you don't know if she's okay or not."

"True." I leaned on the counter as he pressed the grinder top down, and it made a loud racket. I love the smell of freshly ground coffee. It always reminds me of mornings in my parents' kitchen when it was warm and full of happy activity. Mama always made the coffee before daylight, and the rich aroma greeted us kids when we came downstairs for our breakfasts. It's one of those comforting memories that can help me get through all the times when life is less than wonderful.

I'm a terribly impatient person, I've realized. I always want to know endings in books and in real-life mysteries at the beginning. I'm one of those people who flip to the back pages of a book just to see if it ends nicely before I'll buy it. Not that I remember who committed the crime or got the girl; I just remember that it had a nice ending, so I can read it with anticipation instead of dread. Oddly, considering my current situation in being inundated with furry, four-legged creatures, I also have to know if the dog, cat, or other animal is killed off in the book before I'll read it. If the animal dies, in a book or in a movie, I don't want to read it or see it. That's the reason I've never seen *Dances With Wolves,* although I understand it was a lovely movie, and I've always liked Kevin Costner. I've never gotten over the ending of *Turner and Hooch,* which was billed as a comedy, and to my mind, had a horrible ending.

So you can imagine how I felt waiting on the police to call and let me know if Catherine Moore was okay, if she'd shot someone, or if it'd all been a mistake and she'd just shot off her bathroom doorknob.

Those things happen. Bitty still has a bullet hole in her back door where she shot at and missed a falling tree branch. She'd been certain it was a burglar. This is just one of the many, many reasons the good citizens of Holly Springs breathe much easier when her gun is in the custody of the police. It's a heavy, wicked-looking thing, a Colt .45 that's way too big for her to hold steadily. Not that a little thing like a ventilated door bothers Bitty very much. During our annual pilgrimages she passes off the bullet hole in her back door as made by a Yankee soldier. It gets a lot of extra attention. Most tourists don't know that the sun porch used to be the kitchen, and the back door isn't as old as the car my mama drives. Things like bullet holes in doors add an air of danger and excitement.

We took our coffee into the living room, and since the fire had died down to a hot bank of coals, Kit turned on the lights and blew out the guttering candles. Even though I tried to focus on conversation, I kept thinking about Catherine and what was happening in Oxford. Finally Kit reached over and put a hand on my arm.

"Come on, honey. Let's go up to the police station and see if we can talk to the sergeant firsthand. We're more liable to find out what's going on if we're there."

"We should go by and pick up Bitty," I said.

"Will she be awake?"

"It doesn't matter. If I don't tell her what's going on, I'll never hear the end of it. I'd rather her be mad at me for waking her up than for leaving her out."

Kit sighed, but went right along with me when I banged on her front door. I'd already tried to call her, but got her answering machine at the house and left a message on her cell phone. The storm door she uses in the winter was latched, so I couldn't get to the lock for which I had a key. The house was dark and silent, so I knew she was asleep.

"Wait here," I said. "I'll go around to the back door. It's probably unlocked."

"Won't you set off her alarm system?"

"Only if she remembered to set it. I know the code anyway. If she comes to the front door, tell her I'm around back. I think she'd better hear about Catherine from me."

"No argument there. I'm more than willing for you to deal with her."

I left Kit standing on the porch under a chandelier that wasn't lit. Sometimes she forgets to set the switch so the lights come on at dusk. Bitty really needs a house that runs on automatic everything. She'd forget to turn on the electricity if it wasn't already wired.

As I'd hoped, the back door was unlocked. No alarm beeped a reminder to punch in the code when I went in, so I knew she'd forgotten to set the system as well. *Really.* One of these days Bitty was going to be robbed of everything she had, and then she might remember to lock doors and set alarms, I told myself as I went up the stairs and into her kitchen. A low light over the stovetop illuminated a small area, and since I know her house almost as well as my parents', I didn't bother flipping on any lights as I headed for the front door to let Kit inside.

Just as I rounded the corner into the hallway, something big and squishy hit me in the head. I staggered sideways. It hit me again, so I screamed. I wasn't really hurt, but I was alarmed. Had someone snuck into Bitty's house to rob her? While a small part of me thought it was way overdue, the more rational part of me wanted to get rid of the intruder before he did any damage.

This time when the big squishy weapon smacked me in the face, I was ready. I grabbed at it at the same time as I brought up my foot. I caught a brief glimpse of my attacker as I snatched the bulky thing away. I kicked him and heard a gratifying grunt of pain. I could hear Kit banging on the front door and yelling, and I screamed again so he'd be a bit more proactive in my rescue.

It must have worked. I heard glass breaking just as I slung my confiscated weapon toward the intruder, who was squeaking unintelligible words. He was short and wearing a black face mask, some kind of stocking cap on his head, what looked like a raincoat, and a pair of gloves. My blow knocked him for a loop. I saw him reel backward to land on the floor, then he was up and at me again.

This time he had something in his hand that wasn't soft and squishy. It was hard and rigid. I tried to duck, but before I could get out of the way, he hit me right square on top of the head with it.

I saw stars. I heard birds singing and the waves of the ocean crashing ashore. My knees turned to jelly, and I toppled over like a felled tree. I wondered hazily if I'd fallen in the forest, would anyone hear? Then I was only vaguely aware of confusion around me and lights flashing before I slipped away into that safe place behind my closed eyelids.

Something really vile smelling jerked me awake, and I came upright gasping for clean air. To my surprise, an EMT crouched beside me, and just beyond him Kit hovered with a worried expression next to two policemen. What on earth?

At the same time as the EMT guy asked me to tell him my name, Kit asked me if I was all right. I didn't know who to answer first, so I just said, "Get me up off the floor."

The EMT put his hand on my shoulder to keep me from getting up. "I have to take your vitals before I let you up."

"My vitals are fine," I said rather indignantly. "It's my head that hurts. Did you catch the burglar?"

One of the policeman said, "Lady, you *are* the burglar."

Now I was really confused. I looked from the policeman to Kit, who shrugged and nodded. They weren't making any sense. Maybe Bitty could clear—Bitty! Had she been hurt?

"Where's Bitty?" I asked frantically. "Is she okay? Was she hurt? Tell me she isn't hurt!"

"She's fine, unless you consider jumbo size Charmin lethal," the EMT said. "Now please be still while I take your blood pressure."

I was still trying to figure out what toilet paper had to do with Bitty's state of health when she popped up next to Kit. I gave a start. I knew it was Bitty, yet I'd never seen her look quite so . . . un-Bitty-like.

I've seen Bitty's nightwear plenty of times. She always wears a pink cap, pink eyeshades, and usually some kind of pink gown or pajamas. Her slippers are usually pink and frothy with feathers.

This Bitty, however, wore a dark blue terrycloth robe, some kind of blue knit cap on her head, and black eyeshades hung loosely around her neck. I blinked at her a couple times. She lifted one hand and waggled gloved fingers at me.

"You okay, sugar?"

"Who are you, and what have you done with Bitty?"

This time she didn't sound quite as calm. "I hope you know you frightened me nearly to death! And poor Chen Ling—I had to put her upstairs, she was so upset!"

"You were being burglarized. What did you want me to do?"

The EMT sounded annoyed when he said, "Your blood pressure is unstable. Be still for a moment so I can get a decent reading."

I figured my blood pressure was going up faster than the national debt. So I sat still and quiet until he finished, pronounced me fit—or well enough to get off the floor, anyway—and began to pack up the tools of his trade. He seemed to want to escape very quickly, and I was willing to let him go.

Kit helped me up and into the living room where I refused to sit on Bitty's antique and very uncomfortable settee, and sat instead in one of the more comfortable chairs. They're antique, too, but not stuffed with horsehair. Not even a horse would find that settee comfortable.

"Okay," I said when I was situated, "what happened?"

Truthfully, I'd begun to figure it out while the EMT was counting bubbles or whatever it is they count. Bitty's attire was the key. She'd thought I was a burglar, and I thought she was a masked intruder. Apparently we had whacked away at each other in the dark with God only knew what kind of weapons.

"I heard a noise," began Bitty, "so I got out of bed and came downstairs."

"*A* noise?" I echoed. "We rang the bell and beat on the door. Are you wearing ear muffs, too?"

"Don't be silly, Trinket. As I told the nice officers, this was all a terrible mistake. I didn't know it was you in the hallway. I looked at the door and saw this big shadow, so I thought someone was breaking in and called nine-one-one. Then I couldn't find Chen Ling. So I came the rest of the way down the stairs."

"And ran into me," I said. "What did you hit me with?"

"The first time? I just grabbed whatever I could find. It happened to be the super-size package of Charmin mega-roll toilet paper. It felt heavy, so I thought it would work pretty well."

"It did. But that isn't what you hit me with the last time."

"No. When you knocked me down, I found one of Chen Ling's toys on the floor. That's what I hit you with."

There was something she wasn't telling me. Her lips were pressed into a tight line, and her eyes wouldn't quite meet mine. When I glanced at Kit, I noticed that he didn't meet my gaze either. The two police officers still standing in the foyer began laughing. I narrowed my eyes at Bitty.

"Elisabeth Ann Truevine Hollandale, you tell me right this instant what you did. I know it must be something awful," I said.

Bitty's cheeks flushed, and after a moment, she nodded. "Remember when I came to see you at Carolann's shop and brought Chen Ling with me? Well, remember the toy she liked so much?"

For a moment I just stared at her, then it hit me: Chen Ling had latched onto one of Rose Allgood's sex toys and run off down the street with it. Bitty had been forced to buy it since it was damaged once we got it away from the pug, of course.

"You hit me with a *dildo*?" My voice rose on the last word, and again I heard a burst of laughter from the police at the front door. I felt my face get hot, and there was no way I was going to even look in Kit's direction.

To my surprise, Bitty looked just as embarrassed as I felt.

"Well," she said, "it's not like it's ever been *used* or anything. Except to chew on, of course. Chen Ling does love to chew on it."

There was no way I was going to say one more word in reference to the huge rubber dildo. The night had already turned into a disaster, and at that thought, I realized I'd not even mentioned my reason for showing up at Bitty's house in the middle of the night.

About the time I opened my mouth, she held up her hands and said, "I'm wearing these gloves because of the new hand cream I bought that guarantees to get rid of dry skin, calluses, and make them soft again. It stains."

I took her cue to change the subject from Carolann's merchandise.

"Since when have you done anything to get calluses?" I asked, and she shrugged. I shook my head, and that sent a sharp pain from my neck to my eyebrows. Getting hit with hard rubber can be excruciating.

"So why did you come over here in the middle of the night, anyway?" asked Bitty as if just thinking of it. "I thought you and Kit were . . . you know."

That intimation sent another flush of heat to my face, and I glared at her until she had the grace to add, "Having dinner or something."

"Dinner was delicious, thank you," I said, "but I have some news for you that may distress you."

Before she could leap to the wrong conclusion I added quickly, "Nothing to do with your boys."

She nodded. I glanced at Kit, who was sitting with one leg propped over his knee and a hand over his mouth, and then I looked back at Bitty.

"Catherine Moore called me tonight. Someone had broken into her house, she thought, and there was a gunshot before we were disconnected. The Oxford police have been called and are checking on her."

Bitty's eyes widened. "Did she have a chance to tell you anything else?"

"Just that she was sure the intruder was Breck Hartford looking for evidence she has collected against him."

"When will we know what the police have found?"

"I don't know." I glanced over at the police still standing in Bitty's foyer. They were doing some kind of paperwork. "Soon, I hope."

Kit got up from his chair and said, "I'll check with them and see if they've found out anything yet."

He'd gotten about three feet when there was a commotion at the front door. I wasn't that surprised to hear a familiar voice demand to know what had happened to his "sweet little lady."

Jackson Lee Brunetti is a tall, dark, and handsome attorney in Holly Springs, and he's absolutely crazy about my cousin. They make a funny-looking couple, he so tall and dark and Bitty so petite and blonde, but they get along famously. He's the only man I've ever known who thinks everything Bitty does is either cute, sweet, or perfectly legal. If he has to admit it may be illegal, he defends Bitty anyway.

I'm used to seeing Jackson Lee in jeans, a work shirt, and cowboy boots since he owns a nice-size ranch in the area, or dressed in expensive Italian suits for court. The Jackson Lee who appeared in Bitty's entrance hall wore a pajama shirt, sweat pants, and untied Gucci sports shoes. No socks. He looked wild-eyed until he spied Bitty in the living room.

"Sugar bun!"

Bitty quickly pulled off the blue cap and patted her hair into place. "Come on in, honey. I look just awful and shouldn't let you in at all, you know. Why are you here?"

"My secretary called. She heard from her cousin that the police had been called to your address for a possible break-in."

"And you just rushed out in the middle of the night to save me, you sweet thing?"

I swear, if Jackson Lee had a tail, he'd have been wagging it, he was so obviously happy to see her unharmed.

"Darlin', you know I'd walk across hot coals for you," he said, giving her a big hug that lifted her from the floor. "So what happened?" he asked when he set her down.

"Oh, it was just Trinket and Kit breaking in, not a real burglar."

"Lord, you didn't shoot at them, did you?"

Bitty put her still-gloved hands on her hips. "You know I didn't. You made me lock up my gun in the safe. By the time I could have gotten it, real burglars would have had everything out in the street. It's silly to have a gun and not be able to get to it."

Jackson Lee looked relieved. "Just think, though, sugar, that if you'd had your gun on your nightstand tonight, you might have shot poor Trinket."

Poor Trinket sat up at that bit of information and thanked her lucky stars that Jackson Lee had enough influence over Bitty to keep her unarmed. Most of the time.

I said that aloud and Bitty turned to look at me in surprise. "But I thought you felt better when I take along my pistol."

"Since I'm rarely consulted before the fact, I try to make the best of it once I find out you're wagging along a cannon in your purse."

Bitty looked bewildered. "But I have a permit, I practice at the shooting range—or in the back cow lot of Jackson Lee's pasture—and I've never shot anyone by accident. Why are you so against it?"

"For one thing, I've lost twenty percent hearing in my right ear from being too close when you decided to shoot at someone, and for another thing—you've never shot anyone, period. Even when you're aiming at them."

"Honestly, Trinket, sometimes you're very annoying." She turned to look up at Jackson Lee again. "Sugar, we really need to find out about our friend Catherine who lives down in Oxford. Think you could get that information for us?"

While asking, Bitty smoothed the lapels of Jackson Lee's pajama top and flicked away imaginary lint from his sleeve. I could see him melt into a gooey puddle of "I'll do whatever you want, baby" right before our eyes. Trust Bitty to find the quickest and most effective way of finding out what was happening to Catherine.

Jackson Lee was given the details, Catherine's full name, her phone number and address, and disappeared for a short time with the two policemen who had answered the earlier 911 call. When he came back, I saw from his face that the news was not good. So I tensed, and without realizing what I was doing, I reached for Kit's hand.

I was really glad he held on to me, because otherwise I would have fallen on the floor in shock when Jackson Lee said, "There's no sign of trouble at your friend's house. By that, I mean that officers were unable to find any sign of her at all."

"But she said she was locked in her bathroom," I protested. "And I heard someone beating on the door before we got disconnected—and a gunshot. I'm sure I heard a gunshot."

"There were no signs of the bathroom door being forcibly opened, no bullet holes anywhere, no sign of trouble. Are you sure you heard her correctly, Trinket?"

"Yes, yes, I'm quite sure. Kit was with me—did you overhear anything?"

I looked toward Kit, and he slowly shook his head. "I heard only your part of the conversation. From that I was able to determine Catherine was in some kind of trouble, though. Your responses were indicative of her believing an intruder had broken into her house."

"See?" I said, turning back to Jackson Lee. "There must be some sign of her being in trouble, or someone breaking in, or . . . or maybe her getting away. Did they check to see if her car was there?"

"Her car is gone, there's no sign of a B&E—breaking and entering— and she made no call for help. Except, of course, to you. Why would she call you instead of dial nine-one-one?"

"She said they'd never get there in time, and . . . I think she wanted to tell me something but ran out of time. I heard the gunshot, Jackson Lee. I'm not imagining things."

"I believe you, Trinket. You're usually pretty level-headed." When he paused, I expected someone to say, "except when with Bitty," but of course, no one did. Not with her right there listening.

"So," said Bitty, "what do we do now?"

"First thing in the morning," I replied, "we go down there to see if we can find her."

Jackson Lee put up a hand. "I don't want to sound arbitrary, Trinket, but do you really think you and Bitty can find her before the police do?

They've put out a BOLO on her vehicle and personal description, purely as a courtesy since there was no sign of foul play in her home, and it's much more likely that they'll find her than it is for you two to go looking."

"Why on earth would they tie a bolo on her car?" Bitty asked rather crossly. She doesn't like being told she can't do something, even if she doesn't particularly want to do it. She and I both are contrary that way. I'm sure our Truevine ancestry has something to do with it, since our forefathers came from Wales, an entire country full of people too stubborn to surrender to the English eons ago. Throw in a generous dash of Irish, and it's easy to see how my family endured a devastating civil war and burning of our home. It didn't crush us, only sharpened our innate defiance.

None of which has a thing to do with Catherine Moore's disappearance, except to explain how it is Bitty and I can both be stubborn enough to cut off our noses to spite our faces. As the cliché goes.

"*BOLO*, Bitty," I said, "not a necktie, as you well know. It's police jargon for Be On the Look-Out for. Right, Jackson Lee?"

He nodded, still looking down anxiously at Bitty. "So you'll stay right here in Holly Springs, sweet-ums?" he asked. "Won't you? Let the police do their job. You know I'll tell you the minute I hear anything."

Bitty went pure belle on him. She smiled big enough to flash her dimples, which I was amazed to see Botox hadn't erased yet, and purred, "Why, you sweet ole thing you, I just love the way you fuss over me. You know I wouldn't ever want to cause you a smidgen of worry." She reached up to pat him on the cheek with her still-gloved hand, and while I couldn't quite see from my vantage point, I was sure she fluttered her lashes at him, too, as she added, "Don't you fret about it for a minute, sugar. Trinket and I have no intention of doing anything risky."

It really helps that I know how to interpret Belle-speak, and knew exactly what Bitty had in mind.

If Bitty ever runs for a political office, I'm sure she'll get every male vote in our area. She can double-talk and dance around better than any of those jokers in Congress.

I wisely kept my mouth shut. I'm no belle, and if I said anything, I'd give us away in a heartbeat. While we didn't have any intention of doing anything risky, we had every intention of going to look for Catherine Moore ourselves.

Chapter 13

"Why are there so many cars out this early in the morning?" Bitty asked in a tone that said plainly she was not happy to be among them. "People should be at home in bed instead of out roaming around at obscene hours."

"Some people work for a living, Princess Pooka," I said, using my favorite title of the moment for her.

"Did you just call me something nasty?"

"No. Well, not really."

"What does *not really* mean?"

"Don't you remember what a pooka is?" I asked. "Jack used to call you that all the time when we were kids."

My older brother Jack had been fascinated with Welsh and Irish legends and used to tease us with strange names of mythological creatures. It was not his most endearing trait. I *never* liked being called Bloody Bones.

"No," Bitty was saying crossly as she maneuvered her Mercedes onto Highway 7. "Don't tell me this is going to be another Bubba Gump moment."

"Bubba was my favorite character in that movie," I said. "Don't diss him."

"Oh for heaven's sake—so what's a pooka?"

"A fairy spirit that's usually in animal form. Mischievous but not mean. It fits you."

Bitty thought for a moment, then she exclaimed, "*Harvey*! That old movie with Jimmy Stewart, right?"

"Right," I said, pleased that she'd remembered. I started to quote the line from that movie, "'Oh, you can't miss him, Mrs. Chumley,'" and Bitty finished the quote with me, "'he's a pooka!'"

We both laughed then. "A six foot tall invisible rabbit," said Bitty, "suits you better than me. Except for the invisible part."

"Yes, there's certainly nothing invisible about you today," I said. "Your sweater is rather—vibrant." That was an understatement. It was bright green and pink, with a matching silk scarf tied casually around her neck. I wore Lee jeans and a gray hoodie.

Bitty beamed. "Thank you, Trinket. It's new."

Now that she was in a better mood, I decided to run my idea past her. It had come to me right before I got out of bed, and I mulled it over the entire time I was brushing my teeth and dressing. By the time I'd met Bitty for coffee and Kibble—the latter for Chen Ling—I was second guessing myself. I needed another perspective. So I'd waited until we were actually on our way to drag out my thoughts.

"You know," I began, "that when we get there the police are liable to have either roped off her house so we can't go in, or decided she's just gone off by herself and isn't in any danger. So I have a suggestion."

Bitty glanced at me when I paused. "Well, don't be shy, Sherlock. Share your brilliance."

"That was a dramatic pause," I informed her. "Keep your eyes on the road. If Deputy Dawg catches you running another stop sign, you're in trouble."

Bitty mumbled something under her breath, and I ignored her as I continued. "We don't know for certain if Catherine is missing because she's in hiding, or is missing because whoever broke into her house last night took her. Her car is gone. So that must mean that she either took it herself, or the intruder took it. She could be in the trunk for all we know."

"So if we find her car, we may find her, right?"

I smiled. "You're getting very good at this deductive stuff, Bitty. Do you know what she drives?"

"No, but I know someone who does know."

"Someone we can trust not to blab about us being down here?"

"Good heavens, Trinket, you can't have everything, you know. We either take the risk of asking Cady Lee, who is a friend of Cat's, what kind of car she drives, or we wander around aimlessly searching. Which do you prefer?"

"Option C."

"Which is . . .?"

"We call Rayna and get her to track down what make of car and the license plate number."

"Ah. Very good. I like Option C. Oh, precious, did Mummy smush you? I'm so sorry. Here. Let me just—"

"Bitty! You drive! I'll tend to Chitling."

Chitling had decided to abandon her booster seat for some unknown puggy reason. It's high enough that she can see out the windshield while Bitty aims the car wherever it is she's going. Chitling is not always happy to stay in her seat. I don't know why. It has crushed velvet and a super-soft chenille lining—in pink—that keeps her furry behind quite comfy. But this morning Chitling was not happy. No, she had a most disgusted expression on her little pug face, and her beady little eyes kept a close watch on my hands as I attempted to adjust her. It occurred to me that she was probably grumpy because she was wearing a green and gold sweater with a turtle neck that made her look like a mutant bullfrog. I'd be grumpy too if I had to wear something like that.

"Honestly, Bitty," I couldn't help muttering, "do you have to dress her up in all this stuff? I don't know if I'm grabbing clothes or critter."

"She'll let you know," said Bitty serenely, and I jerked my hand back just before Chitling decided that I'd crossed some imaginary canine line. Her teeth clacked together on empty air instead of me.

"Have you been training her to attack?" I asked. "I don't remember this dog being quite so . . . irritable . . . when you first got her."

"Oh for heaven's sake, Trinket, she's just a little dog. Stop whining. I swear, the older you get, the more you act like Great-aunt Imogene."

"That's a horrid thing to say to me," I pointed out with great indignation. "Aunt Imogene was mean to everyone. And she dipped snuff. She sat in a rocking chair on the front porch for thirty years telling anyone who'd listen that the world was a wicked place, and we were all going to hell."

"I know. And that was on her good days. You don't want to end up like her, do you?"

"She lived to be a hundred and three. Every six months she'd summon family to her 'death bed' to say goodbye. After about five years of that, Daddy said we could stop going. I was glad. She used to make me clean out her spit can."

"*Ewwww*," said Bitty, and laughed. "She tried to get me to do it once. When I accidentally spilled it in her lap, she never asked me again."

I looked over at Bitty. "There were great depths to you even back then," I said with grudging admiration. "I never thought of that."

"I'm not always scatterbrained, you know."

The way she said that made me realize that maybe I tease her too much about having "blonde" moments. I resolved to stop. Well, cut back, anyway.

"I know," I said. "You're a lot smarter than most people give you credit for. I forget that sometimes."

Bitty looked pleased. "Thank you, Trinket. I know I get crazy ideas and do some silly things, but sometimes I'm right, you have to admit."

"I'll admit that, if you'll admit that I'm not really too tall and dress cheaply."

There was a long pause, then Bitty said, "Oh my."

Why do I even try? I narrowed my eyes at her, but since she didn't even look my way, my evil stare was wasted. So I exchanged evil stares with Chitling, who never shies away from a confrontation. I hate losing a staring contest to a dog.

I crossed my arms over my chest and tapped my fingers against my elbow and looked out the window for a good ten miles before Bitty offered the proverbial olive branch: "Is this the Tallahatchie Bridge that Billy Joe McAllister jumped off in the song?"

"No," I deigned to say after enough time went by that she knew I wasn't going to make it easy for her. "That bridge is in Yalobusha County—no, wait. Leflore County, by Greenwood."

"Oh. I wonder what he threw off that bridge."

"Some folks said it was the girl's ragdoll."

"What do you think?"

"I think it was just a song."

"Really? I thought it was a true story," said Bitty. "Hollywood even made a movie about it."

I looked over at her. "They made a movie about Francis the Talking Mule, too, but I've never heard a mule say a dadgum thing."

"Remember Mr. Sanders' mule?" Bitty asked. "If he could talk, I wonder what he would have said the day he got his head stuck in that pot of chicken and dumplings."

I couldn't help it. I started to laugh. Then Bitty laughed, and we were over our contentious moment just like that. Best friends and blood relatives seem to do that sort of thing quite often.

"Speaking of talking mules," I said after a moment, "I wonder who that was I overheard talking about someone being dead. I'm convinced they were referring to the professor."

"Could be," Bitty agreed. "Do you think it was Breck Hartford?"

"I don't know. I'd have to hear him talk again to compare. I'm not so sure I want to get that close to him despite what I promised Catherine."

"It could be done, though. Did you tell Cat about it?"

"No, there was never a reason to mention it to her. Maybe now there is. I guess we'll find out when we find her."

"If we find her."

I looked at Bitty, and she glanced at me. Neither one of us said aloud that we may not find Catherine, or find her alive. It was too grim a thought.

It seemed like only a few minutes later that we hit the Oxford city limits. By then I had formulated a plan of sorts. First, we would drive by Catherine's house. If it wasn't cordoned off by police tape, we'd poke around and see what we could find. Rayna was looking up her vehicle information for us, and if she hadn't called back by the time we looked around Catherine's house, then we'd go get some breakfast while we waited.

As luck would have it, there was no police tape strung around her house, not even a patrol car outside. Apparently the Oxford police had decided there was no emergency. From the outside, it certainly looked safe and secure. It wasn't even eight yet, and the street was quiet. Trees filtered the morning sun, leaves drifted softly to the ground, and I saw an older man come outside in his robe to get his morning paper. Just a familiar scene in a small town neighborhood.

Catherine's house is a two-story traditional kind of home, with fieldstone outer walls and surrounded by lots of trees. The walkway goes in a curve from her driveway up to the porch, flanked by mums in bloom and scarlet foliage in front of evergreens. My idea was to march right up to the front door as if we'd come for a visit.

I put my hand on the car door handle. "Why don't you leave Chitling to guard the car while we see if we can get inside?"

Bitty gave me a horrified look. "Where someone can steal her?"

Trust Bitty to worry more about her dog than she did a fifty thousand dollar vehicle. I refrained from rolling my eyes as I tried logic: "Yes. I'm sure there's a huge black market for fat, elderly pugs. If you wouldn't weigh her down with ten pounds of diamonds and velvet, she'd be worth a lot less. It's cool outside, and we're going to be skulking around. Leave her in here where she doesn't get—" I'd started to say, "—in our way," but then I realized that Bitty, being as contrary as she is, would immediately claim that Chitling wouldn't be in our way at all. So I said, "—too stressed if we run into trouble," instead.

"Oh, I hadn't thought about that. I wouldn't want her to get stressed out if we have a problem."

"Good. Crack the windows for fresh air." I got out of the car while Bitty punched the window buttons to give Chen Ling plenty of fresh air. She glared at us anyway. When Bitty shut her door, Chitling began to yodel at us. She yodels very loudly. If anyone was trying to sleep late in the neighborhood, they were out of luck. So much for stealth.

"Poor thing," said Bitty, pausing with a worried look back at her yowling pug. "If I didn't know she hates loud noises, I'd give in and take her with us."

It didn't occur to me what Bitty meant by that last until we were up on the front porch. I started to ring the bell, but Bitty stopped me. "Wait. I have to be ready if there's an intruder still inside."

"What are you talking about?" Then, as she stuck her hand into her Gucci purse, I knew what she meant about loud noises. I barred the door with my body. "If you brought along your cannon, Bitty Hollandale, you can just go sit in the car with Chitling. I'm not about to be shot by mistake or arrested on purpose."

Bitty paused. "Don't be silly. I'd never shoot you by mistake."

I narrowed my eyes at her. "Somehow, that doesn't comfort me. I don't want to be shot on purpose, either."

"Suppose the intruder came back. Who would you rather run into, him or me?"

When I mulled that over, Bitty got exasperated. "Oh for heaven's sake, Trinket, I'm not going to shoot you! I'll just leave it in my purse. Does that make you feel better?"

"Safer, anyway. Besides, if there's an intruder, the police would have found him last night."

"He may have come back. He might be lying in wait for us right now."

"Only if he's some kind of homicidal maniac or serial killer. Any self-respecting killer would be far away from here by now after the police have been out looking around for Catherine."

"Just try the door and see if it's open first."

"I imagine police are very good about locking doors." Still, I tried it, and as I'd suspected, it was locked. I gave it a hearty rattle. "Let me ring the bell. If Catherine's home, I'm sure she'd rather us do that than just break in."

"Oooh, are we going to do that?"

"It was a figure of speech. No, my dear, we are not going to break in."

"Then why are we here? I thought we came to see if Cat's all right."

"We did. Don't make me go through this again. We don't need to break in if we have a key."

"Well, we don't have a key, and I don't know how you think we're going to go in unless we climb through a window. I'd give you a boost, but I can't afford a broken nail. Besides, you're too heavy for me to lift."

"We are *not* going through a window, Bitty."

"If we don't go inside, how are we expected to find out if she's okay?"

I felt like smacking her but said with more patience than I felt, "I never said we weren't going inside."

When we'd stepped up on the front porch I'd noticed a rock that looked different from the others. If it was what I thought it was, an emergency key should be attached to the backside. I felt around it to see if there was a latch or indentation for a finger to pry it open. Since I had to bend over and squat down to reach it, I was at a disadvantage.

"Here, Bitty," I said, and stood up to show her the rock. "See if you can open it with one of those daggers on the end of your fingers."

"Open a rock? Are you kidding? I'd break a nail." She sounded indignant, so I shrugged.

"Not if you don't want to, but I thought since we came all this way it'd be nice to be able to get inside."

"I don't know how you think taking rocks off her porch is going to help. Isn't that vandalism?"

I finally snapped. "Will you stop arguing and just see if you can pry open this damn rock? I think it's got a door key inside it!"

"Oh. It's one of those. Why didn't you say so?"

Bitty bent over, stuck a crimson-coated fingernail into the indentation and popped it open. A key fell onto the flagstone porch with a muted clink. She picked it up and gave it to me, frowning at a tiny chip on the end of her nail.

"I just hate it when that happens," she muttered, and I ignored her as I tried the key in the lock.

It clicked, and I turned the knob. The door swung open without a sound. I stood in the opening for a moment trying to decide what to do first. Behind me, Bitty stepped up so close I felt her breath on my back and her purse nudging my kidneys.

"What do you see?" she whispered.

"Shadows. My eyes are trying to adjust. Wait. I see some furniture. I still think we should ring the bell or call for her before we go all the way inside."

"And I still think I should be armed."

"No." I took a few tentative steps inside. No one hit me in the back of the head or shot me, so I took a few more steps, then a few more until I stood on carpet. It was eerily quiet. There was a faint smell that I couldn't quite place. Sort of sweet, but a little nauseating at the same time.

"Do you see anything?" I whispered to Bitty, but she didn't answer. "Bitty?" I half-turned and saw her still in the doorway. I put one hand on my hip. "Are you coming, Mrs. Braveheart?"

"Can I pull out my gun?"

"No! Stop dawdling."

"It's not dawdling if I'm just trying to be cautious," said Bitty as she took a few steps inside. She sniffed the air. "Something smells funny."

"Yeah. I smell it too. What do you think it is?"

"I have no idea. And I don't want to think about what it could be, either. Do you see anything out of place?"

I'd walked from the entrance hall into the living room. A floor to ceiling fireplace dominated one wall. Parallel to it were two matching white couches, sitting atop a bright rug spread over beige carpet. It was very dimly lit. Curtains were drawn over the living room windows that looked out on the street; a dining room was opposite, facing the back. A large kitchen was on the right, with marble countertops and stainless steel appliances. Double French doors looked out on the backyard, and light came in through them. As my eyes adjusted to the change in light, I saw that one of the French doors was half-open.

My heartbeat escalated. The police wouldn't have left it open. Unless Catherine had returned, no one else should have opened that door. The hair on the back of my neck tightened, and I got the awful feeling that we weren't quite alone.

Almost afraid to turn around, I made myself glance back to see if Bitty was still behind me. She hadn't moved from the entryway. The door behind her was wide open, and she was in silhouette. She had her purse clutched in both hands and held up almost to her chin as she stared at me.

I put my finger up to my lips to indicate she should be quiet, and sucking in a deep breath, I forced my feet to move forward. There was only one way to find out if we were alone, and that was to act like I had no idea anyone else might be close.

The phrase from an old movie, "Feet, don't fail me now!" went through my head as I stepped toward the open French door. Truthfully, I couldn't feel my feet. My entire body had gone numb with irrational fear. Nothing looked out of place in the house. No mess could be seen, no sign that someone may have been forcibly abducted. No sign of another presence, either. Yet I felt in imminent danger.

When I reached the open door, my heart hammering so loud it was all I could hear drumming in my ears, I looked out into the backyard. It was a shaded yard, with tall trees, lots of fading hostas, impatiens and other shade plants, a flagstone terrace, pots of colorful flowers, a wrought-iron patio set, and ornaments scattered across the lawn. Catherine seemed to favor concrete urns and cat statues and had several gazing balls of varying sizes at strategic intervals to reflect the garden.

Maybe I was imagining things, I told myself. After all, it was pretty spooky being in the house of a woman I barely knew. And it was so quiet. The house itself seemed to be holding its breath, as if waiting for Catherine to come home.

I started to turn back to say something to Bitty, and a movement caught my eye. It was in the garden; something had flashed in the biggest gazing ball up on an iron stand. For an instant, I thought it might be a bird or squirrel, but it had been too big, too—furtive.

Hairs along my arms stood straight up, and I had the sudden urge to find the nearest bathroom before I disgraced myself. This was ridiculous, I thought. No killer in their right mind would return to the scene of the crime. But then again, maybe that was a contradiction. People who kill other people aren't in their right minds anyway. There has to be something inherently wrong with them to do such a thing. Maybe this killer was as twisted and evil as a Ted Bundy or Jeffrey Dahmer. Maybe this killer was hiding in wait for his next victim . . . *me.*

Now that I had effectively scared myself into major trauma, I needed back-up. I beckoned Bitty closer. Being of sound mind at the moment, she shook her head. I glared at her.

"Of all times for you to get some common sense, does it have to be *now?*" I asked in an irate whisper.

"Now seems as good a time as any. What's out there?" she whispered back.

"I don't know. There's safety in numbers, though. You can stay here by yourself and hope no one comes up behind you, or you can go with me to see if there's anyone in the backyard who shouldn't be."

Bitty glanced around with an uneasy expression on her face. She had a death grip on her purse, and I hoped her pistol's safety latch was engaged. Otherwise, she was liable to shoot herself in the foot if she held her purse any more tightly.

"All right!" she snapped at me in a whisper loud enough to be heard in Tupelo, "but if someone tries to attack us, I'm shooting him."

"Fair enough."

Bitty tiptoed across the living and dining room to join me at the French doors. She got close enough to be in my shoes if I'd had room, but I didn't protest. At least we presented a united front. And a bigger target, but I tried to ignore that unpleasant fact.

We took baby steps through the open French door until we reached the patio, and I stopped to look around. Bitty's boobs immediately crashed into me, followed by the rest of her, and I stumbled forward.

"You should have signaled that you're stopping," Bitty whispered before I could complain. "So I wouldn't have run into you."

"Next time I'll flash my brake lights," I snapped back at her. My nerves were just about shot. It didn't help that I was positive someone had just run around the corner of the house toward the front. It was a fleeting impression, a glimpse from my peripheral vision, a wisp of motion now gone. Before I could share this info with Bitty, another movement caught my attention. The branches of a tall nandina bush to the right side of the yard shuddered with movement that wasn't caused by the wind.

Bitty grabbed my elbow and dug her claws into me while she hissed, "Bushes at three o'clock!"

Good lord. She was going James Bond on me again.

"I know," I said more calmly than I felt. "Try not to look in that direction. Let's just see what or who it is before we invite trouble."

My idea was to amble around the backyard as if not noticing someone hiding in the bushes. Then, we could move slowly back to the house, and one of us watch from the window while the other went out the front door and around to get a good look at who was there.

That was my idea.

Bitty had another idea.

Before I could share my brilliance with her, she took a step back and brought up her purse. She didn't even open the blamed thing when she fired. A loud shrieking sound emanated from my mouth, followed by me going into a prone position on the grass just in case she decided to aim her Gucci again.

"Would you look at that," said Bitty in a disgusted tone, and when I finally got my eyes uncrossed, I saw our intruder.

It had bolted out of a pine tree and across the yard, a raccoon that weighed at least thirty pounds, fur bristled out and little monkey-paw feet scrabbling over grass and flower beds as it waddled toward a drainage ditch for safety.

"I swear, Trinket," Bitty continued in an exasperated tone, "here you had me all thinking a serial killer was hiding in the garden, and it's only a little ole 'coon."

"Little?" I squeaked. "I've seen grizzlies that are smaller!"

"Now I have a hole in the bottom of my purse. And I could have shot that poor critter by mistake."

"Only if it was sitting in the top of the tree," I said as I got up off the ground and brushed dried grass and leaves from my clothes. "Did you think you were aiming for the giant in the beanstalk?"

Bitty put both hands on her hips, which made me a little nervous since she was still armed, and I wasn't at all sure her purse was aimed away from me. "No, I hit exactly what I was aiming at. I shot that branch off the tree, just like I meant to do to scare the intruder out of hiding."

"Good job. He hightailed it around the corner of the house."

"Are you sure?"

"No. But I think I saw someone running away just as we got out here."

"Then my work here is done if he took off like a cat with its tail afire. I succeeded in my mission." Bitty seemed very proud of herself.

I didn't point out that since we'd scared him away, we didn't know his identity. Or even if he was male or female. Instead I said, "Way to go, Dead-eye." When she looked at me in confusion I clarified, "A marksman, Bitty. A sniper. A good shot."

"Oh." She looked very pleased. "Yes, I am."

"And humble, too."

"Of course."

When I heard a door slam at the house on the other side of Catherine's, I sighed. "Unless I'm very mistaken, the police will be here in about two or three minutes. If you want to be here to greet them, fine. I'd much prefer being a good ways away, myself."

Sometimes Bitty isn't nearly as obtuse as she pretends. She beat me to the car by a good three yard advantage, and we peeled out in the nick of time. A patrol car passed us going toward Catherine's house, and I crossed my fingers and hoped fervently that no one had given them our description or identified Bitty's car.

Chen Ling had gnawed a hole in her special car seat while we were gone, so that her right back leg kept poking through when I tried to fasten her into it. She snarled at me a time or two just to express her gratitude for my efforts, and Bitty was so rattled she didn't even fuss at me for upsetting her dragon. I mean dog.

"Well, that was a waste of time," Bitty said after a few minutes went by and no police car tried to ram us or run us off the road. "We don't know any more than we did before we left home."

"Sure we do."

Bitty glanced at me in surprise. "We do?"

"Yup."

"Well, what?"

"Raccoons aren't always nocturnal animals."

"Honestly, Trinket. I meant something about Catherine."

"I know. Didn't it feel to you like her house had been broken into? I don't mean by the police, either."

"I have no idea," Bitty said rather crossly. "We never left the living area."

"Yet, thinking back, I remember I caught a glimpse of her kitchen off the dining area. Food was out on the counter. A few dirty dishes."

"Is that all?"

"It's enough. Did she strike you as the kind of person who would leave food out to spoil and dishes cluttering the countertop? Me neither," I said before she could answer. "I don't think she or the police left the back door wide open, either. Someone has been in her house, and it wasn't a raccoon."

"I think—"

"And we have to consider that the front door was locked, which suggests that the house was entered from the rear since the key was in place. Or it could be that whoever went in already had a key but left in a hurry when we got there. That may be who took off around the corner when I stepped outside."

"I think—"

"And we didn't make it to the upstairs bedrooms or baths, either. I'm sure we'd find clues there that might indicate if there was a scuffle and she was abducted. Besides a bullet hole somewhere. I distinctly heard gunfire last night," I said, mulling it over.

"I think—"

"I'm pretty sure it was gunfire. Catherine screamed, and she was convinced that Breck Hartford was downstairs and had broken in. If he broke in, that means he doesn't have a key. But wait—did she say he broke in, or did she just say he was downstairs? I can't quite remember."

"I think—"

"You know, I don't even remember if she actually said his name?" I said, and turned to look at Bitty. "Who else could it be, though? I mean, it's not like she has a long list of enemies. Is it? What do we really know about Catherine Moore?"

"I think—"

"What?" I prompted when Bitty paused. "You think what?"

"Oh. I didn't know we'd gone back to a discussion instead of a monologue."

"Honestly, Bitty," I said, "you say the strangest things. So what do you think? I know Catherine was terrified when I saw her, her hands shaking and her voice trembling. Is it possible she's been kidnapped, or do you think maybe she's unwell?"

"Probably the DTs," said Bitty, and turned the big car into a driveway. I looked around. We were at a Sonic drive-in, of all places, and once the Mercedes nosed into a slot, she shut off the engine and turned to look at me. The smell of hot dogs, burgers and fries drifted out the door when a carhop skated out with a loaded tray and headed for the vehicle next to us. My nose twitched.

"Why would she have the DTs?" I asked, but my focus had changed from the main topic of the day to food, so I wasn't really paying attention when Bitty made a snippy comment.

"Is it too early to eat lunch, I wonder?" I asked, eying the carhop's loaded tray. "I bet they serve whatever you want at any time of day."

While visions of fast food danced in my head, my cell phone rang. I had to stop my contemplation of the brightly colored menu lit up with delicious, cholesterol-laden food to answer it.

"Rayna," I said when I finally got my phone open and to my ear. "What'd you find out?"

"I can't believe you two are down in Oxford again," said Rayna. "I'm getting stir-crazy staying in this office all day, so next time you go on one of these jaunts, take me. I need some excitement."

"Do you like getting scared to death by a raccoon?" I asked. "Because that's the most exciting thing that's happened all day. Other than Bitty chipping her nail polish."

Rayna laughed. Then she read me off Catherine's vehicle information while I pawed through my purse looking for my little notebook and a pen.

"Got it," I said at last. "Stay tuned for any police info on Catherine, okay? You have all those scanners and we don't."

When I hung up, I looked over at Bitty. "What were you saying earlier about Catherine? I missed some of it."

"She can drink a two hundred pound man under the table without a blink," said Bitty. "I've seen her do it a time or two. Of course, so can I if I put my mind to it, but I can stop when I want to and she can't."

Finally she had my full attention. "Really?"

"I can't believe you didn't notice. She's been worse ever since her son died."

"Oh." I thought about that a moment, then said, "Poor thing. I can't imagine losing a child."

Bitty nodded. "Neither can I. And for him to commit suicide . . ."

"Are they sure about that? I mean, Catherine seemed so certain her son would never kill himself."

"Wouldn't you believe that, too? No one wants to believe their child would take his own life."

"True." I considered that for several moments, and of course, my daughter came to mind. If anything ever happened to her, I don't think I could stand it. I'm sure every mother feels that way, but I think mothers with only one child feel especially protective. It must be very difficult for Catherine to bear.

That thought led to me asking, "Wasn't there another recent death that was questionable? An Ole Miss student who died?"

"You'd have to ask Brandon or Clayton. They'd know. Why?"

"Catherine mentioned that there had been a death ruled accidental when it was really a murder."

Bitty nodded. "I guess it's possible. But she hasn't been the same since her son died, so I don't know if it's true."

"She's had a really hard time coping," I murmured. "I suppose that could affect her judgment."

"Of course," Bitty continued, "it made it even harder that Catherine and Breck had a torrid affair and had just split up when Monty died. I suppose that's why she's said Breck was responsible for her son's death."

"Torrid," I mused aloud. "Such a descriptive word. So they had an affair, and everyone knew about it?"

Bitty looked astonished that I would ask such a question. "Heavens, Trinket, you can't jaywalk in Oxford without someone finding out about it."

"It's not that small a town," I argued. "It's like Holly Springs, and—oh. I see what you mean."

Bitty nodded. "Good. It's not so much the number of people in a town as it is the number of people willing to gossip about people you know."

"Dear lord." I rolled my eyes and changed the subject. "Are we here to eat or to talk?"

"We can do both. I got quite a scare back there, you know. And my purse! I'm not at all sure it can be repaired."

As if to illustrate her point, she pulled up her purse and stuck her forefinger into the hole. It was quite a large hole.

"Your forty-five, right?" I asked, and she sighed and nodded.

"Maybe you should carry a smaller gun." I thought about that a second and added, "Or no gun at all."

Bitty looked at me with wide eyes. "And be defenseless?"

"There's a difference between being defenseless and being dangerous. I'll grant you that you're a much better shot these days, but I'm still in danger of having my nose shot off every time you pull out that cannon of yours."

"I swear, I'm never taking you target shooting with me again. I was using another pistol, and it ejects spent shells. It was a hot shell that clipped your nose, not a bullet. Besides, if you'd get a little work done, it'd be a lot smaller target."

"If you mean by 'work done' plastic surgery—and I know you do—I'm doing just fine with the nose I have now, thank you."

There wasn't much Bitty could say to that. It's true. Kit Coltrane is a very nice catch. And I did it without Botox or a facelift, just my charming personality, despite what Bitty may say.

"Humph," she said to my remarks, "I should never have told you that you look a lot like Delta Burke. You've done nothing but preen your feathers ever since."

I smiled. "Well, she *was* Miss Florida before being a TV star, you know."

Bitty shook her head. "Forty-five years ago!"

"No, it wasn't. It was . . ." I did a rapid mental calculation and said, ". . . thirty-seven years ago."

"Close enough."

"Maybe in Bitty-years. You've been lying about your age so long I doubt you can even count right anymore."

Bitty sucked in a deep breath, and before things got ugly I said quickly, "My, my, it's so vairy, vairy wahm in heah!"

I wasn't sure our usual conversational life preserver was going to work this time, but Bitty finally let her breath out in a huff of air and said, "That's not going to work every time, you know."

"Just so it works now."

"Onion rings?" she asked after a moment of silence, and I nodded.

"Large order. With lots of ketchup."

After we gorged—daintily, of course—we were in a much better frame of mind. Not even Chen Ling's doggy utterances while she scarfed down a bare hot dog that was probably full of preservatives and a hundred different chemicals soured my mood.

"I'm ready to try again," I said, and when Bitty looked up from untying the pink velvet bib around Chitling's neck, I added, "With a much different approach, of course."

"You mean go back to Catherine's house?"

"Yep."

"Well," she said as she brushed a hot dog crumb off her dog's face, "unless you have an invisibility cloak, Harry Potter, you might as well plan on getting caught."

Chen Ling snuffled out the lost crumb while I said, "I have a plan."

"About what to do after we're caught snooping around Catherine's house?"

"No." I narrowed my eyes at her. "If that happens, we're doomed. My plan entails disguises and secrecy."

Bitty brightened immediately, as I'd known she would. "Really? Disguises? I like it already."

"Good. Where can we find a costume shop in Oxford?"

Chapter 14

We ended up at Jo's Auto Clean-up and Costume Shop on University. Mississippi businesses often like to diversify. It's common to see hand painted signs that advertise proudly, "Snacks & Bait" shops all over the countryside. I try to never eat at those places, but renting costumes was an entirely different proposition.

Bitty was dismayed when she saw the costumes I chose for us. "*Maids?* You've got to be kidding me!"

"No, I'm not kidding. At least these should fit us and not fall down around our ankles." I said the last as a not-so-gentle reminder of one of Bitty's former schemes that hadn't worked out well for me. When Bitty didn't respond, I knew she remembered exactly what I was talking about. That didn't stop her from blowing out an irritated puff of air, but at least I didn't have to hear protests of innocence.

We left the shop with our costumes and a pug wearing a tiara. Don't ask. Bitty has her peculiarities. Chen Ling looked smug all dolled up in a pink taffeta tutu and tiara big enough to fit the average first grader.

Once we were in the car I dropped my next bomb on poor Bitty: "Now we have to rent an old, beat-up car or something that looks like a work van."

I thought Bitty was going to pass out from sheer horror. Finally she found words to go along with her shrieks of protest: "WHY? Are you crazy?"

"Because few maids drive Mercedes, and I thought we'd settled that crazy question a long time ago. Think about it, Bitty. Just for a moment. Does your Maria arrive in a nice, shiny limousine every morning?"

"She doesn't come every day anymore," Bitty replied, a bit sulkily, I thought.

"Okay. So when she does come to clean, what does she drive?"

"Oh for heaven's sake, Trinket, how would I know? Even if I'm up when she gets there, I don't look outside to see what she drives."

I sighed. Sometimes getting Bitty to see reason is a long, complicated process. I gave it one more try. "All right, then, maybe you remember what Mrs. Tyree used to drive when she was a maid for the mayor?"

Mrs. Tyree is Bitty's next door neighbor. She's a lovely elderly lady who came from an entire family of domestics who were clever enough to form their own cleaning company way back in the new liberation era of the early 1970s. Then they diversified into offering yard services as well, and their little company grew large enough to keep Holly Springs well-supplied with help. It ended up being bought out by a larger corporation in the nineties, leaving Mrs. Tyree with enough money to buy the house next door to Bitty, and her children and grandchildren excellent college educations wherever they chose to go. Not that the Civil Rights era changed everything. Some taboos are still firmly in place no matter what the person's race or position in life. Change takes time.

Bitty thought for a moment before she said, "I think she was the mayor's morning help and drove a nineteen-forties Buick. Blue, with huge rust spots on it. It smelled like fish, too, since her husband used it to go frog-gigging at night."

"There. You see? If we show up anywhere wearing maid uniforms and driving a Mercedes, no one would believe it. We have to be as inconspicuous as possible. Besides, your car has already been seen by probably everyone on Catherine's street. We don't want to risk it being recognized."

"Then we can park it a few streets over and walk. I'm not riding in a piece of junk that'll probably fall apart before it gets ten feet down the road."

She had a point. I gave her that one and nodded. "Okay, we can park near a bus stop and act as if we just got off."

"Just as long as I don't have to actually ride on one again," said Bitty. "For two days after riding the last bus, I had exhaust fumes in my hair."

"Oh, Bitty. That's all in your head."

"No, in my *hair*. You need to listen more closely, sugar. Connie had to wash it twice and use extra conditioner."

I gave up. "Fine. Stop at the next Dollar General you see. We need to buy some buckets and mops."

Once we were well-supplied with the outer accoutrements that any maid would use—much to Bitty's amazement—we stopped at a Mapco to change clothes in their bathroom. I looked at Bitty when she came tottering out into the convenience store next to the chips rack, all decked out in a maid's attire of black dress and white apron and cap. However, I have rarely seen maids wear stilettos and pointed that out to her.

She looked down at her feet. "So what should I wear—Army boots?"

"How about flats. Don't you own any?"

"Of course, I do. I even have a pair in the trunk that I wear when it's muddy."

"Then, by all means, let's put them on."

Once Bitty had changed into a pair of $400 Ferragamo red flats—I couldn't be too picky—we set out for Catherine's neighborhood again. I didn't know why I felt so strongly that we had to check out her house before continuing our search, but I did. I'd told myself while munching onion rings that the police would have found any evidence of foul play, so there probably wasn't a thing they'd overlooked or that we would discover. Yet, still, I had to satisfy that little voice in the back of my head that kept nagging me to make my own search.

Bitty parked her car in a lot outside a pizza shop. I expected her to leave Chen Ling and her tiara in the car as before, but she refused.

"No. We're going to be an entire block over, and I'm not taking any chances that some criminal will come along and steal her."

"They'd steal your car first," I said, then realized what that would mean for the bug-eyed little puglet in Bitty's arms. I sighed. "Okay. Just . . . stick her down in your mop bucket so she can't be easily seen, okay?"

"In my *bucket?*" Bitty gasped. "Are you serious?"

"It's clean. She'll survive. Oh, and leave the tiara. It'd be hard enough explaining to any neighbors why we're there without having to explain a dog disguised as a beauty pageant contestant."

"You mean winner, not contestant," said Bitty as she set the pug on the back seat. "Only the winners get the tiara."

"I'm not up on all the rules. Just hurry up and put her in the bucket so we can go and do this before I lose my nerve."

Bitty muttered indignant protests the entire time she got Chitling situated in the blue plastic cleaning bucket. I ignored her. It was nearly noon by now, and we had to get in and get out as quickly as possible. Unless Catherine had turned up in the past two hours, the police would eventually return to investigate her disappearance.

"What are we going to do if we get there and she's home?" Bitty asked me. "I'll just die if she tells people how I'm dressed."

I rolled my eyes. "You better worry that she may *not* turn up. If that's the case, we might have another murder on our hands."

"Well, it's not as if we *have* to do this, you know," said Bitty. "We're just being helpful since we're worried about her."

"Keep in mind that if she's truly missing, the police will consider our helpfulness as interference. We need to get in and out as quickly as possible. I'm not eager to meet up with the Oxford police department."

"Oh, they're very nice," said Bitty, and I looked at her.

"And you know this how?"

Bitty waved a hand in the air. "I had to come down and make a statement the other day. I didn't want to tell you. But they were okay when I told them you don't know any more than I do. Jackson Lee said it was just a formality."

My head began to buzz like a nest of hornets, but we were already in front of Catherine's house, so I didn't press the issue. I had enough to worry about. We walked up the sidewalk to the front door like we were expected, although I could hear Bitty talking softly to the pug in the bucket.

"It's all right, precious, Mama will protect you from crazy Auntie Trinket," she assured the dog. I figured Chen Ling looked at it the other way around, but as long as she didn't bite me or bark and alert the neighbors to two imposters, I didn't care what either of them thought.

The front door was locked again, no doubt by the police, but I still had the key. I let us in, and this time I flipped on a light so it wasn't shadowy as before. The back door had been closed, no doubt also locked, and nothing looked as if it had been touched since we'd left only a couple hours earlier.

"I'm going upstairs," I said to Bitty, who stood owl-eyed in the living room like she'd done before. "If you want, check out things down here. I have a hunch the smell is coming from the kitchen, probably food left out."

When I reached the landing on the second floor, I heard Bitty scolding Chen Ling about trying to eat old food. I smiled. Having Chitling along kept Bitty busy and not as freaked out as earlier, so I began to think it'd been a good idea after all.

No lights were on in the upstairs. Not even Catherine's bedroom light. It didn't make much sense that an abductor would stop to turn out lights, unless there'd been a struggle of some kind. And if police had found her, and if she was dead, there would be a chalk outline on the floor, I was pretty sure. I braced myself, just in case, as I stepped into Catherine's master bedroom.

A king-size bed anchored the middle of the room, flanked by nightstands, and the heavy draperies over the windows were closed. I flipped on the overhead light, and a ceiling fan came on as well. It whisked cool air over me, and I shivered as I crossed to the far wall and an open door that I was sure was the master bath. I don't know what I expected to see. A chalk outline, sign of struggle, bullet holes in the door, maybe the door jamb loose or broken, but I never expected to see nothing.

Nothing was out of place. No sign of the door being forced, no indication that a gun had been fired, and no matter how closely I searched, I found no evidence that a woman had taken armed refuge in the spacious bathroom. A huge garden tub took up one wall, the toilet and vanity were clean and neat, no towels out of place, not even the rug on the tile floor rumpled. The small stained glass window that let in light was clean with no bullet holes, no glass on the floor—nothing. Clean as a whistle. Whatever that means.

I was baffled. I had heard someone beating on the door, a crash and a gunshot. I knew I had. Catherine had screamed, and the line went dead. There should be some sign of a struggle in the bathroom where she'd barricaded herself. Why wasn't there? Did her abductor allow her to clean up first? Had the man, presumably Breck Hartford, tidied up to hide the evidence that he'd taken her?

Maybe I'd misunderstood. Maybe she'd been in the downstairs bathroom. I'd look there after checking out two other bedrooms on the upper floor. One was obviously a guest room, with a neatly made bed, pristine dresser, and family photographs placed on the nightstand as well as on the wall. I paused to look at a photo of Catherine with a young boy who must have been her son. They were both laughing into the camera, and she had her arms around him from behind. Obviously a loving relationship. It had to be terribly hard for her to come to terms with his death.

I knew at once that my guess was right when I opened the door to the next bedroom. It had been her son's, left as he must have left it on the last day of his life. The bed was unmade, covers thrown back as if he'd just risen, and his laptop sat open on a small desk, waiting for his return. A few clothes were scattered about, a shirt hung over a chair, a few textbooks open on the foot of the bed. The full attached bath was as clean and undisturbed as Catherine's own, and I stepped back into Monty's bedroom.

I could almost feel Catherine's grief. It hung in the room, a dense, impenetrable cloud. I quietly shut the door and went downstairs.

Bitty made noise in the kitchen, opening and shutting cabinet doors for some reason, so I went ahead and checked out the downstairs bathroom. As with the other two, it was clean. It was smaller, only a toilet, a custom washstand with the vessel sink atop an ornate chest with cabriole legs, and no evidence of any kind of struggle.

I went into the kitchen. Bitty had obviously dumped the plastic mop bucket since the contents gazed balefully up at me from the floor. I blinked first, as usual, and Chitling looked smug.

"Did you look in the garage?" I asked as I went toward the door leading to it.

Bitty paused in peering into a glass-front cabinet. "No. I'm just checking to see if anything expensive is missing."

I looked at her. "How would you know?"

"Oh, Cat's always bragged about inheriting her mother's china and silver. I can't resist checking to see if it's really as old as she claims."

"So this isn't really about Catherine, it's about you," I said sarcastically, but Bitty just nodded and "hmm-ed" me. I rolled my eyes and opened the door to the garage. "See if you can find out what that smell is," I said as I stepped into the shadowed, stuffy area. I looked around, not surprised that Catherine's late-model Lexus was gone. If she'd been abducted, no doubt the criminal took her car and her with it. If she'd just gone out shopping—which I doubted—the police would end up looking for her vehicle anyway if she didn't return in a reasonable time.

None of this made any sense to me. The police were right. There wasn't a thing to suggest Catherine Moore had been taken from the house against her will. No bashed-in doors, no bullet holes, not even the front door mat out of place.

Yet, I had distinctly heard the panic in her voice and a gunshot. And I had heard a crashing noise as if a door was being forcibly opened. I hadn't imagined it, I knew I hadn't. Kit had been there with me, so I knew it wasn't my overly active imagination.

So—where was Catherine?

I was still mulling over this question when I walked back into the kitchen and found Bitty sitting on top of a marble countertop. Dishes sat around her, blue and white and green, a couple different patterns.

"What are you doing now?" I couldn't help asking even though I was pretty sure I'd regret it.

"I told you. Checking Cat's truth-o-meter. She was pretty truthful. This really is Worcester bone china. See these marks? Seventeen hundreds. Late, I'd say, since this is a piece by Flight and Barr. Very lovely."

Sometimes I forget that Bitty is an antiques hound. I nodded pleasantly and said, "Very interesting, but we need to focus on other things right now. Did you find the source of that dreadful smell?"

"Unfortunately, yes." Bitty slid down from the counter and began putting the dishes back into the glass-front cabinet. "Apparently she left some chicken in the oven. It has little crawly things all over it." She shuddered as she said the last.

I pondered that for a moment. *How long does it take for meat to get maggots in an oven,* I wondered. I didn't realize I'd said that aloud until Bitty answered me.

"Maggots? Ewww! Are you sure she was here when she called you?"

"Well . . . no, I'm not. She used her cell phone. I guess she could have been anywhere."

Bitty nodded. "Maybe she went to her cabin."

"She has a cabin?"

"Of course."

"Not everyone has more than one house, you know," I reminded my cousin a bit tartly. "You could have said something earlier."

"It didn't occur to me. For heaven's sake, Trinket, you're the one who's been BFF with Cat lately, not me."

"BFF?"

"Best Friends Forever. Don't you do email?"

"I don't even do regular mail. When would I have time? I'm too busy running around like a headless chicken these days."

"Really, I think you need to go to the spa for a day. Or a week. You're always so tense and irritable. Armando gives wonderful massages that just take away all the stress like magic."

I rolled my eyes, but Bitty didn't see me. She was too busy putting away the china and poking her nose where it didn't belong.

"A lot of help you are," I muttered, confirming her assessment of my irritability. "I don't suppose you know the location of Catherine's cabin?"

"Why, I do. It's in Pott's Camp not that far from here, back toward Holly Springs. Are you suggesting—"

"No, I'm saying plainly that should be our next stop."

"Well, I'm not wearing these dreadful clothes a minute longer than I have to," she said, "so let's take them back first. If someone sees me in this uniform, I'll just die. And we didn't even need to rent them since not one neighbor has so much as said *boo* to us, much less ask what we're doing here."

As if conjured up by her precipitate assessment, the front doorbell jangled. We looked at each other, momentarily struck dumb. After the doorbell jangled again, I was able to say, "I'll get it. Stay in here and act like you're cleaning."

Bitty gave me a blank look, the doorbell rang again, and I threw my hands up in the air. "Fake it, Barbie," I said over my shoulder. "Pretend you know how to use a dishrag."

When I opened the front door, an elderly woman looked at me suspiciously. She had white curly hair and wore designer sunglasses. "Who are you?" she demanded before I could get out a greeting. "I've never seen you before."

"We're substituting for the regular cleaning service," I said as calmly as I could. My heartbeat had escalated, and my face felt flushed. "Didn't Mrs. Moore tell you?"

"It was late when she left. She usually has me get her mail and newspapers."

"So you talked to her yesterday?"

"No, but I did get her papers this morning. Catherine didn't tell me anything about a new cleaning service."

"It was a last-minute substitution," I lied, feeling myself get deeper and deeper in a sticky web of deception. "I'm sure she'll tell you all about it when she sees you."

"Hmph," said the still-suspicious neighbor, and peered at me over the rim of her sunglasses. "I don't see your van in the driveway."

"We came on the bus." Sweat started to bead on my forehead. My armpits felt hot and damp. I'm not as practiced at lying as Bitty. I get too nervous. Bitty can do it without breaking a sweat, while I look like I've stood under a showerhead. If Chen Ling barked or made any doggy sound, my goose was cooked. The police would be called, and there's no telling what would happen then. I was sure it would involve squad cars and handcuffs, however, so I crossed my mental fingers that this alert visitor would accept my explanation without calling the law.

After another pause, during which she squinted behind me at the living room, she gave a curt nod of her head. "If anything's missing, Catherine will tell me about it, you know."

"I should hope so," I said. It wasn't until she'd turned and crossed the driveway back to her own house that I could breathe easily. I sagged briefly against the door jamb, then stepped back and closed the door.

When I went back into the kitchen there was no sign of Bitty or the pug. I blinked my eyes to be sure she just wasn't under my radar somehow, but nope—no Bitty. "Hey," I called softly. "Where are you?"

The door to the garage cracked about two inches, then Bitty stuck her head in. "All clear?"

"Yes, Joan of Arc, you can come out of hiding now."

Bitty blinked at me. "Didn't they cancel that TV show years ago?"

"No, that was *Joan of Arcadia*. Joan of Arc was—oh, never mind. If I have to explain it to you then it isn't worth it. Let's get out of here."

"It couldn't be too soon for me." Bitty tucked Chen Ling under her arm and headed for the living room. "And I know who Joan of Arc was, so don't underestimate me."

"Hold it, Professor Hollandale," I said. "You forgot her bucket."

"No, I didn't. We're done, so let's just leave."

"I'd like to have a bit of a head start, you know. We don't need to have the police called on us before we can get out of town."

Bitty mumbled and grumbled, but Chitling ended up in the bucket and we left, locking the door behind us. I put the key back where it belonged, and we walked back to the car.

"You know," I said once we'd returned the costumes and were on our way toward Pott's Camp, "Catherine must have taken the time to tell her neighbor she was going to be out of town, or she wouldn't be getting her mail and newspapers."

"True."

"So if she's okay, she's probably at her cabin, don't you think?"

"Well, we can hope."

I thought about all the possibilities as Bitty took Highway 7 out of Oxford. All I could do was hope that Catherine had taken refuge in her cabin and was just fine. It'd be such a relief if she'd been startled by a visitor and the gunshot was just a door slamming.

"But she must have left home quickly," I murmured aloud, "or she'd have taken the chicken out of the oven. No one wants to come home to that kind of mess. Someone must have frightened her badly enough that she'd take off like that."

"Or maybe she just wanted to go off to the wilderness," said Bitty. "It happens."

"Wilderness?" I shuddered. "Let's hope not."

That's how we found ourselves in a desolate spot on the Tippah River, far from a town or even a neighbor, in a heavily wooded area that brought to mind every horror film I'd ever been coerced into watching. Catherine's car sat behind a story and a half house built of logs and roofed with cedar shakes. A deck ran along the backside and around to the front. From where we sat in the blacktop driveway, I could see a pier jutting into the tumbling water that ran past the house. The only sign of life was a buzzard roosting in a tree on the hill overlooking the river. I couldn't help another shudder.

"I'm having second thoughts," I said, and Bitty nodded her head.

"Me, too."

We sat there for another moment in silence. Then I took a deep breath. "We came all this way. We might as well see if she's all right."

"Yes. We should."

Neither one of us moved a muscle. The only thing moving in the front seat was Chitling's nose as she worked it over her plush car seat looking for crumbs. From what, I had no idea. She'd already dedicated a good portion of the drive sniffing out whatever was left from our earlier Sonic meal.

I wasn't expecting a noise of any kind, so when Chen Ling suddenly put back her head and began yodeling and yowling, it scared the bejeezus out of me, and I jumped.

"Agh!" I said to indicate my distress.

"Eeeek!" replied Bitty.

"Row, row, *rooooo*," said Chen Ling. The little dog had her head back, bellowing up at the car's open sun roof. Birds took flight, and the hulking buzzard shifted position on the tree branch.

"Dammit," I said crossly to Bitty, "why on earth does she have to do that?"

Having recovered somewhat, Bitty tried to calm the little . . . dog. "I don't know," she said finally when nothing seemed to work. "She's definitely upset."

"Newsflash," I muttered, and grabbed the door handle. "Now that she's alerted everyone within a half-mile radius that we're here, I suppose we should go on up and knock on the door."

"Yes," said Bitty. "You go ahead. I'll catch up."

I gave her a scathing glance. "Yes, I'm sure you will. Leave your pistol in your purse. And leave your purse in the car."

Bitty just blinked at me, and I said something else under my breath, then got out of the car and walked several yards to the back deck. The house was very quiet. No sign of human presence. Which I found a little odd since Catherine's car sat in plain view. Yet there seemed to be something eerie about it.

Since I've been correctly accused of letting my imagination run amok, I decided I was overreacting to the ungodly howling of Bitty's own personal coyote. Chitling still bayed and yodeled at whatever had caught her attention.

I peeked in a window as I passed on my way to the door, but saw nothing amiss. Everything looked tidy. A couple couches flanked a wide set of windows that looked out on the river, and the back door led directly into the kitchen. I walked to the door to knock, but saw that it was slightly ajar. I stood there a moment. The hair on the back of my neck prickled, and I was pretty sure all the hairs on my arms were standing straight up, too.

I gave myself a stern lecture. Nothing was wrong. Nothing had been wrong at the house in Oxford, and nothing was wrong here. I was, as usual, overreacting. It's a fault of mine, a vivid imagination that leads me down the wrong path all the time.

So I knocked on the glass window of the door, calling for Catherine as I pushed it open a little wider. "Catherine? It's Trinket Truevine. Are you awake? Catherine?"

There was no response. Nothing but a blanketing silence that seemed far too eerie. I glanced back toward Bitty. She was still sitting in the car, and Chitling was still singing her loud coyote song. No help there.

I took the bull by the horns and opened the door and stepped inside. My heart was pounding so hard my ears rang, and it took a moment for me to calm down. Then I called for Catherine again, but with the mounting sense that she wasn't there to answer.

The living room was empty, the drapes open, a small enclosed sunroom door left ajar. I peeked into the sunroom and didn't see anything amiss. So I turned and went across the living room past a huge fieldstone fireplace that took up nearly an entire wall, and turned down a hallway. A faint smell of smoke hovered in the house, like an old fire. Two bedrooms opened off the hall, both of them seeming undisturbed. When I turned, I saw another door, closed. Splinters of wood stuck out at odd angles from it, and my heart started up again with a beat loud enough to fill my ears.

Where the devil was Bitty? I wondered. Probably sitting out there waiting to see if I survived or was chased by a killer. There are definitely moments when I find my cousin less than endearing. Slowly, I pushed against the door, not at all surprised to find it was a bathroom. Towels lay on the floor, and an odd round little hole in the wall caught my immediate attention. Yes. This had to be it. This had to be where Catherine was when she called me. That hole was definitely a bullet hole, I was sure of it. And there was a red smear on the side of the white and gray-streaked granite washstand that didn't belong. I got a queasy feeling in the pit of my stomach. Blood? Oh lordy . . . and not a sign of Catherine.

Maybe . . . maybe she got away. Maybe she was out on a boat in the river or sitting on the banks somewhere fishing. No. Catherine didn't seem the kind of woman to fish. Carefully, so as not to disturb anything should this end up being a crime scene, I backed out from the bathroom, my hands shaking and my knees weak.

When I heard a noise behind me I said, "It's about time you got out of the car." I started to turn when something struck me hard against the back of my neck. Everything became a blur of motion like a tornado, whirling me into darkness, then—nothing.

Chapter 15

I really do hate it when people hit me. It's always so unnecessary. I mean, I'd be more than glad to stop doing what I was doing, or do whatever it is whoever might want me to do, just about anything to avoid getting bashed in the head. Or neck.

If asked to cease and desist or otherwise I'd suffer a knock on the noggin, I'd be quite pleasant and do so. And yet, no one has ever given me the choice in moments of crisis.

Suffice it to say, this makes me cranky. That's why, when I finally began to swim up from the dark pool of unconsciousness where I'd been floating for heaven knew how long, I came up kicking. Normally, I'd say that was pretty much out of character from my usual calm demeanor. After the last year, however, I'm not at all sure what's in character for me anymore. Maybe my real personality is surfacing after decades of dormancy beneath my proper upbringing and adherence to some of society's rules, if not most.

Whatever it is, as I began to regain consciousness, I lashed out with both my feet when I perceived a presence too close. I have long legs, which as a child earned me several unkind nicknames, but they come in handy at times. When my feet connected with something solid, I heard a sound very similar to *"oof!"* It was a gruff kind of sound. Catherine had a husky voice, but not that deep. I wriggled backward, flailing frantically with both my feet.

More sounds erupted in the form of interesting swear words. In the distance I heard unearthly howling. My vision cleared just in time to see my assailant take off for the other side of the house. He wore a gray hoodie pulled up over his head, faded jeans, and grungy tennis shoes. That's all I could tell from the back.

With a little effort, I pulled myself to my feet using a cane-back kitchen chair and staggered after him. Of course, he was too fast for me to catch, but I hoped to get a glimpse of his face or maybe the car he was driving.

By the time I got to the front deck looking out over the river, the only thing I saw was a gray blur booking it through trees and banks of fallen leaves. He disappeared in a thatch of brush.

A sudden noise behind me startled me, and I whirled around to see my cousin and her gargoyle peering at me from the doors opening onto the deck.

"Well," she said, and I knew she was irritated by the way she said it, "how nice of you to let me know you've decided to stay a while." She looked around, then said, "So is she here?"

"I don't think so. There was someone else here, unfortunately."

Bitty looked at me with wide eyes. "Who? Was it Breck Hartford?"

I frowned. I had to admit, "I don't know."

"What do you mean, you don't know? Where's Catherine?"

"I haven't seen her, so I don't know that either."

"For goodness sake, Trinket, what have you been doing in here for so long if you still don't know anything?"

I narrowed my eyes at her. "Mud wrestling. What do you think I've been doing?"

She looked at me uncertainly. The growth on her chest *woofed* at me. "Oh. Did you fall down?"

"Yes. I tend to do that when I'm given a karate chop on the neck."

Bitty's gasp of concern was only slightly comforting. "He hit you? Are you hurt?"

"Not very. More irritated than hurt. Did you get a look at him?"

"At who?"

I sighed. "At the guy who hit me. He just ran out of here like a scalded cat."

"No, I didn't see anybody. Are you sure it wasn't Breck Hartford? He's the kind of person who would do something like this."

"Like this—you mean, he has a history of violence?"

"Oh, I don't know about that. It's just that he was always on the edge, you know? Back in our college days. He used to get in a lot of fights, on and off the football field."

I pondered that for a moment. Breck was a big guy. Tall, and weighing over two hundred pounds at least, I'd say. The guy who had just hit me and run away was tall, but not hefty. More on the wiry side. So I shook my head.

"I'm pretty sure it wasn't Breck Hartford who hit and ran just now. This guy was smaller. Younger."

"So you did get a look at him."

"No, it's just the impression I got. You know."

"Honestly, Trinket, you're such a target. I suppose that your being so tall has a bit to do with it, but you'd think these people would take into consideration that you are a woman, after all."

"By *these people*, I'm assuming you mean the criminal element we seem to attract lately."

Bitty blinked at me. "We?"

"Yes, Sister Serenity, *we*. You don't think I'm in this by myself, I hope."

"You have an alarming tendency to overreact, Trinket. Of course, I'm sure it has a lot to do with the fact you keep getting hit in the head, but still, it'd be best if you could dial it down a little."

My face got hot, and I was pretty sure I was a nice shade of crimson as I said to my dear cousin, "Perhaps I wouldn't keep getting hit in the head if I had a back-up taking the same risks I've been taking."

"Don't be so sensitive. I'm going to check out the downstairs, and then I guess we should leave."

I was pretty sure steam was coming out of my ears as I followed her inside and to the kitchen area. She opened a door to a flight of stairs that led down to a lower level I hadn't known was there. It was an open area with a desk, computer, a couple of covered couches that probably made into beds, and wide windows along one wall that looked out over the slope down to the river. A set of French doors opened onto a shaded terrace, and another door led to a bathroom. I checked the bathroom quickly, and it was empty.

Then I heard Bitty scream. I knew even before I reached her what she must have found, so wasn't that surprised to see Catherine Moore tucked into a small storage closet under the stairwell. Her crumpled body was only half-hidden by a mop, broom and large bucket. She appeared to have been strangled by a wire noose around her neck, and her head lolled forward so that her chin almost rested on her chest.

"Is s-s-she d-d-dead?" Bitty stuttered, and I made myself step forward to put a finger against Catherine's neck to find a pulse. I felt nothing, no sign of life at all, just cold flesh, and took several steps back.

"Yes. She's dead. Don't touch anything. And don't even *think* about trying to move her anywhere, either."

"Why would I do that? Honestly, Trinket, you say the strangest things at times."

"I'm sure I do. It has nothing to do with the present company, of course."

Our brief verbal skirmish had the effect of getting Bitty past her initial horror so that she could cope with her discovery, and helped me, too. We went back upstairs and I put in a call to the police. Potts Camp has their own small police force, and they showed up quite quickly.

One officer took Bitty out on the front deck, and another officer kept me in the kitchen to question us separately. Frankly, I was very familiar with the drill and had to wonder what that said about my life experiences. Being familiar with police procedure is hardly something I wanted to put on my résumé.

After I ran through all the events that led up to us searching for Catherine, the officer questioning me looked at me quizzically. "So you're what—private investigators or something?"

"No, not really. We're just concerned citizens."

"Did it ever occur to you to call in the police?"

"As I already told you, we tried that. It didn't work out so well."

"This is still a police matter, ma'am. It's not safe to run around looking for a killer. You'd be lucky to just get arrested. You could end up dead."

"Yes, I'm aware of that," I said. "In our defense, I'd like to point out again that we did try to involve the police and weren't that successful."

"Tell me again about the man you say you saw."

"I *did* see him. He was tall, maybe six feet, kind of wiry, and wore a gray hoodie and faded jeans."

"Race?"

"White, I'm pretty sure. I mean, I didn't get a good look at him except from the back. Oh, and he wore gloves. Some kind of workman's gloves, gray with red stripes. Tennis shoes, scuffed and dirty."

"Older, younger?"

"I don't know . . . younger, I think."

"What makes you think he's young?"

"Hm, the way he moved, maybe. Quick. Agile. He leaped from the upper deck to the ground and took off through the woods. I guess an older person could do that, but it seemed to me like he was more athletic. If that makes any sense."

The policeman, also fairly young, with a buzz cut and glasses, nodded. "It does. If we have any more questions, can we reach you at this address and these phone numbers?"

"Yes. Of course." I'd given them the usual information at the beginning of our interview, my home and work numbers as well as my cell number and home address.

The other officer was still talking to Bitty, and I went out the back way to get a breath of fresh air. To my faint surprise, I was shaking. My hands trembled, my stomach felt like I'd swallowed a lead weight, and my knees were all quivery. If I let my mind wander, it went straight to how I'd last seen Catherine Moore, and that made me feel worse, so I did my best to think of other things. Anything else would do, yet I pondered the few things I knew about her.

Her son Monty had died nearly two years before, and since that time she'd been obsessed with proving his death was murder instead of suicide.

She had been convinced that Breck Hartford was connected to Monty's death. And she had identified the intruder in her home as Hartford while talking to me. She drank too much, she smoked incessantly, and she worked in the Administration offices at Ole Miss, where Sturgis and Hartford were faculty members. But what else did I know? Not much. Nothing about her private life except for what I heard from Bitty. Did she have a current boyfriend? Lover? How long had she been divorced, and had it been amicable? Was Monty's father in the picture at all? Was Catherine independently wealthy, or had her money come from another source? Her job at the university didn't pay enough for her to afford Jimmy Choo purses and a second home, that's for sure.

There were a lot of variables to be considered, and I was sure the police would put their heads together and figure it out. It was time we stepped back and let them do their job. I, for one, was getting weary of being assaulted.

Another official vehicle arrived, and two plainclothes men got out. A uniformed officer was stringing yellow crime scene tape around the house and across the driveway, and enclosed Catherine's Lexus in the loop. The new arrivals paused to chat briefly with the uniformed officer, and then all three looked my way. I tried not to notice.

When Bitty came outside with Chitling clutched tightly in her arms, the detectives approached us. We were once more separated and questioned. Notes would be compared with the police officers, I was pretty certain.

When it was finally over, we walked to her car without speaking. A uniformed officer lifted the crime scene tape that hemmed in the Benz so we could leave. It wasn't until we were headed back out the driveway that we looked at each other.

"That was awful," said Bitty. "You know, I can't say Cat was my best friend or anything, but no one should have to die like that."

I agreed, and we drove in silence back to Holly Springs. Even Chitling was subdued for a change. Bitty parked her car outside the garage and close to the back door, and we went inside. It was quiet, but the fragrance of recently prepared food still spiced the kitchen air.

"I smell lasagna," I said, and Bitty nodded.

"I got one out of the freezer last night, heated it up, then didn't feel like eating it." We both headed for the refrigerator-freezer cleverly disguised by wood doors to blend in with the cabinetry.

"I don't know why you bother to hide your fridge," I commented as we took out a glass pan filled with lasagna just ready to be reheated and eaten. "We still find it with alarming regularity."

"I know. But it's always such a nice surprise. Do you think we need more cheese on top?"

"Definitely," I replied, and after distributing more ricotta over the already cheesy delicacy, we microwaved it. I did the honors since Bitty has to stand on her toes to punch the over-the-stove microwave's buttons.

While we waited, we poured ourselves a nice California merlot. I leaned back against the granite kitchen counter, swirled my wine and studied Bitty. Her hair was a mess, an unusual occurrence for her since she kept it sprayed as stiff as steel wire most of the time, and her eyes still held a hint of horror at what we'd found earlier. She also still wore her red Ferragamo flats that made her much shorter than I was used to seeing her, and she seemed suddenly vulnerable. It made me want to protect her, but I had learned the harsh lesson that it wasn't always possible to protect others.

I took a nice sip of my wine before I said, "I think we both know the killer," and Bitty looked at me over the rim of her wine glass.

"So you think the same person who killed Professor Sturgis killed Catherine?"

"Absolutely. It has to be the same person. Who else would want to silence a possible witness?"

"But if she really *knew* the killer, wouldn't she have gone to the police? They'd pay attention to a credible witness."

"Her son's death was ruled a suicide, and she's been insistent that it was murder all this time. Maybe they'd think she was just being hysterical."

"Yes, police do tend to jump to that conclusion far too often. A pity. After all, she was pretty messed up by losing her only child, just as anyone would be. Not that I'd nominate her for sainthood or anything. Cat could still outdrink most men and had a wit and the vulgar tongue of a brick mason. Bless her heart."

"Brick masons are vulgar?" I wondered aloud, and Bitty gulped a healthy taste of her wine before shrugging.

"Just those of my acquaintance."

"You lead a secret life that I cannot imagine, you know. Garden club meetings, massages, brick masons, charity functions, target shooting, massages, ice cream socials, community committee affairs, massages—"

"You've been to one of my ice cream socials," Bitty defended herself, and I nodded agreement.

"Yep. It was lovely. Did I mention your massages?"

Bitty said something pithy, and I laughed just as the microwave announced our supper was hot at last. I was tempted to ask if Jackson Lee knew about her masseuse, but since I figured he wouldn't care if he did, I just focused on the lasagna.

We ate at her kitchen table in front of the white-shuttered window. Bitty poured more merlot into our glasses, and I buttered another generous slice of crusty French bread. It wasn't until we'd finished eating and cleaned up our supper dishes to retreat to the cozy parlor with glasses of wine that we talked about Catherine's death again.

Bitty sat opposite me in the overstuffed, formerly slipcovered chair. She'd kicked off her shoes and sat with her feet tucked under her, Chitling ensconced in her usual place on her lap.

"Did you get your slipcovers cleaned?" I asked over the rim of my wine glass. "I notice you don't have anything on the furniture now."

Rather glumly, Bitty shook her head. "They can't get the purple dye out of the linen. I had to order new ones for summer. My winter slipcovers should be ready soon, so I have to be careful until they get here."

"So says the brave woman sitting with a glass of merlot in her hand," I replied with a laugh. Bitty stuck out her tongue, and I made a mental note not to be the one to have the first spill. The parlor furniture is white under the slipcovers.

I carefully placed my wine glass on the nesting table next to the chair and said, "I can't get Catherine out of my mind. I keep seeing her there in the closet . . . I wonder if it would have made any difference if we'd gotten there earlier."

"I doubt it. I think I heard the coroner say she'd been dead at least twelve hours."

"So if I'd known where she was last night, I might have been able to save her."

Bitty leaned forward. "Trinket, none of us knew where she was, and even if we had, I doubt the police could have gotten there in time to save her. She was probably killed within minutes after you talked to her."

To my surprise, my hand shook slightly as I reached for my wine. "It's so horrible to think about what she must have been thinking, how helpless she felt . . ."

"Not Cat. She never felt helpless. I'm willing to bet she gave just as good as she got, and that some guy is out there looking like the bottom of a farmer's boot."

I paused in sipping my wine. "Bitty, that's true! If it was Breck Hartford who killed her, then he should have scratches on him."

Bitty's eyes opened wide. "Do you think we should go down there to check him out?"

"Good lord, no! The police will do that for us. I'm sure they've already thought of that."

"But why would they? I mean, unless they found out that Catherine has always suspected Breck of being responsible for her son's death, they wouldn't know to talk to him, would they? We do, though."

"Bitty, I told them what she said about Breck being downstairs. I wouldn't go down there to talk to Breck Hartford anyway. Especially if he's the killer. I'm tired of getting smacked around. My head hurts, I've got a crick in my neck, and my eyeballs are going to be permanently crossed if I get hit one more time. So no, I have no intentions whatsoever of going back to Oxford any time soon."

"You're just going to let him get away with killing her? And her son?"

"I'm not convinced anyone killed her son." I pondered that a moment, and added, "Although Catherine's murder does give more weight to her suspicion that Monty was killed rather than committed suicide."

"See? We could solve two murders at once."

"Are you insane? I'm content with letting the police handle it. Sergeant Maxwell seemed really serious about charging us with interference if we got in the way again."

"Honestly, Trinket, I'd think you'd want to see justice done."

"I do. Oh, I do. I just don't want to get in between the police and the killer. That leads to uncomfortable and frightening scenarios, and I hate those, I really do."

I thought for a moment that Bitty intended to argue some more, but then she shook her head slightly and sipped her wine without responding. That was a relief. The idea of going back to Oxford and facing a man who might very well be a murderer was less than appealing to me. I was tired, my neck still ached, and I had to be at work early the next morning. Arguing with Bitty took more energy than I had at the moment, and I was only too glad that she changed the topic of conversation to plans for the annual Holly Springs Pilgrimage coming up in April.

"That's so far away," I protested when she asked had I decided yet if I wanted to wear a hoop skirt and pantalets. "Let's get past Thanksgiving first."

"That reminds me, Rose called a few days ago and asked if I was interested in getting involved in the Wish Tree Carolann's putting up in the shop after Thanksgiving."

"It's a worthy cause. Carolann thought of it. Every ribbon represents a donation made by someone. Blue will be for five hundred dollars or more, red for one hundred dollars or more, and yellow for fifty dollars or more. Green will be for any donation made that's under fifty dollars."

Bitty smiled. "I get a gold ribbon."

My eyes probably bugged out of my head. "Bitty! You donated a thousand dollars to the Wish Tree?"

"Don't tell anyone. And don't act so shocked. Not only am I not the only one to donate, I'm not the first to get a gold ribbon. Jackson Lee pledged quite a bit more than I did. Carolann said we could choose one of the three main charities we want to receive our donations, or split it between all three."

See what I mean about Bitty? She can be annoyingly self-absorbed, then turn around and do the most endearing things. Whatever else might be said of her, she has a very generous nature.

When I left Bitty's to go home, I smiled most of the way, thinking about her soft heart and how completely selfless she can be at the most surprising moments. It gave me a warm feeling, which came in handy since the night had gotten pretty cold. My breath frosted in front of my face once I parked my car just outside the garage and started for the house. Maybe I'd make a space for it inside the garage when the weather got worse. Scraping ice and frost off my windshield is not one of my favorite things to do.

Just as I got to the front porch my cell phone rang. Naturally, it was somewhere in my purse, probably at the bottom under Kleenex, Chapstick, pens, a hairbrush, and loose change that always seemed to be floating around. By the time I found it, it had stopped ringing. The light blinked out before I could see the caller's name, and I said something I'd heard Bitty say a time or two. It made me feel much better.

Daddy had left the front porch light on for me, and I stuck my key in the lock to open the door. As it creaked on hinges that obviously needed a shot or two of WD-40, my cell phone rang again. Yet another reason I'd resisted buying one, I told myself, irritated that I couldn't seem to manage two tasks at the same time. Naturally, I dropped my purse and keys and barely caught the phone before it hit the porch floor. Rather irritated, I'm sure my tone was sharp when I answered without looking at the Caller ID.

"Hello!"

There was a brief pause, then a muffled voice said, "Stop snooping around, or you'll end up just as dead as your friend."

"Who is this?" I demanded.

"This is your only warning. Don't be stupid."

That was it. Whoever the caller was, they hung up before I could ask another question. Caller ID read Unknown Caller. For several moments I stood in the fuzzy light from the overhead porch lamp and thought about my options. The reasonable thing to do would be to take the caller's advice.

That was the reasonable thing. Why would I be unreasonable?

Chapter 16

"I think you should tell the police." Gaynelle peered at me over the rim of her tea cup. We were sitting in her living room, a cozy area decorated in a vintage style with big comfy furniture and potted plants. "You've obviously stepped on the murderer's toes, and you know what can happen when you do."

"Yes." I sighed. "Going to the police won't be much help, though. After all, they would probably agree with my caller since we've already been told to butt out of police business."

"That might be a good idea," Gaynelle said after a brief pause. "Y'all did find the last two victims. I worry that one of these days you'll both end up victims."

"It's crossed my mind more than once," I said. "I'm not at all sure how my life's taken such a strange turn. It's almost a year since I came back home, and I've seen more dead people in the last eleven months than I've seen my entire life."

"Opportunities *have* opened up in that direction, I've noticed," Gaynelle replied drolly. "Perhaps you should consider a career in law enforcement."

"Or the mortuary business."

"That, too," she agreed. "Not that you're alone. Other Divas seem to have the same problem as you and Bitty."

Alarmed, I said, "You don't mean—"

"No, no," Gaynelle quickly assured me, "no more bodies have been found. Not that I know of, anyway."

"I ran into Miranda Watson the other day," I said after breathing a sigh of relief, "and she asked me how everyone in 'the murder club' is doing. I told her that was a tacky thing to say, even if it does seem to be terribly true lately." I paused, then added, "I didn't say that last part, of course. No point in giving her any more ideas."

"You're definitely right about that. Miranda comes up with enough ideas on her own without any of us giving her help." Gaynelle took a sip of her tea and frowned.

Since I'd stopped by Gaynelle's to discuss my mystery caller of the night before, I hoped for advice that would make me feel better. And safer.

"Since there have been no more calls," Gaynelle said after a moment of silence, "I suppose the best thing to do is just wait and see what happens. And refrain from doing any more investigations on your own."

"Right. That would be the reasonable thing to do. Try telling that to Bitty."

"Does she know about your threatening call?"

I nodded. "She called me at work today about a half-dozen times, all with the same suggestion—we find out who it is. I told her I'm not that curious. I'd much rather *not* know who wants to kill me."

Gaynelle set her cup and saucer down on the vintage coffee table. "I understand that. Still, in one way Bitty has a point—knowing who threatened you would be a great help. Are you certain you don't want to go to the police?"

"I'm not certain about anything. On one hand, I don't want to know who called me. Yet on the other hand, knowing who it is might be safer. The problem is, looking for the person is not only risking arrest, it's risking my life."

"Quite true. I have a suggestion that may or may not appeal to you, but I'd like for you to hear me out."

"Uh oh. Why do I get the feeling that I'm not going to like this?"

"Probably because you won't like it." Gaynelle smiled primly. "There's safety in large numbers, you know. Herd animals instinctively know this. It's always safest in the middle of a crowd than it is to be ahead or behind."

"I get the feeling you're going somewhere with this line of discussion."

"Indeed I am. To keep you safe, any further involvement should be conducted as a group."

"As in a gaggle of Divas?"

"Geese come in gaggles. Divas come in—"

"Droves?"

Gaynelle laughed. "Most of the time. Truly, Trinket, I think you need to be very cautious. You have been personally threatened. If we all get together, we can investigate as a team instead of individually. What killer in his right mind would try to take out an entire group?"

"Bitty and I were discussing that very thing not so long ago—that someone who is capable of killing a human being cannot really be in their right mind. The act precludes the definition of sanity."

"A good point, but hardly helpful at preserving your safety."

I sighed. "True. Okay. Maybe we should all put our heads together and see what we can come up with to get this situation resolved. Once the murderer is caught, I'll feel a lot safer."

"So you don't believe Professor Sturgis's wife killed him."

Gaynelle's question caught me by surprise. I thought about it a moment, then said, "Despite Bitty's insistence, I'm not at all sure that she's the killer. As you pointed out, it took an act of strength to subdue and strangle Sturgis. Emily Sturgis just doesn't look like she's strong enough to do it."

"I agree. Not to say she couldn't hire a killer, of course."

"Oh, that's it. Throw a wrench into the works," I said, only half-kidding. "Just when I think we can rule someone out, I can't. So who do you think is responsible for killing not just the professor, but Catherine Moore?"

"Breck Hartford is still at the top of my suspect list. He had motive, opportunity, and means."

"But wasn't there friction between Hartford and Sturgis? The professor may not have allowed him close enough to put himself in danger."

"There's a difference between disliking someone and thinking them capable of murder. Sturgis may have been caught by surprise."

"Catherine Moore thought Hartford more than capable," I said. "She also said he was the man who broke into her house right before . . . before she was killed."

I still couldn't quite accept that she had called me for help, and I hadn't been able to save her. If I'd known she was in Potts Camp instead of Oxford, I might have been able to get police there in time, but even then it may have been too late. The feeling that I'd failed her nudged aside any hint of satisfaction that could come from finding her killer.

"Trinket," said Gaynelle, and leaned forward to put a hand on my arm, "you did everything you could to help Catherine. Don't feel that you failed in any way."

I managed a smile. "How did you know what I was thinking?"

She sat back. "Because it's what I would be thinking if I was in your shoes. The truth is no one could have gotten there in time to save Catherine. You did your best to get her help. That's all you could do."

I leaned back against the soft couch cushions. "I always feel better when I talk to you, Gaynelle. You're the only voice of reason in a crazy world."

"Since you largely dwell in Bitty-World, I can well understand that."

We both laughed, and some of the dark thoughts that had been haunting me grew lighter.

It was the main topic of conversation at our next Diva meeting. We met two days later at Cady Lee Forsythe's house. She lives in a house called Magnolia Hill, a two-story white house near the cemetery. The entire yard is enclosed by a black iron fence topped with fleur-de-lis and shaded by magnolia trees over a hundred fifty years old. Those ancient trees have lived through a civil war as well as two world wars and are gnarled with age but a stately reminder of times long past.

Bitty, Gaynelle, Rayna and I had ridden together in the Franklin Benz and parked at the curb in front of the house. Morning sunshine warmed chilly temperatures and glinted off the wide, waxy leaves of the magnolias. Cady Lee's yard service had cleaned under the trees, leaving distinctive rake marks in the black dirt.

The front porch was decorated with straw bales, pumpkins, gourds, and a couple of scarecrows. White rocking chairs flanked a small table that held a pot of overflowing ivy with glossy green leaves. A periwinkle vine added splashes of creamy color.

Cady Lee answered the doorbell's summons herself, swinging open the solid oak door with leaded glass panes and beckoning us inside. "It's getting cold out there. Come in!"

There was a decided bite of chill in the air. Cady Lee had crockpots full of chili, pots of navy bean soup simmering, with rounds of cornbread and crusty loaves of fresh-baked bread set upon a sideboard. The table was set with a cornucopia spilling autumn bounty over a muted gold, green, and red table runner, and expensive china waited on the antique sideboard next to the crockpots. Several bottles of wine leaned inside crystal coolers of ice. In the butler's pantry situated between the dining room and kitchen, I saw platters of desserts on one of the narrow counters. Hello calories, goodbye waistline.

"Brain food," Cady Lee replied breezily when I complimented her on the cheese and cold cut trays brought out and placed on the dining room table. "Helps soak up the fat and carbohydrates and promotes mental health."

I looked at her. "Really?"

"No. But it sounds good, doesn't it?"

"The best reason I've heard yet for cream cheese and onion dip. Whole-grain crackers?"

"A few. I don't like to clutter up the trays with too many healthy things."

"A woman after my own heart."

While I sampled roast beef, Swiss cheese, potato chips and onion dip, Bitty and Gaynelle dipped chili over bowls of cornbread wedges. Rayna had the navy bean soup with diced carrots and a hunk of pork swimming in her bowl, and as the other Divas arrived we depleted a large portion of not only Cady Lee's offerings but casseroles, pies, chicken salad, pimento cheese, and other goodies. Deelight Tillman had brought a Hummingbird cake that looked beautiful on the sideboard. My contribution had been a French silk pie. Bitty had brought wine—of course—and Rayna and Gaynelle each brought home-baked chocolate cakes. Rayna's had caramel in the icing. Be still my heart. I already had my piece staked out.

By the time we'd all eaten, the table and sideboard looked like they'd been visited by a swarm of hungry locusts. We retreated to the cozy parlor where a nice fire burned in the vintage grate.

"Are you certain we can't help you clear the mess, Cady Lee?" asked Gaynelle. "It wouldn't take any time."

Cady Lee flapped her hand at Gaynelle. "Heavens no. I have my help do that. It's her kitchen, not mine. I can barely find a spoon, but Pearl knows where everything goes."

Cady Lee has been accustomed to having help ever since she was born. Rumor has it that Ruby Mae Wilson raised Cady Lee and her sister and brother, because her mother spent all her time at committee meetings, club meetings, and on trips to the Gulf coast to spread more philanthropic cheer. The Forsythe family had morning maids, afternoon maids, and evening maids, as well as a full-time nanny. Most of the help stayed with the family for a lifetime. Ruby Mae has a small, neat bungalow over near the new grade school. I see her sometimes out in her garden, bent with age but still nimble enough to raise turnips, tomatoes, and rows of beans in her back yard. She raised Cady Lee's mother, too. Pearl is her great-granddaughter.

Bitty—sans pug—took a chair near to the fire, and I went to sit across from her. We all had drinks, either warm or cold, and now circled our wagons, so to speak, to talk about what to do next.

"I say we get a good hold of Emily Sturgis and squeeze her until she tells us everything we want to know," said Bitty.

I looked at my cousin. "What is this vendetta you have against Emily Sturgis? I haven't seen or heard a thing that links her to so much as a whisper of evidence against her, Bitty. Why do you think she's involved?"

Bitty waved a hand. "Instinct. She's in it up to her freshwater pearls, I guarantee you."

I rolled my eyes. "Do I detect a hint of snobbery, Miz Hollandale?"

Before Bitty could form a properly scathing reply, Rayna interrupted. "You may be right, Bitty, but Emily's alibi for the professor's time of death is rock solid."

Bitty looked crestfallen, but managed to rally enough to ask, "Are you sure?"

"Pretty sure. A dozen or so witnesses placed her at the preparations for The Grove party. She even stayed the night with Susan Lantrip so they could get up early to take the food over."

Never one to go down without a struggle, Bitty said, "Well, I don't know how she did it, but I'm willing to bet she managed somehow."

"So what is the timeline of how things happened?" Cindy Nelson wanted to know. She's a mother of active children who participate in sports, so always must know who has to be where when.

"Between the hours of nine thirty AM and eleven thirty AM, Professor Sturgis was strangled to death," said Rayna. "Somehow he was moved without anyone noticing, and left in Brandon and Clayton's dorm room. As we now know, at approximately three thirty PM, the professor was discovered by Bitty and Trinket and relocated to the back of a Penske truck that was behind the Trent Lott building. From there, the truck was taken back to Jackson, Mississippi, where it had been rented by Randall Klein, a student.

"Randall has a solid alibi for the time period of the professor's death, being with several other students at the Student Center who vouched for his presence. The Caldwell boys were with them, as well as Bret Hartford and Heather Lightner."

"*Bret* Hartford?" I echoed. "Any kin to Breck Hartford?"

Rayna nodded as she paused to take a breath. "Yes. His son. He's a freshman this year."

"How on earth did you get all this information?"

Rayna smiled. "I'm a snoop and very good at it. I've managed to find out quite a bit just by asking questions and doing computer research."

"Oh, that skip-trace thing you do?" Bitty said.

"Uh, not quite, but close, hon. In this case, I limited my legwork to a few cops I know well enough to ask questions. Rob wants me to stay out of these things, you know."

She said the last almost apologetically. We all knew her husband's point of view on our "extracurricular" activities. He held the same view as most of the Holly Springs police force. "Yes, yes, we all know what Rob thinks," Bitty said. "Not that he's always right, but I do understand that we have to keep some things quiet. Let's get straight to the point of why we're here. We all have to group together. Safety in numbers, last zebra feeds the lion, blah, blah, blah. Basically, Trinket's life has been threatened, and we can't take that lightly."

She looked around at all of us. Her cheeks were slightly flushed, and I wasn't sure if it was because of the fire or the wine. Someone had gasped, and I looked over to see Deelight Tillman with a hand over her mouth. Her eyes bugged out, and she looked upset.

"Trinket, you've been threatened?"

"Basically," I said. "I got a phone call warning me to stop snooping, or I'd end up like my friend. I'm pretty sure they were referring to

Catherine and not Bitty."

Gaynelle nearly choked on her wine. "I should think so," she was finally able to say, "since ending up like Bitty wouldn't be such a bad fate."

"Tell me about it. Being blonde, beautiful, and rich doesn't sound bad at all," I said, mostly to keep Bitty from punishing me or Gaynelle for making fun of her. She has her methods.

"Back on topic," Rayna said when Diva giggles subsided, "we need to have a plan. And we need to do any investigating in groups of at least three or more. Whoever is behind the murder of the professor and Catherine is obviously intent upon getting away with it, and if that means another murder, I don't think he or she will hesitate."

"So who do *you* think it is?" Sandra Dobson asked Rayna. "You've done some investigating on your own, so you must have at least an idea of who might be behind the murders."

"Not really. I hate to form an idea until I have a lot more pieces of the puzzle. I have a tendency to get wedded to my suspicions and sometimes miss important clues."

Carolann Barnett had remained uncharacteristically quiet during our discussion, but now she suddenly spoke up. "I never went to college, so I don't know that much about the relationships between students and professors, and between all the teachers. But if you ask me, there seems to have been a lot of rivalry between Sturgis and Hartford, from what I heard."

"What did you hear, Carolann?" asked Rayna.

Flushing a bit, Carolann toyed with one of the wild curls that always looked alive on her head, and said, "People come into the shop, you know. Well, sometimes they say things and don't think about who might be around. I don't mean to eavesdrop, I swear I don't, but there are times I can't help but hear them."

"So what did you hear?" I leaned forward and asked. "You know it won't go any further. What's said to the Divas, stays with the Divas."

Carolann glanced over at Cady Lee and took a deep breath. I understood her qualms. Cady Lee does get carried away sometimes. She doesn't do it to be malicious. She just can't help herself.

So I said to the group, "We all promise not to tell where we heard what Carolann is about to tell us, right, Divas?"

Of course we all agreed, and Carolann nodded. "Okay. It may mean nothing, of course. I mean, we have to consider the source and all, and even if she is a dear old thing, her information isn't always reliable."

Ah. A *"dear old thing."* I knew what that meant: old as the hills and nutty as a fruitcake. In my childhood, most "dear old things" wore flower-print dresses with lace collars, clunky shoes, small hats, and carried embroidered hankies. Now they're just as likely to be wearing Spandex and carrying a tennis racket. Modern medicine isn't always an improvement, in my opinion.

Nevertheless, we all encouraged Carolann to go on telling us what she'd heard by eavesdropping.

She gulped down more wine and continued. "Well, I was standing over by the display of the new Laura Ashley line, and Mrs. Jarvis came in. Well, she had her great-granddaughter Fronie with her, and while Mrs. Jarvis was looking over the silk chemises, they started talking about the murders of the professor and Catherine Moore. It seems that Fronie—her given name is Sofronia, but no one calls her that—goes to Ole Miss and had Professor Sturgis for her ancient history class. Fronie stood right there and told her great-grandmother that it was a well-known fact that Sturgis and Mrs. Hartford were having an affair. Someone caught them in a clinch in the law library, although why they were both in there no one has a clue, since neither one of them were law professors.

"Then Mrs. Jarvis said, 'Why Fronie, you know that Victoria threatened to beat Catherine Moore to death if she caught her with her husband again, and I vow she must have done it this time.'"

"Is this Victoria Hartford?" I asked when Carolann paused to take a breath. "Breck Hartford's wife?"

Carolann nodded. "Yes. Maybe everyone already knows this? That the professor and Victoria were having an affair?"

"Not everyone," said Gaynelle. "There were whispers about Catherine and Breck, but not as much about those two, to my knowledge."

Cady Lee flapped a hand. "Oh heavens, I thought it was common knowledge. Vicky and Spencer were hot and heavy for a while. That was right after Catherine and Breck got together, I think."

"Why am I just now hearing about this?" I asked no one in particular. "This could change things, you know."

"Really?" asked Bitty. "How?"

"For one thing, it adds another name to the suspect pool."

Bitty shrugged. "They should all already be in that pool up to their adulterous little necks, if you ask me. They're all guilty of something, even if it's just poor judgment. Not that Emily has a shortage of flaws. I tell you—"

To keep from having to hear her state that Emily Sturgis was the murderer again, I said quickly, "Bitty may actually be right. Do they all have alibis for the time of Sturgis's murder?"

Rayna said, "Emily's alibi is rock solid. Victoria Hartford has a pretty good alibi as well. She was away at some triathlon event. Breck Hartford, on the other hand, doesn't have an iron-clad alibi. There's a space of a half hour he can't account for, but I don't think he's at the top of the official suspect list. At least, not according to the information I got."

"Is a half hour long enough to get into the professor's house, kill him, then cart his body over to the student dormitory where it was found?" I asked dubiously. "It seems to me it would take a lot longer than that. Even the most organized killer would have to be moving pretty fast to get that done. And how would he disguise the body? Surely someone had to notice if he had the professor slung over his back."

"Unless he used the same method you and Bitty used to get Sturgis out of the dorm room and into a moving truck," Gaynelle pointed out. "Don't you find it a bit too convenient that the laundry cart was right there in the twins' room?"

I nodded. "It has to be what the killer used to get the professor into the dorms and up the elevator. I'm still curious as to why Brandon and Clayton's room was chosen, but it could have been a random choice."

"Of course it was," said Bitty. "I can't imagine why anyone would want to cause trouble for them deliberately."

"Wasn't using a wire coat hanger a bit too much of a coincidence?" asked Cindy Nelson. "I mean, he was strangled with a wire coat hanger, he has fresh laundry hanging in the hallway, and then he's carted over to the dorms in a laundry cart. Are we sure it wasn't a laundry man who killed him?"

"We're not sure of anything at this point," said Rayna. "Except that two people are dead, and both of them were killed with wire coat hangers. There has to be a common connection."

"Three people," I said, and when Cady Lee turned to look at me, I added, "Cat told me that her son was hung from his closet rod. Does anyone know if he was hung with a wire coat hanger?"

Silence fell. Then Rayna said, "I'll check on that. It would definitely mean that these murders are all related, and that Monty's death was ruled a suicide when it wasn't."

It was something to think about. Catherine may have been more right than she realized.

Then Rayna said, "These are facts I'm sure the police have already considered. I don't think we know more than they do."

I thought about that. It's usually true that the police are nearly always way ahead of us in solving murders. But this time maybe we had—or we believed—facts they didn't. It hadn't seemed to impress them that Catherine had named Breck Hartford as the intruder, but then, it hadn't impressed them when she said he'd killed her son, either.

"So," I said aloud, "it sounds like Breck Hartford is the common denominator in all these relationships. He and the professor had a history. He and Emily have a history. He had a history with Catherine Moore. And his wife had a history with Spencer Sturgis. It all seems to revolve around him."

"Or around Sturgis," Gaynelle pointed out. "I wonder what kind of history he had with Hartford that would lead to wife-swapping?"

"Do you think that's what they were doing?" Cindy Nelson asked with a gasp. "In *Miss'sippi?*"

Gaynelle bent an amused gaze on Cindy. "It's not exactly restricted to certain areas of the country, dear."

"But I mean—*here?* It just doesn't seem proper, that's all. Not so close to where we *live.*"

I regarded Cindy with a feeling of amusement mixed with faint regret. When had I become so jaded as not to be so shocked by immorality? Maybe it was after finding my first corpse, but to be honest, I'd already seen a lot of the seamier side of humanity when working for hotel chains. The things some people did when they thought themselves anonymous or unobserved were amazing, I'd discovered. None had ever led to murder, however, and I considered that crime the most shocking immorality of all.

"It's not like we have it going on here in Holly Springs," drawled Cady Lee. "I mean, that's all the way down in Oxford."

"True enough," Deelight commented. "Not that it couldn't happen here. Could it? Happen here? Why, it might be happening right now, for all we know!"

"Trina Madewell would be right in the middle of it, I'll bet," said Bitty with her usual gift for insulting yet another arch-enemy. "Except that she can't find anyone else to marry her."

"I heard she's dating Rowdy Hampton," Sandra Dobson said around a bite of cheese ball and cracker. "You know, the guy who runs the towing service."

Bitty looked thoughtful for a moment. "Isn't he the one who just did twenty down in Parchman?"

"No, that was his daddy," chirped Marcy Porter. She took a sip of wine before adding, "Howdy let Rowdy run it while he was doing his time, and now they run it together."

"Howdy and Rowdy?" I couldn't help asking. "Is there a Doody in there somewhere?"

"You're dating yourself, Trinket," said Bitty. "Of course, the *Howdy Doody Show* was way before my time."

"Why, don't you remember watching it with me when you got your first color TV?" I asked sweetly.

"Oh, I remember that," said Cady Lee. "Bitty's parents were the first in Holly Springs to go up to Memphis and buy a color TV. We all came over to see it."

Bitty drained her glass. "I'm sure I don't remember that," she said loftily. "You must be mistaken."

"No," Cady Lee said thoughtfully, "I'm right. Don't you remember us watching the *Howdy Doody Show* the next morning after we slept over one Friday night?"

"We were only five or six, Cady Lee. How do you remember that?"

Apparently Gaynelle decided to drag the conversation from wife-swapping and wooden puppets back to murder, because she said, "Ladies, I think we should find out if Breck Hartford's alibi stands up. If he's responsible for Catherine's death, it's a good possibility he also killed Spencer Sturgis."

"I remember," Cady Lee answered Bitty, "because my daddy went up to Memphis and bought *two* color TV sets the very next week. Mama was appalled he'd bring such bourgeois appliances home, but Daddy said we had to keep up, or people would talk."

"Ladies?" Gaynelle interrupted. "Hello? Please remember why we're really here today. We need to figure out our game plan to keep Trinket safe and be sure the killer is caught."

It was a sobering reminder. I nodded. "One thing we haven't yet considered is that there may be two killers."

Gaynelle looked at me closely. "Two? Why do you say that?"

"It makes more sense if there are two. One to establish an alibi for the time of the murder, and the other to establish an alibi for the time it would take to move the body."

Bitty frowned. Or as close as she could come to it with so much Botox. "I don't follow. How could a killer establish an alibi for the very time she commits murder?"

"We've been looking at this as if the killer had to have enough time to strangle the professor and then move his body. What if he didn't? What if the killer murdered him, and then had someone else move the body?"

"An accessory after the fact," Rayna murmured thoughtfully. "That might work. It might just be what happened. No one has mentioned an accomplice. We've all been so focused on Hartford."

"And Emily," chirped Bitty. "Don't forget Emily."

Rayna rolled her eyes. "How could I when you keep mentioning her? Don't worry about Emily. You need to worry about keeping Trinket safe. Can she stay with you for a while?"

Just as I opened my mouth to object, Bitty said, "Always. I'll do anything to keep her safe. She's the sunshine beneath my wings."

I might still have found a reason to explain why I needed to stay in my own home for safety instead of with Mrs. Malaprop, but then Rayna said, "If someone's out to hurt Trinket, they might do harm to her parents as well. You're right here in town and have an alarm system that Trinket won't forget to set. What do you think, Trinket?" she turned toward me to ask, and by then I knew I was doomed.

"I'm thrilled," I croaked, and even managed to smile. "Really."

Chapter 17

"Are you sure you want to risk being in jail or the hospital this close to the Thanksgiving holiday?" Mama asked me when I carried my overnight bag downstairs. "Emerald and Jon will be here next week."

I pondered for a moment, and Mama put her hands on her hips.

"Eureka May Truevine," she said in her stern tone that had once had the effect of reducing me to a quivering lump of jelly, "if I didn't know better, I would think you'd gone as crazy as Bitty. Now, we all know she's prone to getting herself into messes, but she usually manages to get out without too much damage. You weren't born under the same lucky star. You're more likely to end up in a hedgerow somewhere while Bitty goes off on a Mediterranean cruise."

Daddy came into the kitchen just in time to hear the last part of her sentence, and he said, "Anna, I thought you weren't going to tell her about our Mediterranean cruise yet."

A cold chill shot from my head down to my toes. I began to shiver. "Cruise?" I repeated somewhat numbly. "You're taking a Mediterranean cruise?"

"Honestly, Eddie," said Mama, "you made Trinket turn white as a sheet. Here, honey. Sit down for a minute."

Mama helped me into the wooden kitchen chair since my knees seemed to forget how to lock into position to keep me upright. I plopped onto the smooth seat polished by years of Truevine rear ends.

"You'll be fine," Mama assured me when I whimpered.

I wasn't as sure as she was about that.

"Cruise?" I whined. "Mediterranean? With pirates roaming the waters and Greece nearly bankrupt? Unless your crew is made up of Navy Seals, you'll end up being held hostage on some foreign shore."

"Don't be silly, Trinket," said my mother calmly. "It's probably less dangerous for us to go on a cruise to Somalia than it is for you to stay with Bitty right now."

She had a point. Somali pirates may be a pesky problem, but Bitty and I under the same roof too frequently ended in disaster. Nevertheless, I wasn't quite ready to give up.

"Just when are you planning this cruise, and why wasn't I informed?"

"You've been rather busy lately avoiding arrest and being murdered," my sweet mother replied tartly. "This must stop, Trinket. Your father and I would like to get a good night's sleep without waiting for police to ring the doorbell, or a murderer to show up and kill us all in our sleep."

I looked over at Daddy. He stared down at the wood floors and fidgeted like a ten-year-old schoolboy. I sighed.

"Okay. I understand. I won't say anything more about your cruise into infinity, and you will just smile and nod when I go stay with Bitty."

"That's nice, sugar," my duplicitous mother said with a kind smile. "Just be sure you're alive and not in jail next week when Emerald and Jon get here."

"I'll do my best."

"I know you will. Now. I'm putting together the Lane Cake today since it needs to sit a week to let the bourbon mix with all the other flavors. Is there anything else special you want for our Thanksgiving dinner?"

"Valium pie would be nice. If not that, a strong wine will suffice."

Mama just rolled her eyes, but Daddy looked concerned. "You aren't drinking too much, are you, punkin?"

"Not yet. Give me a little more time. I have to save something fun for my golden years." I stood up and picked up my overnight bag. "If anyone calls here for me, tell them I've moved to Siberia."

"Does that include Bitty?" Mama asked as I headed for the door.

"Especially Bitty," I said without turning around. "I'll be back in a few days or as soon as Bitty decides I'm safe, whichever comes first."

As the back door closed behind me, I heard Daddy say, "She used to be the smart one."

Rather glumly, I reflected on the actions that had rendered me stupid as I drove into Holly Springs. Since moving back home, I had allowed Bitty to talk me into doing things I normally would never have done. Now I'd joined the ranks of the dumb and dumber. How depressing.

"What's the matter with you?" Bitty asked after we'd poured ourselves a glass of wine and retired to her cozy little parlor. Chen Ling regarded me with an expression that I took to be annoyance with my presence. Or it could have been the outfit she wore, a pink silk robe that matched her doting caretaker's. She even had a matching nightcap.

"Chitling looks like a pink nightmare," I said, paraphrasing a line from the movie *A Christmas Story*. "A deranged Easter bunny."

Of course, Bitty picked up on it immediately. We're like that. We've watched lots of movies in our lifetimes. Bitty stuck out her tongue at me.

"I'm not Aunt Clara. And *Chen Ling* is a girl, so pink is appropriate."

"I bow to your superior fashion wisdom, Lady Gaga."

Bitty sniffed. "For heaven's sake, I just like some of Lady Gaga's shoes."

"Well, she is a couture maven, I suppose."

"And you'd know this—how?"

I said something suitably rude, and we smiled at each other. Some of my earlier tension eased. Maybe my IQ had dropped a few points lately, but no one understood me as well as Bitty. Which was a frightening thing to consider.

It was warm and cozy in the parlor, with a fire lit in the small fireplace and gray shadows creeping into the corners. "Your new slipcovers came in," I observed as I took off my shoes and propped my feet on the ottoman. "They're pretty."

"I think so, too. It took forever for them to be done, but they're worth the wait. I never can be sure if I'll like them until I see them on the furniture."

"Is this chenille?" I asked in surprise as my bare feet slid across the material. "It feels good."

"It's soft. And I thought the sage green would be restful for the winter."

"The muted pattern is very restful," I agreed. "I like a nice floral that doesn't jump out at you. And these new chenille fabrics don't pull like the older ones do."

"Now that we've danced all around the subject," Bitty said dryly, "tell me who you really think is threatening you."

I made a face. "Well, it's not Emily Sturgis. It was a man's voice."

"Breck Hartford?"

"I don't know. I'm not familiar with him or his voice. I only met him that once. I don't know if I'd even recognize the voice if I heard it again. When I do talk to Hartford again, I may be able to connect him to the voice I overheard at Proud Larry's the night of the professor's murder. Whoever it was knew that the professor was dead, I'm convinced of that."

"Do you think he was serious or just trying to frighten you?"

"If I had to risk my life on it, I'd go with serious. This isn't something I'd want to be wrong about."

"I feel the same way. I think I should hire a bodyguard for you."

Her comment took me by surprise. "A bodyguard? As in a former wrestler or NFL player?"

Bitty nodded. "I have just the one in mind."

"If you say Jerry Lawler, I'm going home."

"He's too busy. No, I was thinking about our cousin Jobert."

For a moment I thought I'd pass out. "*Jobert?* But you hate Jobert!"

"Yes, but as mean as he is, I'm sure he could keep you safe."

"No. Not just no, but H-E-double-toothpicks *NO*. He's not just mean, he's sneaky and deceitful. And when was he ever a wrestler?"

"*H-E-double-toothpicks?* Really, Trinket. You're regressing to the third grade." When I stuck my tongue out at her, she said, "See? Maybe you need something stronger than wine. I just don't know how I'm going to keep you safe if you're uncooperative."

"Great. An inebriated third grader guarded by a gigantic Neanderthal is your idea of keeping me safe. I feel so much better."

"Well," she began rather crossly, "I suppose you have a better idea?"

"Yes. We set your alarm and check all the windows, including your basement. Then we eat dinner and watch a little TV before bedtime."

"And that will keep you safe from some homicidal maniac?"

"No. It will keep me from checking into a motel for the night."

"Oh." Bitty thought about that for a moment. "Sharita left dinners in the freezer that we can heat when you're ready."

I accepted the olive branch of truce. "That sounds good. Is this a new wine?"

Bitty started talking about her extensive wine cellar and the new bottles she'd just gotten in, using words like "gusto, woodsy, piquant, bold," and I pretended to listen with interest. It's like when she talks about antiques. I'm interested up to a point, but my interest wanes after about sixty seconds, unless I'm either looking at a beautiful piece of furniture or sniffing a "full-bodied Bordeaux" before I get to sip it.

Finally, Bitty must have noticed my eyes beginning to glaze over because she said we should go ahead and check the basement now.

Snapped out of my daze, I asked, "Why?"

"It's getting dark outside, and I don't like to go down there too late. Besides, we may need another bottle of wine from the cellar."

"I hope you're not planning a night of alcoholic debauchery," I commented as I got up to follow her and the prancing pug across the hallway toward the kitchen. "If the wine in your cooler isn't enough for our night, we may need reinforcements to help."

Bitty passed up the new wine cooler installed under a granite countertop to open the door to the basement. A whoosh of chilly air washed over us as we descended the stairs. Not long ago Bitty had redecorated the basement into what I deemed a Sopranos mob-style, with black leather furniture, an electronic dart board, and a foosball table. A TV bigger than her sports car hung on one wall.

Headed toward her wine cellar in the far corner, Bitty said over her shoulder, "I saw something on cable TV that I've been thinking about doing down here. What do you think of a home theater?"

"I can honestly say I've never thought about a home theater at all. Why do you want one?"

"We can play our favorite movies, and when the boys come home for the holidays they can gather down here with their friends to watch movies."

"They do that anyway. Haven't you heard about the economic recession?"

"What does that mean?" Bitty turned and looked at me, and I was pretty sure she had forgotten her recent bout with financial depression. I sighed.

"It just seems a waste to spend so much money when you already have a big TV and place for the boys to watch it." I looked around the basement. A nice Berber carpet covered the floor, windows were locked, and the back door had two deadbolts on it, no doubt courtesy of Jackson Lee's insistence. "I hope that's unbreakable glass in the windows," I said as Bitty opened the door to the wine cellar.

"It is," she said, her voice emanating from inside the temperature controlled area lined with racks of wine. "I think it's got some kind of wire in it or something. Jackson Lee said it's smash-proof."

While Bitty toured California and France's bottled offerings, I prowled the room to be sure all was well. There was no sign of anything wrong, and I breathed a sigh of relief that Bitty had agreed so easily to turn on the house alarms. For some reason, I was a little jumpy. I don't like being threatened. Especially by someone I don't know. It's a nasty feeling.

"Here, Trinket. Take these up, will you?"

I took the two bottles of wine Bitty held out. The labels were French and Italian. I had no idea why she was restocking her upstairs wine cooler, but I also knew better than to ask. Involved explanations regarding wine usually leave me yawning. There are really expensive wines that I think smell like old shoes and Bitty claims are truly "piquant" or some other silly adjective, so I refrained from any questions. If I ever ask for a "buoyant" or an "ebullient" wine, I'll need to check into Whitfield for a long stay. Preferably a padded cell with room service.

While Bitty closed the door to the wine cellar and checked the index and temperature controls, I made a final check of the basement doors and windows. All nicely locked. We went back upstairs, and Bitty put one bottle in her kitchen wine cooler and two others in a built-in wine rack. I got our frozen dinners out and popped them into the microwave. While we waited, we uncorked a nice burgundy to go with our Chicken Marsala and talked about everything but murder. It was quite refreshing. When the microwave beeped an announcement that our food was ready, Bitty fixed us each a tray, and we went back into the parlor to watch TV while we ate.

"Good gawd," I said when Bitty chose a program, "when did you start watching shows named *Lizard Lick?*"

"When I saw these two guys get dipped in mud trying to repossess a truck," she replied serenely. "It's funny. If you don't like it, we can always watch *Criminal Minds*."

"Did your cable get cut off?"

"Of course not. Why?"

"Because if my only choice is between lizards and serial killers, I'd much rather read a book or discuss politics," I said.

"Oh for heaven's sake. I thought you liked *Criminal Minds*."

"I do. Just not when some psycho is out there waiting for me to make a mistake so he can strangle me with a coat hanger. It's a little too close to home."

Bitty rolled her eyes. "Fine. Here." She punched the remote. "We can watch people buy houses that cost as much as the national debt, if you like that better."

I smiled. "Right up your alley. Thank you."

A couple hours later we'd demolished our dinners and a bottle of wine and grown tired of watching strangers choose houses. I stifled a yawn and saw that Bitty's eyes had a kind of glazed look in them.

"I hope you're ready for bed," I said. "I've got to go to work in the morning."

"Past ready," said my amiable cousin. "I'll close the fire screen, and you get the lights."

As I reached for the lamp, I heard Bitty close the mesh fire screen over smoldering embers, and we both headed for the kitchen. Chen Ling's toenails clacked against the wood floor as she trotted behind us. I made a final check of the downstairs alarm system, but was then informed that Chitling had to go out one more time. I stared at Bitty.

"Again? She's a leaky faucet. Have you thought of toilet training her?"

Bitty ignored me as she entered the code into the back door alarm pad. It beeped at her, and she opened the door to let Chitling down the stairs, through the sunroom, and then out into the backyard for her nightly deposit. Bright moonlight illuminated the dog as she trotted across grass still green from the summer. Security lamps attached over the garage doors flashed on, and I could see her tail curling over pink satin and her pudgy little rump as she sniffed around for a place to squat.

After several minutes passed, I nudged Bitty. "Is she looking for gold or a place to pee?"

"Don't be so impatient, Trinket. She's picky about where she likes to go."

Since I was standing behind Bitty where she couldn't see me, I rolled my eyes. "I can't believe you haven't built her an inside mini-toilet yet."

"I have thought about one of those little boxes planted with grass that I've seen for sale. Maybe I could put it here in the sunroom."

"You're kidding, right?"

Bitty tilted back her head to look at me. "No, why would I kid you about that?"

"I dunno. Maybe because it's one of the silliest things you've ever said?"

"What's silly about providing an indoor toilet area for Chen Ling for the winter? It sounds sensible to me. It gets so cold outside."

"We don't live in Alaska, Bitty. It gets cold, but there aren't many snowdrifts to keep her from going out in the yard."

Rather indignantly, Bitty said, "We get ice and snow every winter, you know we do. Her little paws get cold. She could get frostbite."

"And I could get bitten by a King Cobra, but both those possibilities are pretty remote."

"Don't be so heartless. Honestly, Trinket, sometimes you're just plain ornery."

I couldn't argue with that. She's right. So I said, "I'll just go on upstairs while you wait on Princess Poo-poo to get through with her business. Remember to set the alarm as soon as she comes back inside—never mind. I'll come back and do it."

Bitty put both hands on her hips and glared at me. "I'm not a child or an idiot. I think I can manage to set the alarm without your expert assistance."

I hesitated. She was right in that she could set the alarm. The problem was that she usually forgot. This was a sticky situation. Dare I rely on Bitty to set the alarm?

Just as I opened my mouth, Chitling gave a shrill bark that startled both me and Bitty. We jumped at the same time. Bitty started out the door, calling for the dog. When I moved to follow there was a loud crash in the area of the garbage cans. My heartbeat went into triple time. I grabbed for Bitty and held on to the sash of her robe.

"No! There's someone out there. Come back inside, quick!"

Bitty jerked free of my grasp. "Not without my dog, I'm not. Chen Ling! Chen Ling! Come to mama!"

Before I could grab her again, Bitty took off across the yard. One of her slippers flew off and landed on the brick driveway. She didn't even slow down. I stood frozen in the doorway, uncertain whether to follow

Bitty or stay where I was. The pug was in the middle of the yard, still barking so shrilly I was surprised paint didn't peel off the side of the garage.

"Bitty!" I yelled after my brainless cousin as she headed straight for her yowling dog. "At least be careful!"

I wasn't sure what she was to be careful of, but there must be something that had the dog so upset. Every time she barked again, her two front paws lifted off the ground as if to give more weight to her indignation. The garbage cans rattled even louder.

Bitty reached the dog in record time, despite the loss of a slipper, and scooped her up from the grass and into her arms. Chitling struggled, still barking loudly and trying to escape her rescuer. The hair on the back of my neck tingled. I strained to see what could be disturbing the dog, but had already talked myself out of going closer to investigate. Even with the motion-sensor lights on the garage, I had no intention of putting myself in danger. Not with the warning about my possible demise still ringing in my ears.

So I held open the door for Bitty and barking pug. Whatever was in the garbage cans could stay there as far as I was concerned. I felt the same way about Bitty's slipper, but she obviously didn't since she scooped it up on her way back.

By the time she reached me, Bitty was gasping for air. Chitling was still yodeling over her shoulder in the direction of the garbage cans. Just as I pulled the door closed behind Bitty, I saw a shadowy form dart from the garbage cans and across the driveway. When it passed beneath the security lamps I recognized the portly shape of a raccoon. I didn't know whether to laugh or cuss.

I decided to do neither. I waited until we were both up the sunroom steps and in the house with the door shut and the alarm engaged before I said, "I saw the intruder."

Still breathless, Bitty flashed me a startled glance. I nodded. "Chitling needs to learn the difference between burglars and wildlife."

"What . . . are you talking . . . about?" she got out in little gasps for air.

"A raccoon. Granted, it does look like a bandit with the little mask it has, but it was rummaging in your garbage cans, apparently, and that's what scared Chitling."

"A . . . drink," Bitty said next. "I need a . . . drink."

Feeling much better now that I knew no insane killer lurked in the yard, I poured Bitty a Jack and Coke. Ice tinkled against the glass of the tumbler as she drained it in one long swallow. Chitling glared at me from the safety of Bitty's arms. Her little pink nightcap was askew on her head.

"More?" I inquired politely when Bitty held out the empty glass. She shook her head.

"No. That'll do for now."

I set the glass on the counter. "Feeling better, then?"

"No. You nearly scared me to death, Trinket! Why did you panic like that?"

"Me? Panic? It was your dog that went berserk out there, not me."

"Well, really, all this fuss over a little raccoon. I swear, I nearly peed myself out there trying to get Chen Ling before some sadistic monster grabbed her, and you just stayed in the house yelling at me."

"No point in both of us getting killed," I said mildly. "Besides, someone had to stay alive to call the police."

Bitty just looked at me, and her bug-eyed dog snorted in my direction. I gave Chitling a stern look. "That'll do, pig," I said.

Bitty's lips twitched. She recognized my quote, of course, since both of us were hopelessly addicted to even kids' movies like *Babe*.

"You should be saying that to Miranda Watson's pig, not to my precious Chen Ling," was all Bitty said, and I knew I'd been forgiven my act of pure cowardice.

"I doubt Miranda would recognize the quote. I'm tired. All this exercise has made me exhausted. Can we go to bed now?"

"Lead the way, Tonto," said my fearless cousin, and I promptly headed for the staircase before she could think of something else for us to do. Behind me, Bitty clicked off most of the lights, leaving on only the kitchen nightlight. Light gleamed through leaded glass windows into the entrance hall, reflections of the porch chandeliers shifting gently in the evening wind. A single light gleamed on the second floor landing, one of those lamps with a thick shade that provided just enough illumination to see where you were going, but not enough to see obstacles like doorstops.

When I stubbed my toe on a heavy flatiron outside one of her boys' bedroom doors, I muttered something under my breath but didn't slow down. Bitty laughed softly.

"'Night, Trinket," she said as she headed toward her room, and I went in the opposite direction to my guest room.

"Goodnight, Valerie and Scooby," I said back.

"*Rut ro*," Bitty replied with another laugh, and then I heard her bedroom door close behind her.

Once I was safely in the guest room with its half-tester bed, canopy, and full bath, I took my shower and changed into my nightgown. It was flannel and worn thin through the years, but one of my favorites. I'd also brought my big, fluffy slippers. They were a lot newer and looked as if they'd once belonged to Big Foot. I didn't care. Comfort was a major thing with me lately. I might sell lovely lingerie during the day, but at night I was a devoted slob. Unless a date with Kit was imminent, of course. Then I took advantage of my store discount and donned slinky silk. There's something indulgent and decadent about the feel of silk next to my skin. I do love my creature comforts.

Bitty's antique furniture creaks and groans at times, but the mattresses are pure twenty-first century. A nice pillow-top cushioned my aching body, and by the time I turned out the light and my head hit the feather pillows, I was asleep.

Unfortunately, my restful slumber was short-lived, and a real-life nightmare took its place.

Chapter 18

A noise woke me from my deep, sound sleep. It was a furtive bump in the night, like a mouse scurrying across the floor. Groggy, I lay there for a moment listening to the house. Old houses have their own peculiar noises, creaking of boards, the settling deep into the foundations, but those are oddly comforting sounds.

This wasn't.

Tension worked its way down my spine. My muscles began to ache from being so tight, and as quietly as possible, I sat up in the bed. Windows let in plenty of moonlight through billowy sheers. Furniture sat darkly against the walls. I blinked to clear sleep fog from my vision, but saw nothing out of place in my room.

Slowly, I lay back down in the bed and stretched out. My imagination must be to blame, I figured. It wasn't like I hadn't had enough on my mind lately. Time stretched into the night, but even though I held my breath, I didn't hear the sound again. At last I began to relax. Sleep hovered within reach, and I closed my eyes.

It seemed like I'd just barely gone back to sleep when a brittle sound jerked me awake again. Irritated, I decided to get up and see what had made the noise.

I'd barely swung my feet over the side of the bed when I heard it again. This time it sounded as if someone had dropped something. Since I knew the house alarm had been set, I figured it was probably Bitty scrounging around in the kitchen for a midnight snack. I might just smack her for scaring me. Or maybe I'd join in the feast. I didn't bother with my slippers, but crept barefoot out my bedroom door and down the hall.

When I reached the upstairs landing, I moved more cautiously. The lamp cast a limited glow, but the downstairs looked completely dark. Usually the outside lights shone through the leaded glass door and windows into the entrance hall, but now it was dark. It was a small detail that I may not have noticed at one time. But my recent experiences had sharpened my senses, so this time, I noticed.

Instead of continuing down the staircase, I retraced my steps to the upstairs hall and went to Bitty's room. I didn't knock. If she was downstairs she wouldn't hear me, and if she was asleep she wouldn't hear me.

Somehow I managed to turn the doorknob without making any noise and eased open her door to peek inside. Two lumps lay atop the high antique bed, covered by white striped damask comforters. Snores emanated from the smaller lump. I stepped inside and tip-toed to the side of the bed.

Chitling had her own mini comforter to match Bitty's. I rolled my eyes. Bitty was covered to her chin so that all that was visible was a pink eye mask and pink silk cap over her head. She looked like something out of a 1930s movie. Maybe a W.C. Fields comedy. I briefly debated on how to waken her without either one of us wetting ourselves. Scare tactics were clearly out of the question.

I hit upon the perfect method: I poked Bitty's Mini-me with my finger and let her wake Bitty.

An indignant *ruff!* made Bitty sit up immediately. Blinded by her sleep mask, she put both her hands out to feel for the dog. Chitling obliged her with a nip that was no doubt meant for me.

I quickly put my hand out of reach and whispered, "Bitty, hush."

"Wha—?" She clawed at the mask over her eyes and blinked up at me. I could see the whites of her eyes by her illuminated clock. It was 2:04 AM. "What—Precious, are you okay?"

"Precious is fine," I hissed at her. "But we may not be. I think someone's in the house."

Bitty still blinked at me. She looked pretty silly with her sleep mask under her chin. "That's impossible," she whispered. "We locked the doors and set the alarm."

"I know. But either you have really large rats or an intruder. Call nine-one-one."

"Did you see someone?"

"No, but I know I heard something downstairs." I paused, straining to hear if the noise below repeated. We were whispering, but sometimes sound travels in old houses. I picked up her bedside phone and held it out. I knew it's a land line and connected to the alarm monitoring service.

"Call it in to your service," I whispered as I waggled the phone in front of her.

Bitty took the phone, put it back on her nightstand, and reached for a small black square that dangled from a chain. She punched a button and all hell broke loose.

Sirens started going off. Lights flashed on and off, all while sirens shrilled and Chitling yodeled protests. My first reaction was to hit the floor. I prostrated myself on the Persian rug by the bed and put my arms over my head as I'd been taught to do in the first grade A-bomb drills. If the Reds had ever nuked us, I'm not sure what good a flimsy wooden desk and my arms over my head would have done to protect me from a nuclear blast, but nonetheless I automatically revert to my grade school days in times of great stress.

I was vaguely aware of Bitty getting up and looking for her slippers—one of which was under my right knee—and Chitling trying to out-scream the sirens. Lights blinked on and off. Noise bounced off walls. It took me back to my youth and the disco craze of the 70s. It wasn't a nice trip.

"I am just sick and tired of this," Bitty said loudly enough that I could hear with her bending over to get her slipper, and then she added, "I'm going to get the shotgun."

Bitty jerked her slipper from under my knee, I lifted my head to see her scoop the still howling pug into her arms, and she headed for the bedroom door. I scrambled up and attempted to stop her.

"Bitty, wait! Don't go downstairs until we know it's safe!"

She ignored me. If I hadn't been alarmed that she'd run into some hulking brute intent on stealing her silver—or a homicidal maniac looking for me—I'd have let her go. Instead, I followed behind trying to out-scream the shrilling sirens.

"Bitty! Bitty! Stop! Wait!" I yelled in vain. Sometimes I'm very slow to grasp the obvious. I finally realized that if I wanted to stop her before she got downstairs, I'd have to get a bit more proactive. So when I got close enough to her, I grabbed the back of her billowing pink nightie.

It turned out to be a robe over pink satin pajamas, and Bitty shrugged out of it on her way down the last flight of steps. I muttered something ugly under my breath, although I needn't have kept my voice low. The alarm was loud enough to wake all of the dead at Hilltop Cemetery a half mile away. Bitty continued on her quest to be armed and dangerous, so I tossed the robe on the landing railing and took the next three stairs in a single leap to catch up to my brainless cousin.

Unfortunately, I had forgotten I was no longer twenty and limber. My bare foot caught on something, and I pitched forward, the momentum of my falling body carrying me a lot farther than I wanted to go. Not only did I catch up to Bitty, I nearly obliterated her.

When I crashed into her, my weight toppled us both off the last step and onto the floor. Our combined weight carried us forward, and we slid across the entrance hall on the highly polished wood. I felt my flannel nightgown scrunch up around my waist as I tried to stop our progress. It wasn't the easiest thing to attempt. Nor was it the most graceful. I felt—and I'm sure I looked—like a spasmodic monkey in my floor-polishing trip across the entrance hall. Beneath me, Bitty made grunting, squeaking sounds that I could barely interpret over the relentless wail of sirens. She was a pink, plush, protesting pillow that cushioned my floundering body.

We came to an abrupt stop at the far edge of the entrance hall. My foot connected with something thin and hard, and I realized an instant too late that I'd somehow kicked over the small mosaic table that held a retro-style French phone. It toppled over and landed on my right leg. I said, "*Ow!*" but couldn't hear my own voice in the racket around us.

Then a rude shove rolled me completely onto the floor. Bitty sat up, Chen Ling clutched tightly to her chest. The dog's little bug eyes were probably crossed, but there was definitely no loss of movement. Or attitude. Still clad in her pink nightwear, Chitling wriggled free of her doting owner and landed indignantly on the floor. Then she took off for the kitchen area. I decided to turn off the blamed alarm before I lost what was left of my hearing. It took a couple tries before I managed to get up from the floor and stand a bit shakily on my bare feet. My big toe on my right foot throbbed. Apparently I'd stubbed it before my ride down the staircase.

After only two tries, I put in Bitty's code on the alarm system, and the sudden silence was nearly deafening. It felt palpable, as if I could reach out and touch it. Then I turned on the lights. I blinked a few times while my vision adjusted to the onslaught of illumination. So where was our intruder? Had he done the sensible thing and gotten out while the getting was good? I hoped so.

"While you're over there," said Bitty from the floor, "turn on the lights." She sounded a bit irritable. I couldn't blame her. Or could I? If she hadn't taken off down the steps neither one of us would have ended up polishing the floor.

"They're already on, as if you didn't know," I replied in what was decidedly a peeved tone of voice. I felt she deserved that much. "Call the alarm company to tell them there's been a mistake. I'm sure it's too late now, but—"

"Trinket?" She sounded a bit shaky, and I looked up from rubbing my bruised big toe just in time to hear her shriek, "I can't see! I'm blind! Trinket, I'm blind!"

I shook my head in disgust. "No, you're not. Your silly little nightcap is over your eyes. Take it off, and you'll be just fine."

"Oh. Well, I called myself taking it off." Bitty dropped the mask she held in one hand, fumbled with her nightcap, and got it pushed back on her head. "Ah. Much better. Now I can see."

"Glory be, a miracle! At last Bitty can see."

"Are you being sarcastic?"

"Why on earth would you think that?" I limped toward my cousin still sitting in the floor like a pink satin frog. "Since no one has tried to kill us yet, or has appeared with the family silver in a pillowcase, we'll just wait for the police to check things out."

Bitty looked startled. "Police?"

I stared at her. "Don't you hear the sirens? They'll be here in three-point-two seconds by the sound of them."

"Well, they can look for the intruder, but whoever it was probably took off when the alarm went off. If he did, it's up to you to come up with a good explanation of why we punched the panic button."

"Good thing I happen to have one handy—truth will just have to do. Maybe we just gave in to panic."

"Don't tell them *that*. You'll make it sound as if we're just two hysterical women again. I'm getting tired of them looking at me like I'm crazy."

I looked down at my cousin. She still wore her pink nightcap. It tilted over one ear in a warped, drunken fashion and looked as if a blob of Pepto-Bismol had been plopped atop her head. Her blonde hair stuck out in erratic spikes. She blinked up at me. I smiled. "Bless your heart."

Bitty's eyes narrowed. She recognizes an insult when she hears it. Before she could share what would undoubtedly be an offensive retort, there was a banging on her front door.

"Police! Open up!" came the shouts, accompanied by more fist banging.

"They're playing our song," I said as I walked to the front door, belatedly aware of my rumpled state and ratty old nightgown. I smoothed down the flannel as best as I could and opened the door. "There's been a mistake," I began to say, but quickly found myself pushed back by several uniformed officers of the law.

They shot so many questions at me simultaneously that I reeled backward. One of them grabbed me by the arm to steady me. "Is this a medical emergency?"

"Where's the intruder?"

"Do you need an ambulance?"

"How many people are in the house?"

"*Is* there an intruder?"

I didn't know how to answer without looking stupid. Or more stupid. I shook my head. "I don't know. We haven't seen anyone since we came downstairs. But I know I heard someone."

Two uniformed officers hustled Bitty and me out onto the front porch while they looked for our dangerous robber/killer/invisible man. I didn't know how else to classify it at that point. My nerves were shot. Being threatened isn't fun, but I had to face the fact that it was becoming a regular occurrence in my life.

So we stood out on the front porch in our nighties, shivering while police did a thorough search of the house. Lights atop police cruisers strobed the night, and no doubt revealed far more than either Bitty or I needed to show. We finally sat down in wicker chairs still on the porch. One of the officers had brought Bitty her pug, and Chitling sat grumpily in Bitty's lap. I looked at my cousin.

"We need to stop doing this."

"It's not my fault we're sitting out here freezing to death," said Bitty, sounding every bit as grumpy as her dog looked. "I'm probably getting frostbite."

"I doubt that. It's fifty degrees out here."

"But cold enough to do skin damage," Bitty persisted. "It's so damp."

"I'll give you damp and cold, but forget frostbite. Not even if you were stark naked could you get by with that claim."

Just as Bitty opened her mouth to reply, the front door opened, and one of the policemen said, "Mrs. Hollandale, can you tell me if the window in the laundry room was already out?"

"Already out?" Bitty repeated with a blank look. "I don't know what you mean."

"The window glass has been removed." He said it slowly as if talking to someone with senile dementia. "Did you remove the glass, or have it removed?"

"Why . . . no. I didn't." Clutching the dog to her chest, Bitty stood up. "So now the glass is broken?"

"No ma'am, it's not broken. It's been cut out."

"Cut out? Wait. I want to see."

"We're processing the area right now. There's a ladder up against the outside of the house, so we're dusting it for prints, too."

Bitty began to pace. I sat in the wicker chair pondering the situation. Okay, so I'd been right, and someone had broken into the house. Not a random intruder, since the glass was cut out and not broken. That meant someone wanted in and knew Bitty had a security system that may actually be in use. Which also meant, that whoever wanted in had a very good idea of what they wanted and was willing to risk arrest to get it. Or get rid of it? The last thought made me shiver.

Apparently Bitty saw that because she said, "I told you it's cold out here."

"I'm not shivering because of the cold." I stood up and leaned close to Bitty. "If someone broke in tonight, it's for a specific reason. I think the same person who killed Catherine thinks I have or I know information that can incriminate them."

Bitty's eyes widened. "But—do you?"

I thought for a long moment. It was becoming obvious to me that Catherine had left behind information she thought I was smart enough to figure out. Unfortunately, she had made a grave error in judgment. I had no idea what she left behind, and even if I did find it, she'd probably disguised it so that I doubted I'd be able to correctly interpret it.

All I could think to say was, "If she left something for me, I haven't found it."

Nodding, Bitty said, "Well, we'll find it, sugar."

"I hope when you say 'we' you're talking about you and Chitling, because I have no intention of getting any more involved than I already am," I said firmly. "This is it for me. Some madman or crazed killer is trying to kill me, and I don't even know anything. I can't imagine what would happen if I did."

"Don't be silly, Trinket. Once we find out who it is, you can tell the police, and then they'll arrest the murderer and it will all be over."

I looked at her. "Do you really believe that?"

She blinked at me a few times. "Don't you?"

"No. Well, not necessarily. Sometimes the police show up a little late. I hate being bruised. Especially when someone is trying to kill me."

"Well," said Bitty a bit crossly, "this would be a lot easier if we just knew what it was Catherine wanted to tell you."

"Yes," I agreed. "It would definitely be a lot easier. I wish she'd had time to tell me what kind of information she had, or where to find it."

"It's just like Cat to get herself murdered before she told you who she thinks killed her son."

"Oh, she already told me that. Breck Hartford."

"But you don't believe her."

"Well, it's not that I don't believe her, it's just that I don't know why he would kill her son and make it look like suicide. It doesn't make any sense. Then Sturgis—and it was all supposed to be over an accidental death?" I shook my head. "It's too crazy sounding to be real."

"If Emily killed Sturgis, it's possible she had a reason to kill Monty."

"I don't think Emily killed her husband."

"Well for heaven's sake, why not?" Bitty sounded exasperated. "Maybe she was having an affair with Monty, and Spencer found out about it, so she killed him."

"Killed Monty, or killed Spencer?"

Bitty started to wave her hands in the air in agitation, but Chitling began to bark, and the police gave us strange glances, so she stopped and whispered, "Both of them, for all we know. Just think about it, Trinket.

What other reason would there be to kill them both? Maybe the professor killed Monty, so she killed him . . . you know, a revenge motive."

I rolled my eyes. "Somehow I can't see Emily Sturgis with Monty Moore. He was a kid. What, twenty or twenty-one? She doesn't seem the type."

Bitty blew out a sigh. "That's true. It seems more like Cat's style than Emily's. I give up then. I guess we won't ever know what it was Cat meant to tell you."

"Looks like," I agreed. "Ah, here comes your knight in shining armor now. I was wondering what was keeping him."

A silver Jaguar swept into the driveway behind a police cruiser and stopped on a dime. Jackson Lee stepped out, once more half in pajamas, half in sweats, come to his fair damsel's rescue. Bitty patted her hair, shifted Chen Ling to her other arm, and put on a big ole smile to greet her frantic beau.

"This is getting to be old," said Jackson Lee when he reached the porch, and his worried gaze went straight to Bitty. His dark hair flecked with gray, normally combed in a neat style, stuck up all over his head. When he raked his hand through it, the reason for that was pretty obvious. "Sugar, I can't stand you being in danger all the time. You go get some clothes. You're going to come stay with me for a little while. At least until all this is over. I insist on it, Bitty. Go upstairs and get packed."

I couldn't help it. I lifted an eyebrow and looked over at Bitty. The smile was still on her face, but I could see that he'd surprised her. This should be interesting. Bitty is always open to cajolery, pleading, especially to bribes, but a demand? I wasn't at all sure how she'd take that, even from Jackson Lee.

"Why, Jackson Lee," she drawled after a moment, "Trinket and I are just fine right here. It's sweet of you to worry, but I don't think we need to be going anywhere."

I looked back at Jackson Lee. He seemed to realize his error, and being the practiced lawyer that he is, he immediately switched tactics. "Of course, sugar plum, you can stay here if you feel safe, but I'm just so worried about you."

I tilted my attention back to Bitty. She wore the same sweet smile. "Honey, you don't need to worry about me. I've got Trinket and Chen Ling for protection."

Wait a minute—isn't it me who needs protecting? I thought but didn't say aloud. I looked back at Jackson Lee to see his next move. He didn't disappoint.

"And nice protection they are, sweet-ums, but I can hardly let you out of my sight when I know you're just fine, so you'll just have to humor me when I worry about you with some homicidal idiot running around and breaking in to your house." He paused to take a breath, then added, "Why, I'd just go crazy if even one hair on your head was harmed, you know I would."

Some of Bitty's tension eased, and she reached up to pat him on his cheek. If he hadn't already been hovering over her like a cloud, she would have had to move closer. He put his hand over hers and smiled so happily I felt like a third thumb and fifth wheel. Good thing we weren't alone, or he might have just swept her up in his arms and stormed up the inside staircase à la Rhett Butler and Scarlett O'Hara.

As it was, I could see him struggle to find something ordinary to say to break the awkward moment. Finally he took a step back, dropped his hand, and seemed to recall he and Bitty weren't alone on some mountaintop. His gaze flicked to me, and he gave a start, then recovered.

"Oh, er, Trinket . . . I have something of yours in the car. I ran into one of the Potts Camp officers in court today, and he said there was something of yours in the evidence room."

"Something of mine? Potts Camp?" I couldn't make a connection for a minute. "I don't know why he'd have something of mine."

"It's in a plastic case, and it has your name on it. A DVD of some kind. A movie you must have loaned Catherine Moore."

"A movie?" I was mystified.

"Yes, they had to check it out, you know, just to be sure it was what it said on the cover, but it's just a movie. He thought you might want it back."

I had no idea what he was talking about, but maybe I'd remember once I saw it. Although I was sure I hadn't loaned Catherine any movies, maybe there was a reason she thought it belonged to me.

But even after Jackson Lee went to his car and came back with the movie, I had no clue why Catherine had thought it might belong to me. I'd never heard of it.

"*Dead at Seventeen*," I read the title aloud, hoping a memory would pop up to provide me with a clue. Nope. Not a thing, even after I said it a few times and ran it past Bitty, who was once more holding court in the parlor since the police had finished and left at last. It had to be three in the morning, and I sat there on Bitty's overstuffed chair staring at the movie, the actors' names, and the cover as if it would provide an answer.

"Have you ever seen this?" I asked Bitty. Jackson Lee sat beside her in the huge chair, much to Chen Ling's dissatisfaction. The dog eyed him warily. He ignored her.

"It's not yours?" Jackson Lee asked, although I could tell he was less than interested in my reply or my puzzlement.

"No. I never heard of it."

"Well, since it's obvious we're not going to get any more sleep tonight, put it in the player," said Bitty. She stifled a yawn. "Maybe you'll remember it after you see some of it."

"I'm quite sure Catherine and I never even discussed movies, much less swapped a couple," I muttered even though no one was listening. Jackson Lee was cuddled up next to Bitty and completely oblivious to anything or anyone else. Bitty was accepting his adoration as her just due, and Chen Ling seemed in danger of falling asleep at last. Her bug eyes were at half-mast.

It took me a few minutes to figure out how to work Bitty's state-of-the-art DVD system, only to learn that it was a Blu-Ray and incompatible with the HD movie in my hand. So I ended up going up to my guest bedroom and popping the movie into the DVD player set inside an antique armoire. I crawled up onto the high bed, crossed my legs, and hit the Play button on the remote.

Forty-eight minutes into the movie, I knew why Catherine Moore had put my name on the plastic case. And I knew what had happened to Monty, and who had most likely killed Spencer Sturgis as well as Catherine . . .

Chapter 19

"What are your plans?" Bitty asked me for what must have been the sixth time since we'd left her house. "I thought you weren't going to get involved in investigating the murders anymore. And why couldn't we use my car?"

"Because we don't want to advertise our arrival," I replied without looking at her. "It's right here, Rayna. Park just beyond that driveway."

It had been two days since I'd watched the video Catherine left for me. We were now on a mission. Since our mission involved secrecy, I had involved Rayna and her car. Actually, I'd had quite a discussion with her about us getting as involved as we were, and so we'd come up with a plan. Our plan branched out to include Bitty and Gaynelle, Bitty only because she threw a fit when she found out where we were going.

Gaynelle sat in the front passenger seat, while Bitty and I occupied the back of the SUV. Even though it had been decided there was a lot more safety in numbers, I resisted endangering others until Rayna pointed out it'd be best to have more witnesses.

Gaynelle looked over at Rayna. "What'd Rob have to say about you doing this?"

"Oh, nothing." There was a moment of disbelieving silence before she added, "I didn't tell him."

"A wise decision." Gaynelle nodded approval. "Now you'll only have to listen to him once instead of twice."

"True."

We all knew there was no doubt Rob Rainey would be livid when he learned about our jaunt down to Oxford. But we also knew there are times it's easier to ask for forgiveness than permission. Not that Rayna would have asked permission, but she would have normally at least informed him of her intention.

I leaned forward to say, "If it works out like we hope, Rob may not be able to say anything but, 'Good job.'"

"Oh, Trinket," said Bitty, "when have our investigations ever worked out like we hope? It always gets screwed up somehow."

"Don't jinx us, Bitty," begged Rayna, while Gaynelle just laughed. I managed a weak smile and indignant glance at my cousin, who was still pouting because we had left behind her furry mutant accessory. I cleared my throat meaningfully.

"That's okay. By the end of the day, we should know what happened and who all was involved. But right now, my main idea is to confront Breck Hartford."

Bitty looked out the window then back at me. "I hate to tell you this, Sherlock, but if you want to talk to Breck Hartford, you're at the wrong house."

"Yes, I know that, Bitty. He's not the only suspect, you know."

She brightened. "Really? You're finally agreeing with me that Emily killed him?"

"No. I'm here on a fishing expedition."

I left Bitty to mull that over and turned to Rayna. "We have a pretty good idea of what happened, and the info you got helped out a lot. Now that we're here, maybe we can figure out what's missing and fill in the blanks."

Rayna nodded. "The ball is in your court."

Bitty sniffed audibly. "That's a silly cliché. Having a ball in your court just means you have to bat it somewhere else."

"Exactly." I smiled. "So, let the game begin."

"Just how many players are allowed in this game?" asked Bitty. "If you know things I don't, you need to share. What info did Rayna get that I don't know?"

"It's better you don't know. Not yet. I need it confirmed or disproven. You have a way of blurting out things best left unsaid. Ladies? Shall we begin?"

With Bitty grumbling a bit, and Rayna and Gaynelle as back-up, I got out of the car and headed for the Sturgis front door. A brisk wind blew dead leaves across the flagstones of the walkway. With only a little trepidation, I rang the bell.

"She's probably out celebrating her freedom," Bitty remarked rather cattily when no one came to the door after my second push on the bell. "I would be."

"There's a wide gulf between being a divorcee and a widow," said Gaynelle. "I think it might be difficult to celebrate the passing of a husband, so we should be cautious about stepping on her toes."

Bitty rolled her eyes. "It won't be so difficult if Emily's the one who helped him on his way, you know, Gaynelle. I still say she's the one who—"

"Hush," I hissed at Bitty. "I think I hear her footsteps."

Just as Bitty opened her mouth to say something probably bitchy, the front door swung open. I managed to say, "Hi, Emily, I don't know if you remember me, but I'm sure you remember Bitty and Gaynelle? And this is our friend Rayna Blue."

To say that Emily Sturgis was less than pleased to see us was an understatement. I flashed my best *"Don't want to bother you, but"* smile, and she still didn't move from the open doorway to invite us in.

"I'm leaving for the airport in a few minutes," she said coolly. "Spencer's body is finally being shipped home for burial."

"Yes, and I'm sorry to intrude on you at this awkward moment, but I think you can help me a great deal if you'll spare me just five minutes. It concerns your husband's untimely death."

Emily stared at me. It had seemed so much more sensible in the planning stages to arrive on her doorstep unannounced to interrogate her, but right now it only seemed rude. Finally she gave a curt nod and stepped back to allow us inside.

The living area was gloomy, shutters closed, furniture covered with sheets, and no sign of life at all. No plants, no photographs, nothing but a stillness that reflected a sense of loss. Despite Bitty's insistence that Emily had a hand in her husband's death, I didn't agree. Maybe she was involved in a cover-up, but not the actual murder.

So once we stood in an awkward half-circle, with no invitation to sit or have tea forthcoming, I started with that premise in mind.

"I know what happened between you and Breck Hartford," I said bluntly, and she didn't turn a hair. She just lifted one eyebrow and seemed faintly amused, so I followed that with, "Is that the reason you haven't turned him in for murder yet?"

My last question didn't exactly bring the response I had hoped it would. Emily actually laughed.

"You must really think me foolish to believe I'd fall for this silliness. Did he send you here?"

"Why would Breck send us here?" I countered.

"Why not? He loves to play games, not me. And really, if this is what you came to discuss, I have no time at all for it. I'm about to bury my husband."

"At least tell me what Montgomery Moore told Professor Sturgis before he died. I know he had to tell him something, because from what I've heard, your husband intended to use this information to ruin Breck Hartford."

That last was a shot in the dark, but apparently I'm a pretty good marksman on the rare occasion. Emily bit her lower lip and looked down at her feet for a moment.

"He did tell you what Monty said, didn't he?" I prompted as gently as possible. "And maybe that was part of the reason he was killed, too?"

Emily sucked in a deep, shuddering breath. Bitty made some kind of

7

furtive sound so I nudged her before she became too vocal.

It was so quiet I could almost hear the house settling into the rich Mississippi dirt. A brisk November wind clacked elm branches together outside and soughed around the fieldstone walls.

Finally Emily looked up, and I saw a faint sheen in her eyes. "It's my fault. All of it."

"*Aha!*" said Bitty at my side, and I grabbed her arm in a death grip to keep her quiet before she ruined a possible confession.

"I've known Breck since we met in Colorado one Christmas while I was still in high school," Emily said as if Bitty hadn't had a Charlie Chan moment. "We dated long-distance for a short time. Then we changed colleges, and by the time we met up again, he was married to Victoria, and I was married to Spencer. It was crazy, but the spark was still there. I know it was wrong, but I couldn't seem to stop, and Breck . . . well, he didn't stop either. Then Breck helped Spencer when he got into trouble at Harvard, and it seemed inevitable that we'd end up down here eventually. I wanted to, yet I didn't want to. I knew what would happen again. Breck and I . . . Poor Spence. He didn't suspect for a long time. Not until Victoria told him, anyway."

The last was said with definite bitterness.

"What did Spencer do then?" I asked as gently as possible.

Emily crossed her arms over her chest as if chilled and looked past us to the closed-in windows. "He went crazy," she said softly. "Ranting and raving . . . I thought he'd want an immediate divorce. But he didn't."

"He just wanted to punish you," said Bitty.

Emily looked back at Bitty. "Yes. Basically. I should have left him then. I don't know why I didn't. Probably because it was my fault. I never meant to hurt Spence. And I never meant to keep on seeing Breck, not after . . . everything."

"Did you know about Spencer's forged credentials?" I asked, and she nodded.

"Yes. Oh yes. Spence threw it in my face that my lover had arranged for him to be a professor here just so he could see me again. That he'd done all that so we could sneak around and see each other behind his back."

"Did he? Did Breck do all that to get you close again?"

She shrugged, a slight lift of her shoulders. "Perhaps. Oh, probably. I don't know. You'd really have to ask Breck that question. He has all the answers anyway."

"But you know why Monty Moore was killed."

"Do I?"

"Yes. You do. He saw something he wasn't supposed to see, and he was killed for it, just like your husband was killed because he knew too much."

Shaking her head, Emily said, "No, Spence wouldn't tell me exactly what Monty said to him, only that Monty had been part of a crime and couldn't stand the pressure of knowing what had been done."

"But you had your suspicions," I said.

"Yes. I had my suspicions. There was a girl . . ."

There it was. Confirmation that I was right, that Catherine had indeed given me the information I needed to solve the murders. But the information was useless without proof. Evidence. Or a confession.

"And?" Bitty prompted when Emily paused. "What girl?"

"Trisha Atwood. She was a student here. Monty knew her. She died. An accident of some kind. Or supposed to be an accident."

"But it wasn't an accident, was it," I said more than asked, and Emily nodded.

"Spence never came out and said it, but I knew that's what it was. And Breck . . . he was involved somehow."

"I'm sure he was," Bitty muttered before I could elbow her into silence. "Up to his adulterous little eyeballs. A lot of that going around, apparently."

I tried to step on her foot, but she was too quick for me and shuffled sideways.

Emily gazed at Bitty for a moment, then said curtly, "It's not like Spencer was a faithful husband. He wasn't."

"I know," said Bitty, and when Emily lifted a brow she added, "The professor and Victoria in the library."

I thought but didn't say, *"With a candlestick."* Sometimes I can't help what pops into my head. Old board games of *Clue* aside, it was obvious Emily Sturgis knew more than she'd told the police. At this point, she probably knew more than I did. I was still on my fishing expedition.

"So it's true about Spencer and Victoria?" I asked. "They were having an affair?"

"More like a fling. It didn't last long." Emily shook her head. "It wasn't a big deal at all. He made sure I knew about it, of course."

"Of course," said Bitty, nodding her head wisely. "Otherwise it wouldn't have been revenge."

A faint smile curved Emily's mouth. "I suppose that was it."

"Oh, that was it," Bitty assured her. "It usually is. Not that I would know about it firsthand, but my late husband the senator used to always say revenge was sweetest when it was with an opponent's wife. And he would have known, believe me."

Before Bitty could quote any more wisdom from her dead ex-husband, I said quickly, "How was Breck involved with the dead girl?"

Emily gave me a wary look. "You'll have to ask him about that. Now

I must ask you ladies to please leave since I can't miss my flight."

And with that, we were quickly ushered out of her front room and onto the front stoop. The door closed behind us with a click of finality, and I still didn't have all the answers I needed. I looked at Rayna, and she nodded as she pulled off her sunglasses.

"Okay," I said, "on to the next victim."

Rayna saluted me. "Off we go."

"I wish you'd tell me what we're doing," grumbled Bitty as we walked toward Rayna's SUV. "I would have brought my calling cards if I'd known we were going to visit half of Oxford."

"How quaint," Gaynelle remarked with a smile. "My grandmother used to have the prettiest calling cards with her name in a lovely cursive script. I think I still have some tucked away in a box. That was a much more genteel time period."

"Genteel, maybe," said Rayna, "but not nearly as enlightened in most ways."

"True," Bitty said. "Before we go on about missing the good ole days, we need to remember that it wasn't that long ago that women didn't have the vote, and there were no such things as microwave ovens."

"Equally important, I'm sure," Rayna remarked with a laugh.

"You bet," said my cousin with a firm nod of her empty little head. "Try cooking a lasagna in ten minutes without one."

"She means reheating," I explained to Gaynelle, who also knew better. "If Bitty cooks, the fire department shows up."

Rather irritated, Bitty said, "I declare, burn down a house just one time, and you never hear the end of it."

A beep sounded as Rayna hit the remote to her car, and we all piled into it as before, Gaynelle in the front passenger seat, and Bitty and I in the back. When Rayna slid into the driver's seat and started the vehicle, Bitty turned to fix me with a steady eye.

"Do you know what you're doing here? Because if you don't, pulling the tiger's tail could get us all into a lot of trouble."

"I assume you mean Breck Hartford?"

Bitty nodded. "That's the tiger I mean, yes. I've told you how competitive he was in college, and I see no sign of him having mellowed. If anything, he may have perfected the art."

"Of winning?"

"No, of stomping out the competition. He doesn't like to just win. He likes to obliterate his opponents."

"Interesting. Very interesting."

"Don't forget dangerous—very dangerous."

"Really, Bitty," said Rayna from the front seat as we pulled away from the curb, "you make it sound like Hartford has been running around killing people for years."

"Maybe he has. I think he's certainly capable of it if he thought the professor was important enough to kill."

That made me rethink: Who would benefit most from Spencer's death? The easy answer was his wife, Emily. But if events had happened as I believed Catherine tried to show me, it was indeed Breck Hartford who benefitted most. If he'd killed Trisha Atwood and Sturgis found out, then Breck could have silenced him. I just had to make that all-important connection between the dead student and Hartford.

Gaynelle turned in the passenger seat to look back at me. "So what do we do next, Trinket?"

I sucked in a deep breath. "We get a confession from Breck Hartford."

"Then you're convinced that he killed Spencer?"

"I think he was involved in the death of Trisha Atwood. I also think he enlisted the help of his son and Montgomery Moore to help him make it look like an accident. When Monty had an attack of conscience and wanted to go to the police, Hartford must have killed him as well. If Professor Sturgis found out somehow, he had to kill him, too."

"Good gawd," said Bitty in a shocked tone. "He's a serial killer."

"Not so much a serial killer as a murderer who has to keep silencing those who can betray him."

Bitty flicked her fingers at me. "Same thing. Multiple murders by one person. So he must have killed Catherine, too."

"Probably. She certainly thought him capable of it. The last time I talked to her I heard the terror in her voice." My throat tightened at the memory. "No one would believe her, and she died for trying to tell people the truth. I didn't even believe her . . ."

"Now, Trinket, it wasn't your fault. I've already told you that," said Gaynelle briskly. "And you're certainly doing what you can now to find her killer. I'm sure Catherine would be the first to tell you that."

I smiled. "Thank you for saying that, Gaynelle."

Bitty huffed. "Well, I tell you that all the time, and you never thank *me*."

"You're family. I know you're always on my side."

Somewhat mollified, Bitty nodded. "That's true, sugar. I am."

"Okay," Rayna said as she wheeled the big SUV around a corner, "we're turning onto Jackson. Where do I go from here?"

"Jackson Avenue West toward the university," I said, scrambling in my purse for the map. Since I wasn't that familiar with Oxford, I'd downloaded and printed out a map on Bitty's computer. "It's past Country Club Drive, Parkview . . . off Troon Road, near a lake. Let me turn it this way . . . St. Andrews Drive, St. Andrews Circle . . . oh good lord."

"What is it?" asked Rayna.

"You can't get there from here."

"Nonsense," said pragmatic Gaynelle. "Give me the map."

Rather grateful to be relieved of navigation duties, I gladly handed it over. It took Gaynelle a lot shorter time than it would have me to guide us from Jackson Avenue to Troon Road. The houses were very large and fairly new in an established neighborhood. One of Oxford's nicest areas, I would imagine. Definitely a house suitable for an assistant coach at the university and his family.

"So what are you going to say?" Gaynelle asked me when we parked at the curb of a two-story house with a small front lawn boasting a fountain and half-circle driveway.

I had to confess, "I don't have a detailed list of questions. Just a few main ones I hope will catch him off-guard."

"That should be enough," said Rayna. "With what we know, all we have to do is get him to incriminate himself."

"What do we know?" asked Bitty.

"I think you should be careful about how you pose the questions," Gaynelle said. "If you spook him too badly, he's liable to destroy any evidence he may have."

"What do we know?" asked Bitty.

"True," I said in response to Gaynelle's comment. "I hope when we confront him, he might be taken back enough to realize it's useless to deny his guilt."

"What do we know?" asked Bitty.

"I'm amazed Hartford's still in town," said Rayna. "He should be somewhere in the Azores or a remote island in the North Atlantic, with the paper trail he left behind. It was almost too easy to find. He's either extremely arrogant or convinced of immunity."

I nodded. "I can't figure out why the police don't act on just what *we* know."

"What do *we* know?" asked Bitty.

"Because they're hindered by things like 'probable cause' and proof," Rayna answered me. "We're not."

Just as I opened my mouth to point out that we were hindered by things like being assaulted or arrested for trespassing, Bitty let out a grinding shriek that scared the liver out of me. I jumped, my purse fell onto the floor, and the contents spilled over the new floor mats.

"What on earth is the matter with you?" I demanded of my cousin as soon as I recovered a little from my fright. "You nearly scared me to death!"

"You've been ignoring me. I hate being ignored. I want to know what we're supposed to know that all of you seem to know, but I don't."

I eyed her for a moment. Her blue eyes were bright, and her face was red, probably because she'd broken a blood vessel or two with her shriek. Her expression was plainly irate. "It wasn't so much that I was ignoring you," I finally said. "It was that I hoped you wouldn't keep asking."

"Why?"

"Because you somehow manage to tell everything you know at the wrong time. It's best if you don't know some things."

Bitty lifted a brow and gave me a look that told me she wasn't happy with my reply. Then she smiled. "Really. I know a lot of things I haven't told to anyone. Like the time you forgot to wear panties to school, and all the boys kept asking you to pick up their pencil off the floor for them. I had to tell you why at recess that day. Then there was the time—"

"Maybe it's okay if you know a few things," I said hastily before she got any farther down Memory Lane. "Rayna did some investigating, did her magic on computer, asked a few judicious questions of her informant in the police department, and found out quite a bit about Breck Hartford's recent activities."

"Goody. That sounds like something useful. So what did we find out?" She'd stressed the *we*, so I knew better than to hold back too much.

"Breck Hartford has been a busy little bee," I began, "so Rayna managed to ferret out useful info using his credit card trail. Once I heard what she discovered, I knew I was on the right track. It all started with the movie Catherine left for me."

"That Seventeen movie?" Bitty asked on a note of disbelief.

I nodded. "Yep. I'd never seen it or heard of it until Jackson Lee gave it to me, but once I watched it, I knew what she was trying to tell me."

"And what was that?"

"For one thing, she was probably right about her son being killed rather than him having committed suicide."

Bitty blinked at me. "A movie told you that?"

"First I'll tell you what I think happened, then Rayna can tell you what we know as fact. But pay attention, Bitty, because if you say the wrong thing to Hartford, it could be a disaster."

"The *Titanic* was a disaster. This would be unpleasant."

I rolled my eyes. "Whatever. So here are my theories, but I've been up late for two nights going over all this, so don't expect me to be brilliant."

"Oh, I never do, honey," my sweet cousin demurred with a smile, and I knew she hadn't quite forgiven me yet for keeping things from her. So be it.

I quickly summarized the movie's plot about three boys who accidentally killed a teenage girl at a party and the cover-up that followed. One of the boys had an attack of conscience and said he was going to confess to the police. So he was murdered, and it was made to look like a suicide. Only the dead boy's mother refused to believe he took his own life. Just like Catherine had refused to believe Monty committed suicide.

"I kept racking my brain," I finished, "trying to figure out what clues she might have left me, when Jackson Lee gave me that DVD with my name written across it. It had been in Catherine's cabin when she was murdered. Whoever killed her didn't bother to take it or didn't make the connection."

"Police found a folder of papers burned in the fireplace," added Rayna. "There wasn't enough left to reconstruct the contents, but they were probably her notes on what she'd learned about Hartford, his son Bret and Trisha. Catherine had bought her own software to track public records and even private records on Sturgis and Breck, so she probably already knew what I just recently learned."

"So why haven't the police discovered this?" Bitty asked dubiously. "You'd think they could do the same thing you and Cat have done, only a lot sooner."

Rayna nodded. "I'm sure they can and probably have, but since the police are constrained by law to gather enough evidence for an arrest warrant, there has to be credible proof of a crime. Trisha's death was ruled an accident. Then Monty Moore's death was ruled a suicide. Again, no reason to continue an investigation. If we're right, Breck Hartford got off cleanly with both those deaths and would have no reason to kill anyone else. So Professor Sturgis had to have some kind of proof of Hartford's actions and intended to betray him somehow."

"What on earth could he have or know that would implicate Hartford?" Bitty mused. "I can't see Monty Moore confessing to Spencer Sturgis. He wasn't exactly a student favorite. And that isn't *proof*, anyway. It's hearsay."

When she looked at me, I nodded. "True. Emily admitted that Breck forged the credentials to get Spencer into Ole Miss." I paused. "Yet that would hurt Hartford as well as Sturgis. So, I think it *must* have to do with Trisha Atwood."

"You mean the professor knew that Breck had killed them both and told him that he intended to go to the police?" Bitty's brow furrowed. "Wouldn't he have known that was dangerous?"

"He should have, yes."

"Maybe," Gaynelle said, "Spencer was willing to risk it to see Breck behind bars. He could have rationalized that if he informed on him, Hartford wouldn't dare be rash enough to try to harm him. Or maybe he didn't tell Breck Hartford what he knew, but Breck found out somehow that the professor intended to go to the police."

"All are possibilities." I glanced out the window up the street to the house where Hartford and his family lived. A second-floor balcony overlooked the front yard, and behind it huge trees led down to a lake in the distance. It reeked of success. "There's another theory, of course. Breck Hartford could have been protecting his son, like the parents in the movie protected their guilty son. Otherwise, I can't understand why Hartford would risk his career, much less his freedom, by such reckless actions. Murder is the ultimate act of idiocy."

Rayna answered, "Impulse control. Men like Hartford who are used to having their every whim met don't react well to being told no. Maybe Trisha Atwood refused him, and he killed her. To give him the benefit of the doubt, it could have been accidental. Still . . . murder or manslaughter, a man like Breck Hartford would hardly allow himself or his son to be taken to jail if he could help it."

"Which brings me to my next theory," I said to Bitty. "Monty Moore either found out what had happened to Trisha, or he was there, as in the movie. So to stop him going to the police, Monty was murdered and his death made to look like a suicide."

"That's sad," said Bitty. "If it's true, then Catherine really was right all that time."

I nodded. "I know."

Bitty sighed. "Now I feel bad about not believing her."

"So do I. The best thing we can do for her now is see that her son's killer faces the law for his actions."

"Or her actions," Bitty said. "I still say Emily did it. It's always the wife."

I rolled my eyes again. "You are the most stubborn woman I have ever known."

Bitty looked pleased. "Aren't I? I'm usually right, too."

"Not this time, Bitty," said Rayna. "Emily simply cannot have done it. She has an iron-clad alibi for the time of her husband's death, and there was absolutely no reason for her to have killed either Trisha Atwood or Monty Moore. And Catherine would never have let Emily within six feet of her if she suspected her capable of doing harm."

"Maybe Emily was trying to protect Breck. It happens." Bitty shrugged. "If she and her lover were covering up his crimes, they could have managed it together."

"All this conjecture," said Gaynelle, "gets us nowhere. We have to go by facts, not what could be, or may have, happened."

It was a timely reminder. I nodded. "Okay, then let's go and see what kind of facts we can get out of Mr. Hartford."

I felt much braver with back-up. Granted, we weren't the Avengers team, but we could be pretty formidable if we chose. In retrospect, presenting a united front probably wasn't the best way to go about it. However, at the moment it seemed like the right thing to do, and we walked two-abreast up the red brick sidewalk to the generous front porch. I rang the bell. It made a gonging sound that reminded me of old horror movies.

When I heard the telltale noise of a bolt being unlatched, I braced myself to face Breck Hartford or a member of his family. It was a bit deflating to see a uniformed maid peer at us inquiringly.

"Is Mr. Hartford at home?" I asked. "We'd like to speak with him."

Shaking her head, the middle-aged woman said, "No, he's out. Mrs. Hartford is home if you would like to speak to her. May I ask who you represent?"

Apparently she thought we were salespeople. I scrambled mentally for a plausible answer, but it was Gaynelle who lied, "The Holly Springs Garden Club. Each April the club hosts an annual Pilgrimage. You may have heard about it?"

"Oh yes, I know about that. Please wait here while I see if Mrs. Hartford is able to meet with you."

We stepped into the entrance hall as she held the door a little wider, and I looked around the house, or what I could see of it from our position. A lovely staircase curved up in a gentle half-circle, with wood banisters atop iron spindles. On one side was the living room, decorated formally in a way I suspected was just for show. On the other side was a formal dining room with a gigantic chandelier that caught light from the Palladium windows and threw it back at us in a rainbow of prisms. Straight ahead lay the family room. From where I stood I saw a deep brown leather chair and a wide-screen TV. A set of weights looked oddly out of place behind the chair, with the bench and steel bars showing signs of frequent use. A towel lay draped over the side of the bench as if thrown there carelessly. It was a rather incongruous thing in a house that otherwise reeked of comfort and money. And I wasn't the only one who noticed.

Behind me, Bitty whispered, "Who's their decorator, a gym teacher?"

I might have answered with a *yes*, but a woman appeared on the staircase, so I did the best thing and kept my mouth shut. She was tall, fairly slender, dressed in a denim skirt and light blouse, the sleeves pushed up to her elbows, and her brown hair was pulled back into a tight French braid. The expression on her face was not welcoming.

"Mrs. Hartford, may we have a moment of your time?" I asked when she halted at the bottom of the staircase. "My name is—"

"I know who you are," she replied tersely. "I can't imagine why you think I have anything at all to say to you."

I smiled. Opposition wasn't going to deter me. "Not even to save your husband?"

"That's not why you're here. You suspect Breck of killing Spencer and probably Catherine Moore too. Well, you're wrong. Both of us have said to the police all that we need to say about their murders."

Gaynelle spoke up: "Are you sure about that? My understanding is that you know a great deal more than you profess. In fact, your entire family is involved."

The silence that fell was thick with tension. I wasn't sure what Gaynelle intended, or how far she should go, but kept my silence. Anything that worked would be helpful.

"Well?" Gaynelle prompted. "You cannot deny that you have not only held back information from the police, but you have lied to them."

"I have no idea what you're talking about," Victoria Hartford said coolly after a moment passed. "Now leave my house at once."

I had to admire her nerve. She kept calm and didn't betray herself or her husband in any way. But I had come here with the intention of getting some reactions, and I didn't want to leave without something useful.

"Just answer one question, please," I said, "and we'll leave."

She didn't say anything, but stuck her chin in the air and crossed her arms over her chest in a defensive position. I sucked in a deep breath before I asked, "How well did your husband know Trisha Atwood?"

It was immediately obvious that she hadn't expected that question. Her face went pale, her arms went out to her sides, and her hands and voice shook. "Get out! Get OUT!"

The last word was a shriek, and she flung herself toward us, waving her arms and curling her fingers into claws as she flailed at me. She was surprisingly strong as I put up a hand to defend my face. Since we were approximately the same height, I shoved her away rather forcibly. She staggered backward, then started to come toward me again, her face contorted with rage.

It was Gaynelle who stepped in to snag Victoria by one arm as she lunged forward. "Stop that this instant!" she said in her sternest school teacher voice. "Control yourself, please."

Victoria jerked her arm free of Gaynelle's grasp and pointed to the door. "Out. If I have to call the police, I'm pressing charges."

I was so mad I was about to spit fire, but I managed to say without snarling, "That would be a very interesting situation, indeed. I'm tempted to stay just to tell them what I know. But I'll wait until after I talk to your husband. Tell him we'll be at Catherine's cabin."

Gaynelle and Rayna had the front door open, and before I knew what she intended to do, Bitty stepped between me and the furious woman. Short as she is, she got right up in Victoria Hartford's face and shook a finger under her nose.

"You listen to me, you mule-faced bitch—if you lay one more hand on Trinket, I'll bounce you off that floor so quick you won't know if you're coming or going. And don't think I can't do it!"

Fortunately, Bitty's bouncing skills weren't put to the test. Gaynelle and Rayna intervened and got us both out the door without more unnecessary violence. When I glanced over my shoulder at Victoria Hartford, I have to say I'd never seen a more murderous expression than the one on her face at that moment.

"Gotcha!" I thought. There was no doubt in my mind that she'd tell her husband exactly what was said. We had successfully laid the trap. Breck Hartford would certainly rise to the challenge, and his reaction would no doubt be swift. We had to be ready.

Once in the car, Rayna organized the recording equipment. A tiny camera small enough to fit in a buttonhole, complete with audio, and a camera fitted to the earpieces of a pair of sunglasses were included in her kit. Bitty was immediately intrigued.

"Oooh, what do I get to wear?"

"A smile," I answered her. "We're taking you home first. I'm not about to risk a hair on your head."

Bitty turned in the seat to look at me. "You've been talking to Jackson Lee," she accused.

"No, I've been *listening* to Jackson Lee. He told me he doesn't want you to ever be in another risky situation. I promised him I'd do my best to keep you safe."

"And you meant it?"

I stared at her. "Of course I meant it, Bitty. Why wouldn't I?"

"Because I'm not going anywhere except with y'all, that's why."

"Look, Rayna and I talked it over before we ever planned this. None of us are that crazy about getting bashed in the head or held at gunpoint. So we're taking precautions. However, as has been proven in the past, the best made plans of mice and men often go awry. We may end up in jeopardy despite our caution. Therefore, we think it best to—"

"If you're going to say, 'Leave Bitty behind,' you better rethink it," Bitty cut me off to say. The look she gave me was narrow-eyed, and her teeth were slightly bared.

"You look like a piranha," I said. "Stop glaring at me."

"Stop trying to leave me out of things."

"But I promised Jackson Lee."

"Just tell him I refused to cooperate. He's familiar with that."

"I bet he is." I sighed. "Okay. I tried. That's all I can do."

Bitty smiled. "Now, what's my part in this going to be?"

"Silent bystander?" I guessed, and she shook her head.

"Not a chance."

"Okay. So, then I'll just outline our plan for you. Rayna had a camera attached to her sunglasses, and we have recorded everything said so far. If we can get Breck Hartford to incriminate himself, we'll have that recorded as well. Then we'll give it to the police and let them decide what to do with it."

"And how do you propose to get him to incriminate himself?" Bitty asked.

"Well, I had hoped to find him home and surprise him, but I'm sure Victoria will tell him everything that was said. So now I expect him to track us down to learn just what we know and if we have any proof."

Bitty looked at me like I was crazy. "So you're luring a homicidal maniac to hunt us down?"

I nodded. "Yes."

"Well, I hope you have a plan to keep us from being his next victims, Mad Max."

"Yes, there's safety in numbers."

"You're saying he can't kill all of us?"

"Something like that."

Bitty looked at Rayna and Gaynelle. "And you two are going along with this?"

"I hardly think he'll gun us all down with an Uzi," said Rayna. "And we don't intend to split up until this is over."

Bitty shook her head. "And if he doesn't decide to look for us today? What then? Do we go home and wait for him to show up in the middle of the night again?"

"I hate it when Bitty is the voice of reason," I said to Rayna, and she nodded her agreement.

"It's rather like finding a talking frog, isn't it," she said.

Gaynelle laughed. "Amazing, but you just know there's a trick to it?"

"I'm sitting right here, you know," said Bitty.

I reached over to pat her on the arm. "I know, honey. And you'll be glad to hear that you have an excellent point. While I think Breck Hartford will tear after us like a bear with his tail afire, he may prefer to wait and catch us alone. It seems to have been his style. Yet I'm thinking he might want to confront us as soon as possible to forestall our going to the police."

"If he's innocent, he may be angry, but he's not going to hunt us down like a rabid dog," said Rayna. "But if he's guilty, as we all think he is, Breck will come after us today instead of waiting."

"Let's hope our armchair psychology is on the right track," said Gaynelle. "If we are wrong, we may be in a lot of trouble setting a trap like this."

"Are you kidding?" I said. "If we're *right*, we're going to be in a lot of trouble."

"Well, we've taken proper precautions," Rayna said after a moment. "We have recording equipment ready, some safeguards in place, and my cell phone is programmed to speed dial the Marshall County police if need be."

"And if they don't arrive in time?" asked Bitty. "What precautions are in place for that?"

"Burial policies," I quipped, but none of us laughed with any real humor.

Bitty rolled her eyes. "Good thing I brought along my gun, then. At least I'm prepared."

"Oh no," I said immediately. "You're leaving your gun in your purse and your purse in the car. I'm not taking a chance on anyone being accidentally shot."

"How do you feel about intentionally?"

"I'd rather take my chances with Hartford."

Bitty looked at Gaynelle and Rayna. They looked out the car windows. She blew out a sigh. "Okay. You win."

I was relieved. "It's about time."

We had set a trap for Breck Hartford, and I hoped he showed up to be caught. It was the only thing I'd been able to come up with to get proof of his crimes. It should work. He'd consider Catherine's cabin to be private enough for a confrontation and would have no idea that we'd already set the stage to catch him.

Just like fishing; bait the hook and reel 'em in. Unfortunately, we were the bait.

Chapter 20

Catherine's cabin sat on a hill above the Tippah River. It wasn't a big house, but very comfortable. Rayna had managed to get the keys to it from a realtor who had been trying to sell it for Catherine. I hadn't even known the house was for sale, but now I wondered who would want to buy a house where there had been a murder.

Of course, Bitty's cabin had been a murder scene as well, and she'd managed to sell it fairly quickly, but that was before the real estate market bottomed out in the area.

"Is everything still working correctly?" Rayna asked for at least the fifth time. She had checked and rechecked all the electronic equipment she'd brought with us. Since her husband Rob is a bail bondsman and an insurance investigator, he has a lot of cool stuff suitable to use for snooping. And, hopefully, also good for catching a killer.

"How would I know if it was working right or not?" asked Bitty as she peered up at Rayna where she stood on a utility ladder fiddling with a camera. "Is there supposed to be a red light or something?"

"Yes. Do you see one?"

"Yes," said Bitty, patting her blonde helmet of hair as she added, "be sure you get my best side, okay? I don't want to look terrible if this is going to be used as evidence in court one day."

"Don't worry about it, Norma Desmond," I said, rolling my eyes. "When you're ready for your close-up, she'll let you know."

Bitty narrowed her eyes at me, then apparently remembered that would produce wrinkles, and her face cleared as she said, "*Sunset Boulevard* was a great movie."

Looking frazzled, Rayna said, "I wish you two would hush. Just tell me if these cameras are too noticeable."

I eyed them critically. "Move that one pointed toward the fireplace a little to the left so it looks part of the corner molding. That's right. Now it's hardly noticeable at all."

"Good. Rob usually does this stuff, so I should have paid better attention. I wish I knew if this is all hooked up right. I'd hate for us to go to all this trouble, not to mention putting ourselves in danger, and then have nothing on tape to give the police."

"You've tested it three times already, and it's working," said Gaynelle. "I think it will be fine, Rayna."

She sighed and stepped down off the utility stool. "Well, we're ready then. This is going to be so disappointing if he doesn't show up."

"If you ask me," said Bitty, "we're better off if he doesn't show up. It's not as if we have unassailable proof, even if he confesses on tape. Is it?"

"It won't be the same as if he confessed to the police, no," replied Rayna. "That doesn't mean it won't be useful. They can play all this back to get a confession from him."

"What do you think, Trinket?" Gaynelle asked.

"I think Bitty's been hiding her vocabulary skills. *Unassailable?* Very good, Professor Bitty."

My dear cousin said something quite sharp and to the point, and I smiled. We needed relief from the tension. My nerves were stretched to the breaking point, and I'm sure the others' were too.

Gaynelle, who had been standing by the dining room window looking out on the parking area, said, "Someone's turning into the driveway."

I think we all gasped at the same time, and Rayna scurried to put away the folding utility ladder and hide any evidence of our spy equipment. I felt rather like James Bond. Or Mata Hari. Her exploits as a spy were legendary. And she was rumored to be a *femme fatale*, so that appealed to me.

But I digress.

So there we were, surrounded by enough technical equipment to apprehend a drug lord, anxiously waiting for the killer to appear. It sounds crazy in retrospect, and even felt crazy then for us to attempt such a thing. Not that our insanity deterred us in the least.

Rocks crunched under tires as the car rolled to a stop next to Rayna's SUV. My heart hammered so hard in my chest I thought it might break a rib. I looked at the others. They looked as tense as I felt. We waited for Breck Hartford to get out of the car and come to the door, and he didn't disappoint us.

The door swung open on his late-model BMW, and he flung himself out of it like a man possessed. We all did a collective *gulp!* as he slammed the door shut and stomped up to the back deck. I'd forgotten how big he was—tall and with the broad shoulders of a linebacker. I could well imagine him playing football and running over the other players with no mercy. I had a brief moment of panic as he reached the back door and pounded on it.

We had pre-arranged our roles in the play we were about to perform, so Gaynelle went to open the door while we scattered to our respective places. "Yes?" she inquired as if greeting an unexpected visitor.

Breck Hartford hesitated as we had hoped. Some of his rage abated, and he looked uncertain. He didn't know Gaynelle well or at all, and so made a visible effort to control his anger as he said, "Tell Bitty I want to talk to her."

Gaynelle's years as a public school teacher often came in handy. She lifted a brow and tilted her head to one side as if chastising him for his rudeness. From my position in the kitchen, I had a nice view of Breck's face as his tan complexion took on a ruddy hue. It wasn't a good look for him.

Breck had grown up in the South where good manners are stressed. I could tell it was an effort, but he added politely, "Bitty invited me. May I please speak with her?"

It was said stiffly and somewhat sarcastically, but Gaynelle stepped back and held the door open for him to enter. "Bitty is in the living room. I'm sure you know the way."

Since the house wasn't that big, it wouldn't have been difficult for a complete stranger to find the living room, but Breck just nodded as he walked through the kitchen and dining area and into the living room. Bitty stood next to the huge fieldstone fireplace. When she wants to be, Bitty can be the very model of good manners and discretion. She greeted Breck cordially but not warmly.

"Hello, Breck. Please have a seat." She indicated a large wingback chair set at an angle to the fireplace.

He glanced around at the rest of us and shook his head. "No, I would rather stand, thank you. I want to know why you came to my house to accuse me of murdering Sturgis and Catherine. My wife is very upset."

"As she should be," replied Bitty without a flicker of an eyelash. "She's married to a murderer."

Breck looked dumbfounded at Bitty's cool response. Then he looked absolutely furious. "Do you know I can file a lawsuit against you for slander? I'm a respected coach and a teacher with tenure, and I won't have any slur against my reputation."

"You should have thought of that before you murdered the professor and Mary Ann. I mean Catherine."

I tried not to laugh, but a snort escaped anyway. When I'm nervous, I do that. Bitty's reference to the old TV show *Gilligan's Island* was probably involuntary, but it was still something I found funny. I glanced toward Rayna and saw her lips twitch, and I knew I wasn't alone.

Breck Hartford's voice rose as he said, "I already told you that I had nothing to do with their deaths, and I'm damn tired of you saying I did!"

Rayna spoke up: "What about Trisha Atwood?"

Hartford's face went from red to white. He looked as if he'd just been shot with a stun gun. He sounded hoarse when he asked, "What do you mean by that?"

"I meant just what I said. What about Trisha Atwood? Does her murder not mean anything to you?"

"Trisha died from an accidental fall."

"You know better than that," Rayna replied. "She was killed and her death made to look like an accident."

"Police investigated. It was ruled an accident," Breck retorted as he seemed to regain some composure. "Your saying it was murder doesn't make it true."

Rayna waved a hand to indicate the rest of us. "I'm not alone. There are others who believe as we do. And before you deny it again, remember that we don't make these accusations lightly. We have some history of being fairly accurate."

Breck's laugh was more a bark of derision. "Oh yes, I've heard of you women up there in Holly Springs calling yourselves the Dixie Divas and pretending to solve murders. Most of the time you just get in the way of the police and hamper their investigations. It's a wonder you haven't already been arrested and charged with obstruction."

Since he echoed similar complaints from not only my mother and Jackson Lee but the Holly Springs Police Department, there wasn't a lot we could say to defend ourselves.

I had been focusing on Breck's voice since he entered the house, and while I was pretty sure he was who I overheard talking to someone the night the professor was killed, he didn't sound very much like the caller who had threatened my life. Of course, on the night I had overheard him assuring someone that the professor was dead, the room had been crowded with people and loud music. I couldn't be a hundred percent certain it *had* been Breck Hartford. And that accusation may never stand up in a court of law. We had to have proof, and our elaborate charade had so far provided very little.

"Mr. Hartford," I began my part in his interrogation, "isn't it true that you had contact with Trisha Atwood the night she died? That, in fact, your Visa card was charged with payments to a strip club in Saltillo right outside Tupelo? Let me answer for you—yes to both questions. Trisha was a freshman still staying in the dorms two years ago, and at night earned extra money dancing at a club. She also moonlighted as a private dancer for men who could afford her, like you."

Hartford grated, "You don't know what the hell you're talking about."

"Yes. I do. Your Visa card was charged with payments at the club where Trisha worked. You had a large cash withdrawal the same night she died. Five hundred dollars. A friend of Trisha's said she was excited that night, that she said she was going to earn five hundred dollars for private lap dances at a steady client's house. Your credit card proves you were a steady customer. Circumstantial evidence now, but trust me, what we don't know the police do. They'll soon have enough to charge you with the murder of Trisha Atwood at the least, and with all three murders at most."

A muscle flexed in Breck's jaw. I noted that his hands had curled into fists at his sides, and his entire body was tense. "You women are crazy. And if you think I'm going to let you defame me without retaliation, let me assure you that I'll hire a lawyer and sue you all for slander."

"You can't sue someone if it's the truth," Bitty interjected. "It'd be like suing me because I'm blonde."

Breck flicked a glance at her. "If you're a natural blonde, then I guess I'm a killer. But the possibility of either of those things being true is remote."

Now, I knew Bitty was a natural blonde, although the color of her hair in recent years was largely due to an expert hairdresser. But there was such an element of certainty in Hartford's tone that I began to wonder if we were wrong. Yet, how could we be? All the evidence pointed to him. Who else would take a five hundred dollar cash advance from his Visa account to use on a lap dancer except him? The account was in his name only. And I just couldn't see his wife hiring him a lap dancer anyway. She didn't seem the type to be that permissive. After all, she'd retaliated in kind when she found out about her husband's affair with Emily Sturgis. And she knew about Catherine.

Bitty's eyes had narrowed, and her hand went to her hips as she looked up at Breck Hartford. "I'll have you know that I *am* a natural blonde, so that must make you a killer!"

"Prove it."

"We will," said Gaynelle. When Hartford turned to look at her, she nodded her head and said softly, "*Fiat justitia et pereat mundus.*"

Not being up to date on my Latin, I had no idea what she'd said until Breck said, "The wheels of justice turn slowly, but grind exceedingly fine."

"Almost." Gaynelle smiled. "'Let justice be done though all the world perish,' is the translation from Ferdinand the First, Holy Roman Emperor."

A mirthless smile played on his lips as he regarded Gaynelle for a moment with an expression I couldn't read. Amusement? Irritation? A combination?

"A history lesson along with accusations of murder," he said finally. "A most intriguing afternoon indeed. I regret that I cannot stay longer, but since I have already wasted an hour of my day listening to crazy conjecture, I intend to go home and call my lawyer."

"Do that," said Bitty with a smile. "You're going to need him."

Hartford looked momentarily taken aback by her comment, but recovered quickly. "I suggest you call yours as well. If you say one word of this tripe to anyone, and it gets back to me, I'm going to sue all of you for everything you have or ever will have. Keep that in mind."

It was deflating. I could see our one chance to get a confession or incriminating evidence slipping away. And there wasn't anything I could do about it.

We were all standing in the living area and had been so intent on trapping Breck Hartford that none of us, not even him, heard the back door opening. It wasn't until a voice from the kitchen/dining area interrupted us that we knew someone had come into the house. And it wasn't just any someone. It was Victoria Hartford.

Since I was facing the dining area, I saw her step into the living room. She looked much different than she had earlier. She was wearing navy blue sweats, athletic shoes, and a dark blue knit cap on her head.

"Well," she said so loudly it made me jump, "isn't this cozy."

Breck turned, looking surprised to see his wife. The rest of us froze. Victoria had obviously come prepared. She had a pistol the size of Bitty's pointed directly at us, and no one wanted to move. It went through my head that she thought we were going to haul him off to the police or maybe tar and feather him. She must have come to his rescue to stop him from confessing, and would drag him out before he could say anything that might be useful.

It never occurred to me that she had a very different plan.

Sounding annoyed, Breck said, "Vicky, what are you doing? Put that thing down and stop being stupid."

"Did you tell them anything?"

"Of course not." He glanced at Gaynelle and added, "There isn't anything to tell. I was just about to leave. You don't need that gun. They won't try to stop me."

"Good God, Breck, you're so damn stupid," she said sharply. "Can't you see that they already know too much?"

"They don't know anything, and won't if you'll just keep your mouth shut," he grated between clenched teeth.

"As usual, you want to wimp out on me. Again." Victoria gestured with the gun. "Tie them up. I thought of a way to do this on the drive out here."

"Did you follow me?" Breck demanded. "I told you I'd take care of this, and you didn't have to worry."

"I didn't need to follow you. I've been out here before. What? You think I didn't know about your affair with Catherine? Please. I know more about you and your silly flings than you ever dreamed. I know about *all* of them."

Breck had an expression on his face like she'd hit him with a two-by-four. He shook his head after a moment. "This is no time or place to talk about all this, Vic. We can discuss it at home."

She waggled the barrel of the gun at him. "We'll discuss it when this is done. Get some duct tape and tie them up. Just their hands. They'll have to walk to the van."

"Dammit, Victoria, stop talking! You're always talking! Can't you just *shut up?*"

Apparently, that was the wrong thing to say to her. She sucked in a sharp breath, and her eyes narrowed with fury. She took a step forward, and I noticed that the barrel of the gun was shaking in an alarming way.

"Shut up?" she repeated softly. "You're telling me to shut up?"

"Hell yes, I'm telling you to shut up! You're going to ruin it all with your stupid big mouth!"

I wanted to tell Breck Hartford that if he kept talking to her that way he was liable to be in serious trouble, but I didn't dare open my mouth. Victoria Hartford was a woman on the edge, and I was slightly amazed that her husband couldn't see it. When I stole a glance at Rayna and Gaynelle, I saw that they were well aware of her instability.

Bitty, however, took a step forward to confront Victoria. "Listen, I don't care if you two argue, but I've had enough of this. You both need to take it outside. Or home."

Victoria didn't even look at her. Her gaze was on her husband. But she let Bitty know that her interference wasn't going to be tolerated: "You say one more word, and I'll shoot you, Bitty."

Wisely, Bitty stopped where she was and clamped her lips tightly together. I was so proud of her.

Breck stared at his wife in obvious disbelief. "Have you lost your mind? Are you *trying* to get us arrested?"

"If it were left up to you, we'd already be serving time in Parchman. Can't you do anything right? Why is it always up to me to clean up your messes? Why do I have to do *everything?*"

Her voice rose on the last word to almost a shriek. I stood transfixed by her rage. Her face was contorted into something almost unrecognizable.

"Vic . . . calm down." Breck cleared his throat, and I saw the alarm in his eyes as he put out a hand as if to touch her, then let his arm fall to his side when she gave a sudden jerk as if repulsed. "It's going to be okay. Just remember why we had to help, okay?"

"Oh, I remember why we had to help," she spat at him. "Because you're always a no-show. No matter what Bret did, he could never measure up to you, never be as good as his father because you were the football hero, the only one in the family to graduate from college, the first one to ever become a professor. But did you ever show up for him? For our son? Were you ever there at one of his baseball games? You even missed his high school graduation because you were off with your slut of the month. And then had the nerve to show up afterward to act like the big shot, taking pictures, pretending to be what you should have been all along—a good father. Oh yes, Breck, I remember why we had to help. Do you?"

Despite the chill of the unheated house, beads of sweat dotted Hartford's upper lip, and his jaw muscles flexed. He sounded slightly hoarse when he said, "I did what I could to keep him from going to jail. I risked my own freedom to help, so don't forget that."

She gave him a scornful, raking glance. "I had to tell you what to do. As usual. You stood there mewling like an old woman, pacing back and forth with your silly hand-wringing while I had to figure out what would work. And it did work. No one suspected that stupid girl didn't die from the fall. I fixed it all. Even when that slut's son threatened to go to the police."

Breck Hartford's chest rose and fell rapidly. "Vic . . . tell me you didn't do anything to Monty. You didn't. Did you?"

She changed the pistol to her other hand, still holding it in front of her. "What was I supposed to do? He would have ruined everything. I couldn't let that happen. Bret has so much more ahead of him than that sniveling kid ever did."

"My God." Breck stared at her as if she was a complete stranger. "I can't believe I'm hearing this."

"Why? Because I had the nerve to do what you should have done? Because I was there for our son when you weren't? You left me no choice."

All my careful conclusions flew out the window. Breck Hartford hadn't killed Monty . . . did that mean he hadn't killed anyone else either? But if not—who? Surely Victoria hadn't killed Spencer and Catherine. Obviously, she'd had Breck help her cover up their son's part in Trisha Atwood's death, and killed Monty when he wanted to go to the police. But the rest? Could she have done it?

"Be a man," she was saying to Breck. "Tie them up. We have to get rid of them in a way no one will suspect it wasn't an accident."

Rayna made a small sound, and I saw Bitty's eyes widen. Gaynelle remained as impassive as usual. She would be an excellent poker player, I thought irrelevantly.

"No," said Breck flatly. "I'm not committing murder. Covering up for Bret was one thing. He didn't mean to kill her, it was just a stupid accident. But this? No. And my God, Vic, I can't believe you killed Monty! He was just a kid!"

"He was going to tell the police," Victoria said slowly as if talking to an imbecile. "I did what I had to do."

Breck ran a hand over his face. He looked wild-eyed. I knew how he felt, and I wondered if I looked as dazed as he did. "Jesus, Vic—what about Sturgis? Tell me you didn't have anything to do with his murder."

Victoria's lips tightened. "Monty had told him what happened. Of all people, to tell Spencer Sturgis! I couldn't believe it when Spence told me. He thought I'd be happy that he had found out something to use against you. Happy! The fool. I was only with him to get back at you. He meant nothing to me."

"But . . . but how? I mean, Spencer was a small man, but a dead weight would be too heavy to carry by yourself."

Her lip curled. "You underestimate me yet again, darling. I've been in training for the triathlon. I'm in excellent shape. All I needed was help getting him out of the house and somewhere his death could be blamed on someone else." Her eyes turned toward Bitty. "I didn't realize it was your sons' dorm room. Not that it matters now. It served the purpose at the moment."

"Did you use the laundry cart to move him?" I couldn't help asking. "We found it in their room."

"Yes." She shrugged. "Spencer never was very observant. He thought I was a laundry deliveryman when he opened the door."

"But the freshly laundered and ironed shirts," I said. "How did you manage to get his laundry?"

Sounding impatient, she said, "They weren't his, of course. I hung them up, then took the extra hanger and came up behind him. It was over quickly. He hardly struggled at all. I needed extra time, so I made a mess so the police would think there'd been a struggle and he'd disappeared. It worked fairly well, too."

"Well, I don't see how it worked," said Bitty in the small silence that fell. "You don't look anything like a laundry deliveryman."

Victoria actually smiled. "I can disguise myself well enough when I choose. I've studied theater. I'm quite good when I want to be."

"I can imagine," Bitty agreed.

Rayna and Gaynelle had said very little since Victoria barged in, and I wondered if they had some sort of plan. I hoped so. It was beginning to look as if we were in for a very rough ride if we didn't figure out a way to get that gun away from her and call the police.

"I'm fascinated," Bitty said to her. "You're much more clever than I ever gave you credit for being."

"I'm not surprised. No one has ever thought of me as anything other than Breck Hartford's wife, the woman who had to pretend not to know about all those other women. Well, I'm a lot more than that. If things had been different, I would have had a career of my own, not just been a faculty wife."

She sounded bitter, and when I glanced back at Breck, I saw him smirk and knew he was going to say something very, very stupid.

"Like what? An actress?" he sneered. "A dancer? You couldn't even keep a part in a grade school play, for God's sake. What makes you think you would ever have had a career?"

Victoria flushed, her face turning a dull red. As I stared at her, I remembered my impression of the person who had attacked me here at the cabin when I had come to find Catherine. Could it have been Victoria that I saw that day, not a young man? It was entirely possible. Apparently her training kept her very fit, and she was tall and slender, and I could have mistaken her for a young man since I only saw someone running away.

Then, Victoria lifted the pistol and pointed it directly at her husband's chest, and all rational thought flew out the window. My heart thudded into overdrive, my palms began to sweat, and my feet turned to ice. Everything seemed to slow down so that each word was long and drawn-out, each action so slow as to take minutes instead of seconds.

"I could have done it if not for you," she said. "But I can change that."

I think I gasped. Or maybe it was someone else.

In the scant seconds it must have taken her to aim, I had time only to say, "No, don't!" before she fired.

The sharp smell of cordite was immediate, the noise terrific. My ears rang, and I could taste gunpowder. Breck Hartford dropped to the floor like a sack of rocks. He made no sound, just collapsed. When I moved as if to help him, Victoria turned the gun toward me.

"Don't touch him. Don't do anything unless I tell you to do it."

"You can't shoot us all," said Rayna, her voice wavering a little. "One of us could get to you before you could do that."

"I don't have to shoot all of you. All I have to do is shoot one of you. Then you'll know I mean business. Care to test me?"

None of us did, of course. We became very compliant. Amazing what a threat can accomplish, especially when backed up with a firearm held by a crazy woman. Usually that woman was Bitty, but now we were dealing with an unknown quantity. Prudence seemed the best option.

"No," Rayna answered Victoria. "I'm good."

On the floor, Breck's right foot quivered. He was still alive. I didn't want to draw his wife's attention to that fact, just in case she decided to finish the job, so I said, "Tell me what you need from us, please. I'm sure we can come to a mutual solution without the need for violence."

What I meant was, *without the need to shoot any of us*, but I didn't think it quite necessary to explain. Not that it would have made any difference. She'd obviously made a plan and intended to stick to it. She waggled the gun barrel at me.

"Where are all your cell phones?" she demanded. "Never mind. I see your purses in that chair. Step back very carefully and slowly. I'm a good shot, so don't think about trying anything stupid." She dumped our purses and found Gaynelle's cell phone, but when my purse provided no phone, she turned to me and gestured for me to empty my pockets.

Anything for the lady with the loaded gun, I thought as I gave it to her. Then she turned to look at Rayna. "Hand it over."

Rayna complied, then Victoria took our phones and tossed them on a table with the others. She turned to Bitty. "Where's your purse?"

"I have no idea," Bitty lied smoothly. "I may have left it somewhere. It's been such a hectic day."

"Right. Well, Miss Hectic, if you don't come up with your cell phone within five seconds, your day is about to get a lot worse."

"Well, why didn't you say that's why you wanted it? I have my cell phone right here." Bitty produced it from the pocket of her Gucci slacks.

Once Victoria had all the phones, she took out the batteries and tossed them on the table. No more GPS system to guide rescuers. She had thought this through pretty well, it seemed.

Switching the pistol back to her other hand, she motioned at me with it.

"I brought a roll of duct tape. You're going to tie up your friends. Ah, I mean your *Divas*." She stressed the last word with enough sarcasm to fill a bucket. I didn't argue.

"There's some rope downstairs," I began, but she shook her head.

"No. The duct tape is in the kitchen. Get it. And I'll be watching you the entire time."

She used the pistol as a wand to wave Rayna, Gaynelle and Bitty toward the dining area where she could keep her eye on me as well. She took a vantage point by the dining room windows so if anyone else arrived she could see them, and had the Divas on the other side of the small table. If any of us made a false move, she would shoot us before we could escape. As she'd said, none of us wanted to risk the other being shot by our precipitate actions.

I walked slowly and reluctantly toward the kitchen, far too aware of the gun trained on me. When would I learn? Or would I ever learn? Maybe Jackson Lee was right, and we all needed keepers. Or maybe Miranda Watson, i.e. gossip columnist, was right, and we'd formed some kind of murder club. Unwittingly, of course.

"Stop dawdling!" Victoria snapped when I paused in the kitchen by the windows. I looked toward the back door. It beckoned invitingly. Maybe I would have attempted to get out and run for help, but that would leave the others alone with a furious, unbalanced woman. Then Victoria turned toward the others when Rayna made a soft exclamation, and I seized the chance to sweep the roll of duct tape off the counter and into the gap between the edge and the refrigerator. When she turned back to look at me, I just stood there staring at the counters, then shrugged.

"I don't see any duct tape. Where did you leave it?"

"Look on the counter by the sink."

"Nope. Not here."

She said something quite vulgar and took a couple steps into the kitchen area. I backed up a step. Of course, the roll of duct tape wasn't on any of the butcher block counters. Victoria shook her head in obvious disgust.

"I thought I brought it in. Well, I'm not about to give any of you a chance to get away, so look for tape. Catherine's bound to have some in here somewhere."

I rummaged through some drawers, taking all the time I dared, hoping against hope rescue would arrive somehow. Finally I said, "All I found is masking tape."

"That will have to do. Bring it here."

She gestured with the gun until we were back in the living room, huddled together like frightened geese. Breck still lay in the floor. He'd stopped moving again. Blood seeped from a hole in his upper torso near his left shoulder. It had made a puddle under him. If he was alive and didn't get treatment quickly, he'd bleed to death.

When I glanced at Rayna, she looked at me and gave a slight shake of her head. I didn't know what to do, but amazingly, Bitty did.

"He's making a mess all over the rug," she said to Victoria. "At least let me move him to the tile floor."

"What do I care about the rug?" Victoria demanded. "It's not mine."

"No, but it's a Fereghan Sarouk from central Persia and very expensive. It'd be a shame to ruin it. I know you appreciate fine furniture and textiles."

"It is?" Victoria looked down at the rug. It had muted colors and a lovely pattern, and I had no idea how expensive it was, but it did look very nice. "Okay," she said after a moment. "Move him off the rug."

"He's too big and heavy. Can Trinket help? She's a big girl and pretty strong."

I glared at Bitty, but when Victoria motioned for me to help her, I did. We bent and managed to pull Breck off the rug and onto the tile. A faint sound escaped his lips as we got him situated near a credenza. Bitty glanced up at me as her hands busily arranged his body where he lay partially on his side.

"Ooh," she said, "this is a Hekman antique credenza, Trinket. Just look at all the ornate details on the door panels."

When I stared at her as if she'd gone crazy, she added, "See the fine workmanship in the floral design?"

Just as I'd decided the stress had sent Bitty into Cloud Cuckoo Land, she hissed under her breath, "Help me turn him so he can breathe!"

Ah. It finally became clear to me. I asked an inane question, something about how did she know what the credenza was, as I strained to turn him to his side.

"Because I recognize the gilded swirls as distinctive to the style," she replied in a loud tone.

About that time Victoria decided we'd had enough time to move the body and admire the antiques. "He's off the rug, so get back over here. Bitty, you tie up the others. I have my gun pointed right at you, remember, so even if I can't get all of you, I can at least shoot a couple of you. Get Trinket first. She's the biggest."

Really. I was getting weary of being talked about as if I'm the size of a Georgia Tech linebacker, and almost said so aloud. Prudence kept my mouth shut, however. We'd done what we could for Breck, so we stood up and joined Rayna and Gaynelle near the fieldstone fireplace. Bitty took the roll of masking tape from Victoria.

"Make it tight, and do several loops around their wrists. No, do it with their arms behind their backs. Like that."

Bitty tied me up first. I tested the strength of the bindings when she moved on to Gaynelle and thought that with a lot of effort, I could break the flimsy tape. While looking for it, I'd seen a roll of duct tape but pushed it back into a corner. We had a better chance of getting free with the thinner masking tape. Thankfully, Victoria didn't seem to know that little fact.

When Bitty had us all tied, Victoria snatched Rayna's car keys, then marched us to the back door, single file, with her pistol pointing the way. We were very obedient. None of us wanted to risk the others by trying to be a hero.

I found it appalling that Victoria didn't even glance at her dying husband as we left. They had to have been married at least twenty or twenty-one years since their son was around that age, but she apparently didn't spare him a thought as we got into Rayna's SUV. She jabbed the pistol at Bitty, the only one of us still unbound.

"Drive. And do exactly as I say, or I'll shoot your cousin first. Understand?"

I made a squeaking sound, and Rayna nudged me. The three of us sat in the back seat like ducks trussed up for dinner, while Bitty got into the driver's seat, complaining all the while.

"I can't drive this big ole thing! It'd be like driving a log truck. I'm used to cars that drive easily."

Victoria wasn't impressed. "It has power steering and brakes. You'll be fine. Shut up and drive."

Bitty started the car with Rayna's keys and adjusted the rear-view mirror. I could see the reflection of her eyes, and she looked caught between fear and outrage. I hoped she didn't do anything too foolish. But then again, this was Bitty, and she's known for foolish. She was in good company. If we hadn't been so foolish as to think we could trap a killer, we wouldn't now be in danger of becoming murder victims ourselves.

I saw that Breck's car was hemmed in by Victoria's as we left the driveway and headed toward the highway a mile or so down the narrow road paved with black tar. Tall trees lined the road, and gravel crunched under car tires every time Bitty got off the road. It was a bumpy ride to the highway, made worse by our circumstances.

I didn't think it could get much worse.

Boy, can I ever be wrong.

Chapter 21

So there we were, barreling down Highway 7 toward Holly Springs, with no idea what our maniacal navigator planned to do with us. Every time Rayna, Gaynelle or I tried to communicate with one another, that blamed pistol would be aimed right at us. I had no doubt Victoria would shoot with or without much provocation.

Next to me, Rayna fidgeted about. I wasn't sure what she was doing, but thought it must be similar to what I was doing—attempting to loosen the tape around my wrists. Up front, Bitty hunched over the steering wheel. She looked like a leprechaun sitting behind the wheel of the huge SUV, but my thoughts went to a horror movie I had been coerced into watching, *Bride of Chucky.* In the movie, a doll was possessed by the spirit of a serial killer. While that described Victoria more than it did my dear cousin, I had a feeling Bitty was not taking this well. It could go either way.

That feeling was not dissipated when she began to mutter to herself. Victoria's eyes narrowed. She sat with her back to the passenger door, not seat-belted, just watchful.

"I don't know what you're saying, but you can stop it. No talking to each other. Or you'll end up like my dear departed husband."

"So how were you able to kill Catherine?" asked Gaynelle. "Did she let you in, or did you have to sneak into the house?"

For a moment I thought Victoria wasn't going to answer. Then she gave a short bark of laughter. "That stupid slut. She had no idea who she was dealing with, I'll tell you that much. She thought my husband had broken in on her. How she thought Breck smart enough to pull all this off without leaving any evidence makes me laugh. He's never been smart, just charming. But charm can only get you so far. Oh, he had ambition, just nothing to back it up. If it wasn't a football play, he was lost. I had to do everything. All of it! While he pretended he didn't know about it so he could be safe."

Gaynelle nodded as if in understanding, but I don't know how anyone could ever understand murder. "Your son Bret—he didn't mean to kill Trisha. It was an accident."

Victoria nodded. "Yes. He was so scared. And Breck, as usual, was off with one of his sluts. I had to take care of it. And I did. I was the one to think of putting her under a dorm window, and I was the one who arranged for her car to be driven to the parking lot. I took care of all the details. I had to, you know. Breck has never been there for Bret or for me. And Bret knew it. I was the one he came to when there was a problem. I always fixed it."

"Like you fixed Monty?" asked Rayna.

"Like Monty," Victoria agreed. "He was going to the police to tell them about that silly girl being killed. Bret didn't mean to do it. There was a struggle, and she fell from the deck and hit something on the way down. It broke her neck. He would have been arrested, and there would be charges . . . I didn't see any reason he should have to suffer for the rest of his life because of that girl. Or because of Monty being such a coward."

"Some might call it having a conscience," I couldn't help saying, and Victoria shrugged.

"Some might. I couldn't let him do it, though. And he was a weakling anyway, just like Breck. He would have broken under interrogation and told everything."

"It was a private party, wasn't it?" I said, remembering details from the movie *Dead at Seventeen* that Catherine had left for me. "And it got out of hand."

"Something like that. Bret used the Visa card to book it, and since it was in his father's name, I knew if police suspected us they could track it unless I did something."

"If it was a party," said Rayna, "then there had to be more people than Bret and Monty there. What about the other boys? Wouldn't they have told?"

"They'd gone home before she fell. Only Bret and Monty were still there. By the time anyone found out about it, Bret and I had already done everything. Monty drove her car to the parking lot while Bret and I put her on the ground under her dorm window. I put on her coat in case someone saw me or the security cameras were on, then I took her key card to go upstairs and open the window to make it look like she'd fallen. No one would ever know. I thought of *everything*."

She actually sounded proud of herself. It gave me the chills.

"You thought of everything except the Divas," Bitty snapped. I felt like smacking her in the back of the head. Victoria did *not* need a reminder. But Miss Clueless went on, "We know. And if we know, then the police know."

"There's a big difference between knowing and proving," Victoria replied coolly. "I left no evidence behind. You four are the last incriminating remnants."

She spoke calmly and emotionless, as if we were minor annoyances that needed disposal. I figured she was a sociopath. No remorse. No conscience. Just tidying up. So now Bitty was dethroned. Victoria was definitely the new *Bride of Chucky*.

For some reason I couldn't help muttering, "'Auday duay dumbalar, give me the power I beg of you . . .'" Of course, transferring souls any place except where they're supposed to be is impossible unless you're in Hollywood making an implausible horror movie with dolls possessed by evil.

Yet somehow Bitty picked up on it. "Lamar Deswayze," she replied, mangling the quote yet keeping it somewhere in the ballpark. I laughed. I couldn't help it. Who else in the world but Bitty and I would be quoting horror movies when stuck in a car with a mad serial killer?

Victoria thumbed back the hammer on her pistol. "Is that code for something? I told you not to talk to each other!"

That stopped the laughter, I can tell you. "It's from a movie," I explained. "*Bride of Chucky*. It's a spell to transfer the soul of a living person to a doll, and—"

"Shut up," said Victoria more calmly. "I think all you Divas are nuts. What kind of stupid club is it, anyway? Just one of those social things where you get together to eat and gossip?"

"No," Bitty defended us. "We drink wine, too. And lately we solve murders."

"Yeah. Good job with this one. You had no idea who killed Spencer or Catherine until I told you. You thought it was Breck." Another bark of laughter sounded way too loud in the SUV. "Idiots. You couldn't figure out how to tie your own shoes, much less solve any murders."

I could see that Bitty was getting irritated when she should be cautiously scared. I wanted to tell her to be careful but didn't want to risk Victoria getting too frisky with the pistol. That would be disaster.

By this time we had reached the outskirts of Holly Springs. Daylight faded early, and street lights were on in the gathering dusk. Neon signs advertising gas, pizzas, fried chicken, and other delights gleamed in a rainbow of bright colors. Just ahead on the right the Holly Springs Police Department had taken over the site of a former medical clinic. It sat on a gentle rise and was easily seen from the highway, one of our main streets in town. So close, and yet so far, rescue waited as it came into sight. Victoria gestured for Bitty to continue down Highway 7 a few hundred yards.

"I may not be that familiar with Holly Springs," she said, "but I looked it up on a map, and I know where we're going. So don't try anything funny. Turn on the next street after J Mash Drive."

"JM Ash Drive," Bitty corrected, and I rolled my eyes. She was going to get us all shot before we could even get to wherever it was this lunatic wanted to dispose of us. The thought gave me pause. Maybe it was better to take our chances in a more populated area than wait until she got us off in the boonies somewhere.

No sooner had I thought that than Victoria said, "If you try anything, don't think I won't shoot you. I don't really care if I'm caught. I've saved my son, and that's the main thing to me. Nothing else matters."

I glanced at Rayna and Gaynelle. Their faces reflected what I was feeling. Fear. I tried to think of something that would convince Victoria not to kill us. Or at the least, give us a long enough distraction to overpower her. I had my hands almost free. The tape had worked loose enough that I was pretty sure I could get it off. If I could do it, I was pretty sure Rayna had accomplished it as well. That made two of us, and with Bitty as a third, maybe we could overpower Victoria. I wasn't as sure about Gaynelle. She's feisty, but she's sixty-five or so and not as able to engage in physical exertion.

Since I didn't know what Victoria planned for our demise—that we were to be done away with was certain in her mind—I knew we had to act soon or she'd succeed. I just didn't know what to do that wouldn't get one or more of us shot. Rushing her was out of the question. None of us was faster than a bullet. That job was left to Superman.

So we passed up JM Ash Drive and the hope of the police department. I wanted to yell at Bitty to pull up into the police parking lot, but we'd passed the street, and the moment was lost. A few hundred yards down we turned onto Lemac Avenue. It's a quiet street with only a few houses spaced several lots apart. It ended at Center Street.

There's a stop sign at the junction of Lemac Avenue and Center Street, and Bitty did one of her famous rolling stops. Then I saw the police car. My heart thudded into overdrive. She deliberately took the corner on the proverbial two wheels, and I waited to hear the wail of a siren. Rescue was at hand!

"Damn you," Victoria snarled, and jammed the barrel of the pistol into Bitty's ribs. "You did that on purpose!"

"I didn't see him," Bitty lied.

"I'm tempted to shoot you right now. You better hope that cop isn't paying any attention. If he stops us I'm going to shoot you right in the heart!"

"This is an expensive sweater," said Bitty calmly. "I'd rather you shoot higher."

Sure enough, about three seconds later a siren pierced the night. Blue lights atop the car popped on, and it did a U-turn and came after us.

"Okay, say one word and I promise I'll shoot both of you," Victoria warned, and emphasized her threat with another hard jab into Bitty's side.

"Ouch," said Bitty.

As luck would have it, Officer Rodney Farrell stepped out of the police cruiser and walked up to the driver's side window. My heart was thumping so hard I was sure he'd be able to hear it as he motioned for Bitty to roll down the driver's side window.

He looked startled when he recognized Bitty. "Miz Hollandale . . . did you get a new car?"

"No. This is Rayna's. I'm just driving it tonight."

I couldn't see her face but hoped she was making some kind of gesture to let him know we weren't in there willingly.

"You did another rolling stop, you know," Officer Farrell went on with a shake of his head. "I'm going to have to give you a ticket this time. You've been warned plenty, so don't try to talk me out of it or say you're going to tell my grandma. I have a job to do, and I've gotta do it."

"I wouldn't dream of doing such a thing," said Bitty. "Why on earth would you think I would?" She cocked her head to one side.

Farrell bent a little lower to look inside the car. He noticed the three of us in the back, and then he looked at Victoria before he looked back at Bitty. "Have you all been drinking?"

"Of course not!" Bitty exclaimed. "You know I don't drink and drive."

"We're just on the way to visit a friend of mine," Victoria said in a pleasant tone.

"Okay." Farrell had his book out and started writing in it. "I'll need to see your license, Miz Hollandale."

Bitty fluttered about for a moment, then reached for her purse on the floorboard of the SUV. "For heaven's sake, you know who I am," she said. "Why do you need to see my license?"

"I need the number." Farrell glanced up and said, "I'll have to call it in. Procedure for a traffic stop."

"By all means," said Bitty, and I knew she was stalling for time.

What would happen if we alerted the officer? Would Victoria really shoot him, and also as many of us as she could? I wasn't sure, but I didn't want to take the chance on it, either.

While Farrell returned to his car, using his shoulder piece to call the dispatcher, I held my breath. Maybe someone had found Breck. Or knew that we were missing. Or had called our cell phones and discovered they were out of use.

"Remember," Victoria warned, "not one word, or I'll shoot him between the eyes, and then the rest of you."

In just a couple minutes Farrell was back. He handed Bitty her license, then gave her the ticket. "You can pay that at the courthouse," he said. "All the information is at the bottom. Pay it by the court date, or a bench warrant will be issued. Okay?"

"Okay," Bitty said slowly. She took her time putting the license back in her wallet and returning it to the purse. The ticket went up on the dashboard. She looked up at the officer again. "It should be public knowledge about a running stop at a stop sign. No one I know ever heard of that law."

Officer Farrell straightened. "You know about it now," he said. "Watch it next time. Good evening, ladies."

Then he was gone, our hope of rescue vanquished. I wanted to cry.

"Good job," said Victoria. "Now drive. Stop at all stop signs and don't speed, either."

As we continued down Center Street I racked my brain trying to think of a way to escape. Fear clogged my survival instinct, and the only thing I could think of was that we were going to die.

"I should have pushed you out of that dorm window when you were a freshman," Bitty said to Victoria. "You were mean then, and you're mean now. I don't know what Breck ever saw in you."

A wry smile twisted Victoria's mouth. "Funny you should say that. A fall is what started this whole mess."

"You are evil, just plain evil."

"And you're just as crazy as I've always heard. You haven't changed much since college."

"You have," said Bitty. I saw her glance in the rear-view mirror. "You were mean, but you weren't this cold back then."

"Yeah, well, life happens."

I craned my neck to look out the rear window of the SUV, but to my extreme dismay and disappointment, no police car was in pursuit. It still sat at the stop sign as if the officer inside had decided to take a nap.

Victoria must have seen me turn to look. She said, "Too bad, huh? I guess it's just not your lucky day." She laughed as if she'd said something really funny, while my hope withered. It looked like we were going to have to make our own luck if we wanted to get out of this alive.

Center Street took us toward the industrial part of Holly Springs, an area with a few businesses left but mostly empty, weed-choked lots. This time of year when dark came so early, very few people would be in the area. Not too far away sat the ruins of the old ice plant, a place where Bitty and I had spent a few memorable moments several months before.

"Turn here," said Victoria, and we turned onto a narrow road that would be dusty in the summer time and was lined with high grass, bushes, and some trees. An attempt had been made at sidewalks, but the dry road was nearly even with the crumbling curb. There were no street lights to illuminate our progress, and the SUV's headlights scrubbed deepening shadows from the road. It looked spooky in the fading light.

"Woodyard Road," said Gaynelle. "It's a dead end."

Victoria smirked. "How fitting."

"I think a pulp mill used to be here," Rayna said after a moment. "Closer to the railroad tracks, maybe."

"It's on up the highway," Bitty commented. "New owners."

"Shut up," said Victoria.

Trivial conversation served to cover up the fact we were all scared to death. The only one not terrified was our abductor. The moment of truth was fast approaching, and we may have only one chance to overpower her and escape. We couldn't even plot an escape since we couldn't converse. Anything we did would have to be a fly-by-the-seat-of-our-pants kind of thing. And I wasn't so sure we were capable of doing something so audacious. Look at what happened when we did have a plan in place. The multitude of things that could go wrong without any plan at all was daunting.

The SUV bumped down the road, and when Victoria pointed, we went to the left of a fork. Then the road abruptly ended, and Bitty braked to a stop.

"What now?" she asked. "Time to walk the plank? Pistols at dawn?"

"You watch too many movies. Turn off the engine and give me the keys."

It got very quiet when the motor died. Headlights speared the evening shadows, and dust or mist floated in the beams of light. Somewhere in the distance a dog barked, and the night song of a bird trilled in the band of trees on the driver's side of the car. Once the headlights went off, it would be pitch black.

And that was definitely in our favor.

I took a quick look at Rayna, and she lifted her chin to acknowledge me. Gaynelle cleared her throat, while up in the front seat Bitty turned to look at Victoria.

"You do know you won't get away with this, don't you?" she asked.

"As I told you earlier, I'm not worried about that. Now do exactly as I tell you. I want you out of the car one at a time."

"And if we don't?" Bitty asked. "It's not like you're going to let us go if we do what you want, so why should we?"

"Because I can make your deaths very, very unpleasant. Do what I say, and it will be over quick. Now get out of the car. You first."

Bitty glanced back at us. "You know I love you guys," she said. "And

Trinket, you were the sister I never had. I missed you so much while you were gone all those years, and now that you're back . . . well, we had fun, didn't we?"

"This is so touching," snapped Victoria. "I'm tempted to shoot you last just for the entertainment factor. Now *move!*"

"Can I at least carry my purse with me?" Bitty asked. "I have pictures of my boys in there. You have a son. You know how it feels to be a mother."

"Spare me. I had to make a choice between my son and yours. You lost. But carry your purse. Just get it and step out of the car."

"I'm going," said Bitty as she opened the car door. "Just tell my boys that I was thinking of them until the end."

"That's not a conversation I'm going to have," Victoria said as she opened her own door and eased out with the gun still pointed at Bitty. "If it makes you feel better, I won't shoot you in the face, so you can have an open casket."

I couldn't believe what I was hearing. Of all the heartless, most brutal women I had ever met in my life, Victoria Hartford had to be the worst. She turned back to us and opened the SUV's back door.

"You three get out. Remember I have a gun and I'm a good shot. Come out one at a time, and slowly."

We looked at each other, and then Rayna started to slide out of the car. I worked feverishly at my bonds, and Rayna looked at me and mouthed, , "I'm free. Help Gaynelle."

My wrists popped free of the tape about that time, and I nodded. I reached behind Gaynelle and slid my fingers through the sticky loops of masking tape to pry it loose. She pulled, and the tape broke. We were free! Now we just had to distract Victoria before she killed us.

"What do we do next?" Gaynelle whispered in my ear. "If we move too quickly, she's liable to shoot Bitty and then turn on us. She can probably shoot faster than we can run."

The three of us stood just outside the SUV while Victoria guarded us with the gun. It was hushed, the night a dark blanket beyond the lights from the car, and Bitty caught in the headlights with a look on her face like a deer on the highway.

Rayna nudged close to me. "Let's rush her," she said softly. "The three of us together."

I shook my head. "We'll just be a bigger target. If we split up, we can have at least a one in three chance to take her."

"Or get shot," Gaynelle whispered. "Come on. We're wasting time that we don't have."

Just as Rayna took a step away from the car the SUV's headlights went off, plunging the area into total darkness. "Go!" I whispered urgently, "go!"

We rushed toward we'd last seen Bitty but it was too dark to see much. I half-turned to help Gaynelle, but she was much friskier than I'd thought she would be and was already ahead of me.

"To the trees," Rayna said in a low tone, and we headed for the darker shadow of trees that were barely discernible from the rest of the vacant lot, running bent over so as not to appear as big enough targets.

It was a good thing we'd all worn slacks, because branches slashed at us as we dove into the brush. I felt a sharp jab in my side, and my sweater tore. I hunkered down in the brush and walked like a duck toward where I'd last seen Bitty and Victoria. I heard their voices, Bitty sounding irate and Victoria sounding threatening. Oh lord. This may go from bad to worse in a hurry.

"You are nothing but common white trash," I heard Bitty say when I got closer. "If you had an ounce of decency, you'd come out of hiding and face me."

"When I see your face," Victoria retorted in a snarl, "I'm going to shoot it! You kicked me!"

"You're trying to kill me! What did you expect?" Bitty shot back at her. "Freshly baked cookies and a pat on the back?"

I crept closer, aware that Rayna and Gaynelle were right behind me. Darkness was our friend right now. As my eyes adjusted to the absence of light, I saw that Bitty was crouched on the ground with her back to us. Her blonde hair was a pale blur against the deep shadows. Victoria was harder to see in her dark navy sweats, but a bit of thin moonlight glinted off the gun barrel so I knew her approximate position.

"I can circle around behind her," Rayna whispered in my ear, and gestured toward Victoria. "What do you think?"

"Find a thick branch and knock her in the head with it," I whispered back. "But be careful. If she sees you, she won't hesitate to shoot."

Rayna sucked in a sharp breath but sounded determined. "I'm going to do my best to knock her head off."

"Good," I said, and heard bushes rustle as Rayna moved away. Gaynelle and I got a little closer to where Bitty and Victoria were still arguing. I feared the minute Victoria could see well enough, she'd shoot her.

"What should we do?" Gaynelle whispered, and I thought about it a moment. We had only one chance to succeed. We weren't armed, and all it would take for Victoria is a single shot to kill one of us.

I finally said, "When we hear Rayna hit her, we run out and try to get the gun away. It's risky, but I can't think of anything else that might work."

"If only there was more light."

"If there was more light, then she could easily pick us off one by one," I pointed out.

As if conjured by the mention of it, two spears of light suddenly rolled over the scene, catching Victoria and Bitty in the twin beams. They stood barely ten feet apart.

"There's my ride," said Victoria, and lifted the pistol. "Be still, and this will be quick."

Bitty had flopped to her side from a standing position, and held her purse in front of her. Before I could move to stop it, to save Bitty, a deafening shot split the air. A flash of muzzle blast, and it was all over. I think I screamed. I didn't care if I got shot or if it was stupid, I burst out of the bushes toward my cousin. She lay still on the ground, dust all over her Gucci slacks, her purse clutched to her chest.

I fell on my knees beside her. A gaping hole was in the purse, and I tried to pull it away to look at her wound. I had basic CPR, maybe I could save her. I *had* to save her.

"Oh Bitty, oh Bitty, oh Bitty," I said over and over again, choking on the words while tears ran down my face. It felt as if a vise was squeezing my chest, and I tugged at the purse again.

"Stop it, Trinket," my dear departed cousin said irritably.

Stunned, I sat back on my heels. "You're alive."

"I know that. Check Victoria. I think I got her."

I turned to look, and Victoria Hartford indeed lay on the ground staring up at the night sky. There was a faintly surprised expression on her face, and the hand holding the pistol was lax.

"Mom!"

Bitty and I both turned toward the cry as a tall young man leaped from the car and left its engine still running and lights illuminating the night. He rushed over and knelt beside Victoria.

"Mom!" he cried again, a heart-rending sound. He looked up at us. "What did you do to her?"

Bitty had sat up by then and hugged her purse to her chest. "Kept her from killing us, that's what we did. Do you have a cell phone?"

He looked dazed. "A cell phone?"

"Yes. We need to call an ambulance."

The young man I assumed to be Bret Hartford fumbled in his jacket pocket for a phone and held it out. Bitty took it and punched in three numbers. Then she looked up at me. Her tone was conversational, as if she was sitting at Budgie's eating pie.

"I have another hole in my purse. Dammit. This is a Versace, too.

That makes two purses ruined this month. Maybe I need to get a smaller pistol."

Even though she sounded calm and collected, her hands were shaking so badly the phone kept bouncing off her ear. I reached down and took it from her.

"I'll talk to them. And forget the smaller pistol. What you have works just fine."

Rayna and Gaynelle came up, and Rayna knelt beside Victoria and began CPR. I didn't think it would help, but I was glad she was trying.

The 911 operator answered, and I stepped away to give her the information. As I did, I saw blue lights flashing, heard the bloop of a siren, and three police cruisers arrived in a cloud of dust and noise. I said, "Never mind," to the 911 operator and hung up.

"That was quick," said Bitty.

Officers erupted from cars and swarmed over the scene, barking orders and taking command of the situation. Rayna relinquished her efforts on Victoria to a uniformed officer and stood up, looking a little dazed. I wasn't sure if Victoria was dead or alive. Her son hovered close by, his face a mixture of horror and disbelief. I knew how he felt.

I was so relieved to still be alive I plopped down on the ground next to Bitty. "You shot her," I said, and Bitty nodded. Her eyes looked huge in the blue lights.

"I did. I had to. I didn't want to, though. It's a huge responsibility, isn't it? She made it look so easy, though. The way she shot Breck . . ."

Bret Hartford overheard and turned to look at us. "My mom shot my dad?" He raked a hand through his dark hair. "I don't believe you. She wouldn't do that. She loved him. She was just trying to keep us all together . . . everything got out of control so fast. No one knew—it was an accident, that's all it was. Everyone should have just left it alone! Why didn't you just leave it alone?"

His voice grew loud, his hands curled into fists, and his face contorted with anger and disbelief. For a moment I thought he was going to attack us, and I hoped Bitty's Versace was still loaded. A deterrent might be needed. Then it hit me—his was the voice I'd heard the night Professor Sturgis was killed. And Bret was probably my threatening phone call. Apparently Victoria had sucked him into her madness.

Then officers pulled him away and took him aside. I heard Bret's voice rise even higher, then it collapsed into sobs. When I looked over at Victoria, I saw that no one was working on her. She must have died. *Oh no.* I had mixed emotions.

"I killed her," Bitty said flatly. "I didn't aim for anything vital, I just wanted her to stop trying to shoot me. But she moved just as I pulled the trigger, and it was too late."

"Honey, you did what you had to do," said Rayna, and Bitty looked up at her.

"I just don't understand why she took it so far. I mean—all these people died, but all she had to do was explain that Trisha Atwood's death was accidental. It doesn't make any sense."

"Murder never does," Gaynelle said. "People who think it's the only solution to a problem have something intrinsically wrong with them."

"Ladies," said an officer, "come with me, please."

Now would begin the interviews and interrogations. It was becoming a familiar routine, which didn't say a whole lot about our extracurricular activities. We would be interviewed by police separately, and I expected Bitty not to be charged with anything. After all, it was self-defense. In Mississippi, if you have reasonable cause to fear for your life, a shooting is ruled defensible as long as the shooter is not the aggressor.

"How did you get here so quickly?" I asked the officer who escorted me to one of the cars. "I didn't even get a chance to talk to the nine-one-one operator."

"Officer Farrell recognized Miz Hollandale back at the stop sign. When he called it in, we knew there was a problem and told him to stand down until back-up arrived."

"Rodney Farrell?" I asked in surprise. "But how did—what do you mean you knew there was a problem?"

"We've been watching Victoria Hartford. She slipped away from surveillance earlier. Sit here in the back, ma'am, until we get the scene secured."

"Wait—what about Breck Hartford? She shot him a while ago, and—"

"Yes, ma'am, we know. He's been airlifted to the trauma center in Memphis."

"At least he's still alive. That's good to know."

Relieved, I leaned back against the seat. Back seats in police cars are extremely uncomfortable, but I didn't care. I felt as if I were the luckiest person in the world. After this, I didn't think anything would ever bother me again.

Chapter 22

"You know Mother is worried about this new direction your life has taken," my sister said. Her disembodied voice drifted to me through clouds of steam and relaxation. We were at Bitty's favorite spa for the day. Nothing was going to disturb me too much, not even my sister's disapproval. I didn't bother opening my eyes to reply.

"And I worry about her and Daddy going off on a Mediterranean cruise."

"That's hardly the same thing. They're unlikely to be confronted with dangerous people who are armed."

"Tell that to the passengers of the *Achille Lauro*."

"Oh honestly, Trinket, you cannot compare what happened aboard a cruise ship in the eighties to modern cruises. Besides, I think it's sweet they're getting to travel a lot."

"Then you can come tend to two hundred cats and a neurotic dog while they're jet-setting around the globe. You might like it. It's probably easier than handling a dozen children."

I pulled my thick terrycloth towel up a bit from where it had slid down on my slick skin. The towel wrapped around my head cushioned it as I leaned against the wall. I could almost feel the tension oozing out my pores along with the "impurities" the perky little spa-therapist had promised. Bitty had opted for the full body polish, and then recommended I get the cellulite package as well as steam therapy and a massage. Since she was paying, I ignored the implication that cellulite had taken over my thighs and just went along with the program. Not only was it easier, but I needed pampering. Bitty had insisted we surrender to indulgence and bought an entire package for herself, me, Rayna, Gaynelle, and even Emerald since she had arrived two days before. The spa was almost as delighted as the rest of us at Bitty's generosity.

Except for my sister's irritating pursuit of information and condemnation, all was well in my world. Emerald had always been a bit on the worrisome side, finding disaster in every corner and tragedy in every outing. I thought that strange since this was the same woman who blithely ignored her offspring climbing bookshelves and teasing rabid dogs, but I suppose everyone has their flaws.

Later, as I was lying on a table with cream smeared on my face and cucumber slices on my closed eyes, I heard Gaynelle explain to Emerald just how we had come to be mixed up in so many murder cases. If I hadn't been involved in them, I would have thought she was lying or exaggerating. It did sound rather far-fetched when listened to as an objective party.

Soft music played in the room, and aroma therapy fragrances filled the air. Despite Gaynelle's recount of terrifying details, I dozed off. When I woke, my masseuse smiled at me.

"Feeling better?" she asked. I had opted for a sweet-faced girl who looked about twelve to do my massage. Having some strange man pound on my naked body wasn't that appealing to me. Cellulite treatment notwithstanding, I'm not that comfortable about my physical appearance.

Kit never complained, but I figured his standards were compromised by the fact he spends a great deal of his time with one hand up a cow's butt.

"Tip-top," I answered the masseuse. "I've been waxed, polished and buffed. I feel like a luxury car about now."

"Just get an oil change and new plugs, and then my job here is done," she said with a laugh. "Ready for your massage?"

I sighed with contentment. "I was born ready."

Much later, on the ride home in Bitty's Franklin Benz, we savored our manicures, pedicures and pampered bodies.

"Bitty," I said, "I now understand your addiction. I could get used to this."

"See? I told you. It makes up for a lot. Armando and Rafael make house calls, by the way."

Since I was sitting up front with Bitty, and the others sat in the rear seat, I turned my head to look at them. "So do any of you have either Armando or Rafael on speed dial yet?"

Gaynelle said primly, "No, but I did get Rafael's cell phone number."

I laughed. "You're a constant surprise, Gaynelle. It looks like walking on the edge helps you."

"I don't know about that. This last time I lost a good three years off my life."

"So tell me," Emerald began, "how on earth did you get so involved with a female serial killer?"

I'd repeated the story so many times I was sick of it, but Bitty summarized it up quite nicely: "She hid the professor's body in my boys' dorm room. I took offense."

"And?" Emerald asked when Bitty didn't add anything else. "That's it? Surely there's more to the story than I read or was told. Mother doesn't go into details about it. She said it makes her head hurt to think of all the trouble you two get into these days."

I felt like a sixth grader being scolded.

"Well, it's not like we go out looking for trouble," I said defensively. "It finds us. Most of the time. Some of the time. It certainly found us this last time, anyway. It is always a big shock finding a corpse in a closet, let me tell you."

My sister, as I have said before, is small, blonde and pretty. I always feel like I'm an Amazon standing next to her. When I was a kid I always wondered if I'd been adopted, but I have since realized that my mother was never a glutton for punishment. She's done well with the hand she was dealt.

Emerald shook her head, then patted her hair with freshly manicured nails. "I can only imagine. Heavens, Trinket, it just worries me to death when I hear some of the stuff you've done lately. If one of my kids did anything like that, I don't know what I'd do."

"Just send them here," I said, getting irritated at her maternal tone. "We can use the help."

Rayna decided to interrupt, which was probably a good thing. Emerald and I had been in close quarters with her kazillion kids for forty-eight hours, and whatever patience I ever claimed to possess had evaporated after the first thirty seconds listening to metal music and screeches. One of the older boys likes to tease the ten-year-old girl. She likes to make sounds like steam escaping a tea kettle. It begins to wear after about five seconds.

"Did I tell you what Rob said?" Rayna asked. "After he got over being so upset about everything, he said we might as well get paid for risking our lives."

"What does that mean?" I asked when she didn't elaborate. "We put together a high wire act?"

"No," said Gaynelle, "we take up lion taming."

"Or shark surfing," Bitty suggested. I looked at her quizzically. She shrugged a shoulder. "What? It's a real sport. Right? Where you surf with sharks?"

"I think the sharks are optional," I said gently.

"*Any*way," Rayna said more loudly, "Rob said we could help with his insurance investigation if we promised not to carry guns or get arrested. The guy he hired didn't work out."

"Really? He didn't like it?" I asked.

"Not exactly."

"He wasn't good at it?" asked Bitty.

"No, he was pretty good."

"Is he dead?" Gaynelle inquired.

Rayna shook her head. "No, he's out of intensive care now and will be fine. He doesn't want to come back, though, and Rob doesn't have time to do everything."

"Sounds like the perfect job opportunity," I remarked.

"You have *got* to be kidding," said my sister. "You're all nuts."

"Welcome to my world, little sister."

Thanksgiving dinner was on the table, and I anticipated a pleasant turkey-induced semi-coma. The dining room table seats twelve easily with the two matching leaves, and if necessary, a couple more can be squeezed in. Emerald and Jon's six children staked their claim on one side where Daddy had put a small bench for the two younger children, and Bitty, her boys, I, and Emerald and Jon sat on the other side. Mama and Daddy took their usual places at the head and foot of the table. It was a veritable feast.

Mama's best dishes held two turkeys, cornbread dressing, sweet potato biscuits, fried okra, field peas with snaps, mashed potatoes and gravy, and cranberry sauce. I swear the table groaned when the second turkey platter was set in the middle. Ambrosia salad, one of Mama's specialties, sat next to green bean casserole. A Royal Albert bowl held fried corn, and cathead biscuits were piled atop a large plate. An array of desserts guaranteed to give me a sugar high that would last a week waited on the kitchen table. Mama had outdone herself. Not only did we have chess pie, but she'd baked a Lane cake and even a Hummingbird cake. There was lemon meringue pie, Karo pecan pie, and buttermilk pie, too.

I fully expected Emerald's kids to be swinging from light fixtures and sliding down the staircase banister. It was the kind of thing we'd done as kids. Everything was so familiar and comforting. Family rituals remained the same, just the ages of the players changed.

After Daddy said grace, there was an immediate rush to fill our plates. Someone got me in the back of my hand with a fork when I reached for the turkey platter. I knew better than to let that deter me. Hesitation could mean an empty plate. I still have scars on the back of my hand from a brief skirmish with my brother Jack over the last pork chop.

For several minutes there were only the sounds of Mama's best silverware against china and "Please pass me's" as we did major damage to the banquet before us. Once some of our initial greed had been sated, small talk began.

It went smoothly for the first five minutes. Then my sweet, big-mouth sister said, "I can't believe you two are going to work as insurance investigators for Rob Rainey. I'd be scared I'd get shot if I was spying on someone."

Silence fell. Bitty and I looked at each other, then back at my sister. "Nothing has been decided yet, Emerald," I said. "Rob just suggested it because he's irritated with all of us for going off on our own."

"Well," said my mama, "that was very foolish of you. I would have thought either Rayna or Gaynelle would have better sense than to do such a thing. You know if you take that job, you're going to have trouble. People get upset when you try to catch them in a lie or defrauding the insurance company."

"I already have a job," I replied. "It's getting to be our busy season for Christmas shopping. I doubt very seriously that Rob was serious anyway. He was just upset."

"Oh no, Trinket," said my clueless cousin. "He was quite serious. He said he'd even train us. I think it sounds exciting."

"I think it sounds dangerous," said Mama.

"I think it sounds stupid," said Emerald.

"I think it sounds like *fun*," said Annie, Emerald's ten-year-old daughter. "Do it, Auntie Tinkle. You can be a crime fighter like the Avengers or Catwoman, or—"

"Or you can be dead like Al Capone," interrupted a deep voice. I turned to see Jackson Lee in the doorway from the kitchen. He'd been invited, but had dinner with his sons first, so was showing up for coffee and dessert.

Bitty immediately went into belle-mode. "Oh sugar, I'm so glad you're here. And none of this talk about being dead, for heaven's sake. It's Thanksgiving. We're supposed to enjoy it."

"Al Capone?" I repeated. "We're not criminals, Jackson Lee. We would be on the hunt for criminals."

"You'd be dead," he retorted. "This last time was much too close. It drives me crazy when you all act like you're invincible."

"Well," said Bitty, "I know it was much too close for comfort, that's true. If Bret hadn't shown up . . . I wonder if he really would have helped his mother kill us and get rid of our bodies?"

"He seemed rather shocked by his mother's actions," I commented. "Of course, he'd helped cover up the first death, then helped move Professor Sturgis, so he's in it up to his ears anyway. And poor Catherine . . . her sister seemed very nice, and I'm glad she was able to arrange for a memorial service. Catherine will be buried next to her son."

"You know," said Bitty, "I told you the wife did it. I just had the wrong wife."

I rolled my eyes. "Whatever you say, Swami."

Jackson Lee had pulled up a kitchen chair to sit near Bitty, and he said, "The police connected Bret to Sturgis's murder by tracing a red plaid blanket that had been in the laundry cart to him. Victoria had bought it using Breck's Visa card."

"She was so careful," I said, "but never thought about the paper trail they left for the police—and Rayna—to trace. It condemned not just her, but her husband and son."

"Breck Hartford has hired a high-powered attorney down in Oxford to try and get them both off. He kept information about Trisha's death from the police so was charged with being an accessory after the fact," Bitty explained to Emerald. "My goodness, he spread himself around pretty good, so I think he deserves to go to jail for being such a—" She paused when Mama cleared her throat and tilted her head at the kids listening avidly. "—stupid man," Bitty finished.

"Who wants seconds?" I asked, and held out my plate for Daddy to put a couple slices of turkey on it. "Extra dressing, please. No giblet gravy."

Later, as the night closed in, and we were all happily stuffed to the gills, Kit came by to share coffee and conversation. I was quite content. The only thing that could have made it better was if my daughter had been able to come, but she promised she'd try her best to show up for Christmas.

It was a cool, crisp night, and I snuggled against Kit with my head leaning back on his chest as we stood on the back deck to watch the last rays of sunlight disappear behind the cherry orchard.

"When are you going to give up getting involved in murders?" he asked against my ear, and I shivered at his warm breath.

"Oh, soon."

"How quick is soon?"

I tried a belle-response: "Why you sweet thing, are you worried about me?"

"Every day," he whispered in my ear.

This time I smiled. It was rather nice having a man worry about me. Even if I didn't take the job with Rob, I had no doubt that Divas would somehow become tangled in another murder. It was just a matter of time.

Bitty and Jackson Lee joined us on the deck, and I looked at my cousin and smiled. There were worse things to do than solve murders, and even though the police had already figured out the killer's identity, we had helped gather enough evidence to see that Breck paid for his part in it. Victoria had paid the ultimate price, but I was just glad she'd never have another chance to hurt someone.

"Did you hear that Cady Lee's sister wrote a book set in Holly

Springs?" Bitty asked, and I shook my head.

"No. Has it been published?"

"It comes out in January. I heard that it's causing a lot of controversy because of the subject. There's a lot of people in town who are madder than a hornet and threatening to sue for libel. It is libel, isn't it, Jackson Lee?"

He nodded. "If it's the written word about someone and printed without their permission, it's libel. I've already had two people come to talk to me about it. Until the book comes out, however, I can't do anything."

"So what's it about?" asked Kit.

"Local domestics and how they were treated before the Civil Rights act. It's bound to be controversial."

"But isn't there another book out about that kind of thing?" Bitty asked. "Why would she want to copy someone else?"

"Beats me. But some of the older families in this town are up in arms about it."

A shiver went down my back. My Spidey-sense told me that there was going to be trouble when that book came out, and Divas were going to be smack dab in the middle of it.

"Well," said Bitty, "you know Cady Lee's sister is going to be in high cotton if that book gets a lot of publicity."

"Exactly," I said. "We just better be prepared."

"Oh sugar, aren't we always?"

Jackson Lee and Kit exchanged glances, and one of them groaned. I think it was Kit, but I couldn't be too sure.

"Here we go again," said Jackson Lee with a sigh.

The End

About Virginia Brown

As a long-time resident of Mississippi, award-winning author Virginia Brown has lived in several different areas of the state, and finds the history, romance, and intrigue of the Deep South irresistible. Although having spent her childhood as a "military brat" living all over the US, and overseas, this author of nearly fifty novels is now happily settled in and drawing her favorite fictional characters from the wonderful, whimsical Southerners she has known and loved.

38059873R00154

Made in the USA
Middletown, DE
12 December 2016